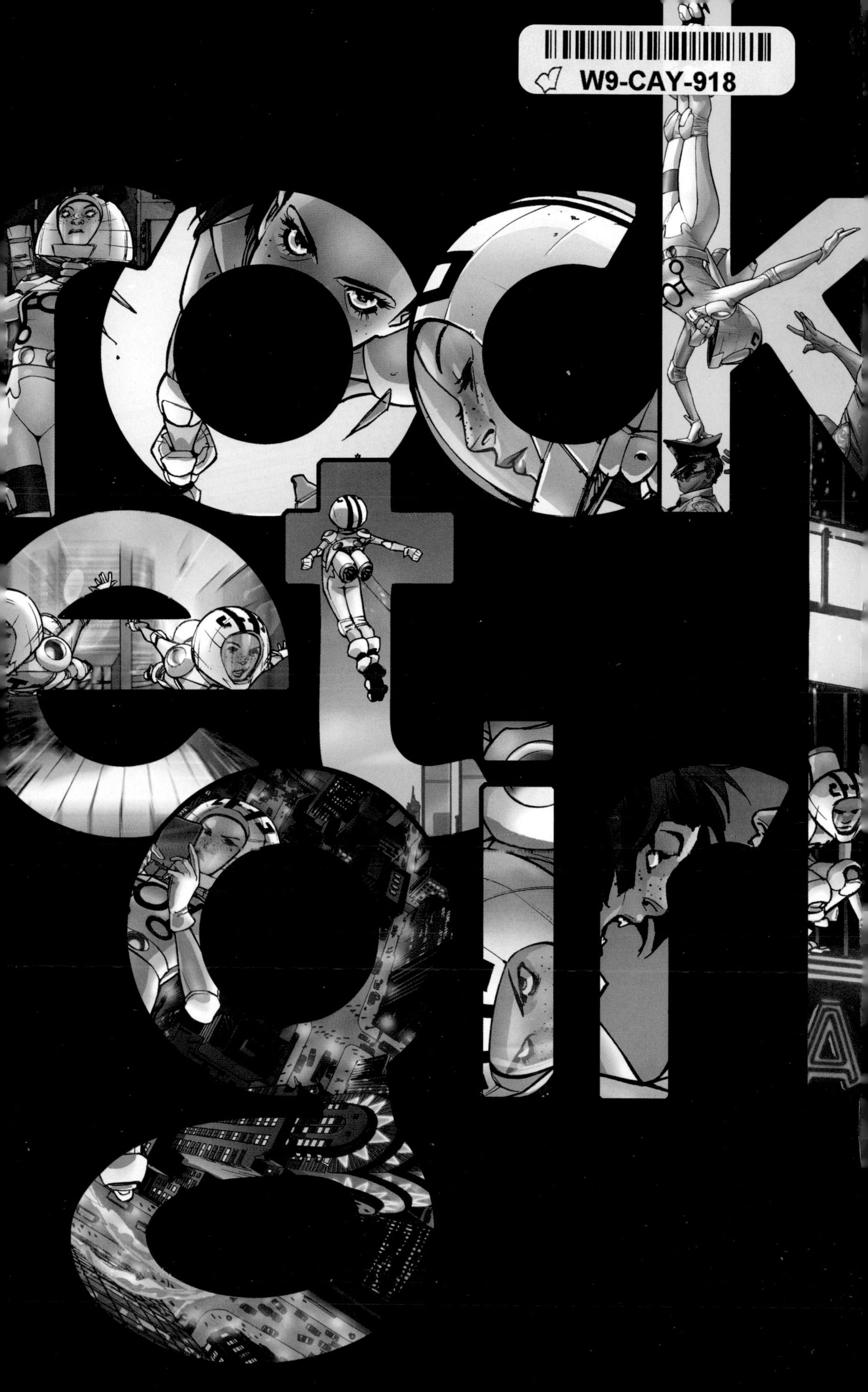
rocket girl

ROCKET GIRL, VOL. 2: ONLY THE GOOD.... First Printing. December 2017.

Published by Image Comics, Inc. Office of publication: 2701 NW Vaughn St., Suite 780, Portland, OR 97210. Copyright © 2017 Brandon Montclare and Amy Reeder. All rights reserved. Originally published in single magazine form as ROCKET GIRL #6-10. Rocket Girl™ (including all prominent characters featured herein), its logo and all character likenesses are trademarks of Brandon Montclare and Amy Reeder, unless otherwise noted. Image Comics® and its logos are registered trademarks of Image Comics, Inc. No part of this publication may be reproduced or transmitted, in any form or by any means (except for short excerpts for review purposes) without the express written permission of Image Comics, Inc. All names, characters, events and locales in this publication are entirely fictional. Any resemblance to actual persons (living or dead), events or places, without satiric intent, is coincidental. Printed in the USA. For information regarding the CPSIA on this printed material call: 203-595-3636 and provide reference #RICH—769879. For international rights, contact: foreignlicensing@imagecomics.com. ISBN: 978-1-5343-0325-6

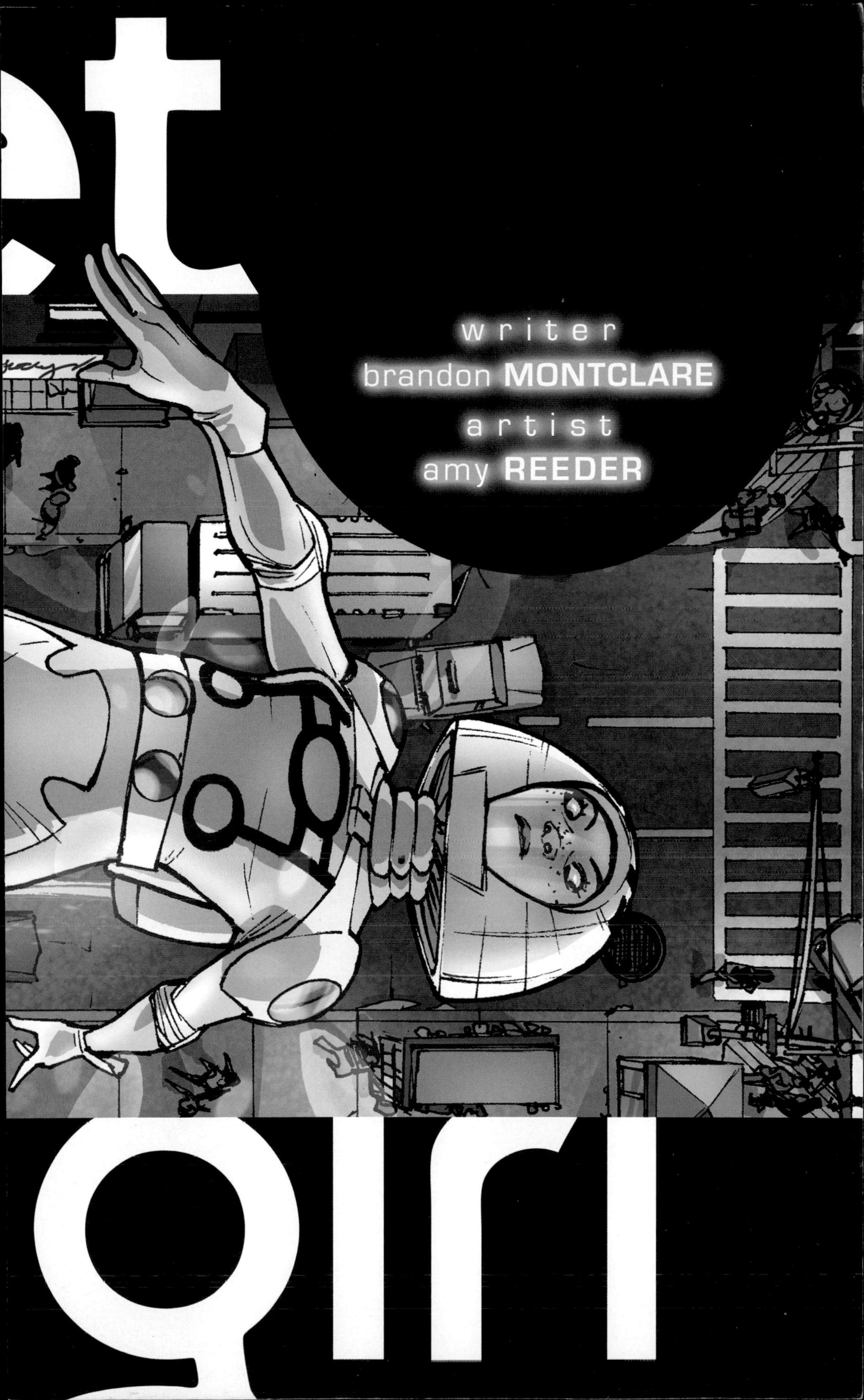
et
writer
brandon MONTCLARE
artist
amy REEDER
girl

rocket girl SO FAR...

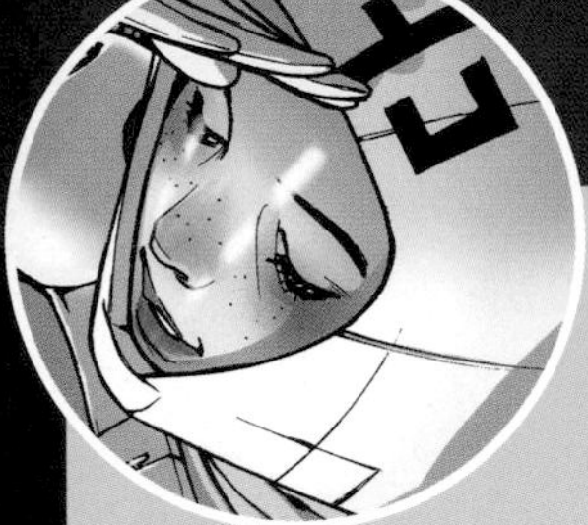

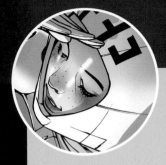

DAYOUNG JOHANSSON

A teen cop from the future--and more importantly, a true believer. She travelled back in time to an 80s Big Apple that was rotten to the core. She's investigating the nascent Quintum Mechanics Corporation for crimes against time.

Known now as Rocket Girl, she believes she's just dismantled Quintum Mechanics' manipulative plans. But that success has destroyed any chance she ever had of returning home. Trapped in the past, she's vowed to forever hang up her jetpack. Let's see how long that lasts...

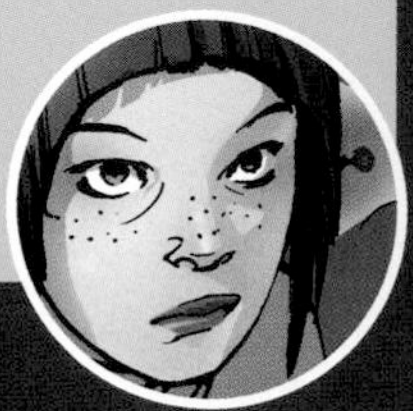

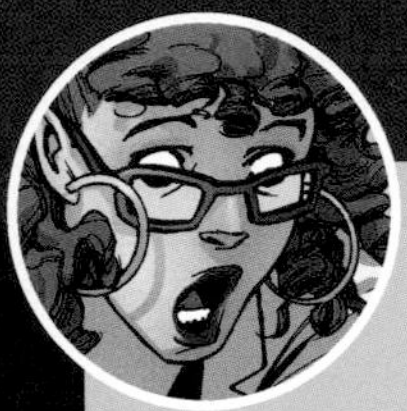

ANNIE MENDEZ

A graduate student researcher at Quintum Mechanics. She's done more than anyone else to develop the Q-Engine and spark a new age of time travel...but she's treated like just another cog in the wheel. Even though she has the opportunity to realize the vast powers of the Q-Engine, she decides to help Rocket Girl sabotage the Quintum Mechanics labs. She's worried it was the biggest mistake of her life.

RYDER, CHAZ, AND GENE

Annie's fellow students. They discover the truth behind Quintum Mechanics and do what they can to help DaYoung and Annie. Now they fear for their future, in more ways than one.

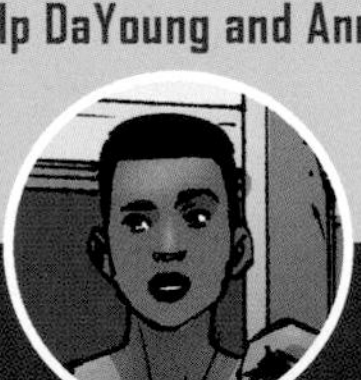

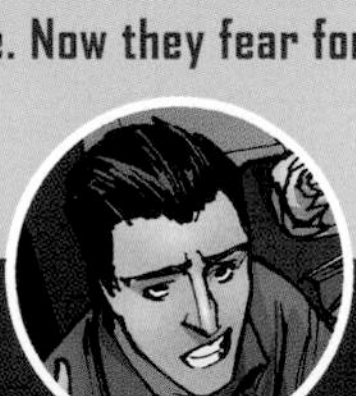

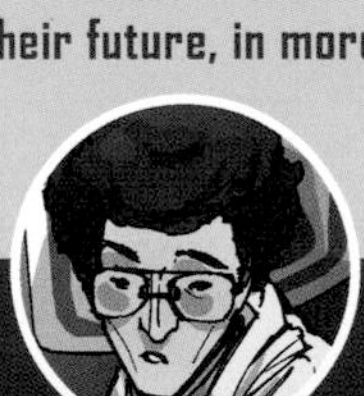

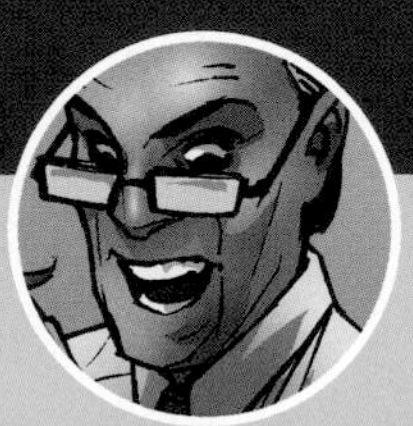

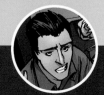

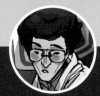

PROFESSOR SHARMA

Sharma is the stubborn head of 1980s Quintum Mechanics. Every time Rocket Girl blows up the Q-Engine, he builds a bigger, better version.

DETECTIVE CICCONE

A veteran of the 1980s NYPD, Ciccone caught the case of the high-flying Rocket Girl. He might be as honest as they come—but that's not saying much in a cesspool of rampant corruption. He's definitely too old for this.

OFFICER DUNN

A crooked cop who only looks out for number one.

OFFICER DUNN

He's also an older version of himself! On orders from his bosses at the 2013 Quintum Mechanics, he followed DaYoung from the future.

OFFICER TWEED

Tweed is Officer Dunn's partner, and just as crooked. His older self didn't make it far upon returning to 1986.

COMMISSIONER GOMEZ

Jim Gomez has dedicated his life to law enforcement. He's thirteen.

LESHAWN O'PATRICK

DaYoung's partner in the New York Teen Police Department of 2013. He wants to do what's right, but never wanted DaYoung to risk it all by time travelling to 1986.

JO$#UA

The mysterious CEO of Quintum Mechanics. Joshua turned informant, providing DaYoung the means to investigate New York City's past-- literally. But it could be the biggest double-cross in history.

Chapter 6_Split Second >>

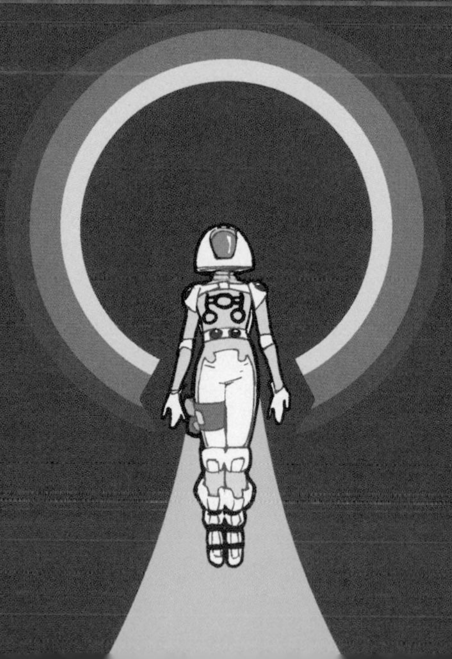

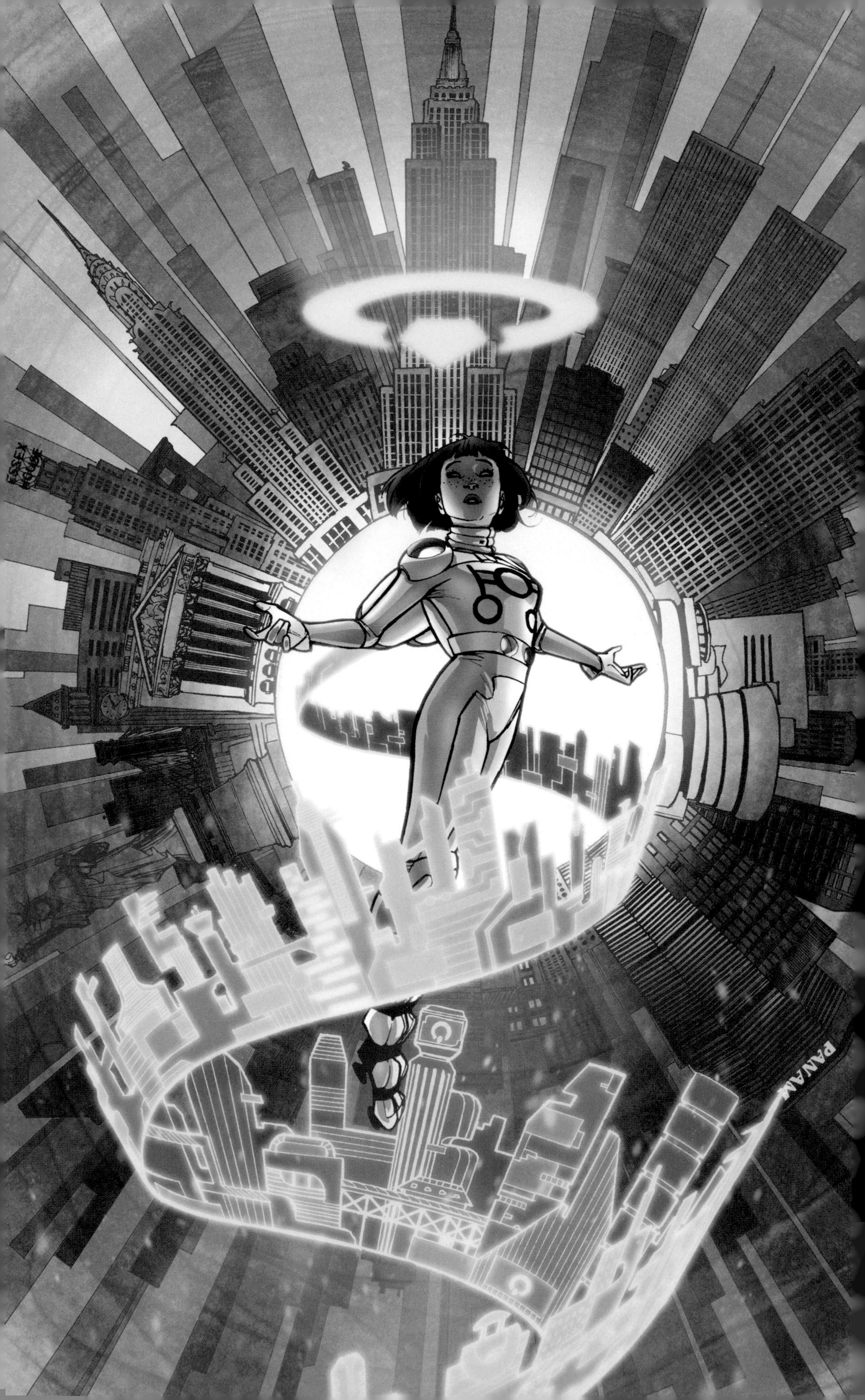
PANAM

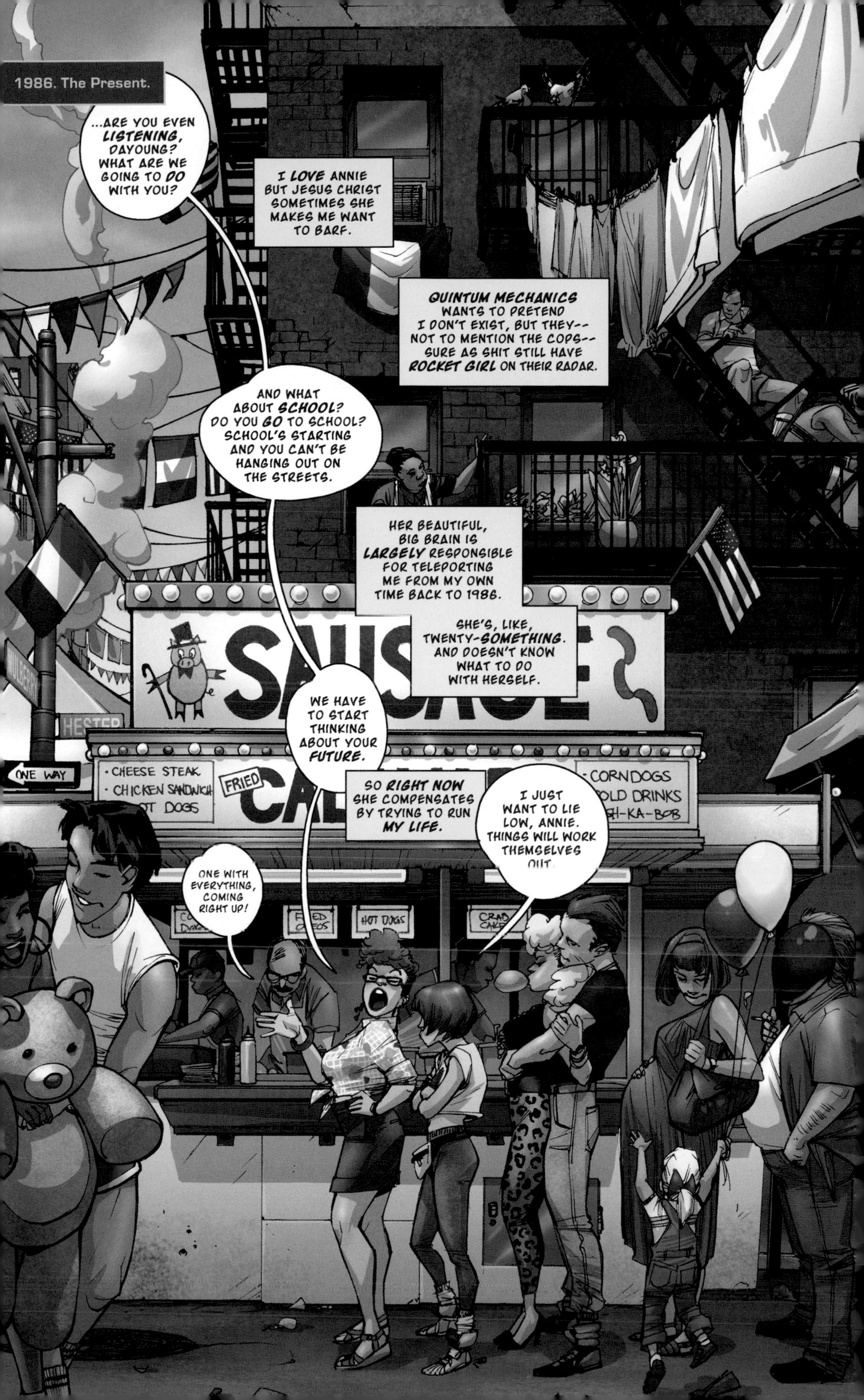
1986. The Present.
...ARE YOU EVEN LISTENING, DAYOUNG? WHAT ARE WE GOING TO DO WITH YOU?
I LOVE ANNIE BUT JESUS CHRIST SOMETIMES SHE MAKES ME WANT TO BARF.
QUINTUM MECHANICS WANTS TO PRETEND I DON'T EXIST, BUT THEY-- NOT TO MENTION THE COPS-- SURE AS SHIT STILL HAVE ROCKET GIRL ON THEIR RADAR.
AND WHAT ABOUT SCHOOL? DO YOU GO TO SCHOOL? SCHOOL'S STARTING AND YOU CAN'T BE HANGING OUT ON THE STREETS.
HER BEAUTIFUL, BIG BRAIN IS LARGELY RESPONSIBLE FOR TELEPORTING ME FROM MY OWN TIME BACK TO 1986.
SHE'S, LIKE, TWENTY-SOMETHING. AND DOESN'T KNOW WHAT TO DO WITH HERSELF.
WE HAVE TO START THINKING ABOUT YOUR FUTURE.
SO RIGHT NOW SHE COMPENSATES BY TRYING TO RUN MY LIFE.
I JUST WANT TO LIE LOW, ANNIE. THINGS WILL WORK THEMSELVES OUT.
ONE WITH EVERYTHING, COMING RIGHT UP!
MULBERRY
HESTER
ONE WAY
· CHEESE STEAK
· CHICKEN SANDWICH
FRIED
· CORN DOGS
HOT DOGS
FRIED OREOS
CRAB CAKES

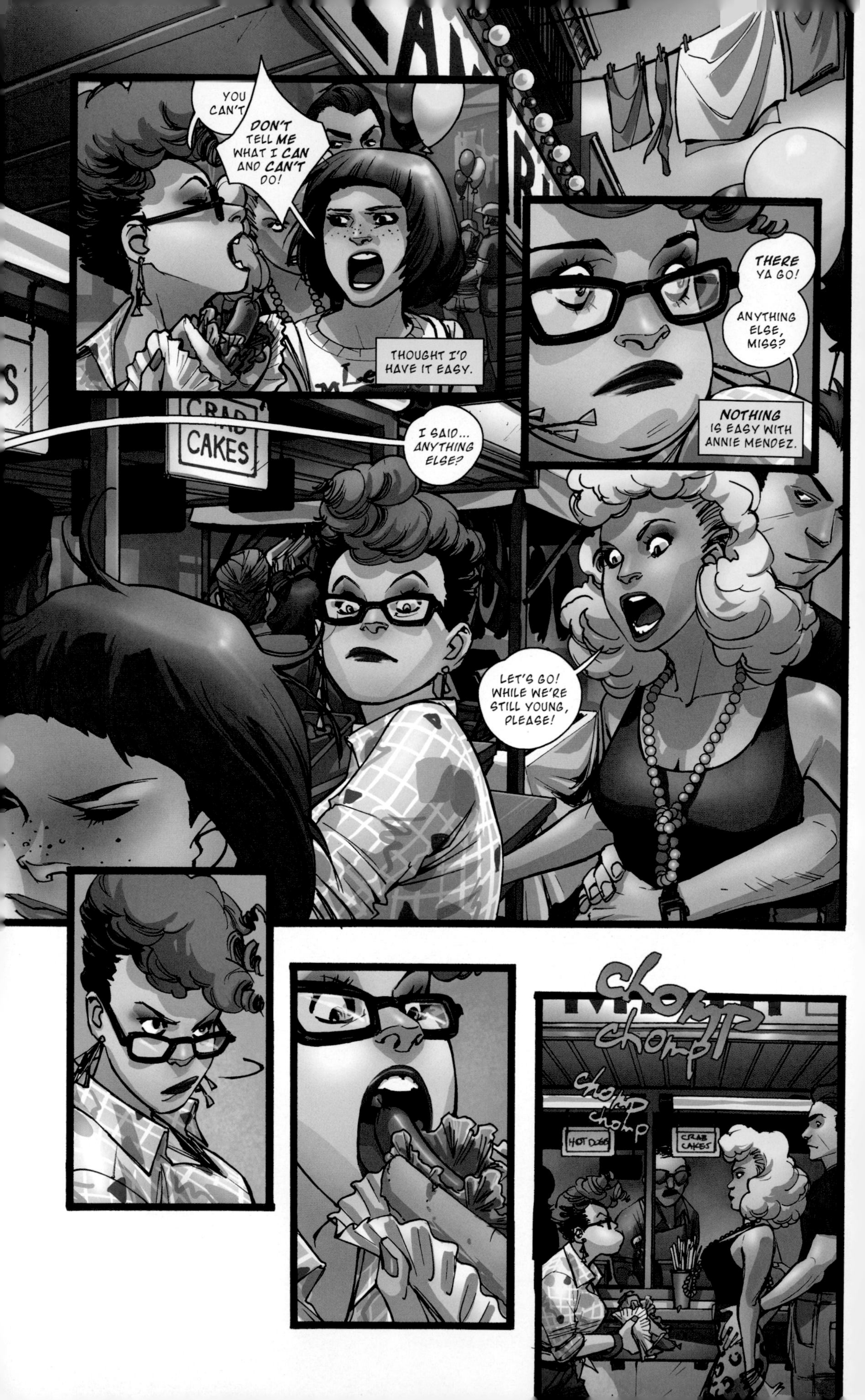
YOU CAN'T
DON'T TELL ME WHAT I CAN AND CAN'T DO!
THOUGHT I'D HAVE IT EASY.
THERE YA GO!
ANYTHING ELSE, MISS?
NOTHING IS EASY WITH ANNIE MENDEZ.
CRAB CAKES
I SAID... ANYTHING ELSE?
LET'S GO! WHILE WE'RE STILL YOUNG, PLEASE!
CHOMP
CHOMP
CHOMP
CHOMP
HOT DOGS
CRAB CAKES

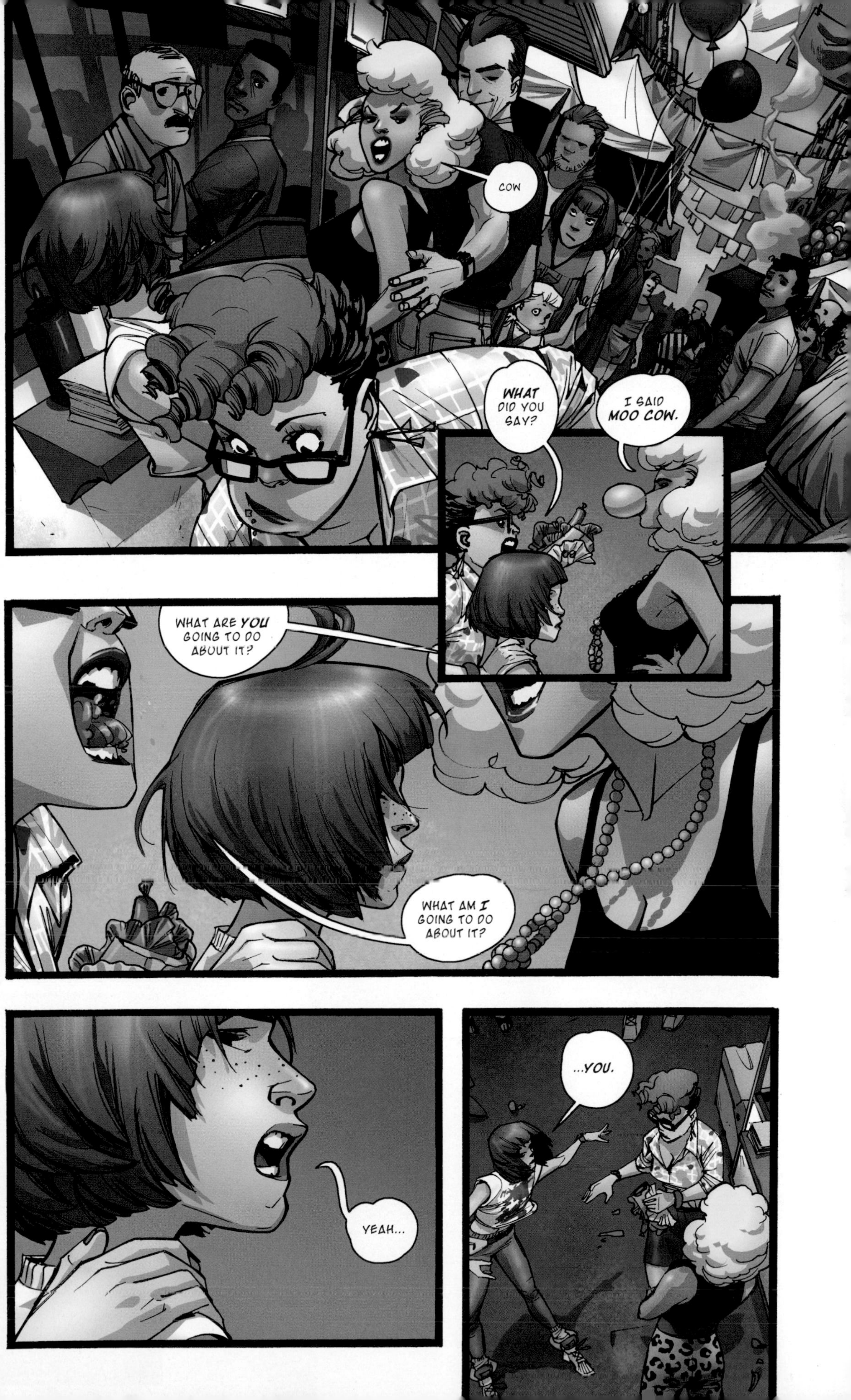
COW
WHAT DID YOU SAY?
I SAID MOO COW.
WHAT ARE YOU GOING TO DO ABOUT IT?
WHAT AM I GOING TO DO ABOUT IT?
YEAH...
...YOU.

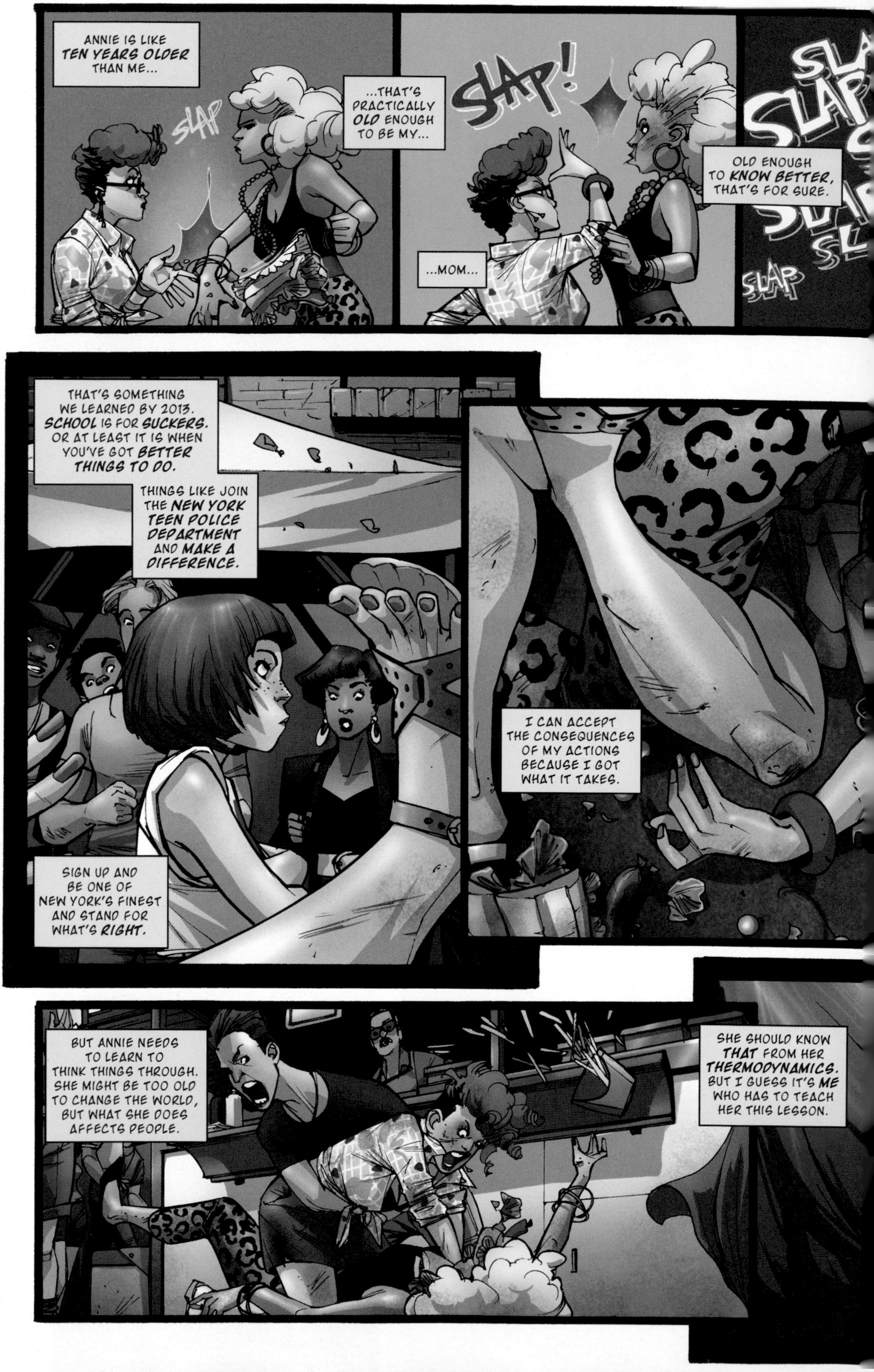
ANNIE IS LIKE TEN YEARS OLDER THAN ME...
SLAP
...THAT'S PRACTICALLY OLD ENOUGH TO BE MY...
SLAP!
...MOM...
OLD ENOUGH TO KNOW BETTER, THAT'S FOR SURE.
SLAP
SLAP
SLAP
THAT'S SOMETHING WE LEARNED BY 2013. SCHOOL IS FOR SUCKERS. OR AT LEAST IT IS WHEN YOU'VE GOT BETTER THINGS TO DO.
THINGS LIKE JOIN THE NEW YORK TEEN POLICE DEPARTMENT AND MAKE A DIFFERENCE.
SIGN UP AND BE ONE OF NEW YORK'S FINEST AND STAND FOR WHAT'S RIGHT.
I CAN ACCEPT THE CONSEQUENCES OF MY ACTIONS BECAUSE I GOT WHAT IT TAKES.
BUT ANNIE NEEDS TO LEARN TO THINK THINGS THROUGH. SHE MIGHT BE TOO OLD TO CHANGE THE WORLD, BUT WHAT SHE DOES AFFECTS PEOPLE.
SHE SHOULD KNOW THAT FROM HER THERMODYNAMICS. BUT I GUESS IT'S ME WHO HAS TO TEACH HER THIS LESSON.

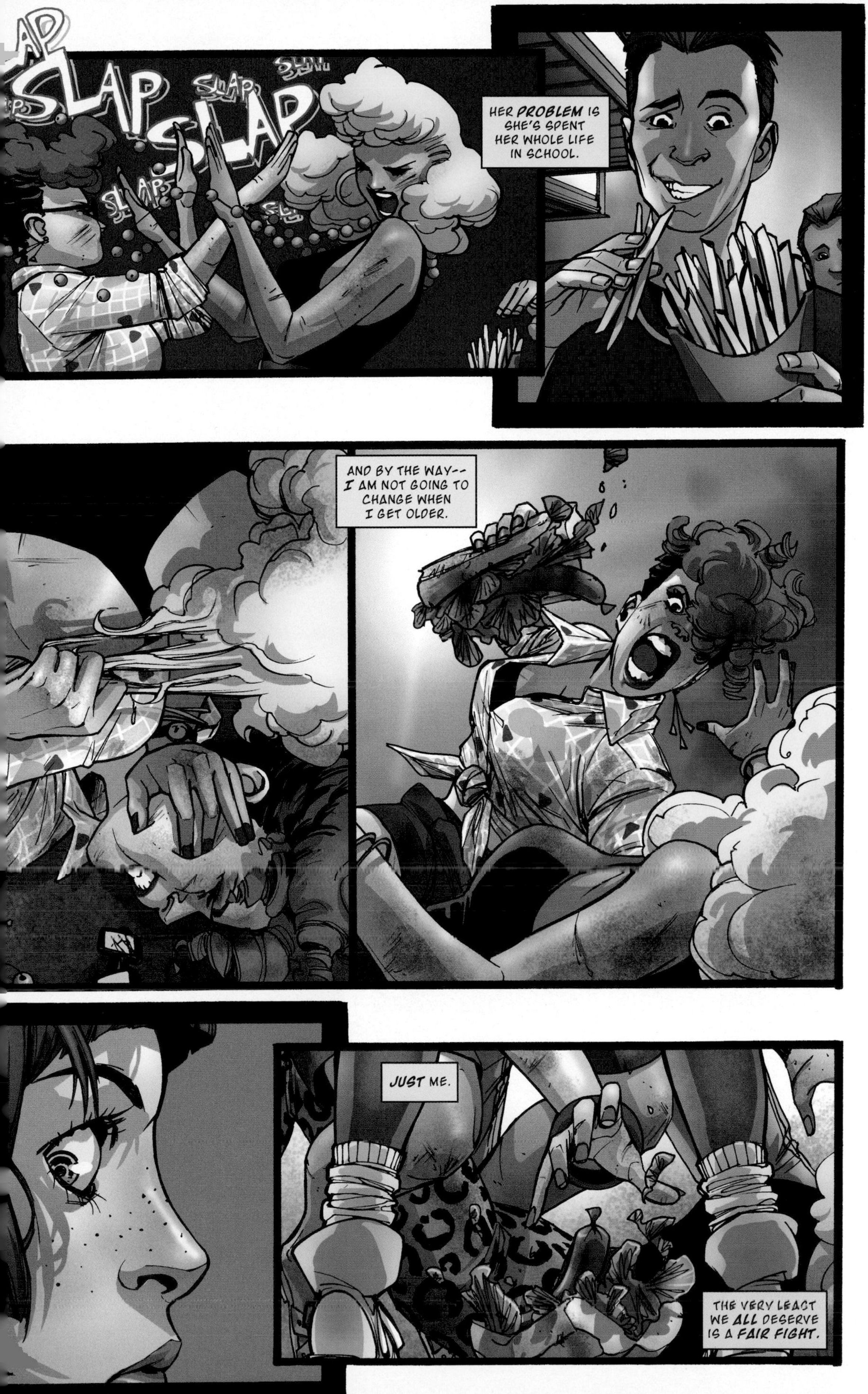
SLAP
SLAP
SLAP
SLAP
SLAP
HER PROBLEM IS SHE'S SPENT HER WHOLE LIFE IN SCHOOL.
AND BY THE WAY-- I AM NOT GOING TO CHANGE WHEN I GET OLDER.
JUST ME.
THE VERY LEAST WE ALL DESERVE IS A FAIR FIGHT.

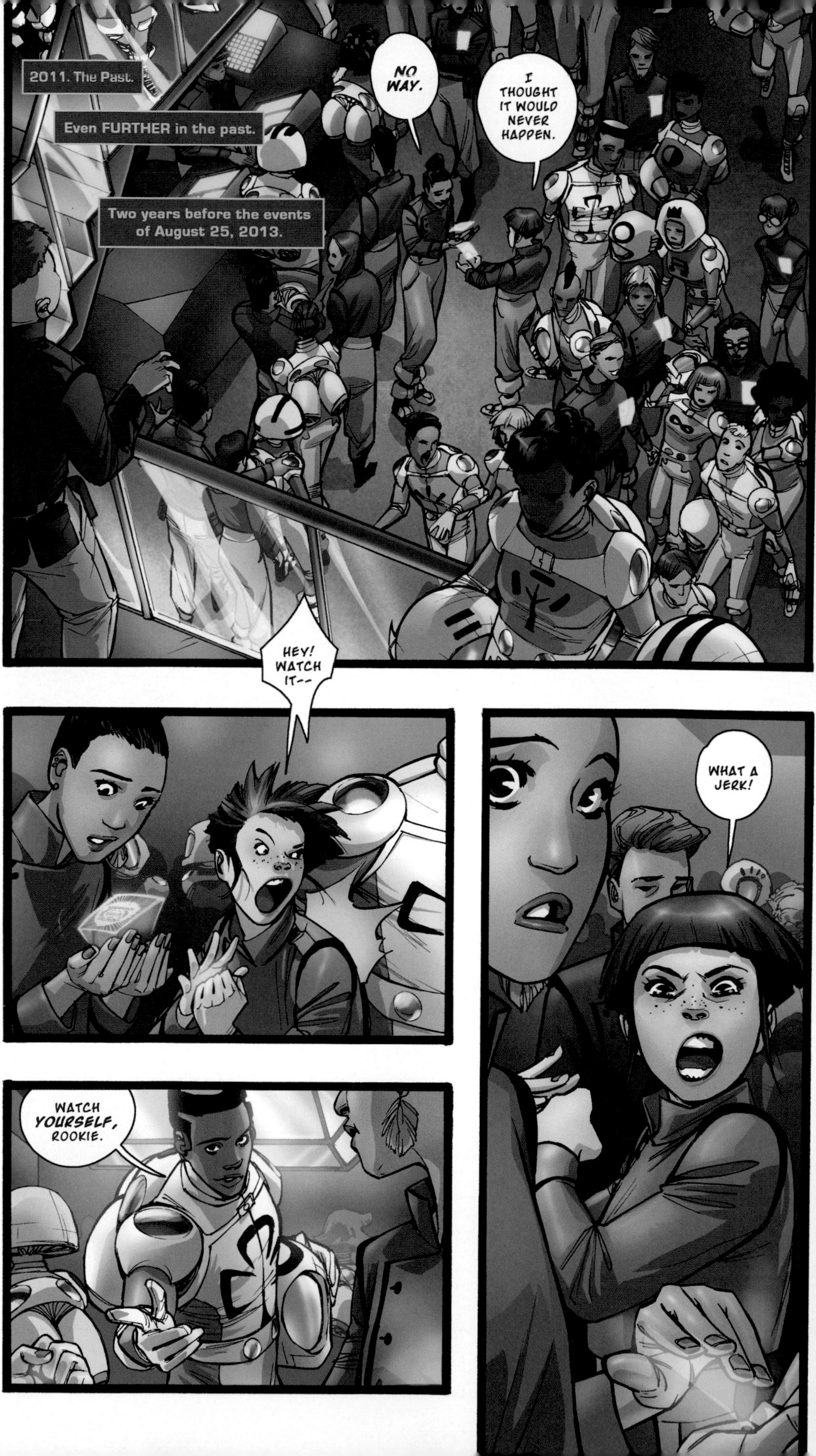
2011. The Past.
Even FURTHER in the past.
Two years before the events of August 25, 2013.
NO WAY.
I THOUGHT IT WOULD NEVER HAPPEN.
HEY! WATCH IT--
WHAT A JERK!
WATCH YOURSELF, ROOKIE.

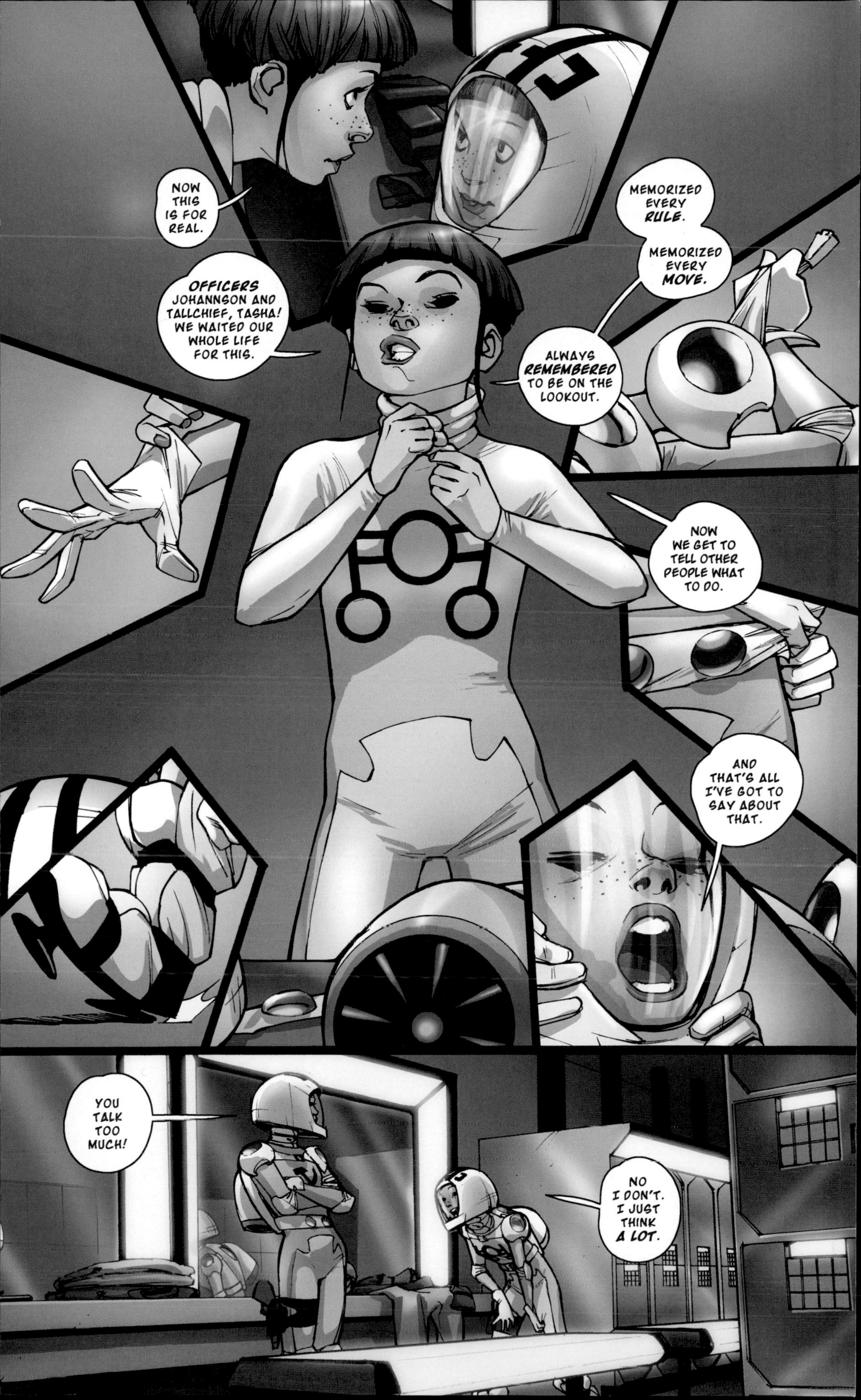
NOW THIS IS FOR REAL.
MEMORIZED EVERY RULE.
MEMORIZED EVERY MOVE.
OFFICERS JOHANNSON AND TALLCHIEF, TASHA! WE WAITED OUR WHOLE LIFE FOR THIS.
ALWAYS REMEMBERED TO BE ON THE LOOKOUT.
NOW WE GET TO TELL OTHER PEOPLE WHAT TO DO.
AND THAT'S ALL I'VE GOT TO SAY ABOUT THAT.
YOU TALK TOO MUCH!
NO I DON'T. I JUST THINK A LOT.

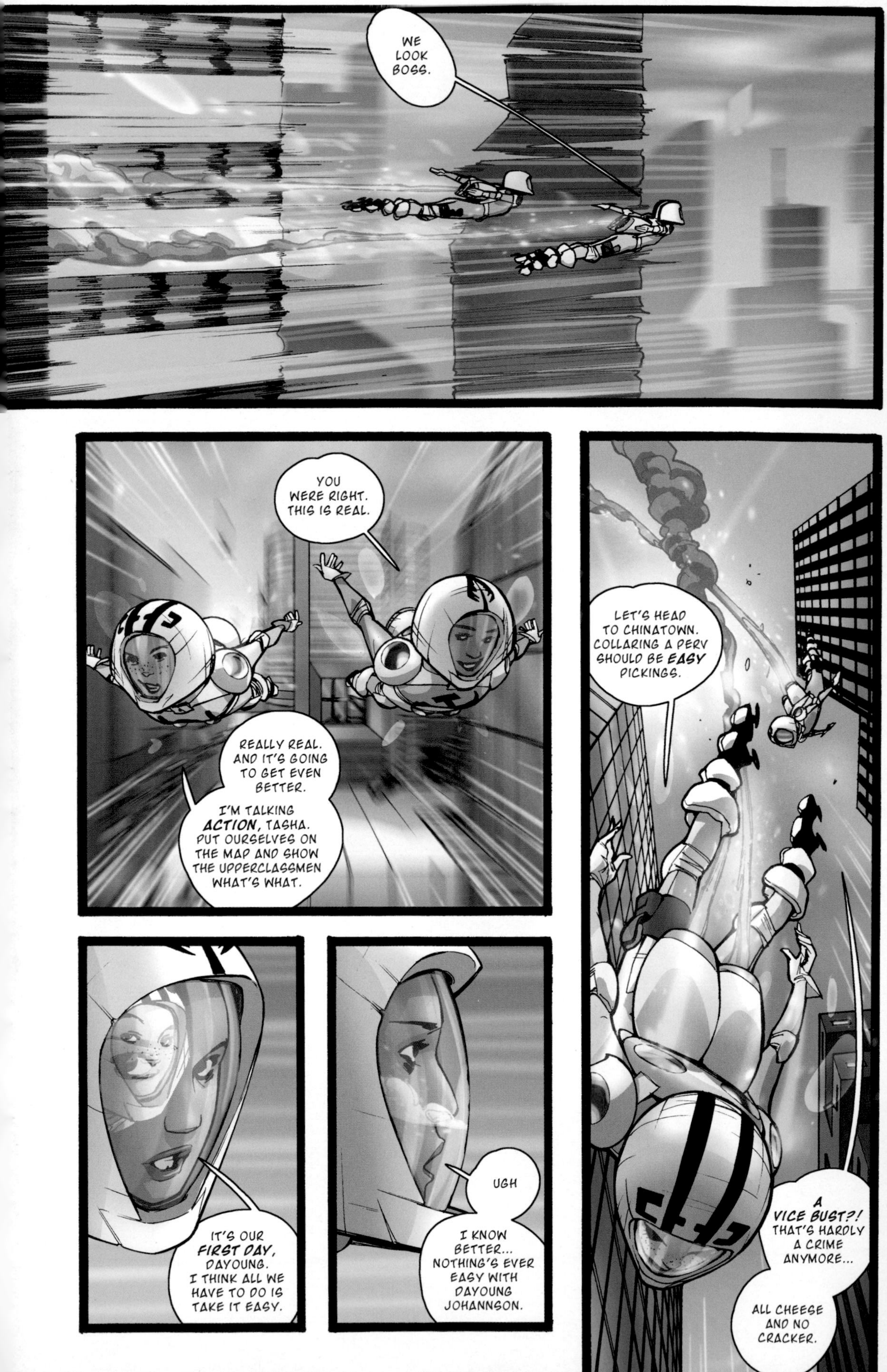
WE LOOK BOSS.
YOU WERE RIGHT. THIS IS REAL.
REALLY REAL. AND IT'S GOING TO GET EVEN BETTER.
I'M TALKING ACTION, TASHA. PUT OURSELVES ON THE MAP AND SHOW THE UPPERCLASSMEN WHAT'S WHAT.
IT'S OUR FIRST DAY, DAYOUNG. I THINK ALL WE HAVE TO DO IS TAKE IT EASY.
UGH
I KNOW BETTER... NOTHING'S EVER EASY WITH DAYOUNG JOHANNSON.
LET'S HEAD TO CHINATOWN. COLLARING A PERV SHOULD BE EASY PICKINGS.
A VICE BUST?! THAT'S HARDLY A CRIME ANYMORE...
ALL CHEESE AND NO CRACKER.

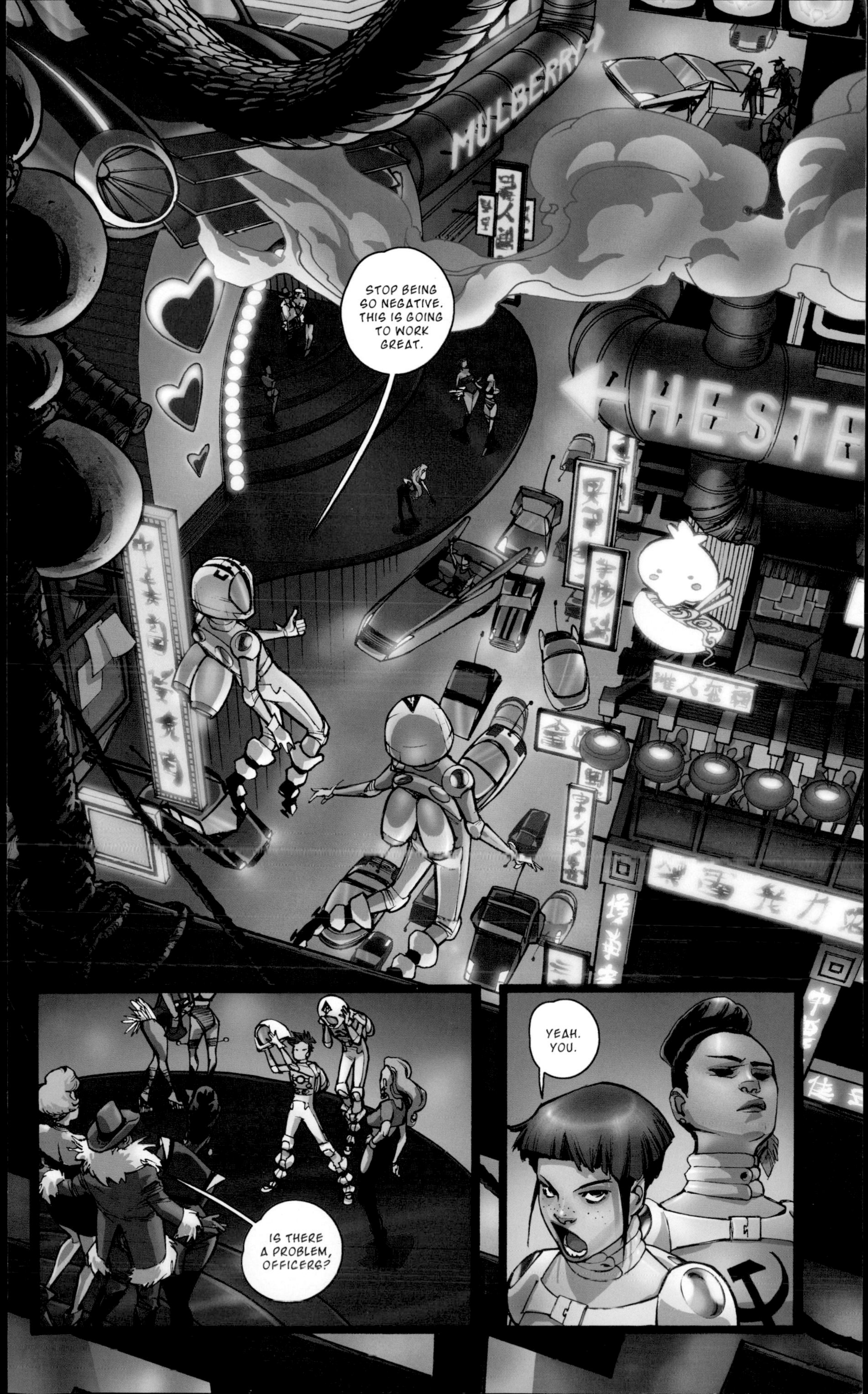
MULBERRY
HESTE
STOP BEING SO NEGATIVE. THIS IS GOING TO WORK GREAT.
IS THERE A PROBLEM, OFFICERS?
YEAH. YOU.

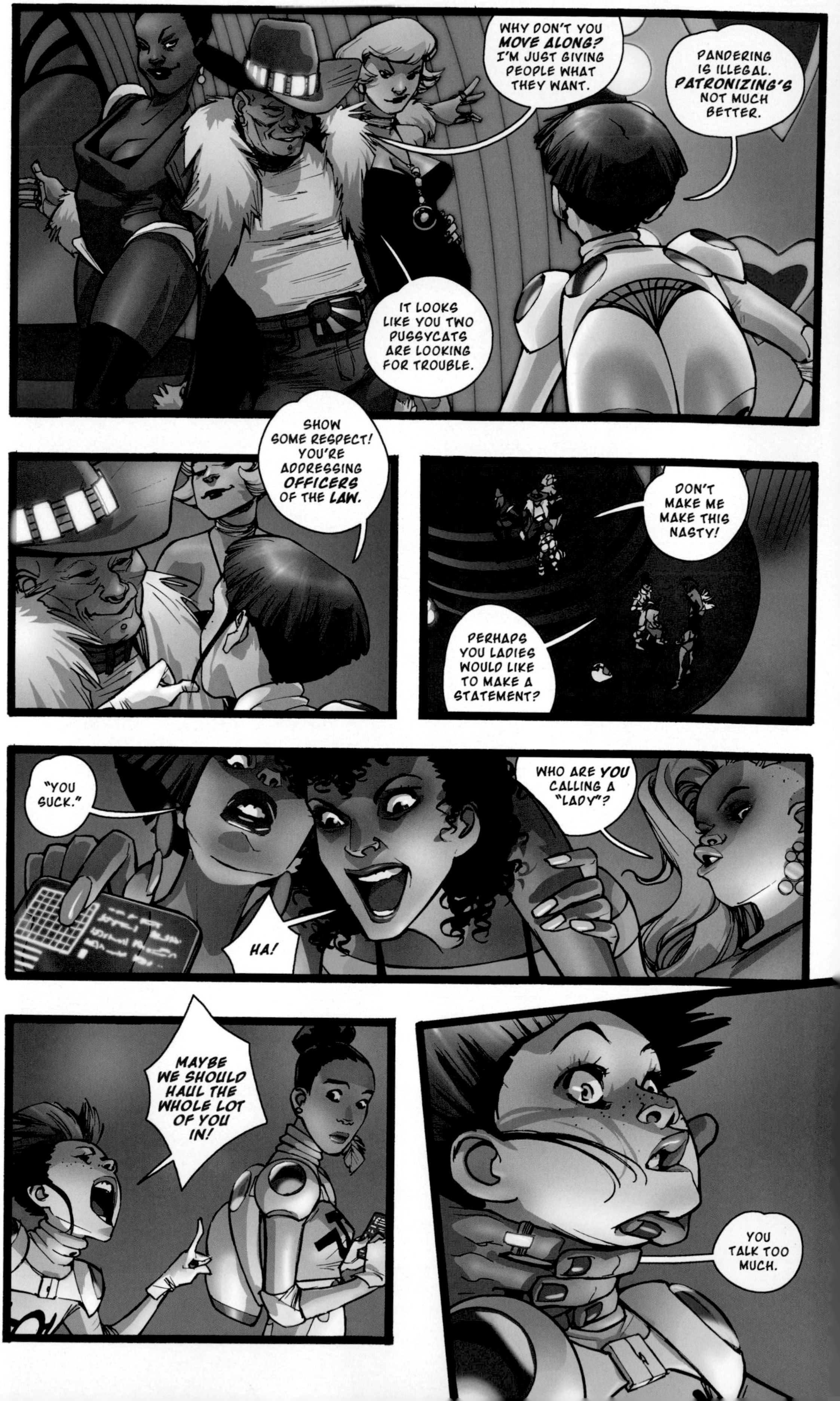
WHY DON'T YOU MOVE ALONG? I'M JUST GIVING PEOPLE WHAT THEY WANT.
PANDERING IS ILLEGAL. PATRONIZING'S NOT MUCH BETTER.
IT LOOKS LIKE YOU TWO PUSSYCATS ARE LOOKING FOR TROUBLE.
SHOW SOME RESPECT! YOU'RE ADDRESSING OFFICERS OF THE LAW.
DON'T MAKE ME MAKE THIS NASTY!
PERHAPS YOU LADIES WOULD LIKE TO MAKE A STATEMENT?
"YOU SUCK."
WHO ARE YOU CALLING A "LADY"?
HA!
MAYBE WE SHOULD HAUL THE WHOLE LOT OF YOU IN!
YOU TALK TOO MUCH.

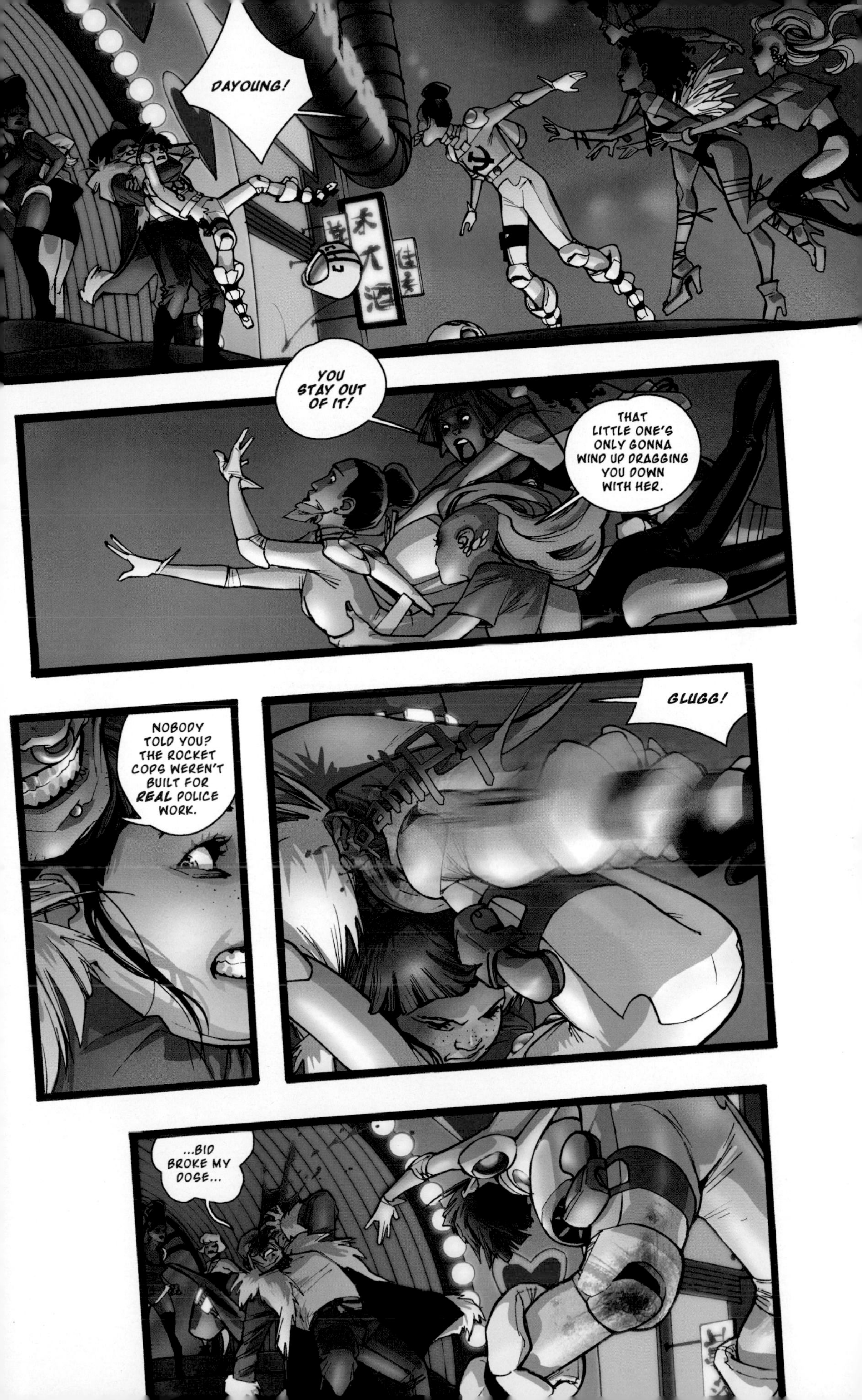
DAYOUNG!
YOU STAY OUT OF IT!
THAT LITTLE ONE'S ONLY GONNA WIND UP DRAGGING YOU DOWN WITH HER.
NOBODY TOLD YOU? THE ROCKET COPS WEREN'T BUILT FOR REAL POLICE WORK.
GLUGG!
...BID BROKE MY DOSE...

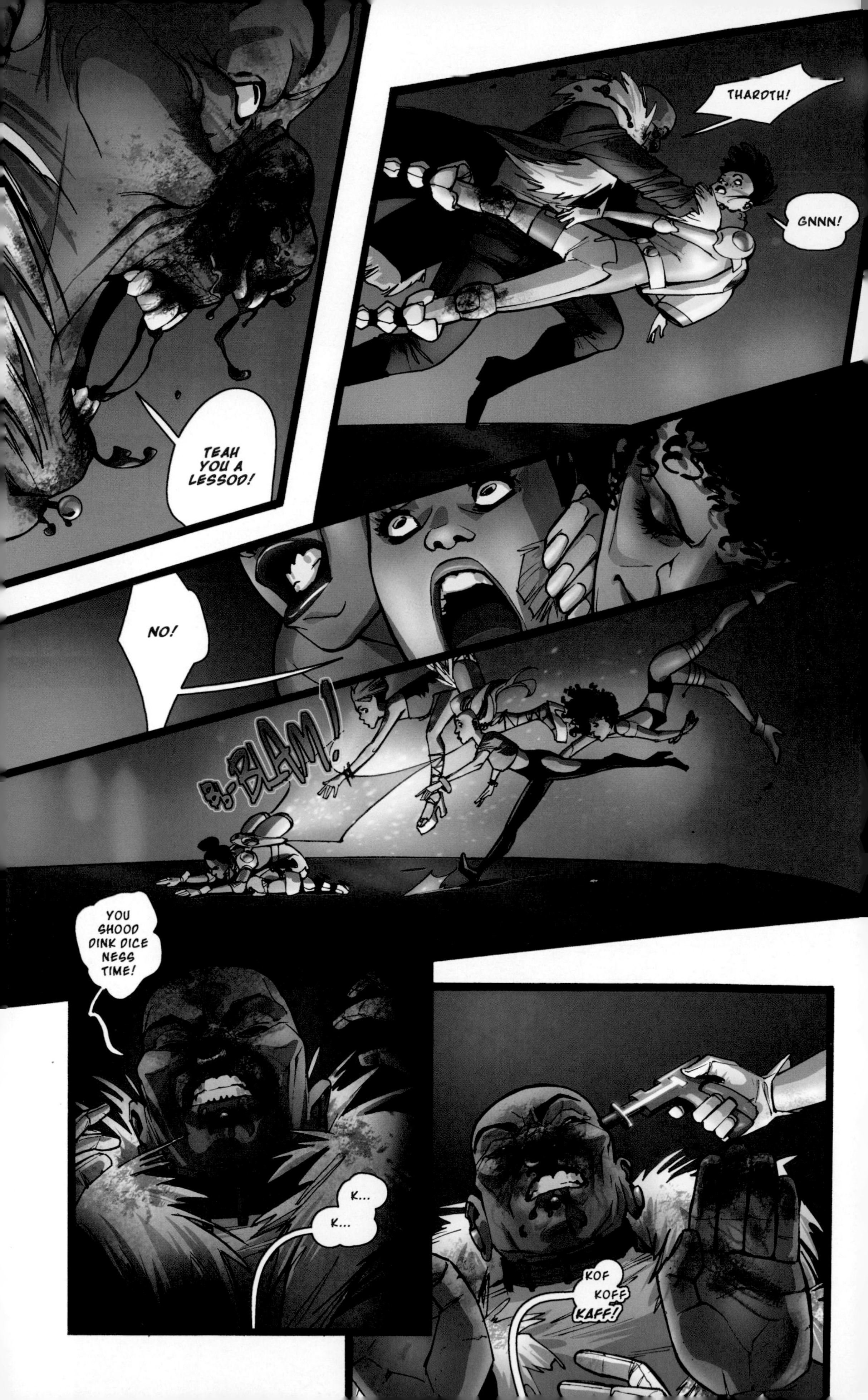
THARDTH!
GNNN!
TEAH YOU A LESSOD!
NO!
B-BLAM!
YOU SHOOD DINK DICE NESS TIME!
K...
K...
KOF KOFF KAFF!

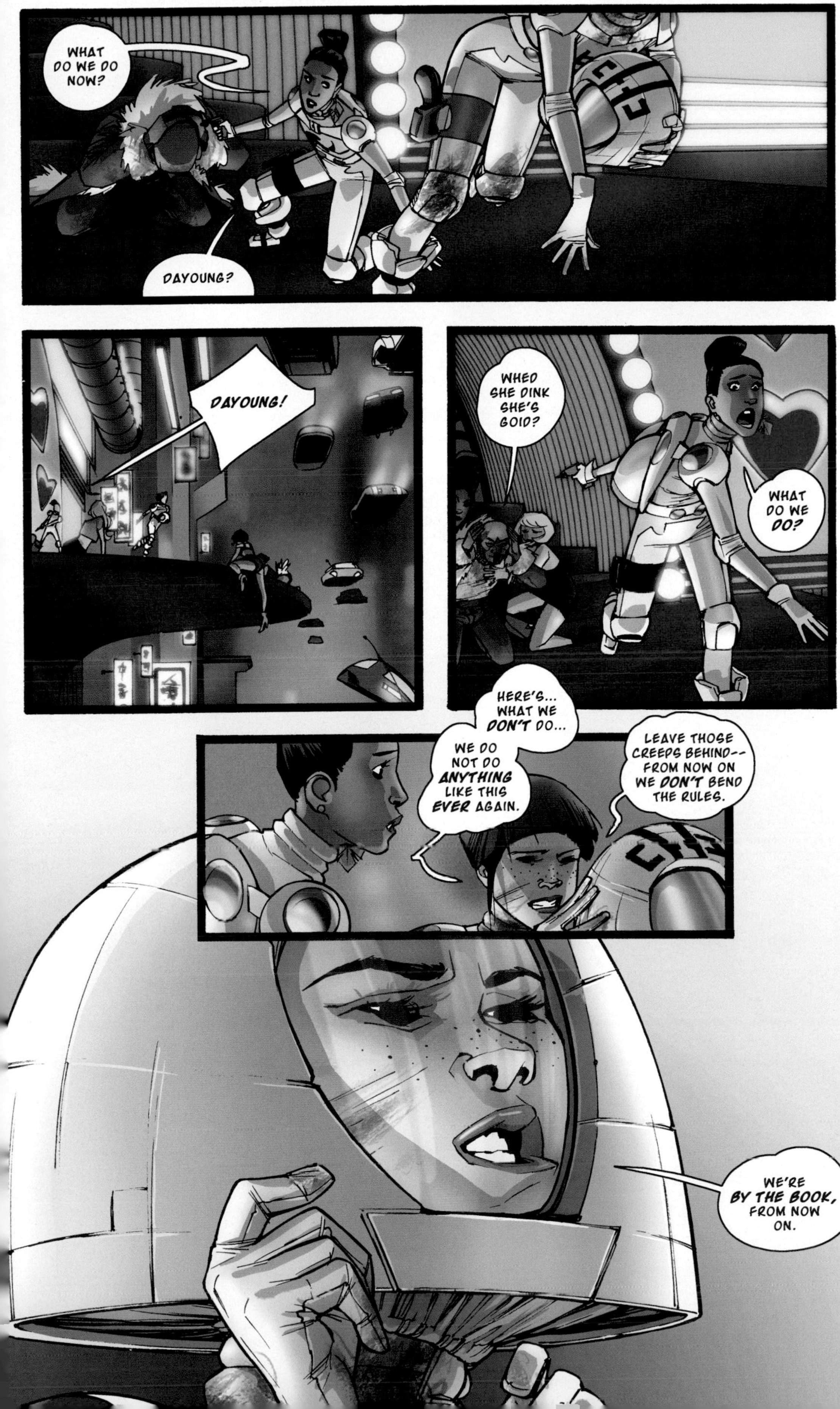
WHAT DO WE DO NOW?
DAYOUNG?
DAYOUNG!
WHED SHE DINK SHE'S GOID?
WHAT DO WE DO?
HERE'S... WHAT WE DON'T DO...
WE DO NOT DO ANYTHING LIKE THIS EVER AGAIN.
LEAVE THOSE CREEPS BEHIND-- FROM NOW ON WE DON'T BEND THE RULES.
WE'RE BY THE BOOK, FROM NOW ON.

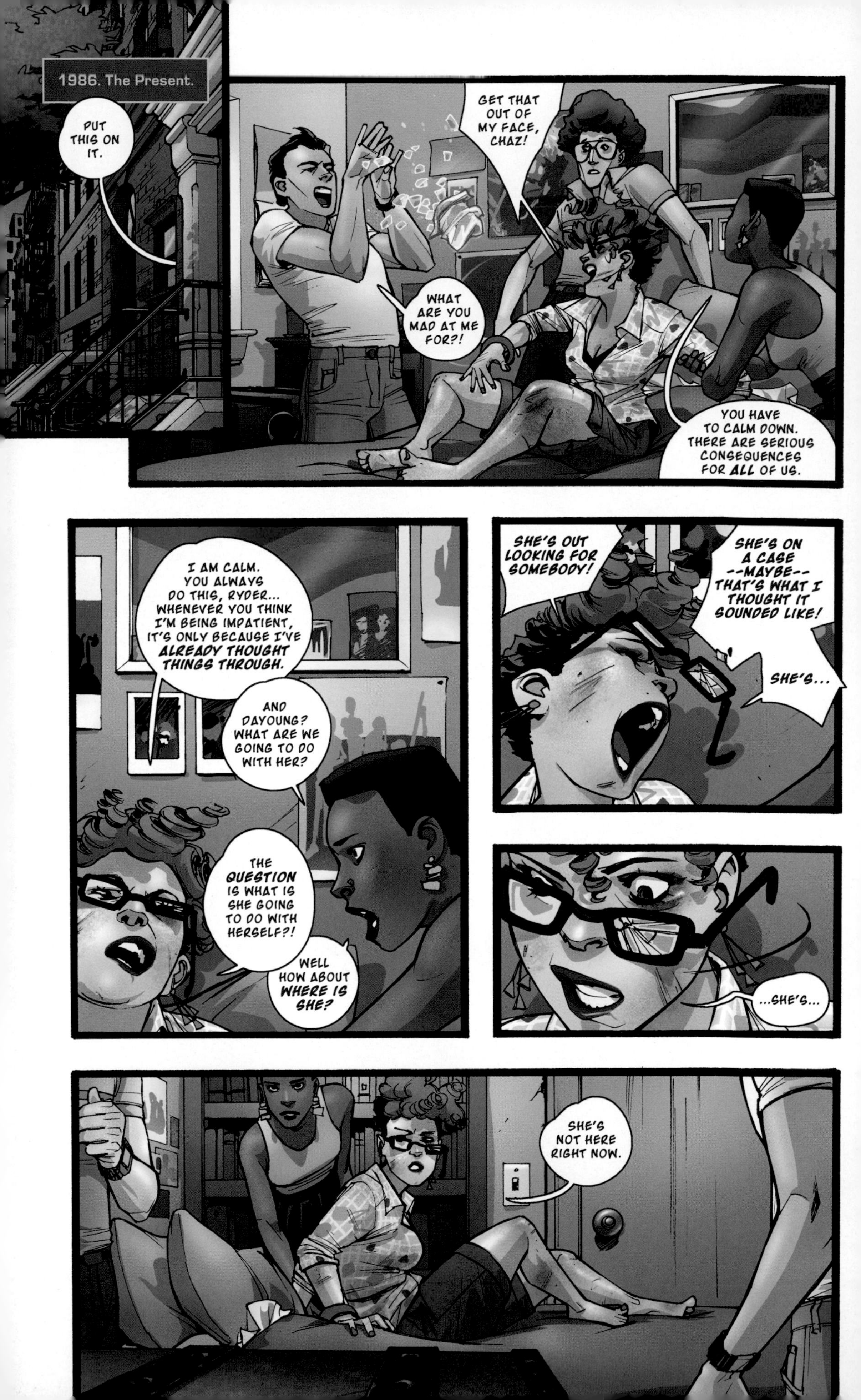
1986. The Present.
PUT THIS ON IT.
GET THAT OUT OF MY FACE, CHAZ!
WHAT ARE YOU MAD AT ME FOR?!
YOU HAVE TO CALM DOWN. THERE ARE SERIOUS CONSEQUENCES FOR ALL OF US.
I AM CALM. YOU ALWAYS DO THIS, RYDER... WHENEVER YOU THINK I'M BEING IMPATIENT, IT'S ONLY BECAUSE I'VE ALREADY THOUGHT THINGS THROUGH.
AND DAYOUNG? WHAT ARE WE GOING TO DO WITH HER?
THE QUESTION IS WHAT IS SHE GOING TO DO WITH HERSELF?!
WELL HOW ABOUT WHERE IS SHE?
SHE'S OUT LOOKING FOR SOMEBODY!
SHE'S ON A CASE --MAYBE-- THAT'S WHAT I THOUGHT IT SOUNDED LIKE!
SHE'S...
...SHE'S...
SHE'S NOT HERE RIGHT NOW.

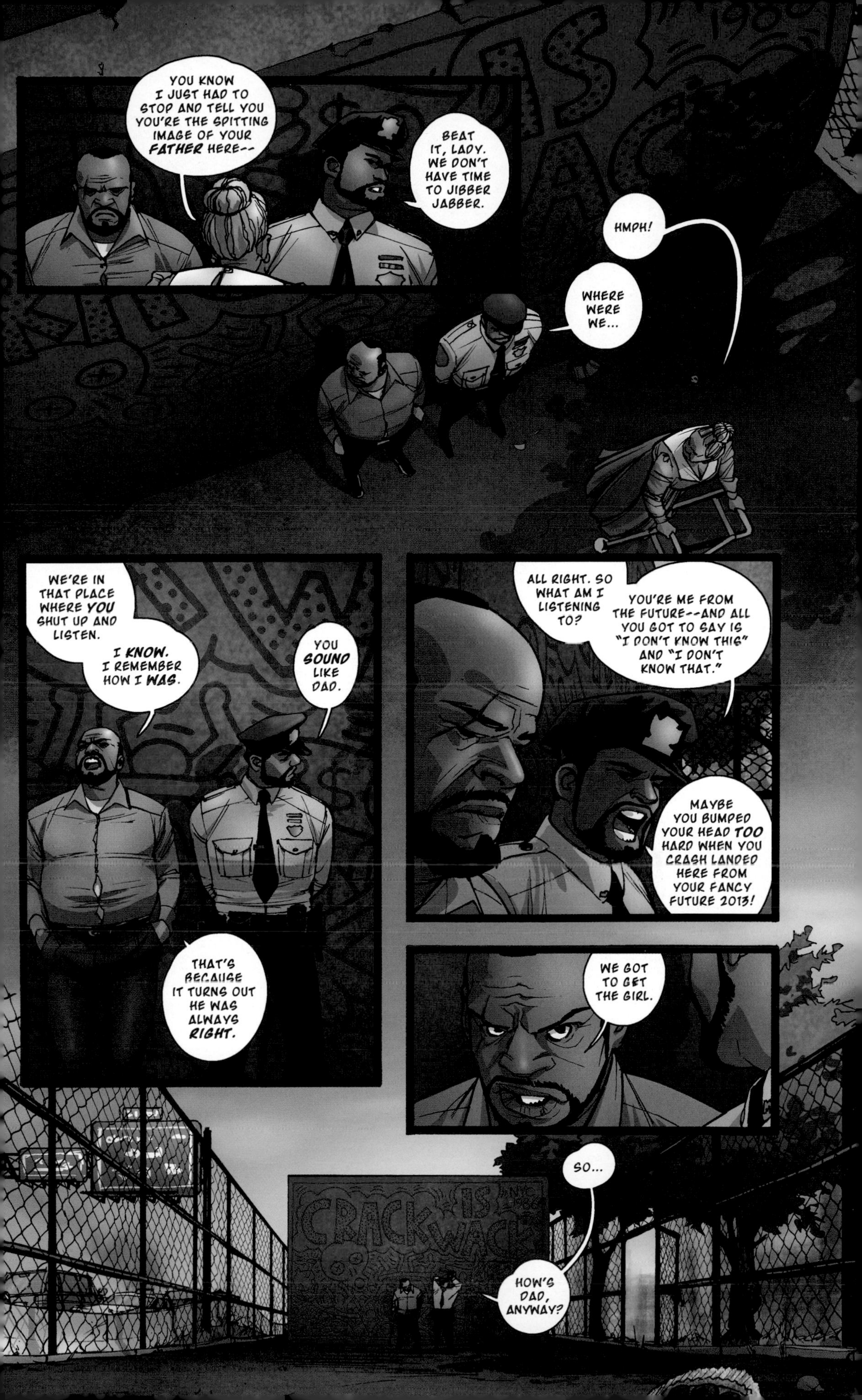
YOU KNOW I JUST HAD TO STOP AND TELL YOU YOU'RE THE SPITTING IMAGE OF YOUR FATHER HERE--
BEAT IT, LADY. WE DON'T HAVE TIME TO JIBBER JABBER.
HMPH!
WHERE WERE WE...
WE'RE IN THAT PLACE WHERE YOU SHUT UP AND LISTEN.
I KNOW. I REMEMBER HOW I WAS.
YOU SOUND LIKE DAD.
THAT'S BECAUSE IT TURNS OUT HE WAS ALWAYS RIGHT.
ALL RIGHT. SO WHAT AM I LISTENING TO?
YOU'RE ME FROM THE FUTURE--AND ALL YOU GOT TO SAY IS "I DON'T KNOW THIS" AND "I DON'T KNOW THAT."
MAYBE YOU BUMPED YOUR HEAD TOO HARD WHEN YOU CRASH LANDED HERE FROM YOUR FANCY FUTURE 2013!
WE GOT TO GET THE GIRL.
CRACK IS WACK
SO...
HOW'S DAD, ANYWAY?

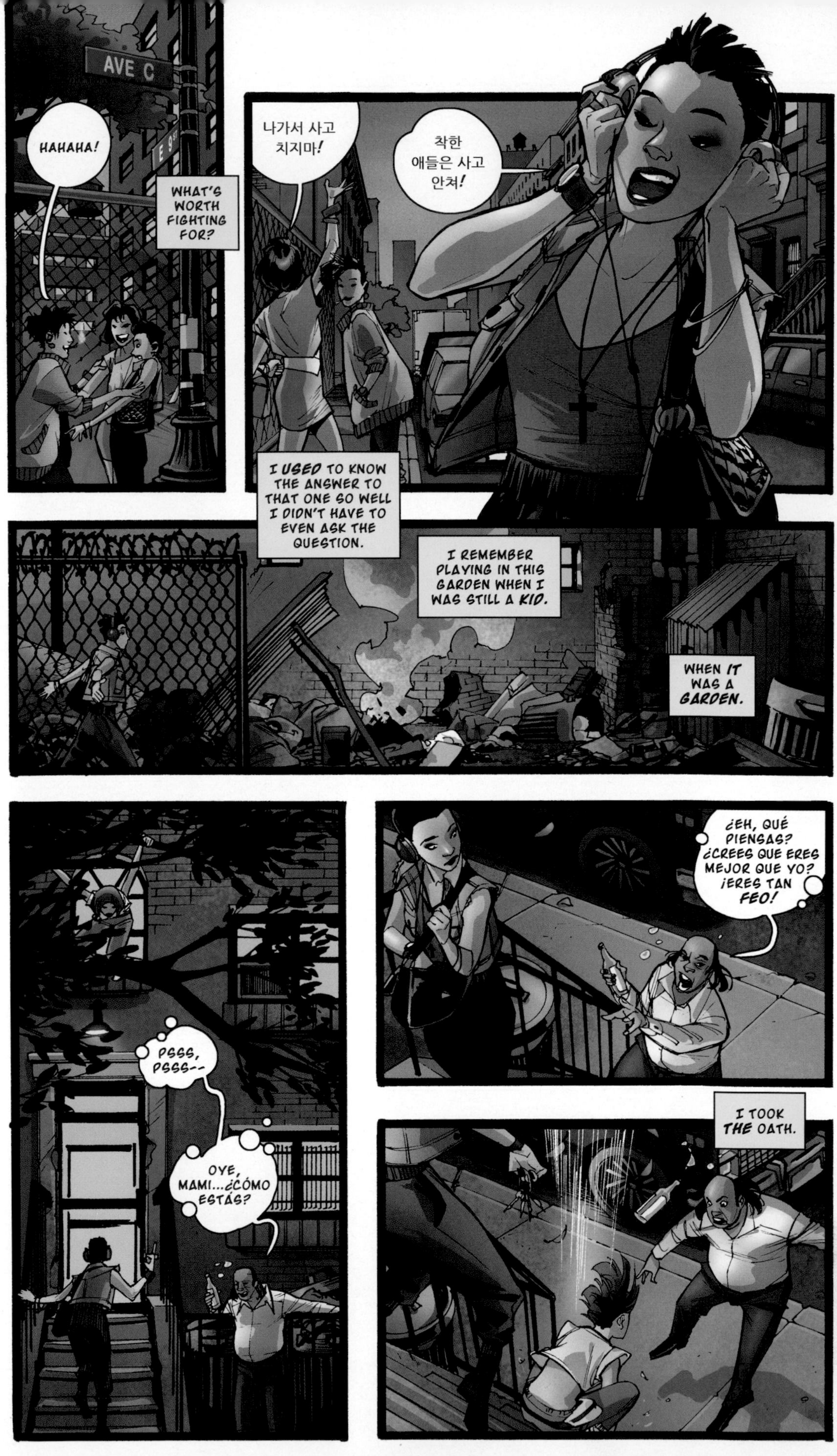
AVE C
HAHAHA!
WHAT'S WORTH FIGHTING FOR?
나가서 사고 치지마!
착한 애들은 사고 안쳐!
I *USED* TO KNOW THE ANSWER TO THAT ONE SO WELL I DIDN'T HAVE TO EVEN ASK THE QUESTION.
I REMEMBER PLAYING IN THIS GARDEN WHEN I WAS STILL A *KID*.
WHEN *IT* WAS A *GARDEN*.
PSSS, PSSS--
OYE, MAMI...¿CÓMO ESTÁS?
¿EH, QUÉ PIENSAS? ¿CREES QUE ERES MEJOR QUE YO? ¡ERES TAN *FEO!*
I TOOK *THE* OATH.

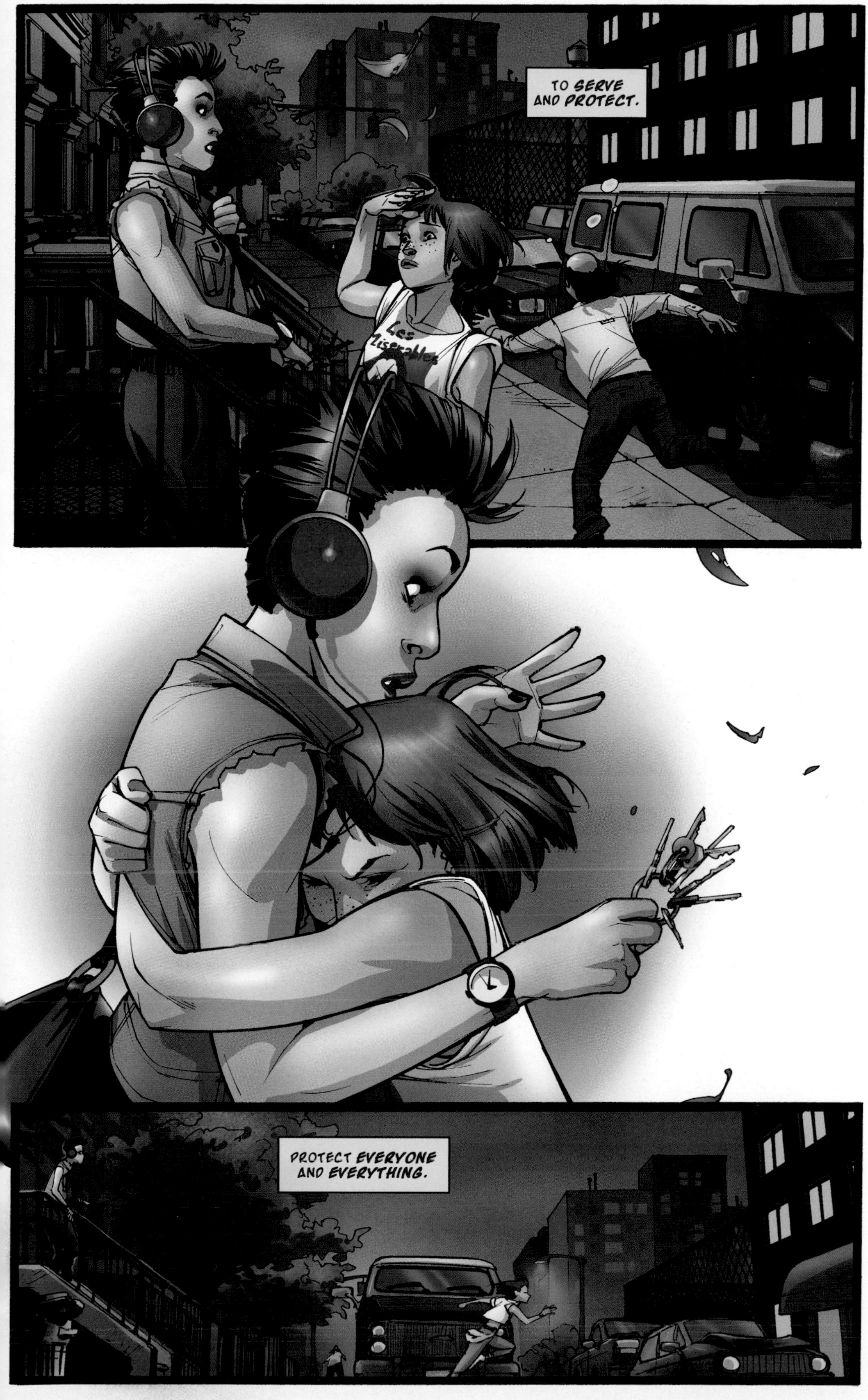
TO SERVE
AND PROTECT.
Les Misérables
PROTECT EVERYONE
AND EVERYTHING.

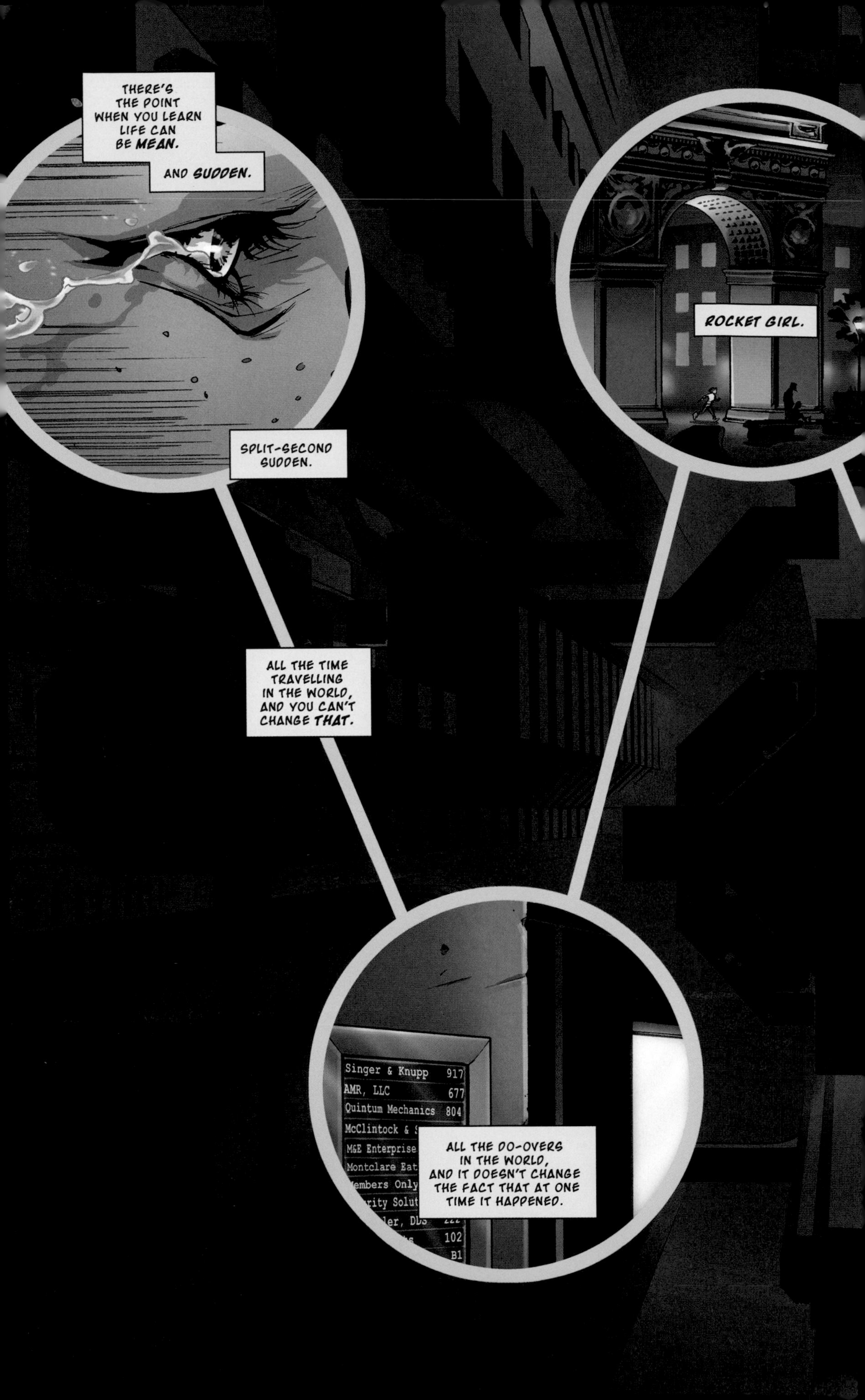
THERE'S THE POINT WHEN YOU LEARN LIFE CAN BE MEAN.
AND SUDDEN.
SPLIT-SECOND SUDDEN.
ROCKET GIRL.
ALL THE TIME TRAVELLING IN THE WORLD, AND YOU CAN'T CHANGE THAT.
Singer & Knupp 917
AMR, LLC 677
Quintum Mechanics 804
ALL THE DO-OVERS IN THE WORLD, AND IT DOESN'T CHANGE THE FACT THAT AT ONE TIME IT HAPPENED.

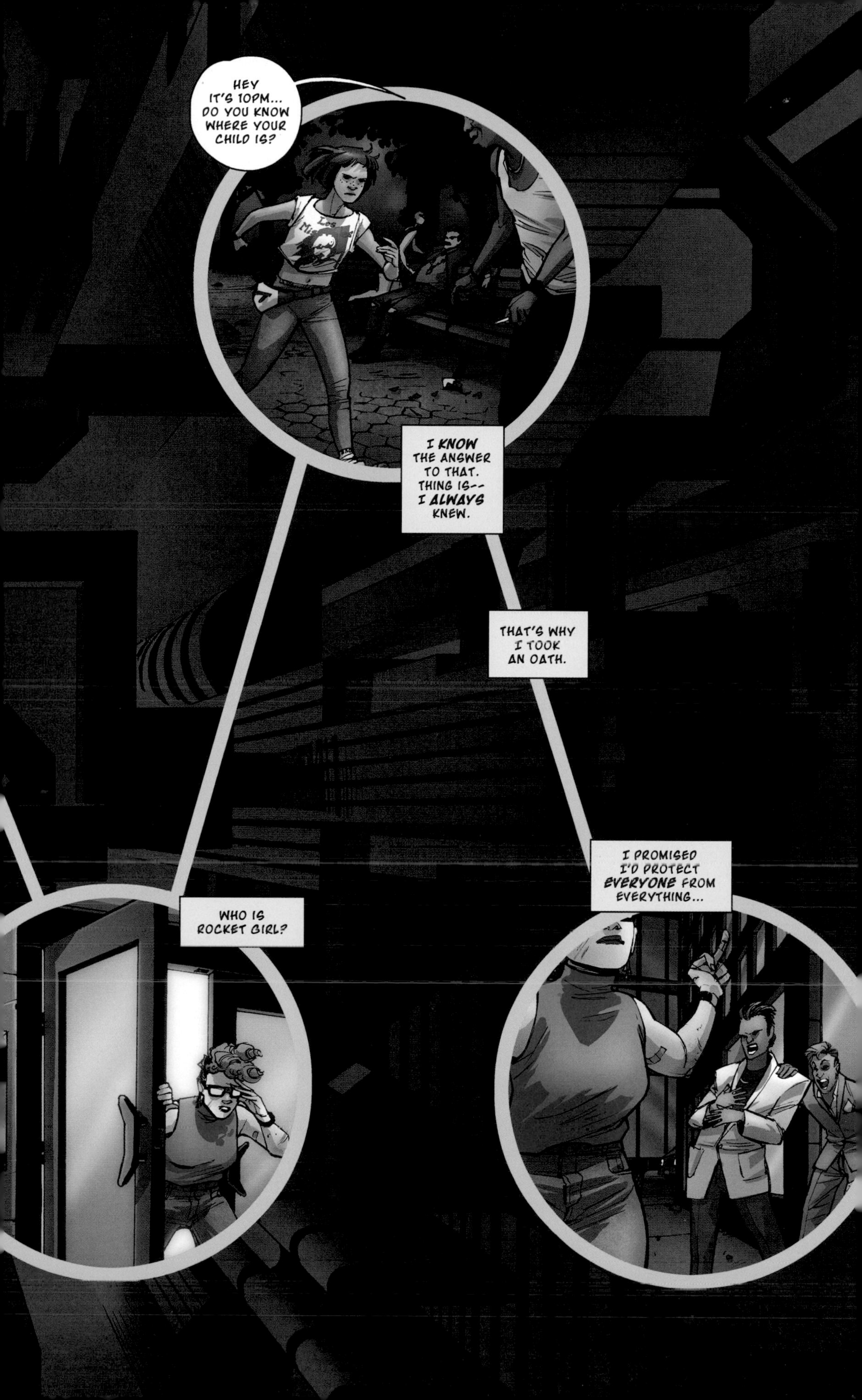
HEY IT'S 10PM... DO YOU KNOW WHERE YOUR CHILD IS?
I KNOW THE ANSWER TO THAT. THING IS-- I ALWAYS KNEW.
THAT'S WHY I TOOK AN OATH.
I PROMISED I'D PROTECT EVERYONE FROM EVERYTHING...
WHO IS ROCKET GIRL?

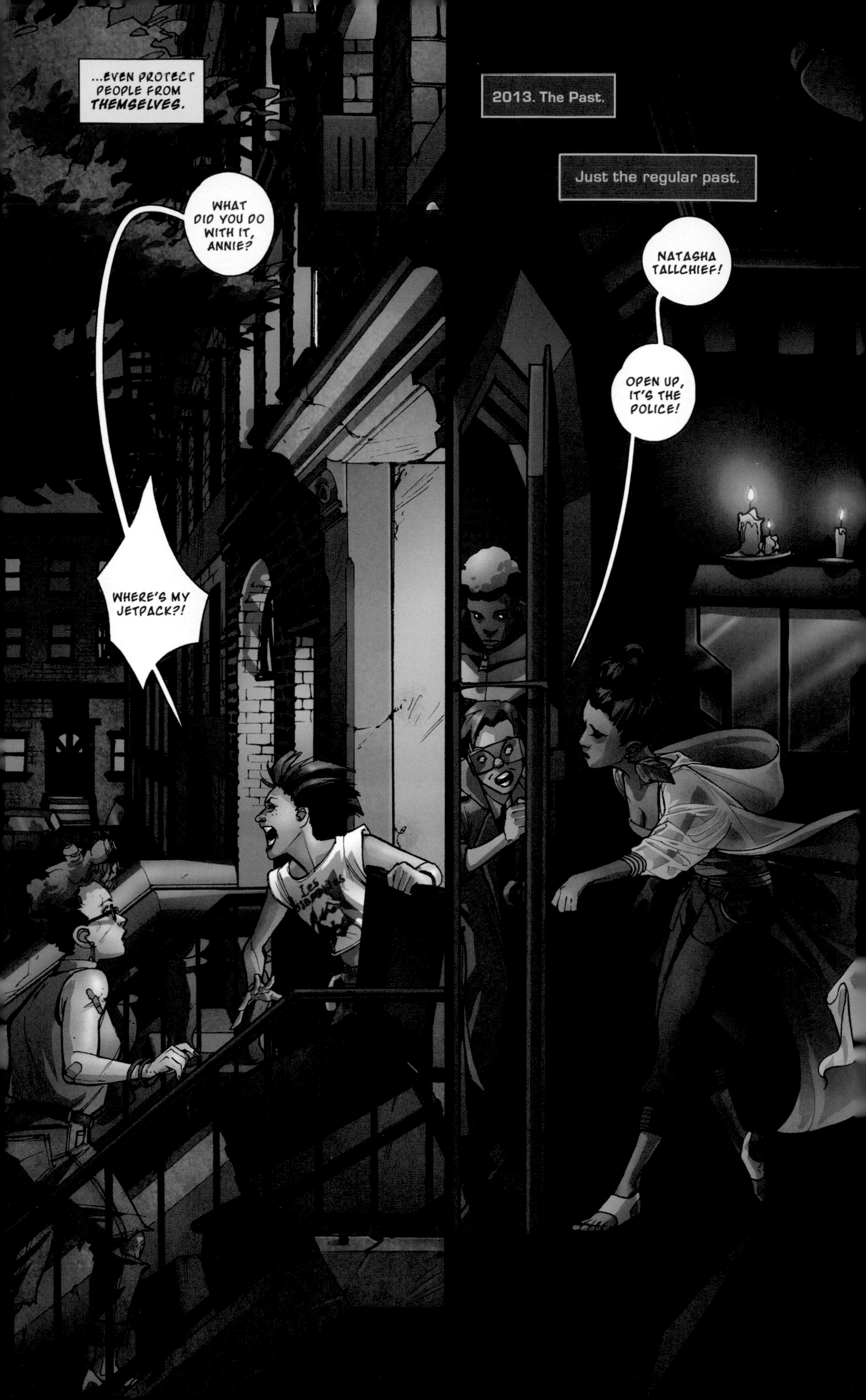
...EVEN PROTECT PEOPLE FROM THEMSELVES.
WHAT DID YOU DO WITH IT, ANNIE?
WHERE'S MY JETPACK?!
2013. The Past.
Just the regular past.
NATASHA TALLCHIEF!
OPEN UP, IT'S THE POLICE!

Chapter 7_Now What?! >>

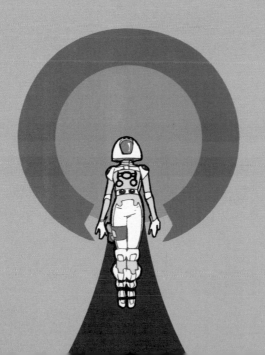

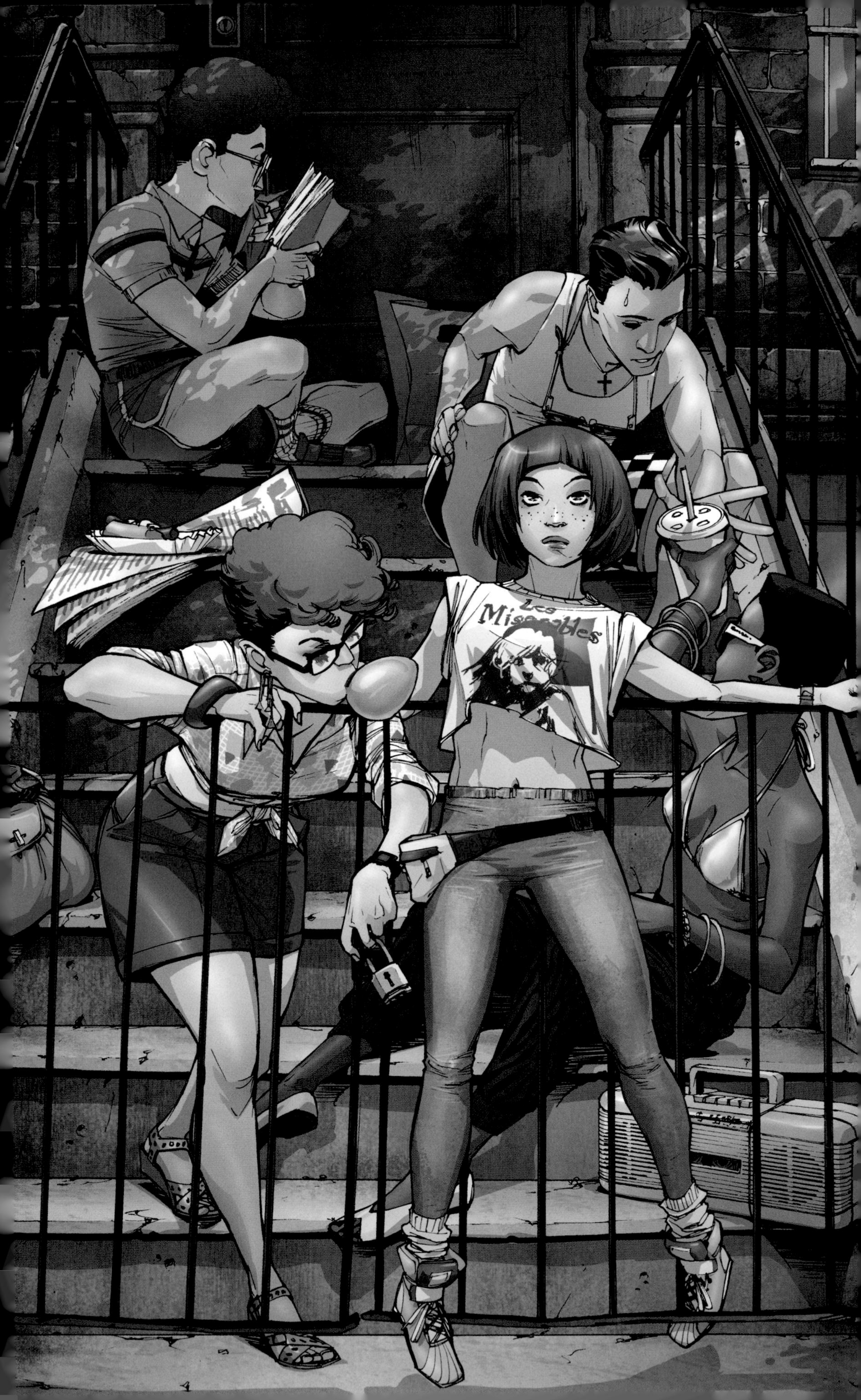

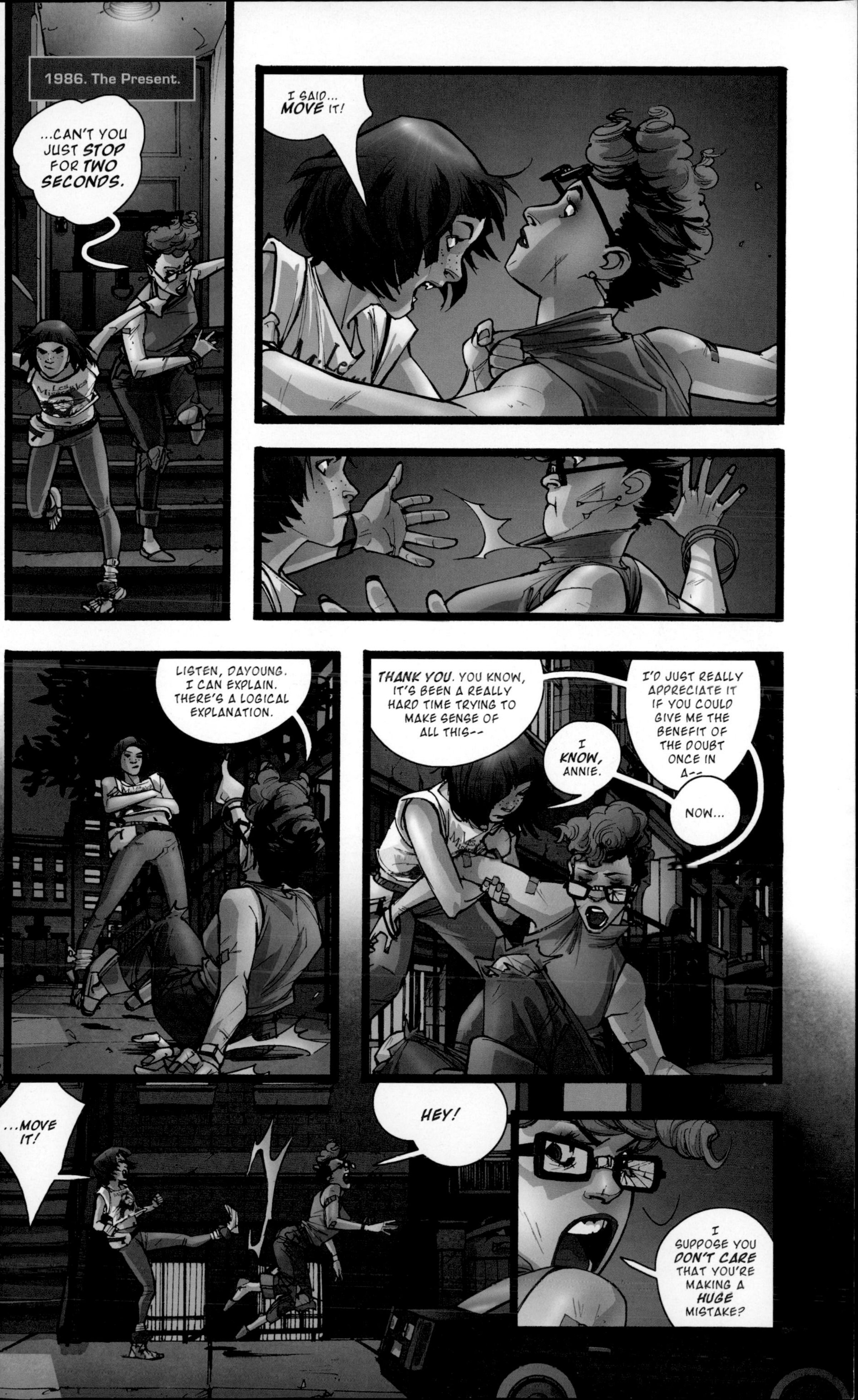
1986. The Present.
...CAN'T YOU JUST STOP FOR TWO SECONDS.
I SAID... MOVE IT!
LISTEN, DAYOUNG. I CAN EXPLAIN. THERE'S A LOGICAL EXPLANATION.
THANK YOU. YOU KNOW, IT'S BEEN A REALLY HARD TIME TRYING TO MAKE SENSE OF ALL THIS--
I'D JUST REALLY APPRECIATE IT IF YOU COULD GIVE ME THE BENEFIT OF THE DOUBT ONCE IN A--
I KNOW, ANNIE.
NOW...
...MOVE IT!
HEY!
I SUPPOSE YOU DON'T CARE THAT YOU'RE MAKING A HUGE MISTAKE?

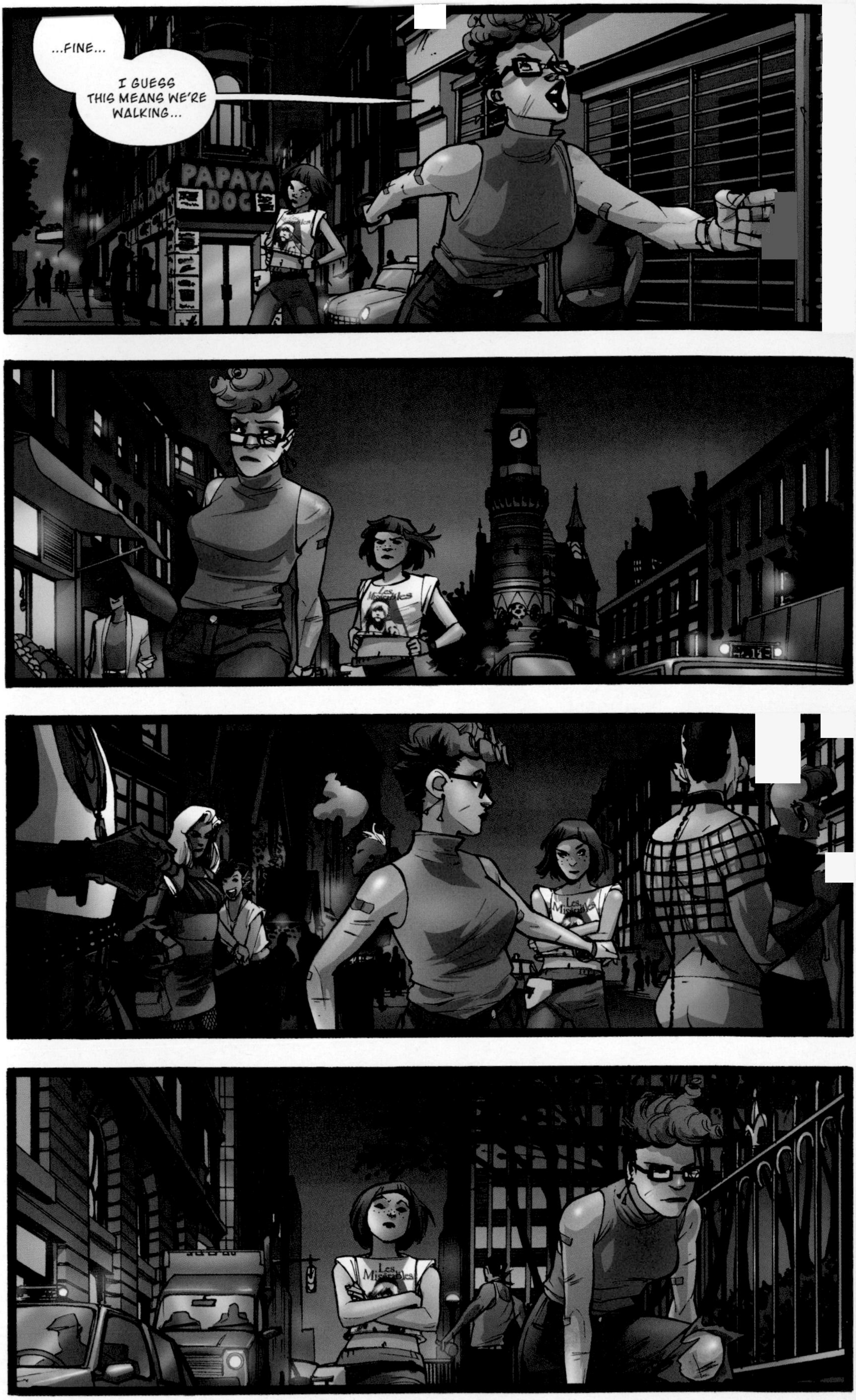
...FINE...
I GUESS THIS MEANS WE'RE WALKING...
PAPAYA DOG

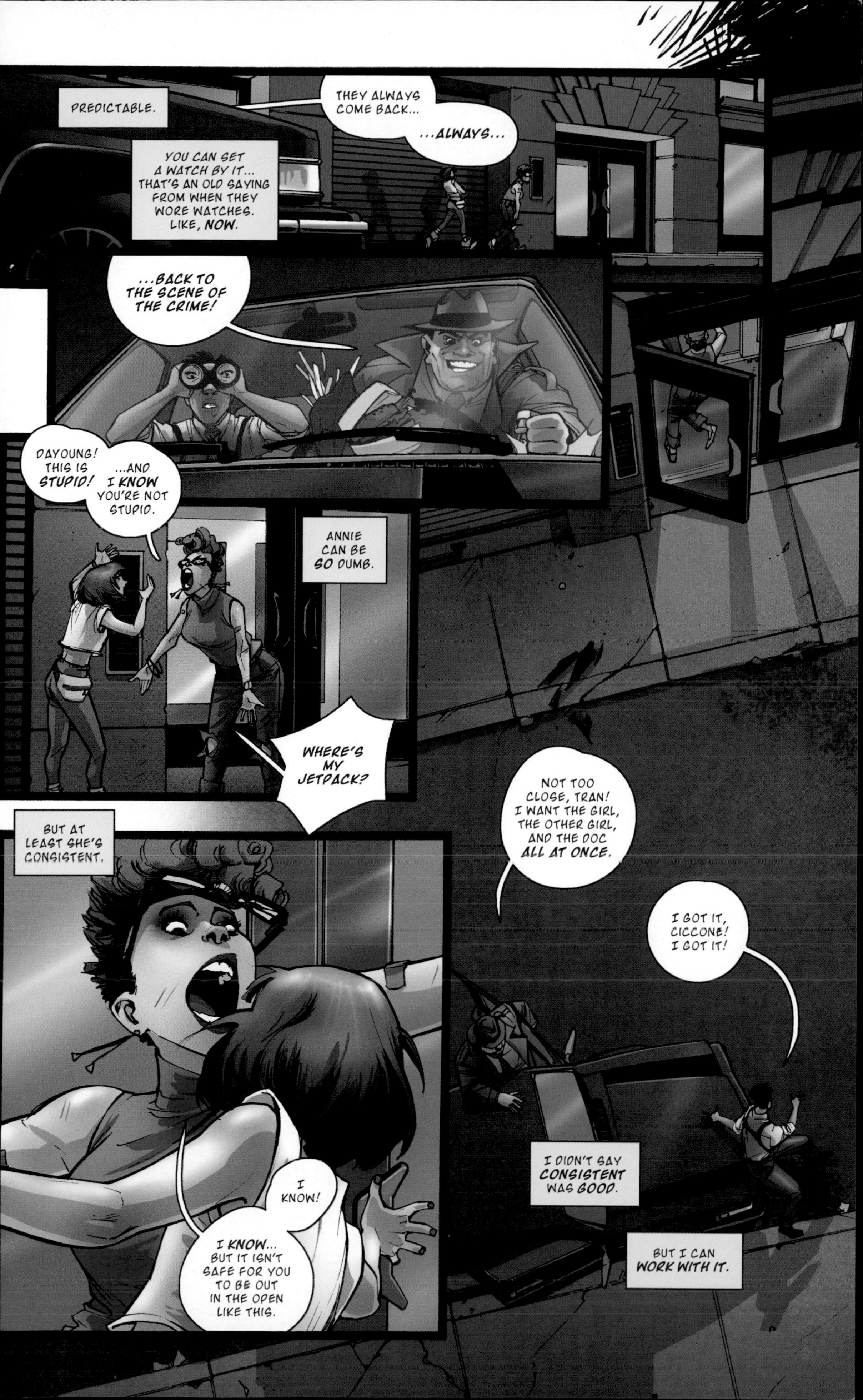
PREDICTABLE.
THEY ALWAYS COME BACK...
...ALWAYS...
YOU CAN SET A WATCH BY IT... THAT'S AN OLD SAYING FROM WHEN THEY WORE WATCHES. LIKE, NOW.
...BACK TO THE SCENE OF THE CRIME!
DAYOUNG! THIS IS STUPID!
...AND I KNOW YOU'RE NOT STUPID.
ANNIE CAN BE SO DUMB.
WHERE'S MY JETPACK?
NOT TOO CLOSE, TRAN! I WANT THE GIRL, THE OTHER GIRL, AND THE DOC ALL AT ONCE.
BUT AT LEAST SHE'S CONSISTENT.
I GOT IT, CICCONE! I GOT IT!
I KNOW!
I KNOW... BUT IT ISN'T SAFE FOR YOU TO BE OUT IN THE OPEN LIKE THIS.
I DIDN'T SAY CONSISTENT WAS GOOD.
BUT I CAN WORK WITH IT.

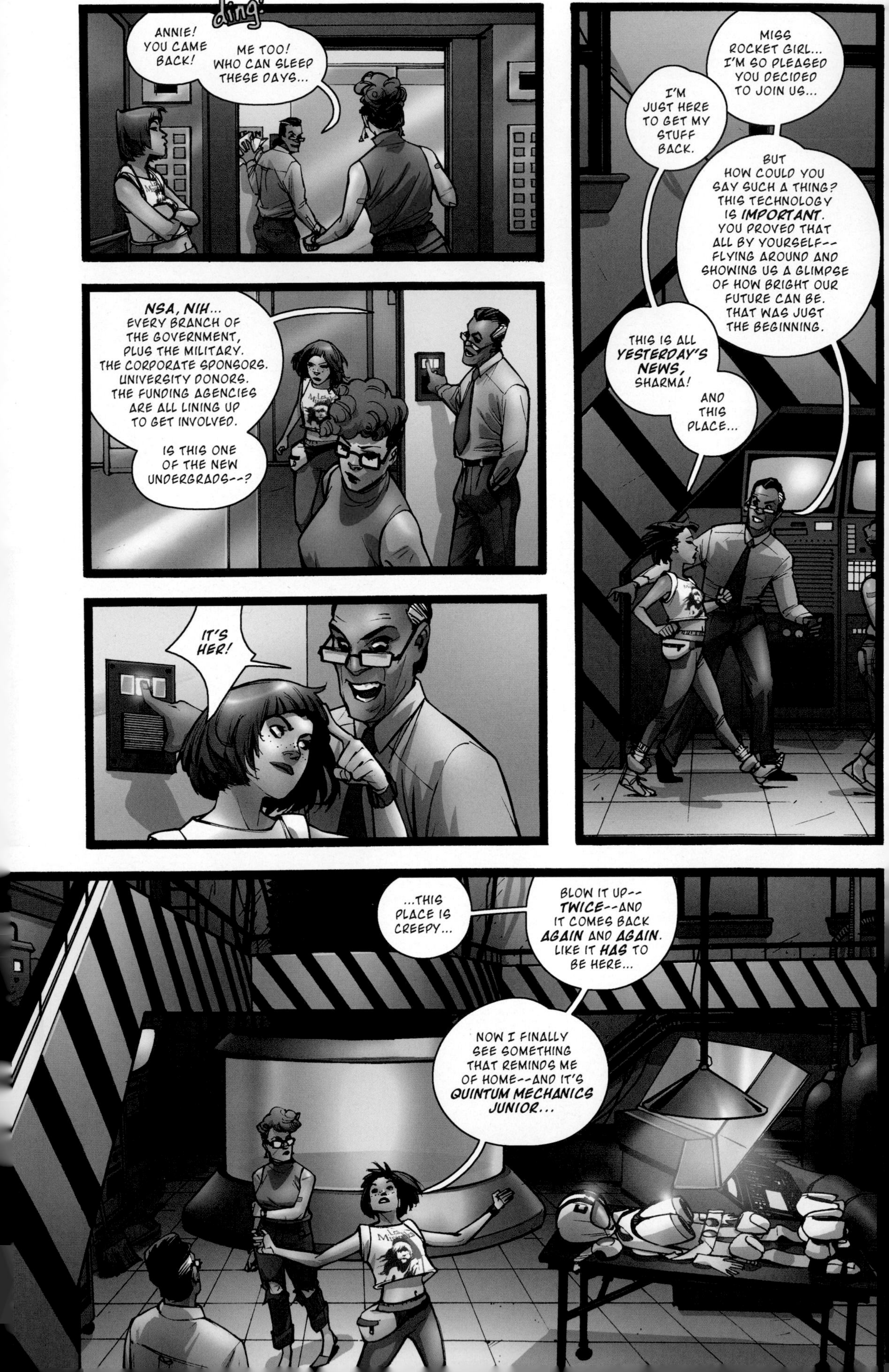
ding!
ANNIE! YOU CAME BACK!
ME TOO! WHO CAN SLEEP THESE DAYS...
NSA, NIH... EVERY BRANCH OF THE GOVERNMENT, PLUS THE MILITARY. THE CORPORATE SPONSORS. UNIVERSITY DONORS. THE FUNDING AGENCIES ARE ALL LINING UP TO GET INVOLVED.
IS THIS ONE OF THE NEW UNDERGRADS--?
IT'S HER!
MISS ROCKET GIRL... I'M SO PLEASED YOU DECIDED TO JOIN US...
I'M JUST HERE TO GET MY STUFF BACK.
BUT HOW COULD YOU SAY SUCH A THING? THIS TECHNOLOGY IS IMPORTANT. YOU PROVED THAT ALL BY YOURSELF-- FLYING AROUND AND SHOWING US A GLIMPSE OF HOW BRIGHT OUR FUTURE CAN BE. THAT WAS JUST THE BEGINNING.
THIS IS ALL YESTERDAY'S NEWS, SHARMA!
AND THIS PLACE...
...THIS PLACE IS CREEPY...
BLOW IT UP-- TWICE--AND IT COMES BACK AGAIN AND AGAIN. LIKE IT HAS TO BE HERE...
NOW I FINALLY SEE SOMETHING THAT REMINDS ME OF HOME--AND IT'S QUINTUM MECHANICS JUNIOR...

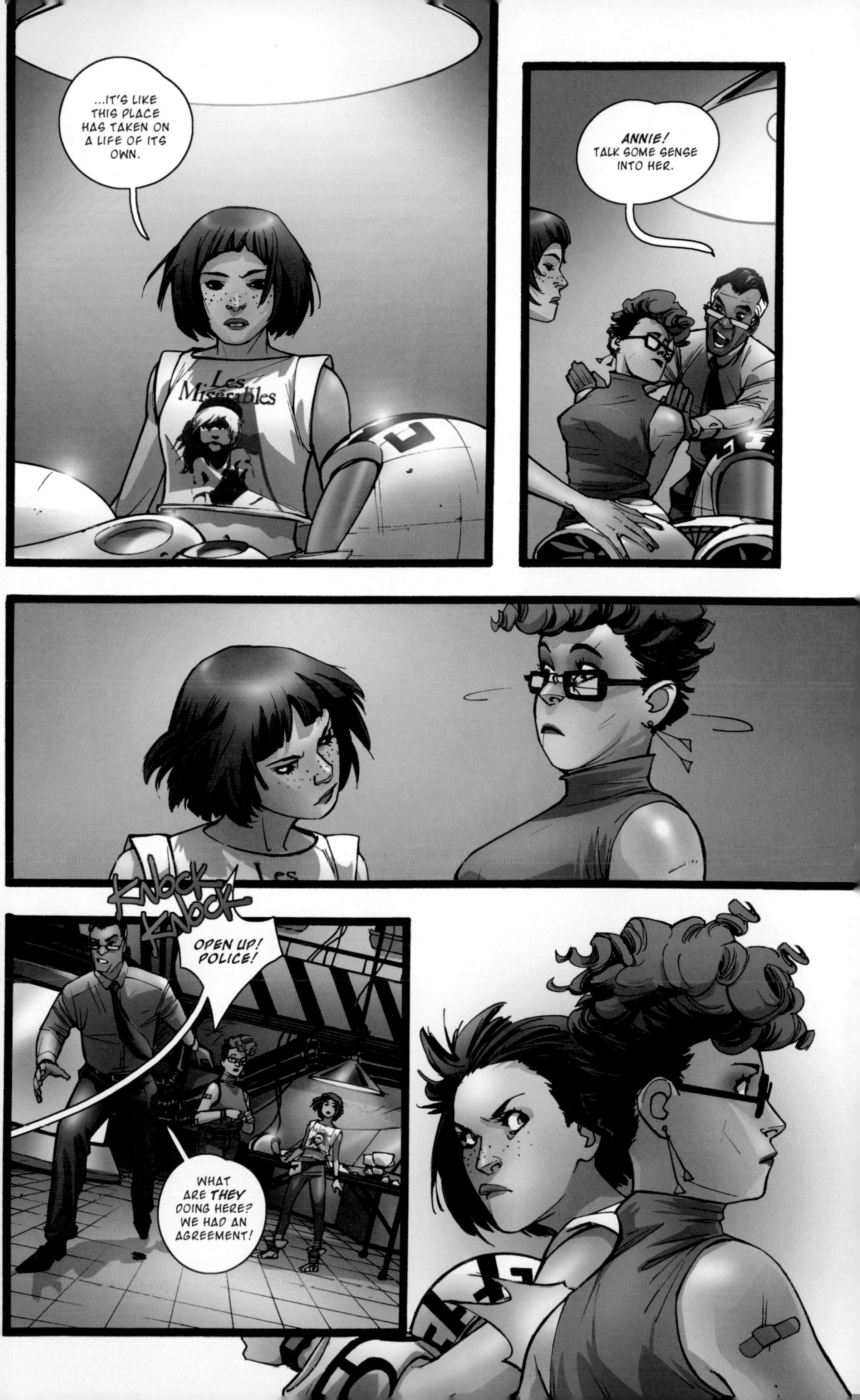
...IT'S LIKE THIS PLACE HAS TAKEN ON A LIFE OF ITS OWN.
Les Misérables
ANNIE! TALK SOME SENSE INTO HER.
Les
KNOCK KNOCK
OPEN UP! POLICE!
WHAT ARE THEY DOING HERE? WE HAD AN AGREEMENT!

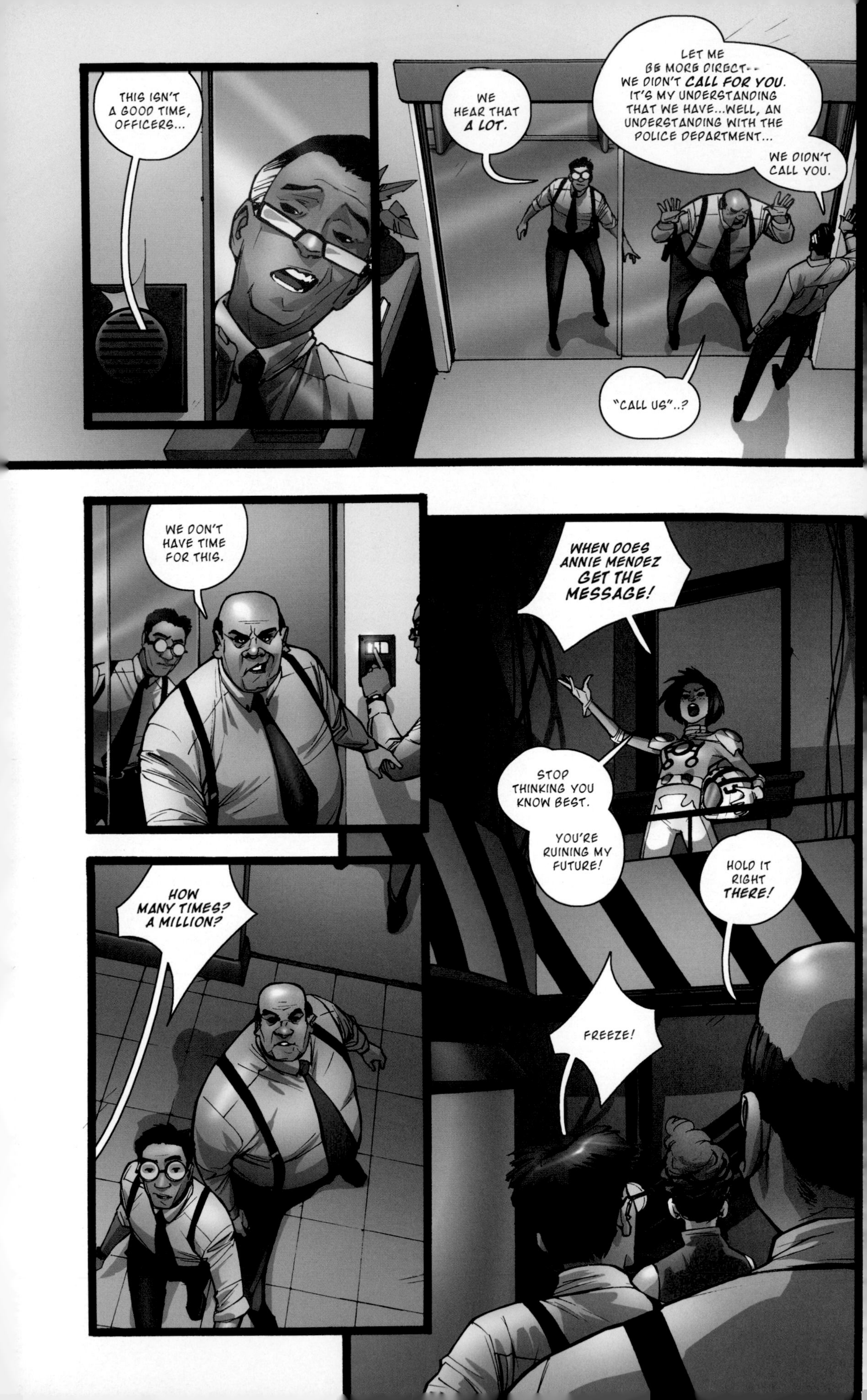
THIS ISN'T A GOOD TIME, OFFICERS...
WE HEAR THAT A LOT.
LET ME BE MORE DIRECT-- WE DIDN'T CALL FOR YOU. IT'S MY UNDERSTANDING THAT WE HAVE...WELL, AN UNDERSTANDING WITH THE POLICE DEPARTMENT...
WE DIDN'T CALL YOU.
"CALL US"..?
WE DON'T HAVE TIME FOR THIS.
HOW MANY TIMES? A MILLION?
WHEN DOES ANNIE MENDEZ GET THE MESSAGE!
STOP THINKING YOU KNOW BEST.
YOU'RE RUINING MY FUTURE!
HOLD IT RIGHT THERE!
FREEZE!

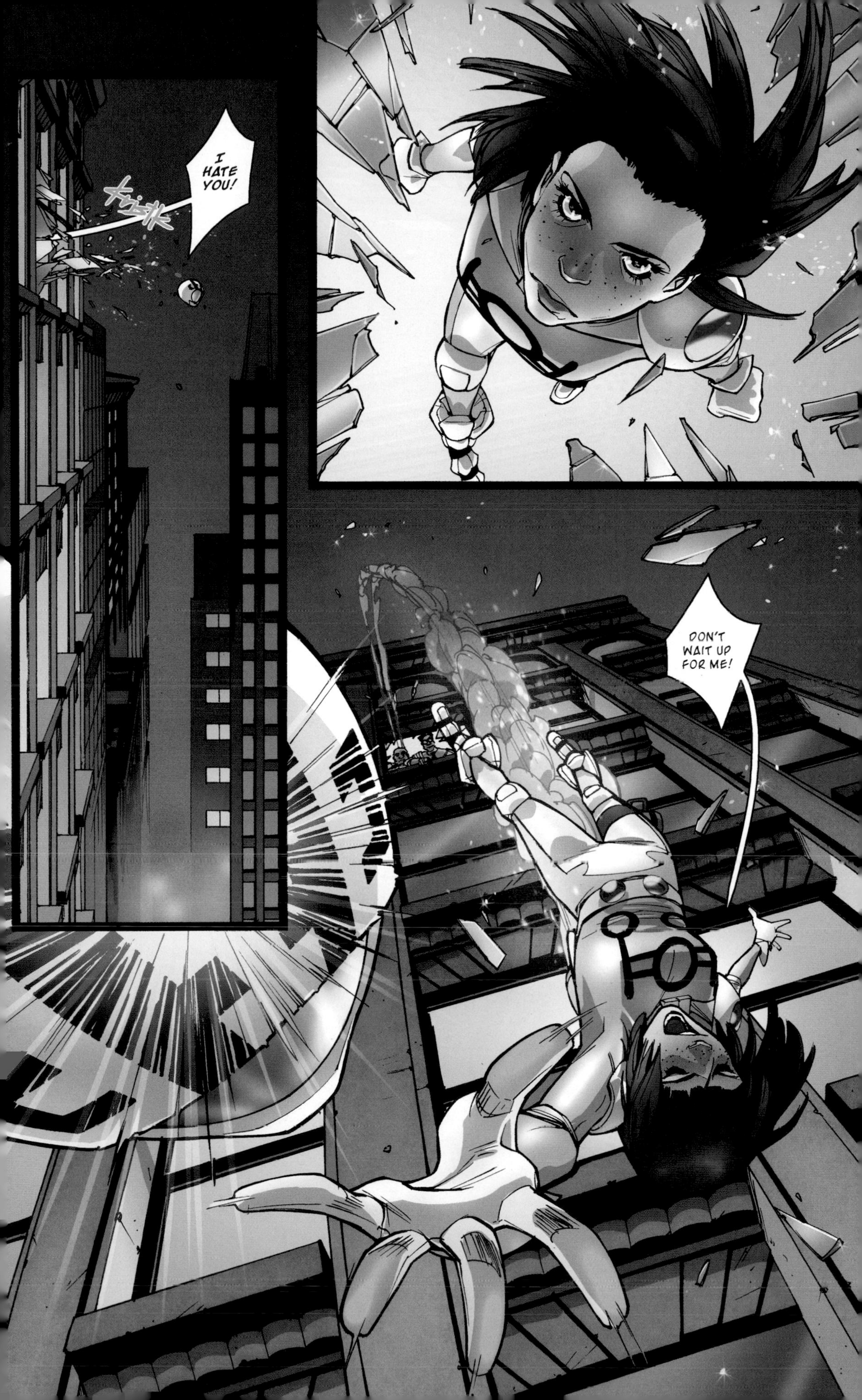
I HATE YOU!
DON'T WAIT UP FOR ME!

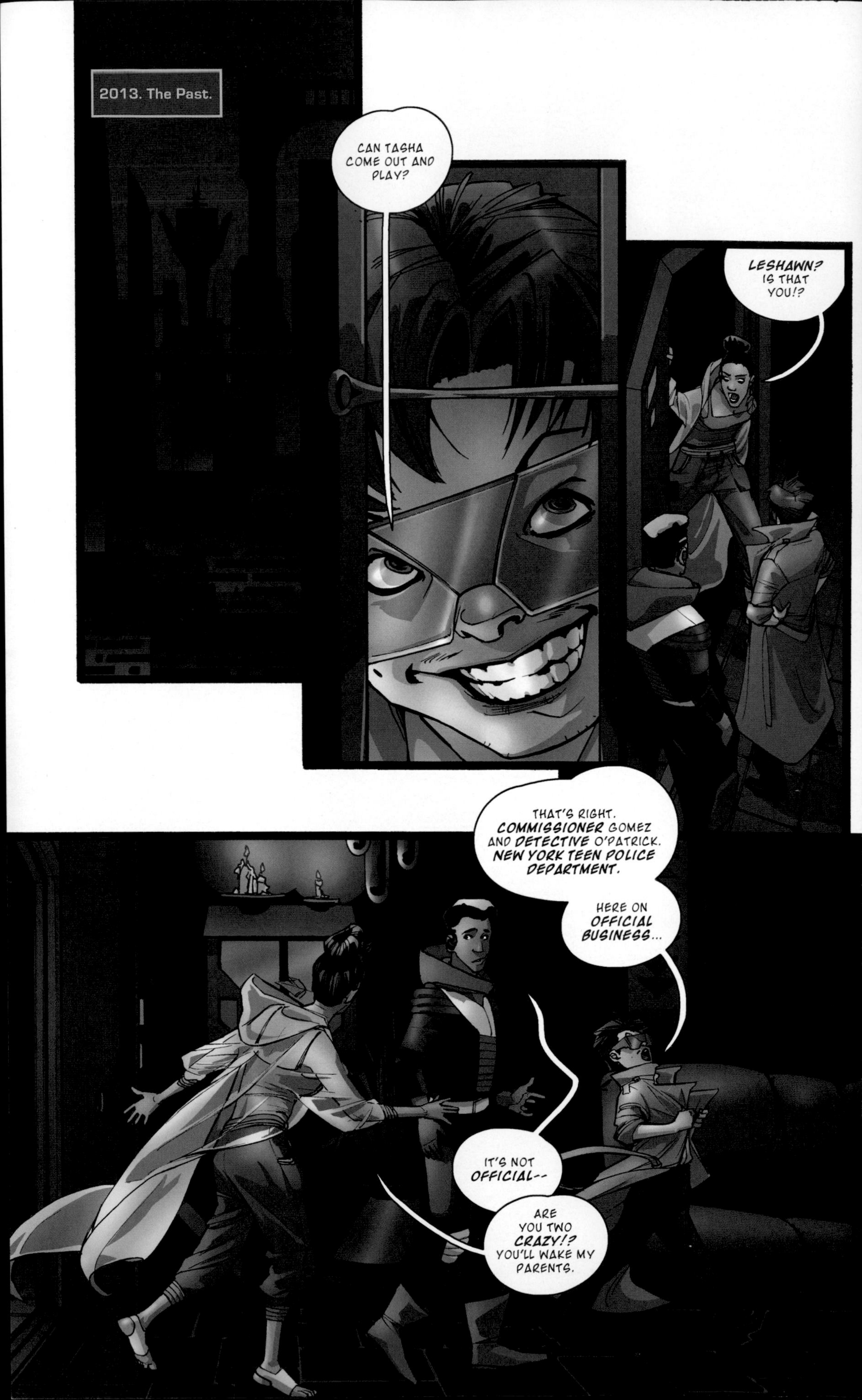
2013. The Past.
CAN TASHA COME OUT AND PLAY?
LESHAWN? IS THAT YOU!?
THAT'S RIGHT. COMMISSIONER GOMEZ AND DETECTIVE O'PATRICK. NEW YORK TEEN POLICE DEPARTMENT.
HERE ON OFFICIAL BUSINESS...
IT'S NOT OFFICIAL--
ARE YOU TWO CRAZY!? YOU'LL WAKE MY PARENTS.

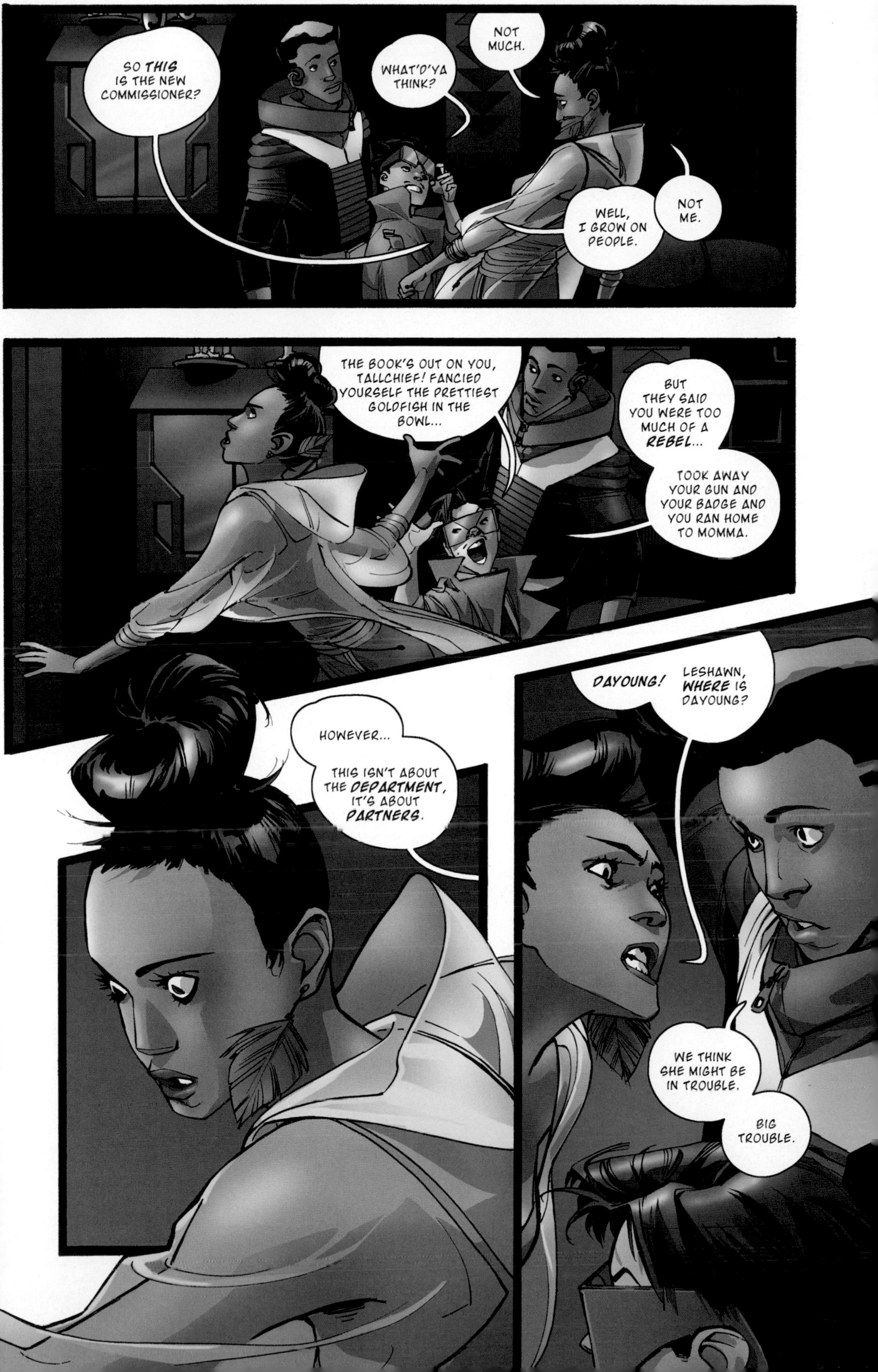
SO THIS IS THE NEW COMMISSIONER?
WHAT'D'YA THINK?
NOT MUCH.
WELL, I GROW ON PEOPLE.
NOT ME.
THE BOOK'S OUT ON YOU, TALLCHIEF! FANCIED YOURSELF THE PRETTIEST GOLDFISH IN THE BOWL...
BUT THEY SAID YOU WERE TOO MUCH OF A REBEL...
TOOK AWAY YOUR GUN AND YOUR BADGE AND YOU RAN HOME TO MOMMA.
HOWEVER...
THIS ISN'T ABOUT THE DEPARTMENT, IT'S ABOUT PARTNERS.
DAYOUNG!
LESHAWN, WHERE IS DAYOUNG?
WE THINK SHE MIGHT BE IN TROUBLE.
BIG TROUBLE.

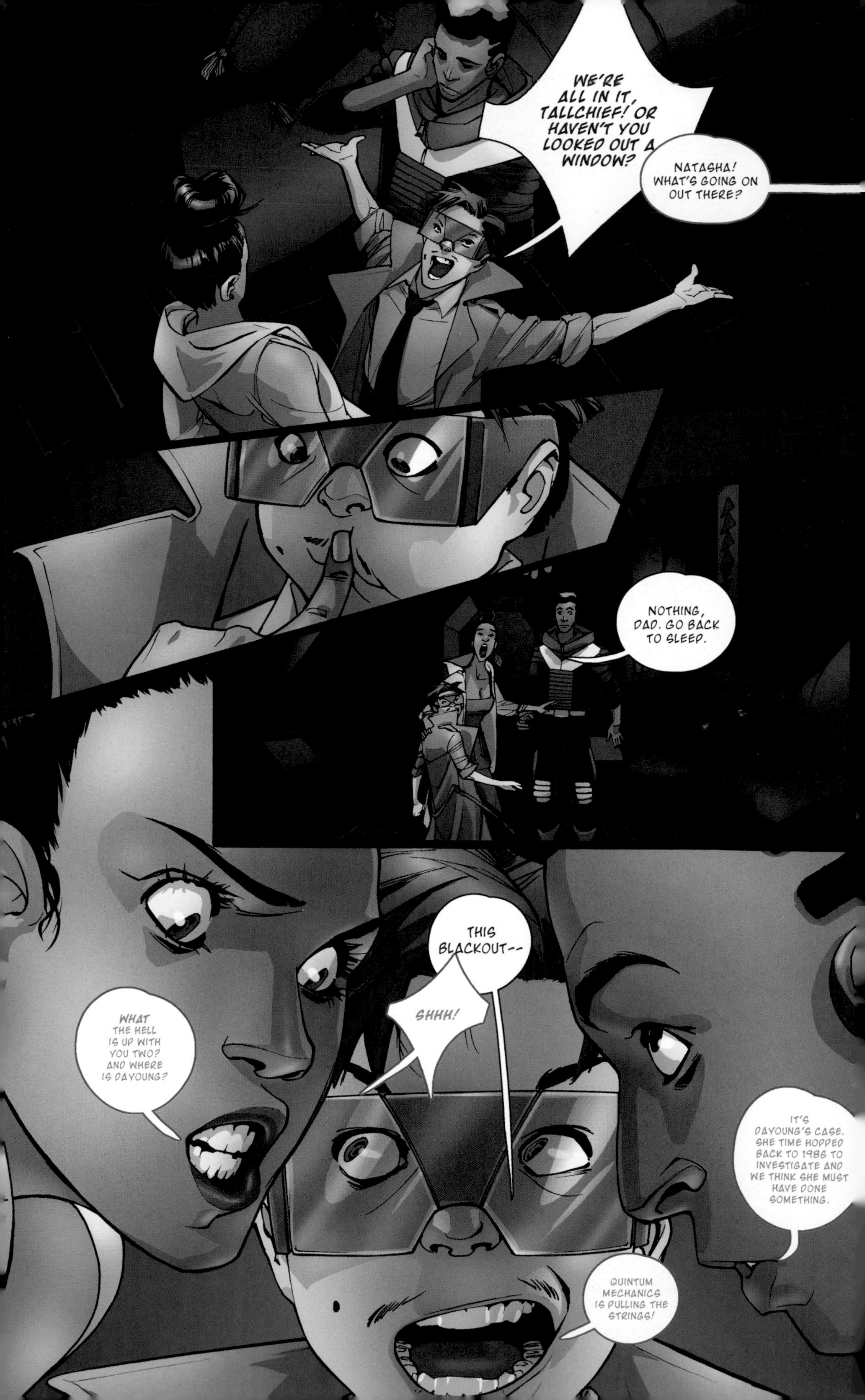

WE'RE ALL IN IT, TALLCHIEF! OR HAVEN'T YOU LOOKED OUT A WINDOW?
NATASHA! WHAT'S GOING ON OUT THERE?
NOTHING, DAD. GO BACK TO SLEEP.
WHAT THE HELL IS UP WITH YOU TWO? AND WHERE IS DAYOUNG?
THIS BLACKOUT--
SHHH!
IT'S DAYOUNG'S CASE. SHE TIME HOPPED BACK TO 1986 TO INVESTIGATE AND WE THINK SHE MUST HAVE DONE SOMETHING.
QUINTUM MECHANICS IS PULLING THE STRINGS!

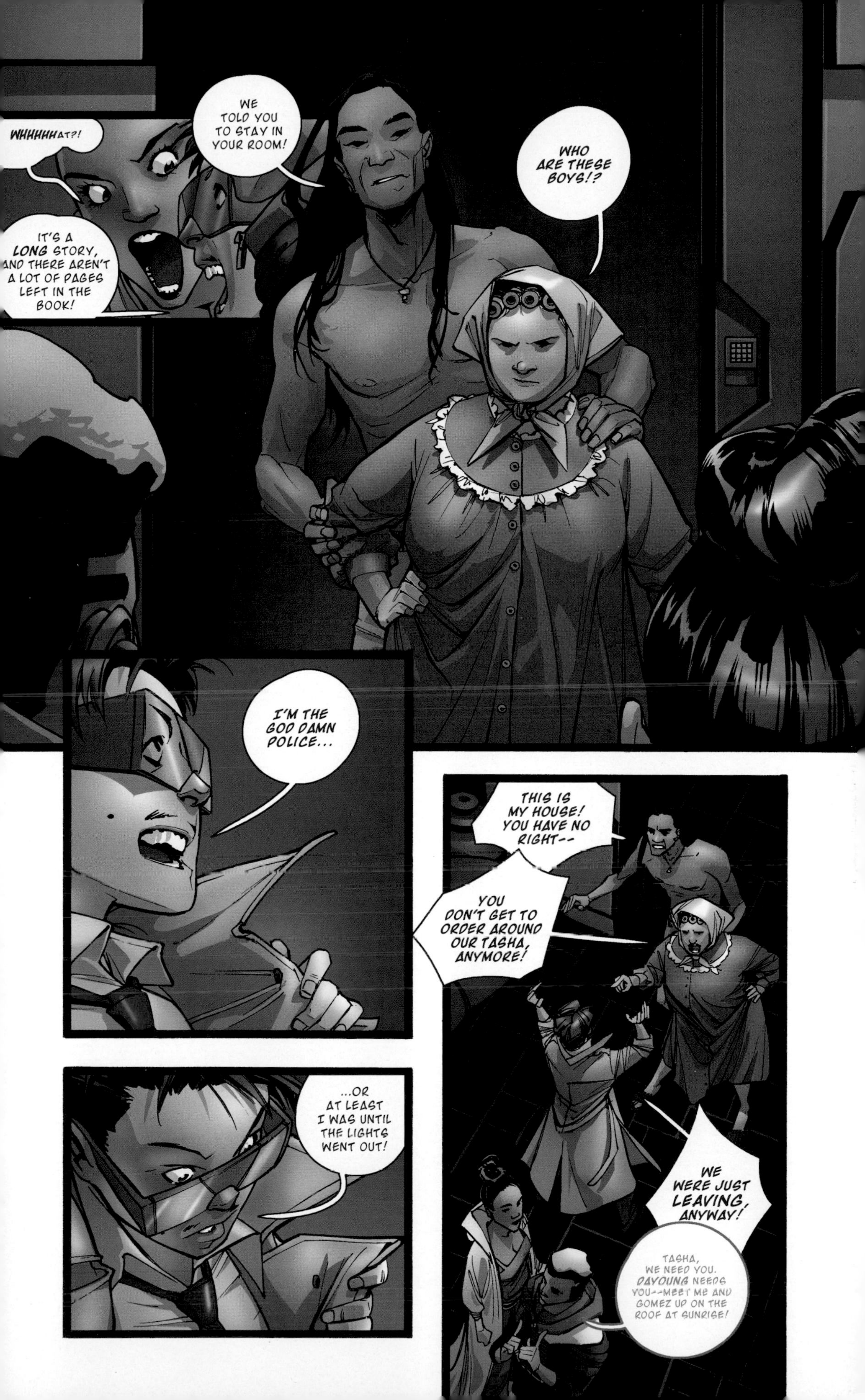
WHHHHHAT?!
WE TOLD YOU TO STAY IN YOUR ROOM!
IT'S A LONG STORY, AND THERE AREN'T A LOT OF PAGES LEFT IN THE BOOK!
WHO ARE THESE BOYS!?
I'M THE GOD DAMN POLICE...
...OR AT LEAST I WAS UNTIL THE LIGHTS WENT OUT!
THIS IS MY HOUSE! YOU HAVE NO RIGHT--
YOU DON'T GET TO ORDER AROUND OUR TASHA, ANYMORE!
WE WERE JUST LEAVING, ANYWAY!
TASHA, WE NEED YOU. DAYOUNG NEEDS YOU--MEET ME AND GOMEZ UP ON THE ROOF AT SUNRISE!

WE CAN DO THIS EASY OR ROUGH, LADY!
AND STAY OUT!
SLAM
THAT DID NOT GO WELL.
WELL... WELL ENOUGH.
LET'S GET OUTSIDE. I CAN'T SEE MY HANDS IN FRONT OF MY FACE IN HERE.
THINK THE STREETS WILL BE SAFE IN THE MORNING?
NEW YORKERS THESE DAYS... WHO KNOWS? THEY'RE SCARED.
FEAR IS GOING TO EVOLVE INTO SOMETHING. LET'S HOPE EVERYONE KEEPS COOL WHEN THE SUN COMES UP.
EITHER WAY, WE CAN'T GO FUMBLING AROUND IN THE NIGHT...

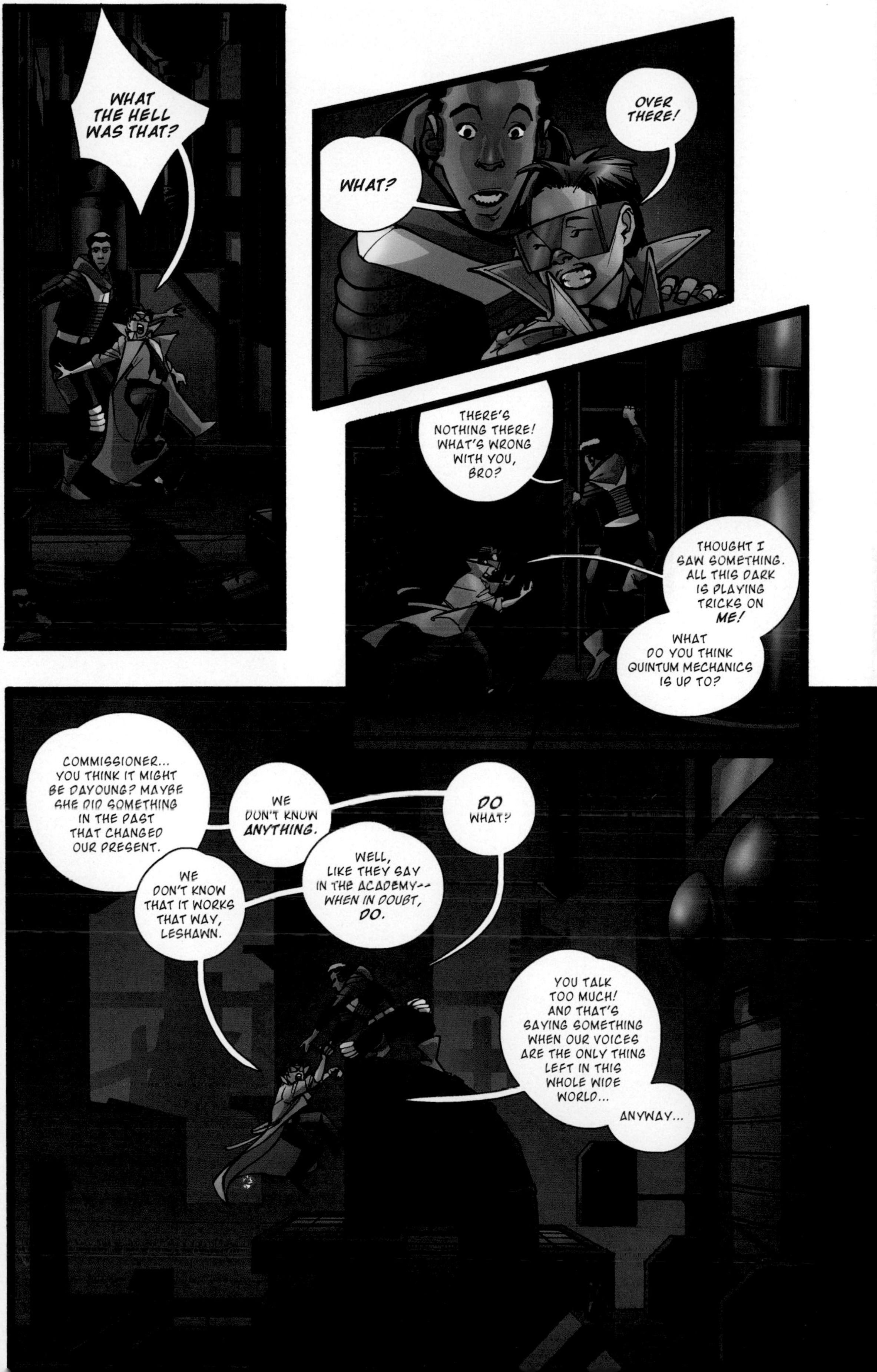
WHAT THE HELL WAS THAT?
OVER THERE!
WHAT?
THERE'S NOTHING THERE! WHAT'S WRONG WITH YOU, BRO?
THOUGHT I SAW SOMETHING. ALL THIS DARK IS PLAYING TRICKS ON ME!
WHAT DO YOU THINK QUINTUM MECHANICS IS UP TO?
COMMISSIONER... YOU THINK IT MIGHT BE DAYOUNG? MAYBE SHE DID SOMETHING IN THE PAST THAT CHANGED OUR PRESENT.
WE DON'T KNOW ANYTHING.
DO WHAT?
WE DON'T KNOW THAT IT WORKS THAT WAY, LESHAWN.
WELL, LIKE THEY SAY IN THE ACADEMY-- WHEN IN DOUBT, DO.
YOU TALK TOO MUCH! AND THAT'S SAYING SOMETHING WHEN OUR VOICES ARE THE ONLY THING LEFT IN THIS WHOLE WIDE WORLD...
ANYWAY...

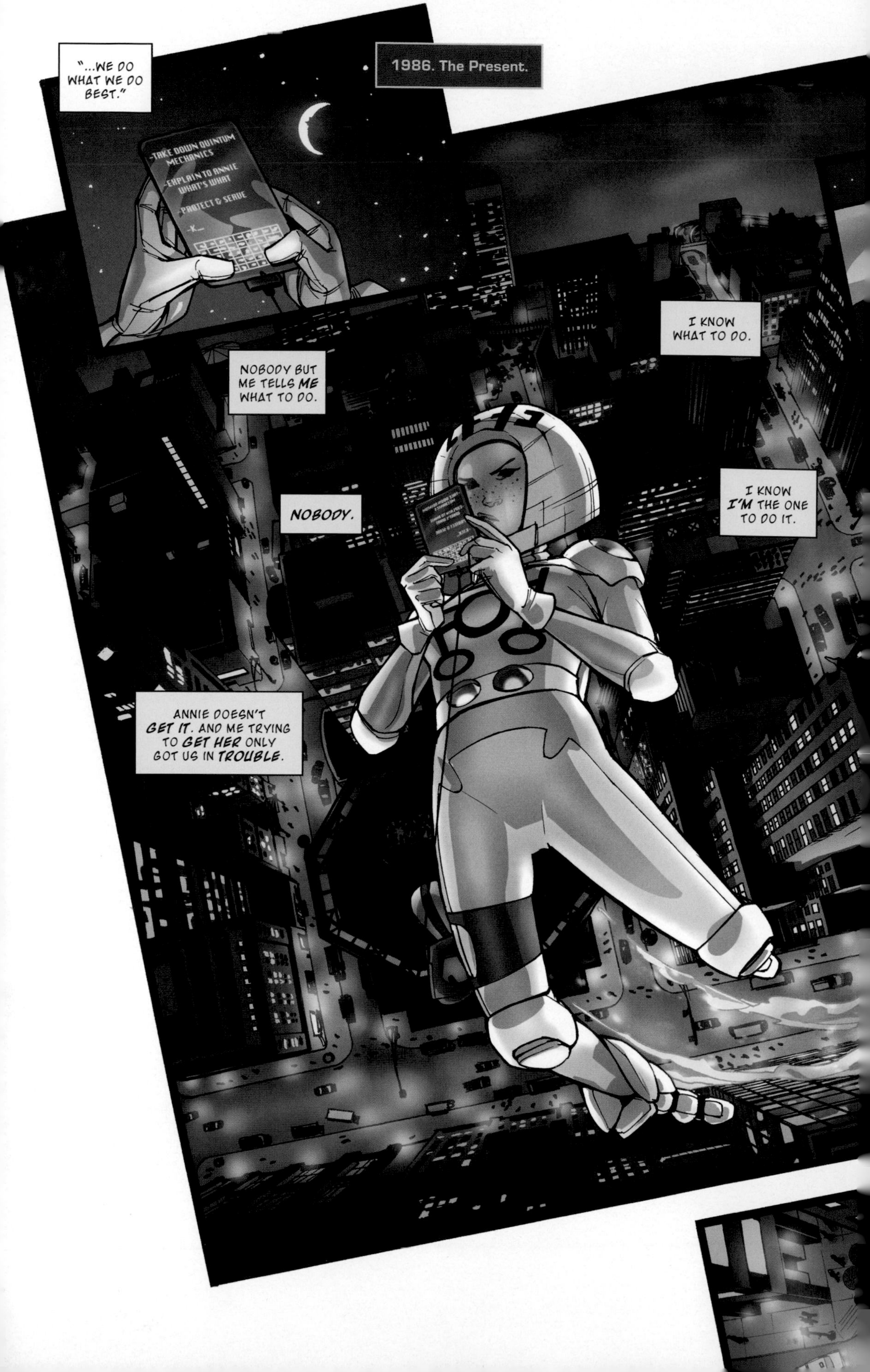
"...WE DO WHAT WE DO BEST."
1986. The Present.
-TAKE DOWN QUINTUM MECHANICS
-EXPLAIN TO ANNIE WHAT'S WHAT
-PROTECT & SERVE
-K_
NOBODY BUT ME TELLS ME WHAT TO DO.
I KNOW WHAT TO DO.
NOBODY.
I KNOW I'M THE ONE TO DO IT.
ANNIE DOESN'T GET IT. AND ME TRYING TO GET HER ONLY GOT US IN TROUBLE.

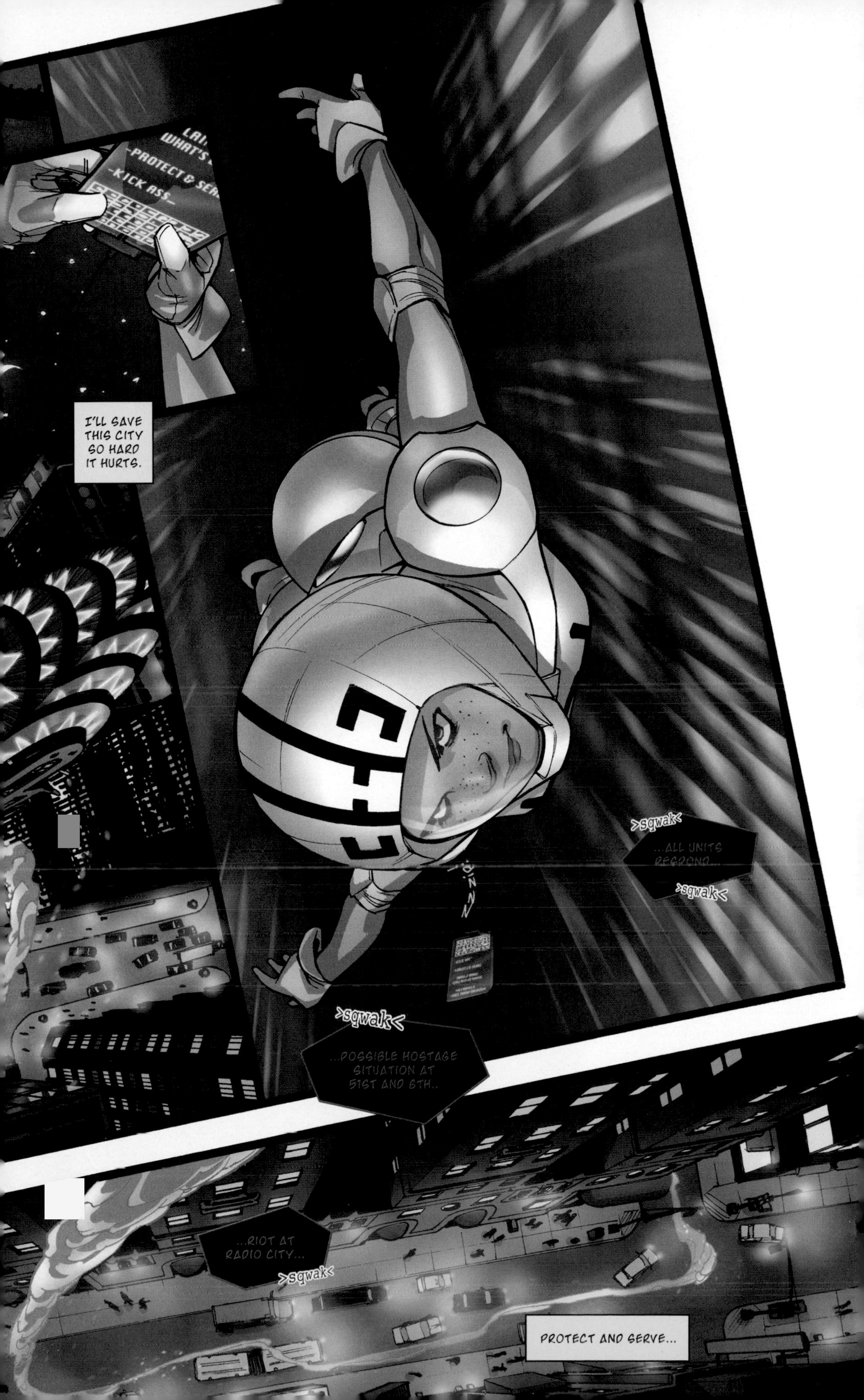
I'LL SAVE THIS CITY SO HARD IT HURTS.
>sqwak<
...ALL UNITS RESPOND...
>sqwak<
>sqwak<
...POSSIBLE HOSTAGE SITUATION AT 51ST AND 6TH...
...RIOT AT RADIO CITY...
>sqwak<
PROTECT AND SERVE...

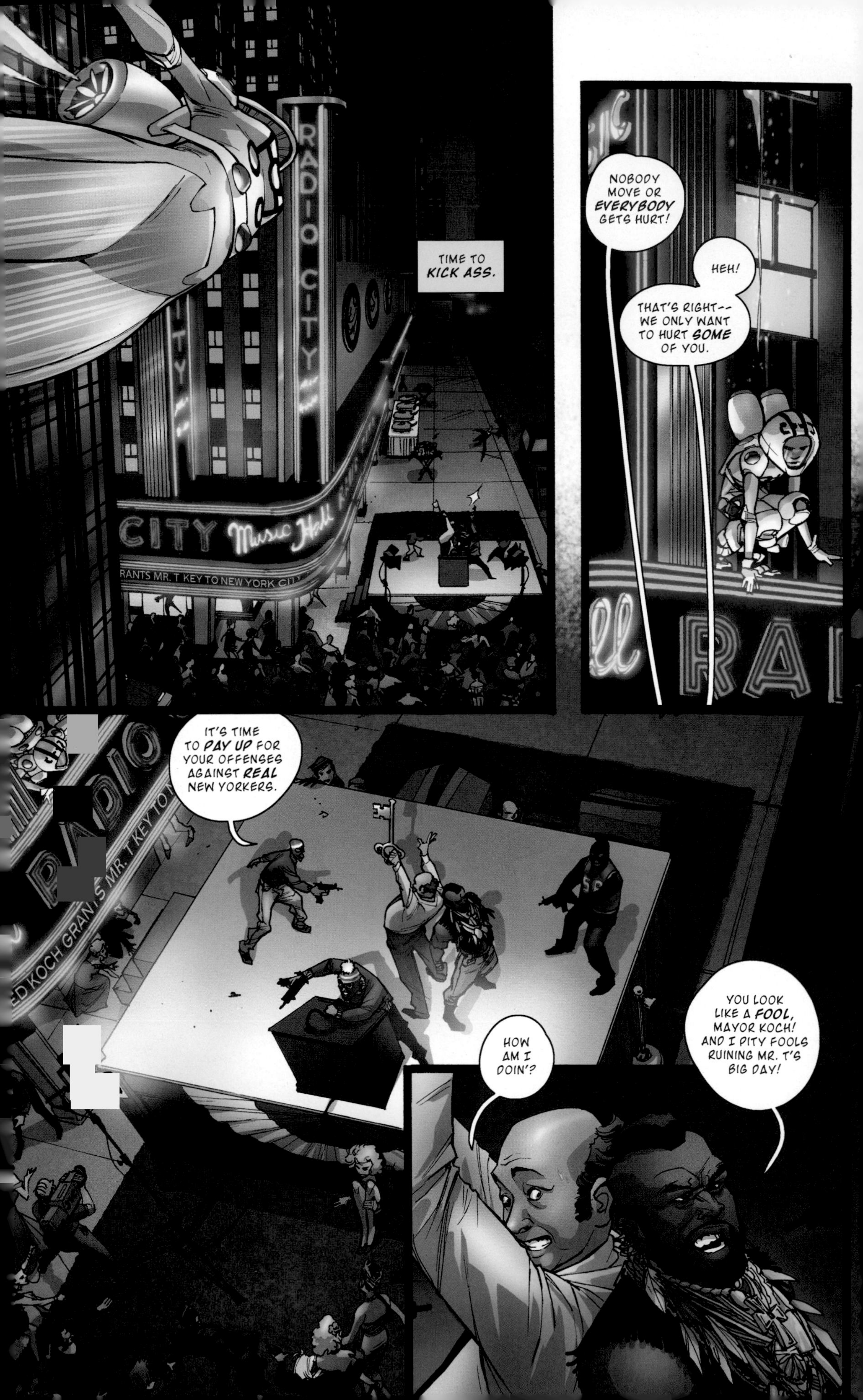
TIME TO KICK ASS.
RADIO CITY
CITY Music Hall
GRANTS MR. T KEY TO NEW YORK CITY
NOBODY MOVE OR EVERYBODY GETS HURT!
HEH!
THAT'S RIGHT--WE ONLY WANT TO HURT SOME OF YOU.
IT'S TIME TO PAY UP FOR YOUR OFFENSES AGAINST REAL NEW YORKERS.
HOW AM I DOIN'?
YOU LOOK LIKE A FOOL, MAYOR KOCH! AND I PITY FOOLS RUINING MR. T'S BIG DAY!

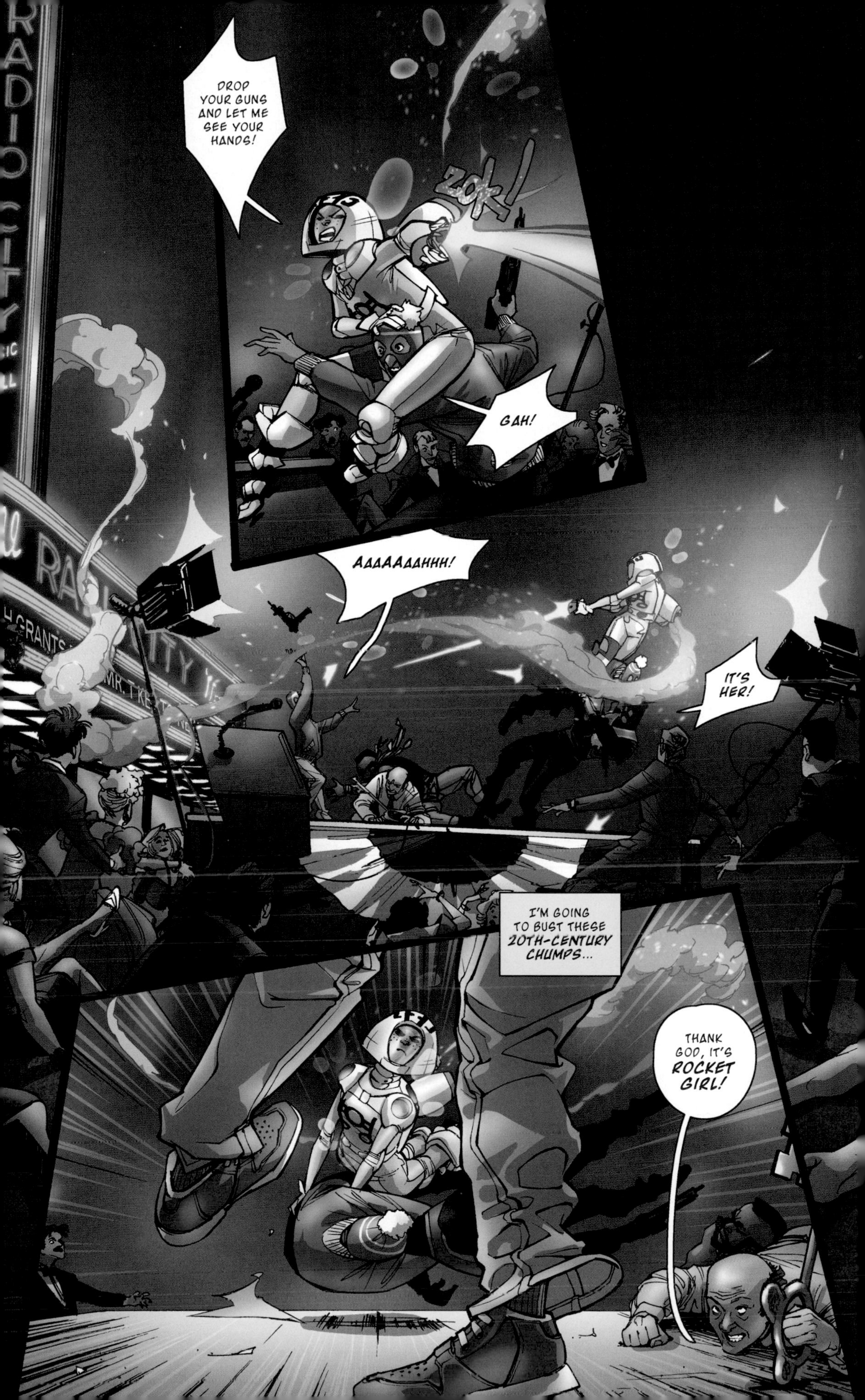
DROP YOUR GUNS AND LET ME SEE YOUR HANDS!
ZOK!
GAH!
AAAAAAAHHH!
IT'S HER!
I'M GOING TO BUST THESE 20TH-CENTURY CHUMPS...
THANK GOD, IT'S ROCKET GIRL!
RADIO CITY

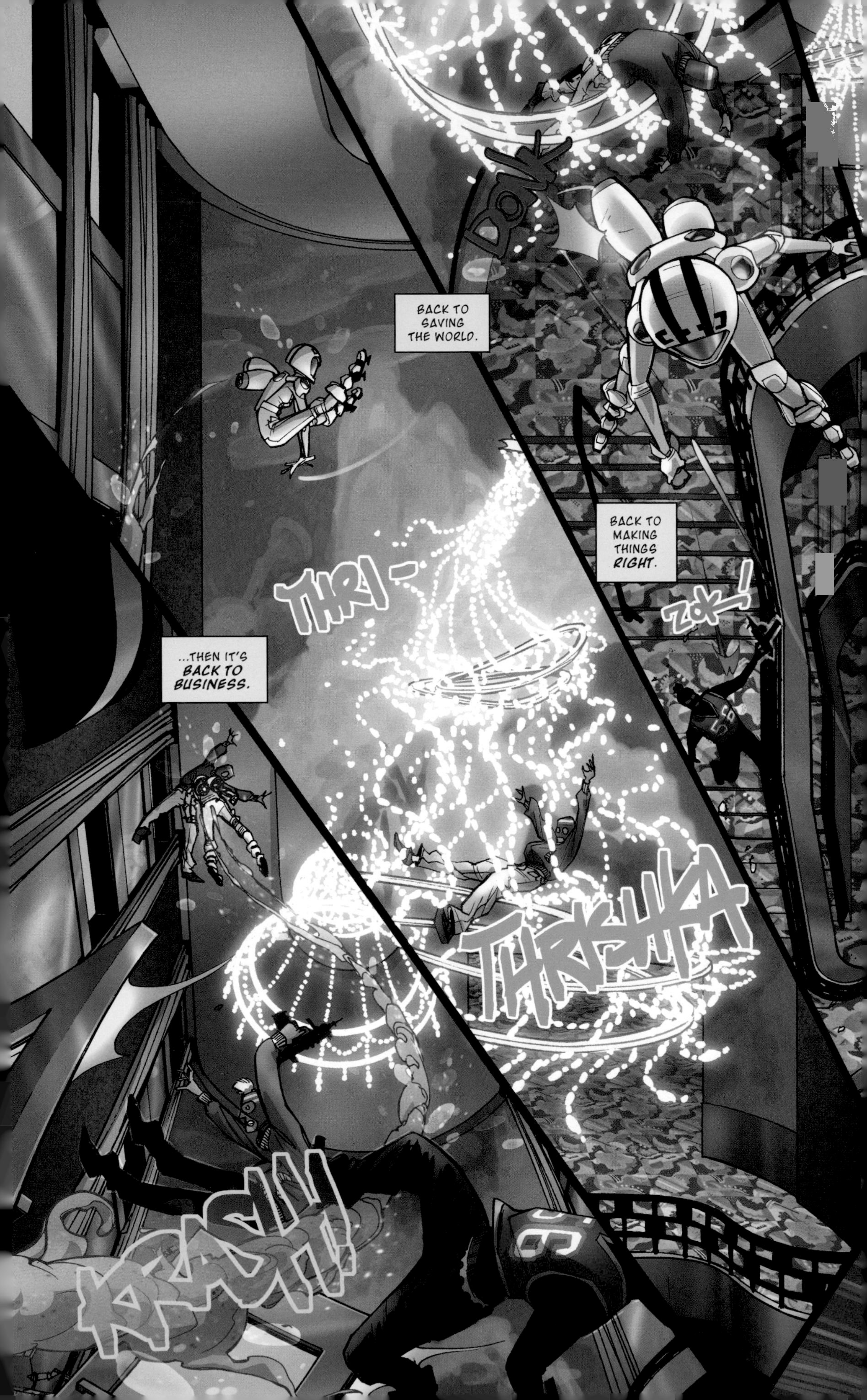
DONK
BACK TO SAVING THE WORLD.
BACK TO MAKING THINGS RIGHT.
ZOK-!
THRI-
THRSHKA
...THEN IT'S BACK TO BUSINESS.
KRASH!!

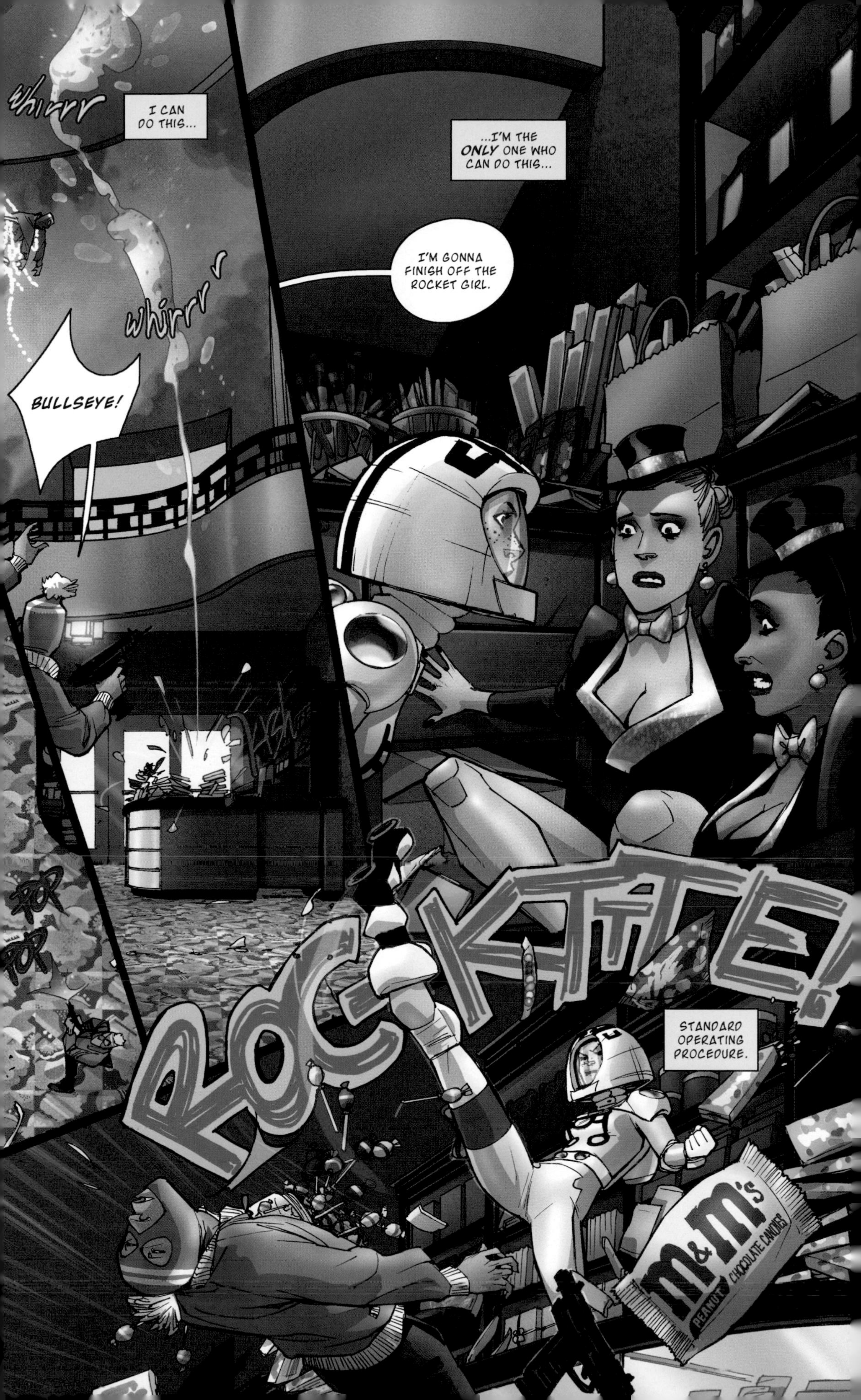

whirrr
I CAN DO THIS...
...I'M THE ONLY ONE WHO CAN DO THIS...
I'M GONNA FINISH OFF THE ROCKET GIRL.
whirrr
BULLSEYE!
POP
POP
ROCKITTE!
STANDARD OPERATING PROCEDURE.
m&m's
PEANUT
CHOCOLATE CANDIES

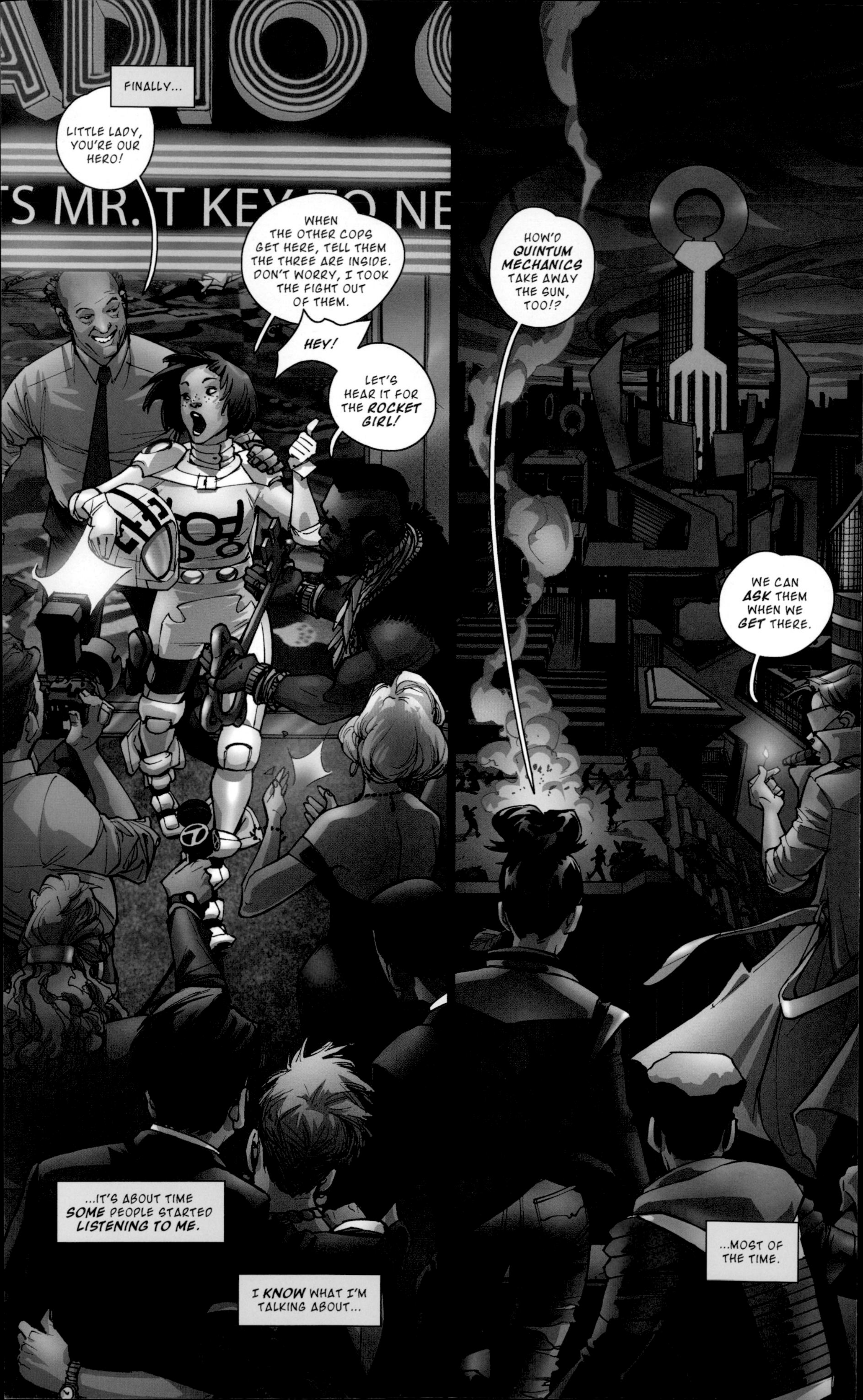
FINALLY...
LITTLE LADY, YOU'RE OUR HERO!
TS MR. T KEY TO NE
WHEN THE OTHER COPS GET HERE, TELL THEM THE THREE ARE INSIDE. DON'T WORRY, I TOOK THE FIGHT OUT OF THEM.
HEY!
LET'S HEAR IT FOR THE ROCKET GIRL!
HOW'D QUINTUM MECHANICS TAKE AWAY THE SUN, TOO!?
WE CAN ASK THEM WHEN WE GET THERE.
...IT'S ABOUT TIME SOME PEOPLE STARTED LISTENING TO ME.
I KNOW WHAT I'M TALKING ABOUT...
...MOST OF THE TIME.

Chapter 8_Big G Whiz >>

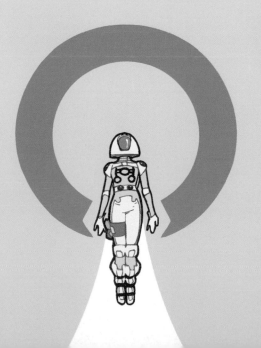

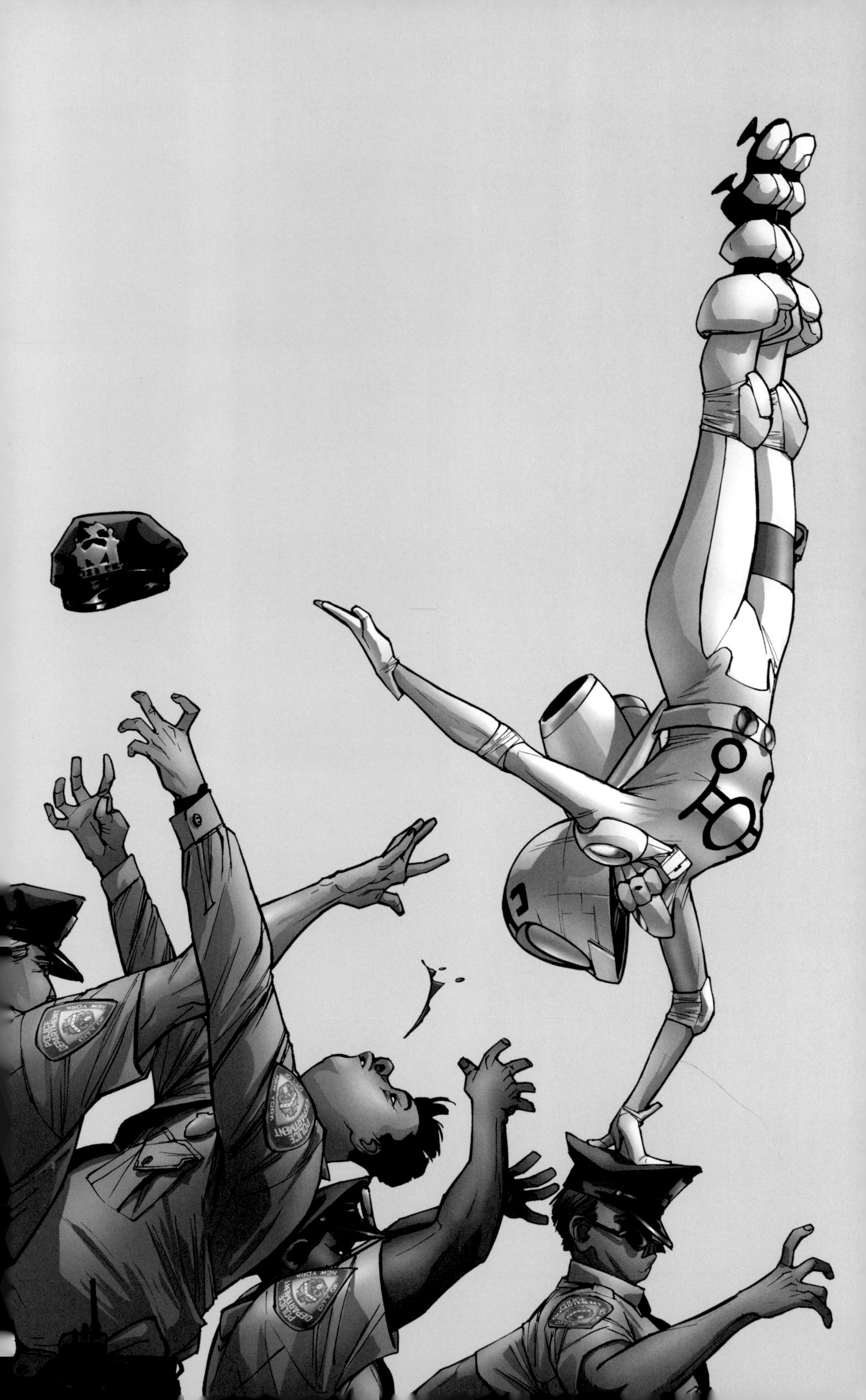

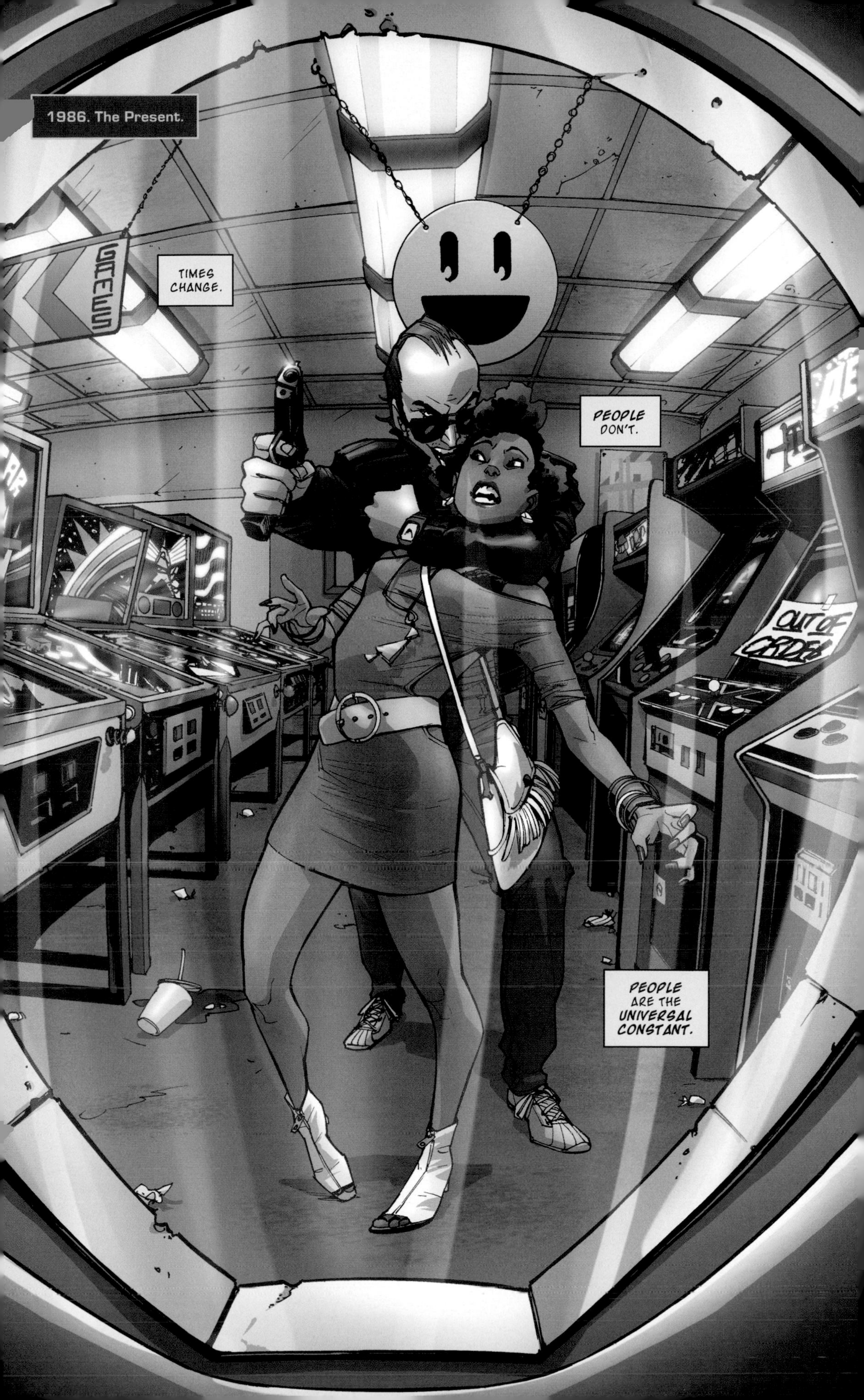
1986. The Present.
TIMES CHANGE.
GAMES
PEOPLE DON'T.
OUT OF ORDER
PEOPLE ARE THE UNIVERSAL CONSTANT.

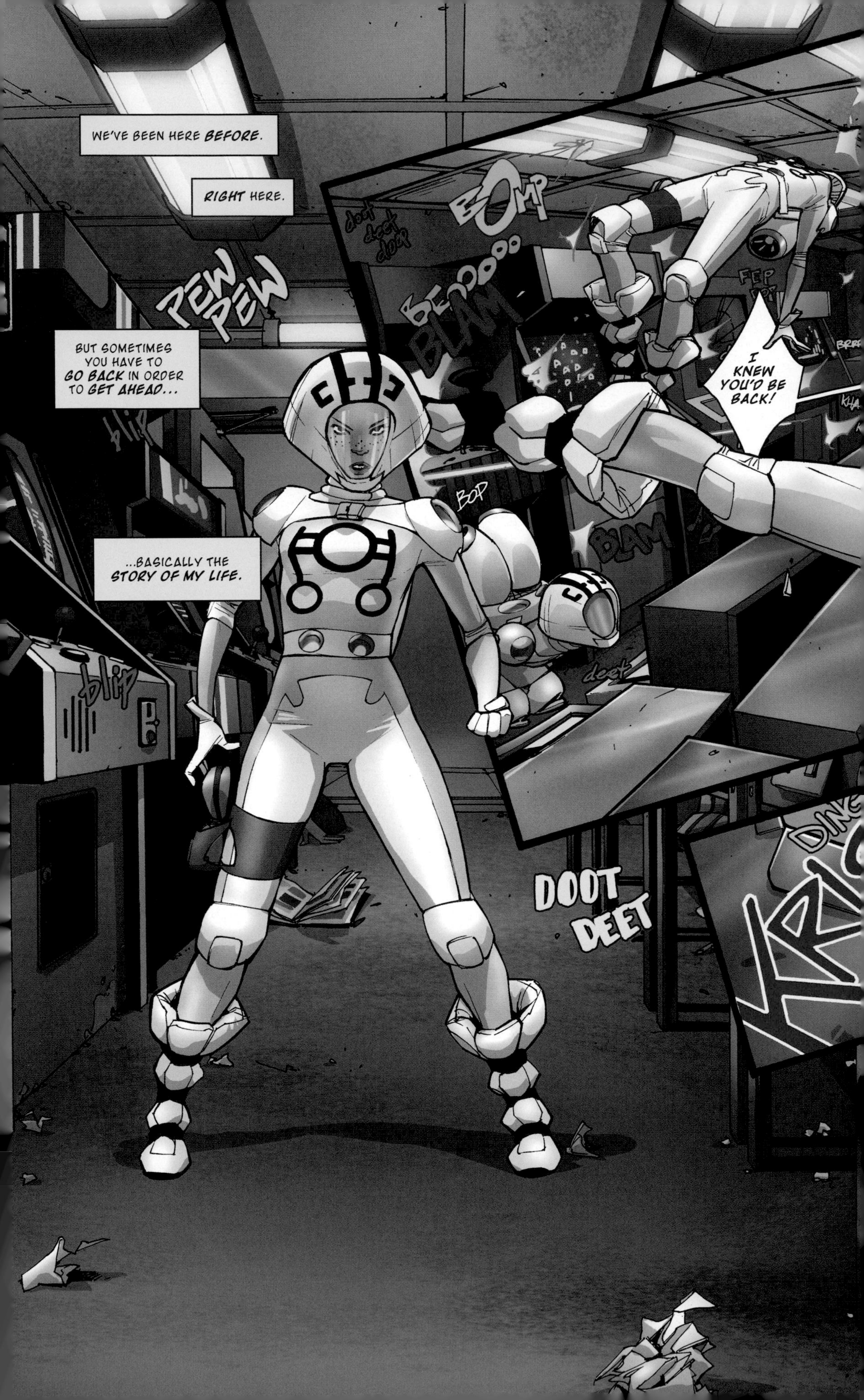

WE'VE BEEN HERE *BEFORE*.
RIGHT HERE.
PEW PEW
BOMP
doot deet doop
BEOOOOO
BLAM
BUT SOMETIMES YOU HAVE TO *GO BACK* IN ORDER TO *GET AHEAD*...
I KNEW YOU'D BE BACK!
blip
BOP
...BASICALLY THE *STORY OF MY LIFE*.
BLAM
blip
deet
DOOT DEET

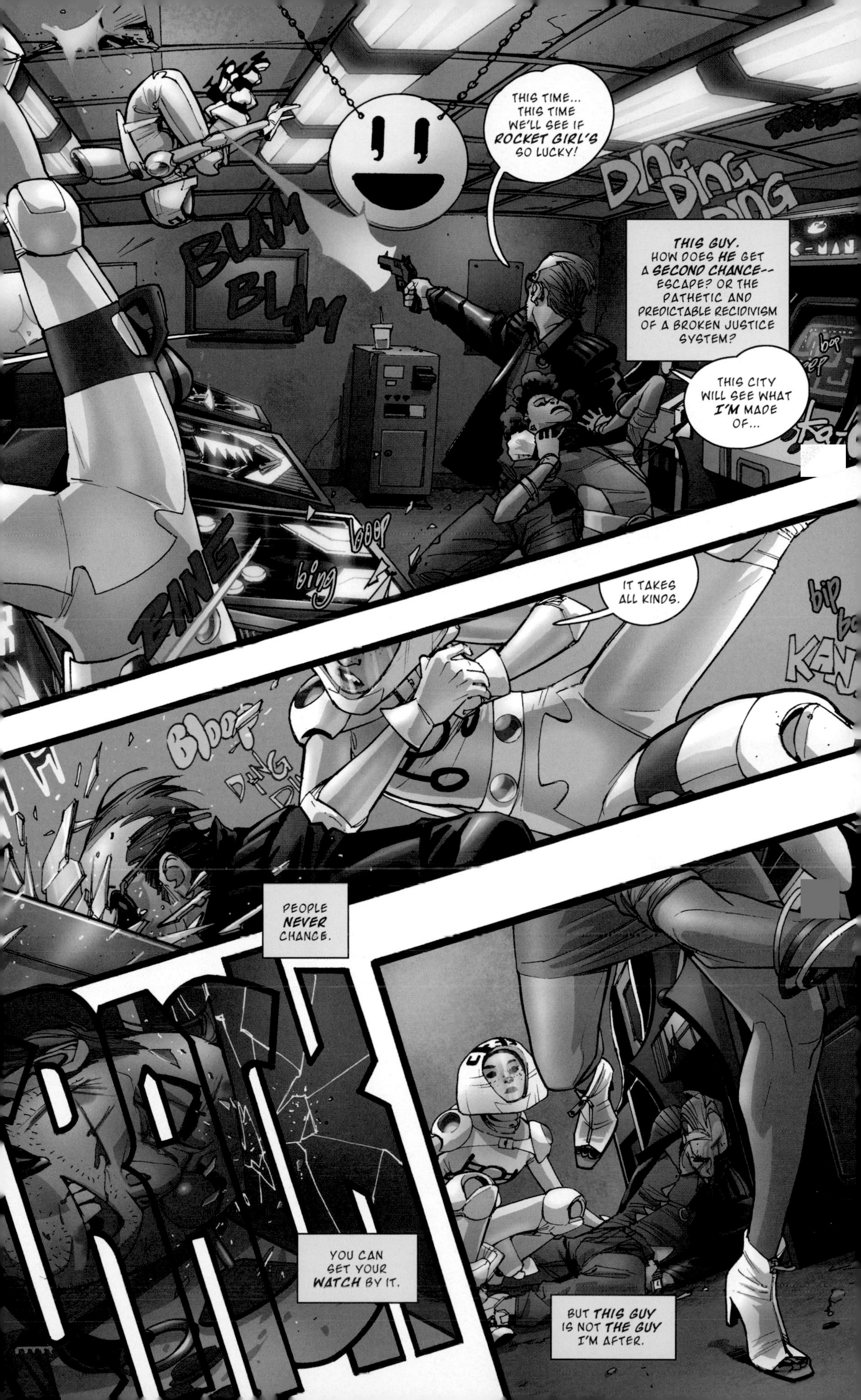
THIS TIME... THIS TIME WE'LL SEE IF ROCKET GIRL'S SO LUCKY!
DING DING DING
BLAM BLAM
THIS GUY. HOW DOES HE GET A SECOND CHANCE-- ESCAPE? OR THE PATHETIC AND PREDICTABLE RECIDIVISM OF A BROKEN JUSTICE SYSTEM?
THIS CITY WILL SEE WHAT I'M MADE OF...
BING
boop
bing
IT TAKES ALL KINDS.
PEOPLE NEVER CHANCE.
YOU CAN SET YOUR WATCH BY IT.
BUT THIS GUY IS NOT THE GUY I'M AFTER.

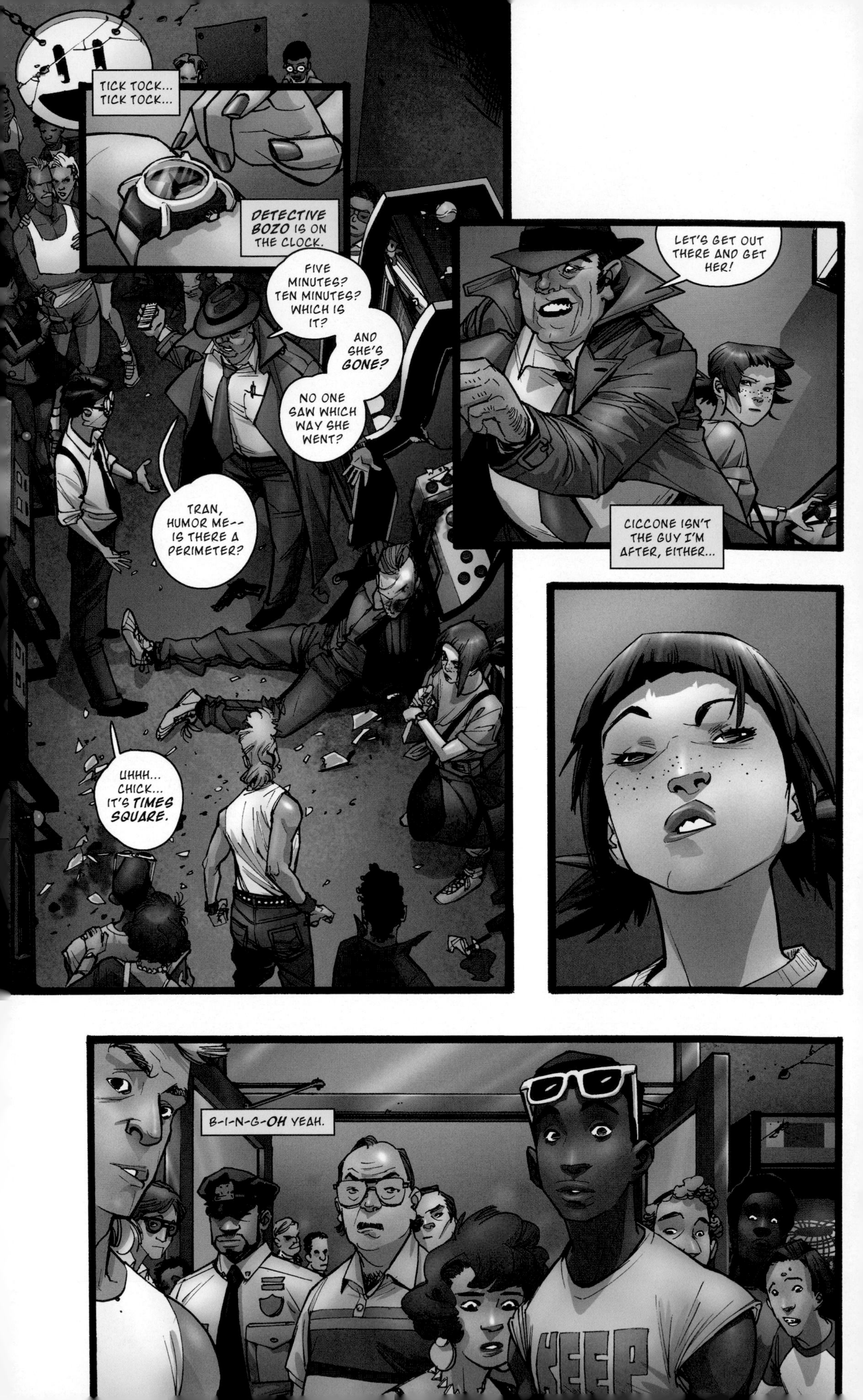
TICK TOCK... TICK TOCK...
DETECTIVE BOZO IS ON THE CLOCK.
FIVE MINUTES? TEN MINUTES? WHICH IS IT?
AND SHE'S GONE?
NO ONE SAW WHICH WAY SHE WENT?
TRAN, HUMOR ME-- IS THERE A PERIMETER?
UHHH... CHICK... IT'S TIMES SQUARE.
LET'S GET OUT THERE AND GET HER!
CICCONE ISN'T THE GUY I'M AFTER, EITHER...
B-I-N-G-OH YEAH.
KEEP

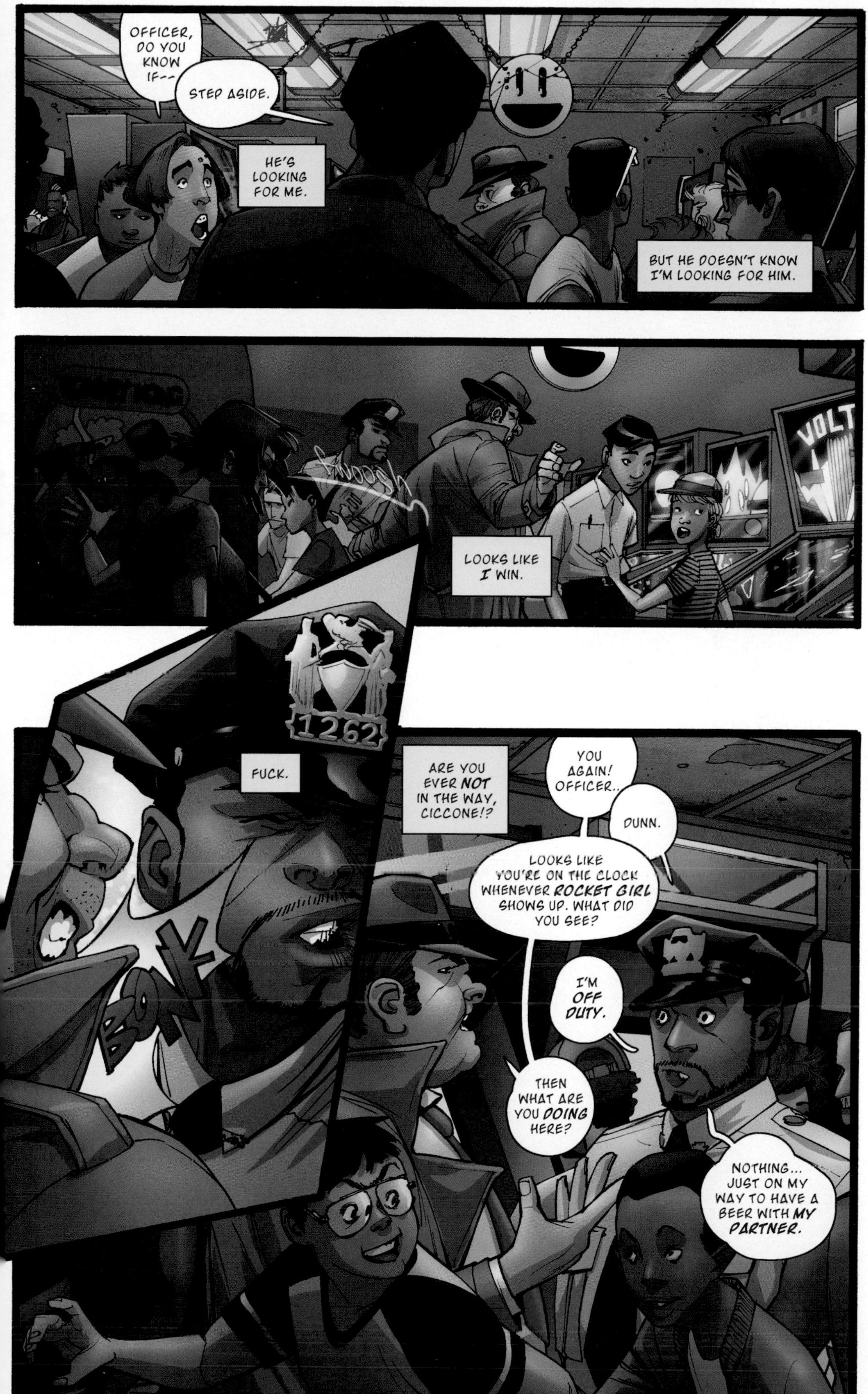
OFFICER, DO YOU KNOW IF--
STEP ASIDE.
HE'S LOOKING FOR ME.
BUT HE DOESN'T KNOW I'M LOOKING FOR HIM.
LOOKS LIKE I WIN.
1262
FUCK.
ARE YOU EVER NOT IN THE WAY, CICCONE!?
YOU AGAIN! OFFICER..
DUNN.
LOOKS LIKE YOU'RE ON THE CLOCK WHENEVER ROCKET GIRL SHOWS UP. WHAT DID YOU SEE?
I'M OFF DUTY.
THEN WHAT ARE YOU DOING HERE?
NOTHING... JUST ON MY WAY TO HAVE A BEER WITH MY PARTNER.

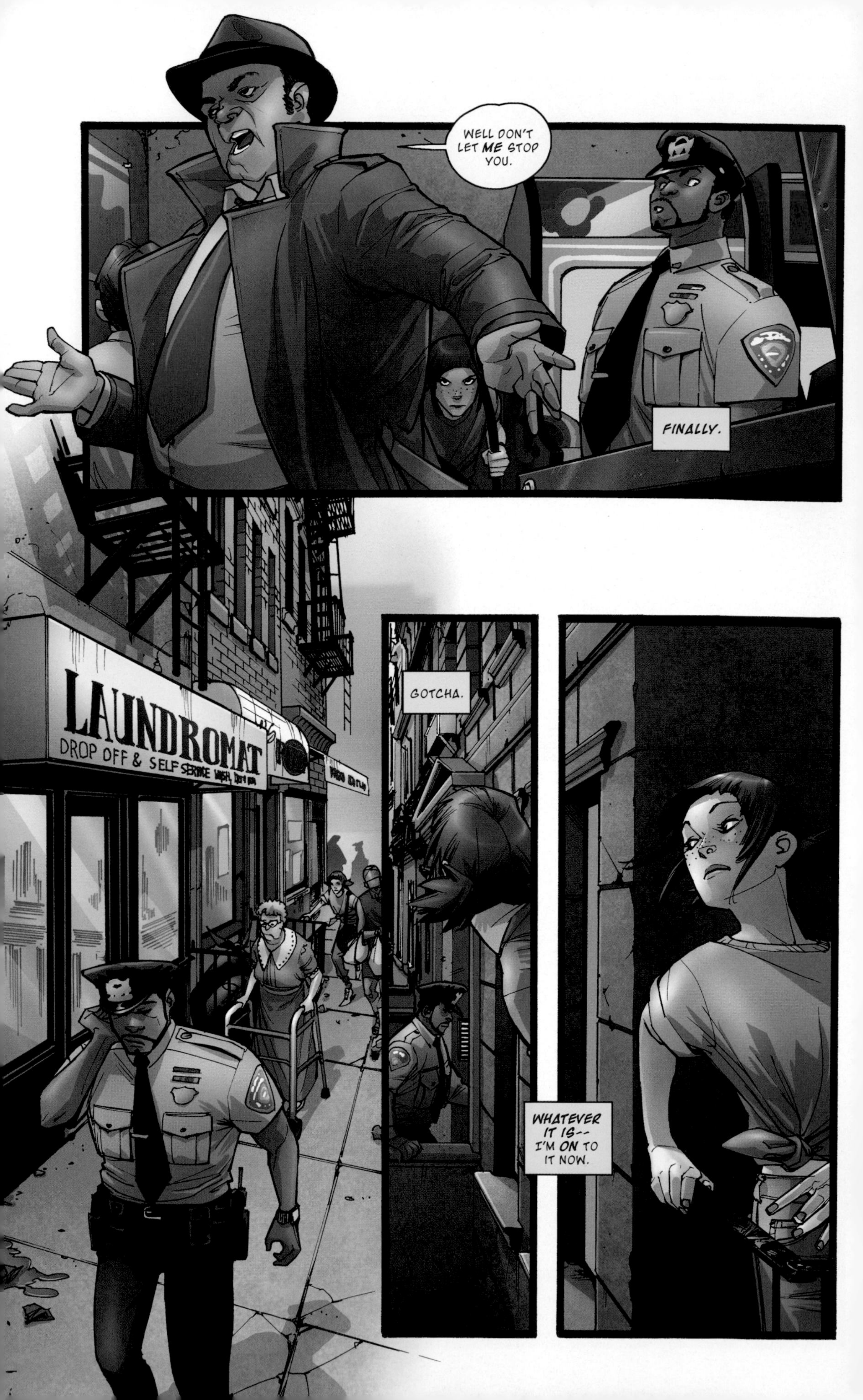
WELL DON'T LET ME STOP YOU.
FINALLY.
LAUNDROMAT
DROP OFF & SELF SERVICE
GOTCHA.
WHATEVER IT IS-- I'M ON TO IT NOW.

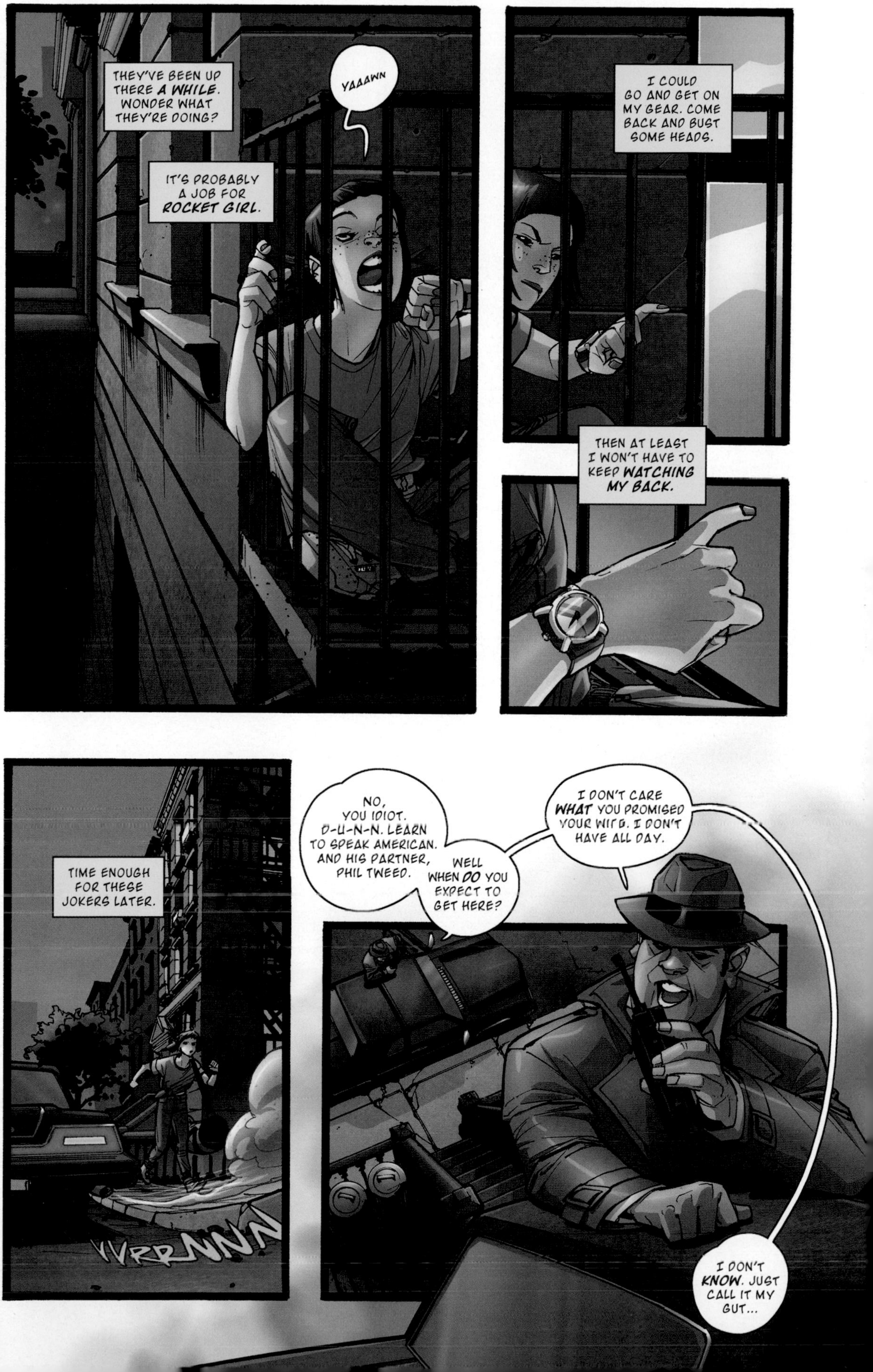
THEY'VE BEEN UP THERE A WHILE. WONDER WHAT THEY'RE DOING?
YAAAWN
IT'S PROBABLY A JOB FOR ROCKET GIRL.
I COULD GO AND GET ON MY GEAR. COME BACK AND BUST SOME HEADS.
THEN AT LEAST I WON'T HAVE TO KEEP WATCHING MY BACK.
TIME ENOUGH FOR THESE JOKERS LATER.
VVRRNNN
NO, YOU IDIOT. D-U-N-N. LEARN TO SPEAK AMERICAN. AND HIS PARTNER, PHIL TWEED.
WELL WHEN DO YOU EXPECT TO GET HERE?
I DON'T CARE WHAT YOU PROMISED YOUR WIFE. I DON'T HAVE ALL DAY.
I DON'T KNOW. JUST CALL IT MY GUT...

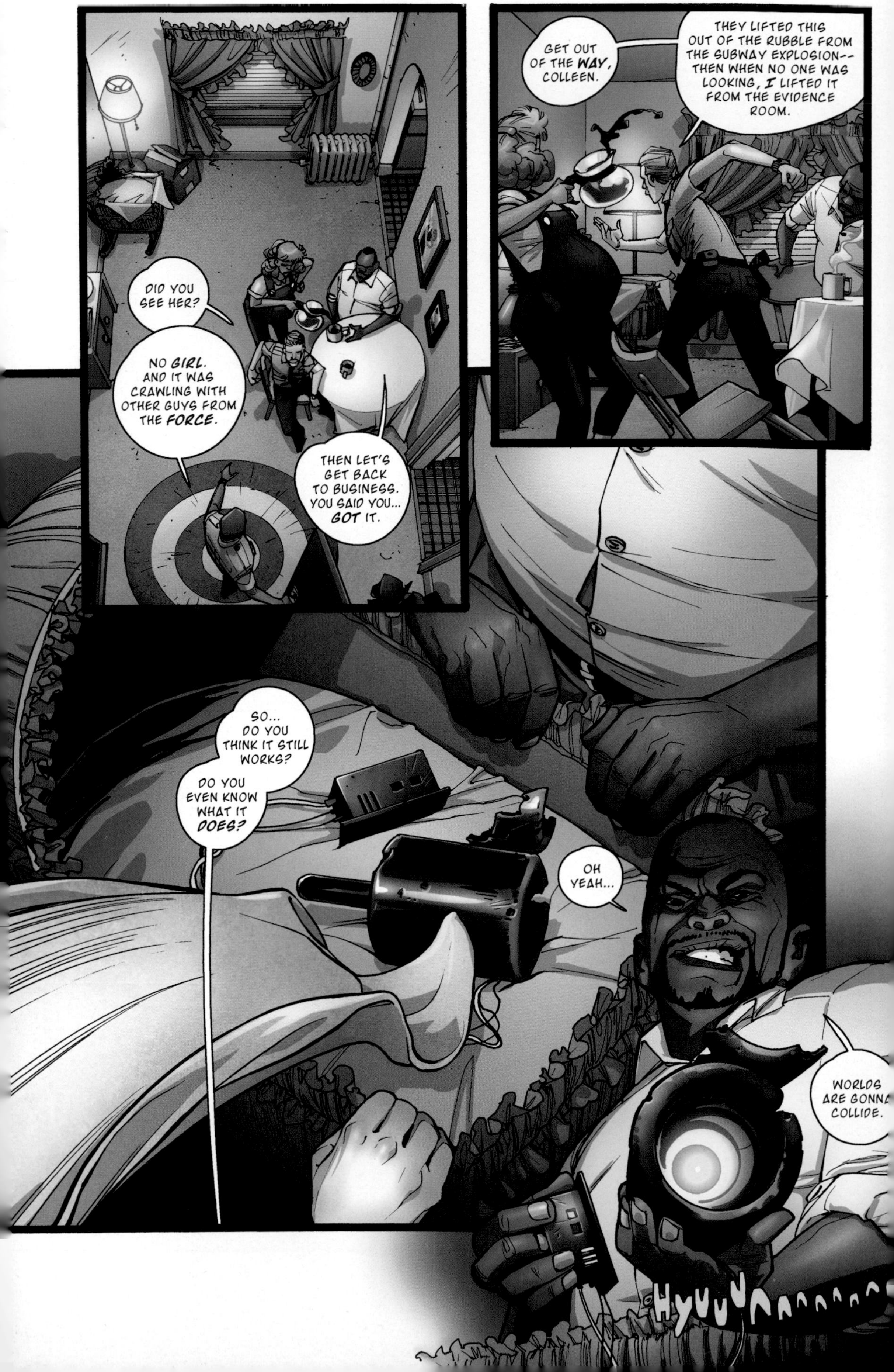
DID YOU SEE HER?
NO GIRL. AND IT WAS CRAWLING WITH OTHER GUYS FROM THE FORCE.
THEN LET'S GET BACK TO BUSINESS. YOU SAID YOU... GOT IT.
GET OUT OF THE WAY, COLLEEN.
THEY LIFTED THIS OUT OF THE RUBBLE FROM THE SUBWAY EXPLOSION-- THEN WHEN NO ONE WAS LOOKING, I LIFTED IT FROM THE EVIDENCE ROOM.
SO... DO YOU THINK IT STILL WORKS?
DO YOU EVEN KNOW WHAT IT DOES?
OH YEAH...
WORLDS ARE GONNA COLLIDE.
HYUUUNNNNNNN

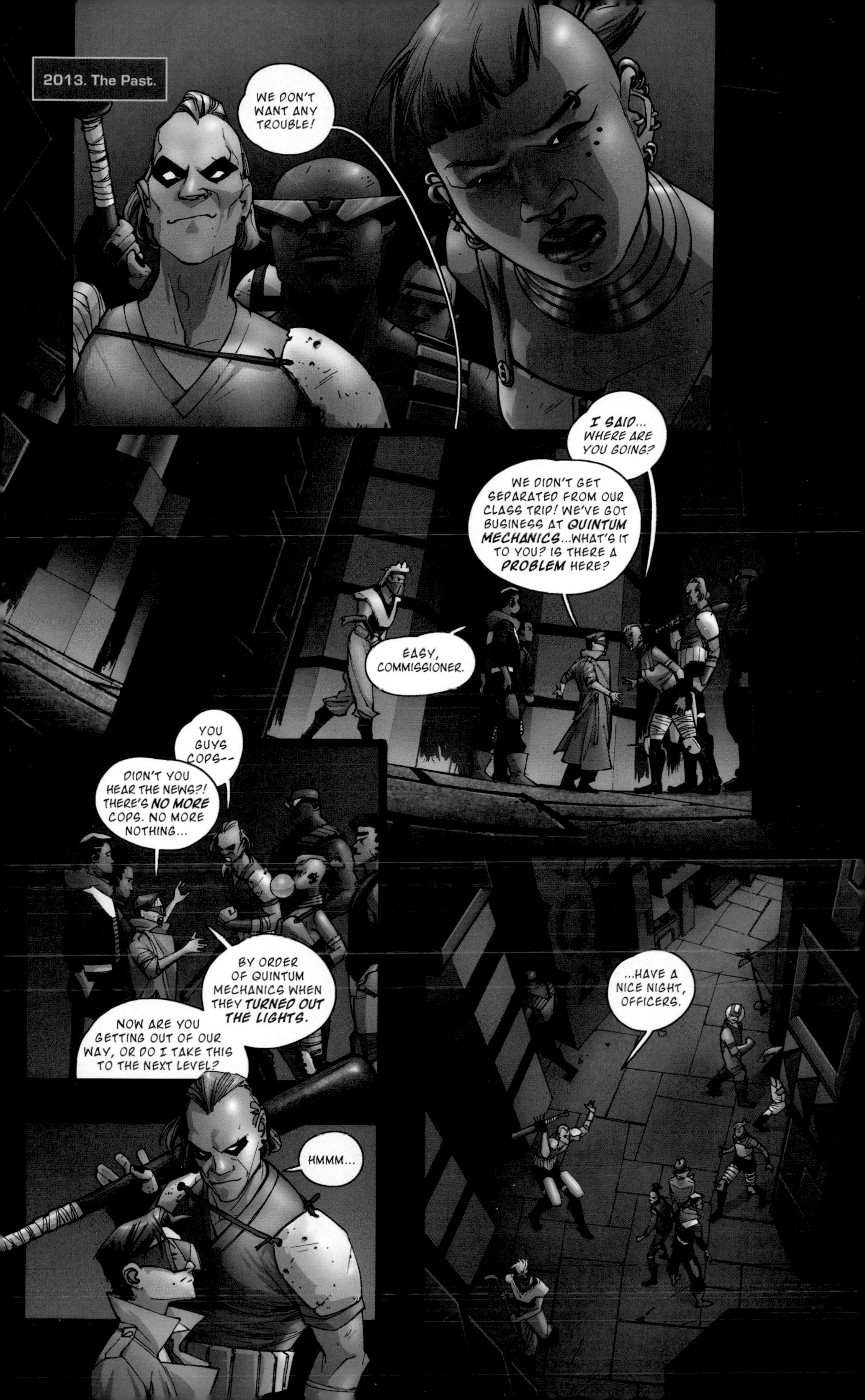
2013. The Past.
WE DON'T WANT ANY TROUBLE!
I SAID... WHERE ARE YOU GOING?
WE DIDN'T GET SEPARATED FROM OUR CLASS TRIP! WE'VE GOT BUSINESS AT QUINTUM MECHANICS...WHAT'S IT TO YOU? IS THERE A PROBLEM HERE?
EASY, COMMISSIONER.
YOU GUYS COPS--
DIDN'T YOU HEAR THE NEWS?! THERE'S NO MORE COPS. NO MORE NOTHING...
BY ORDER OF QUINTUM MECHANICS WHEN THEY TURNED OUT THE LIGHTS.
NOW ARE YOU GETTING OUT OF OUR WAY, OR DO I TAKE THIS TO THE NEXT LEVEL?
HMMM...
...HAVE A NICE NIGHT, OFFICERS.

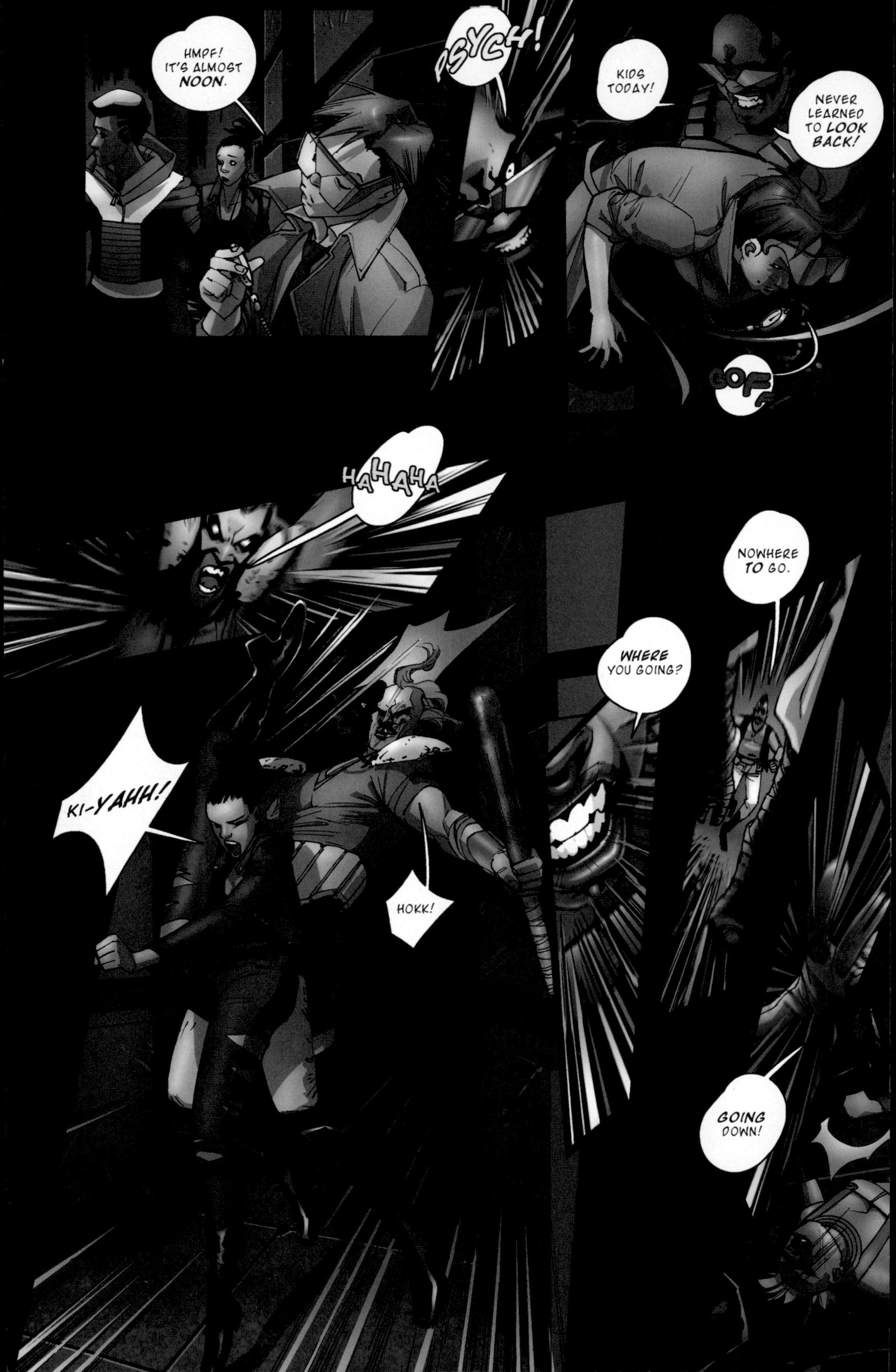
HMPF! IT'S ALMOST NOON.
PSYCH!
KIDS TODAY!
NEVER LEARNED TO LOOK BACK!
GOFF
HAHAHA
NOWHERE TO GO.
WHERE YOU GOING?
KI-YAHH!
HOKK!
GOING DOWN!

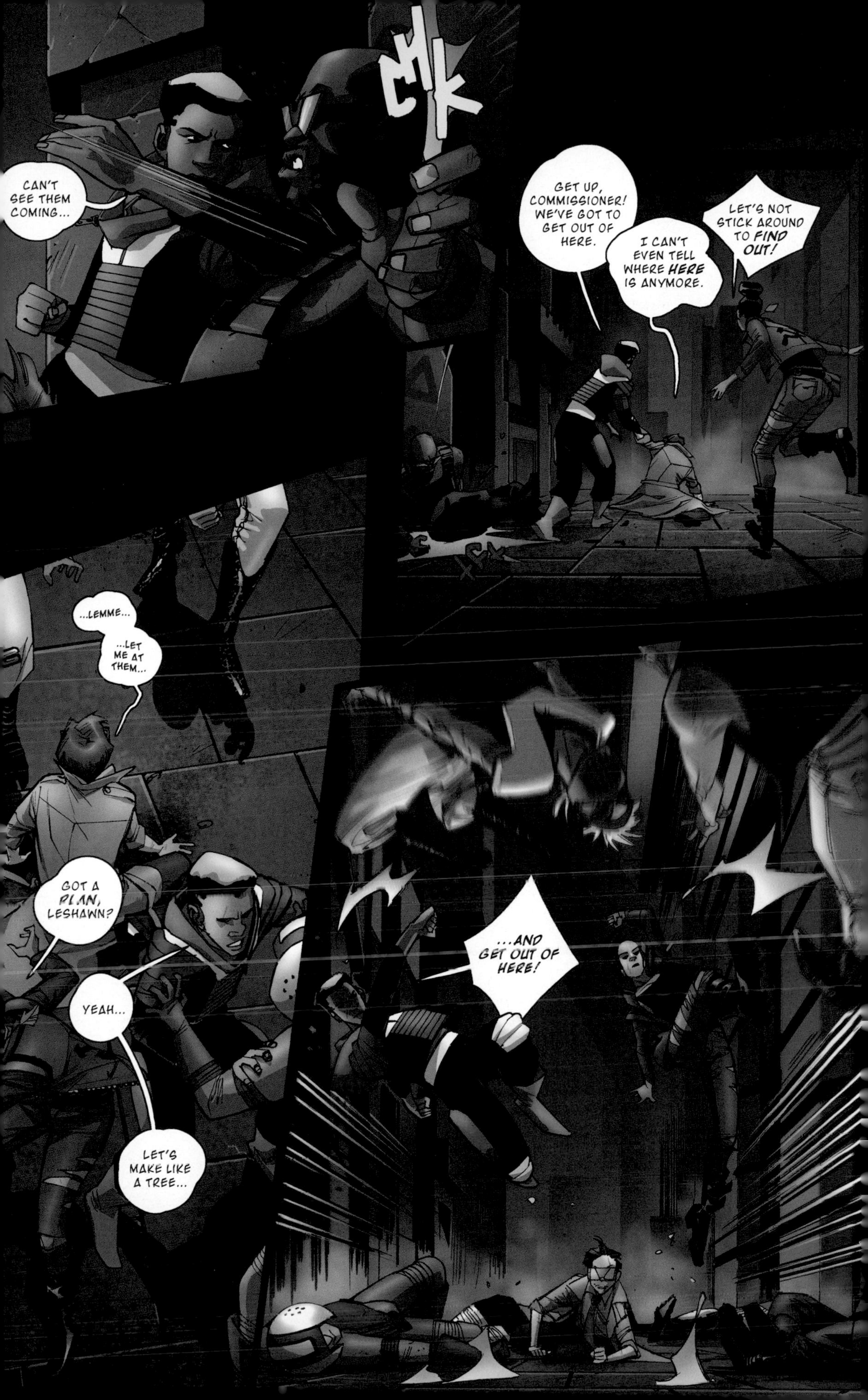
CHK
CAN'T SEE THEM COMING...
GET UP, COMMISSIONER! WE'VE GOT TO GET OUT OF HERE.
I CAN'T EVEN TELL WHERE HERE IS ANYMORE.
LET'S NOT STICK AROUND TO FIND OUT!
...LEMME...
...LET ME AT THEM...
GOT A PLAN, LESHAWN?
YEAH...
LET'S MAKE LIKE A TREE...
...AND GET OUT OF HERE!

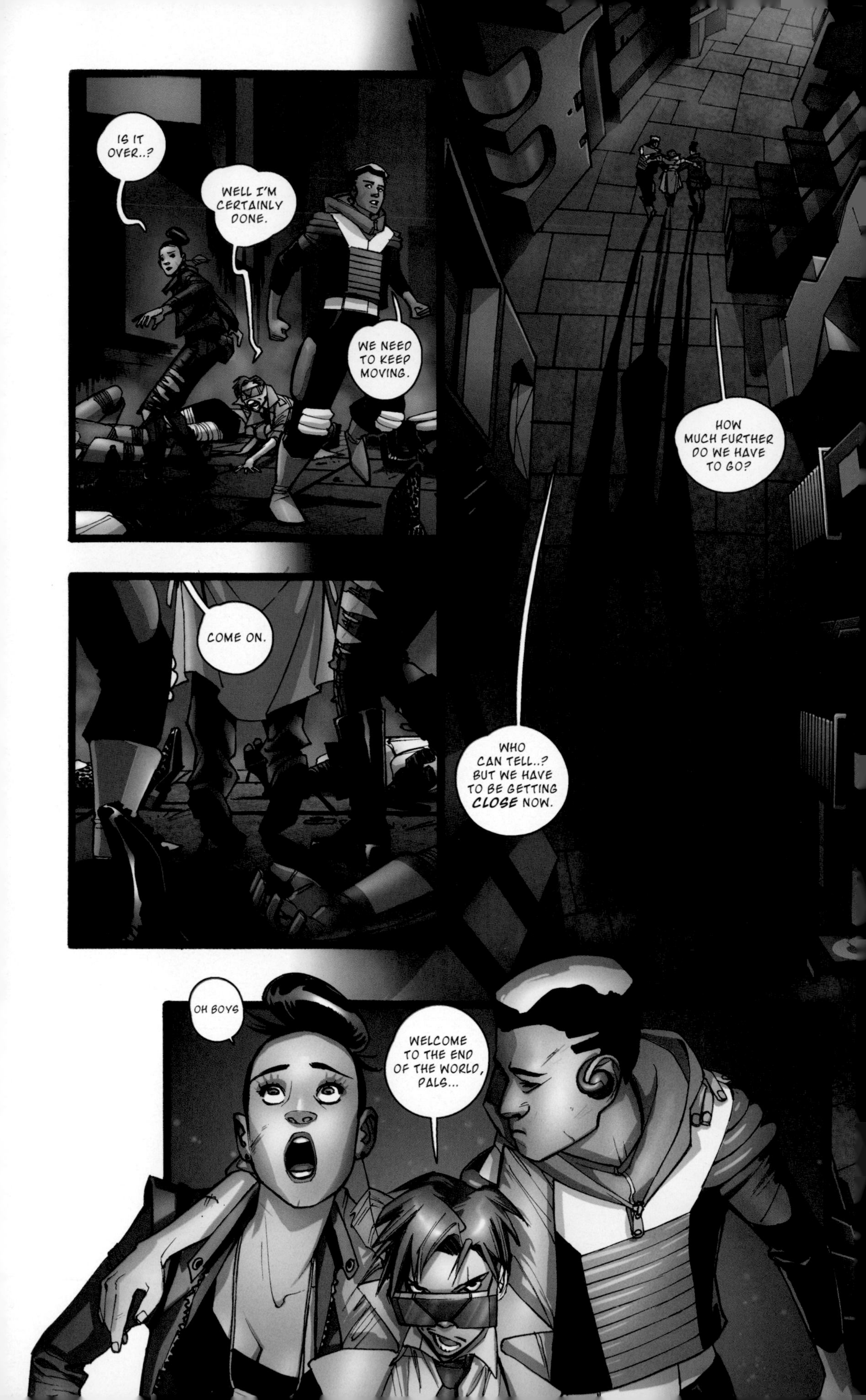
IS IT OVER..?
WELL I'M CERTAINLY DONE.
WE NEED TO KEEP MOVING.
COME ON.
HOW MUCH FURTHER DO WE HAVE TO GO?
WHO CAN TELL..? BUT WE HAVE TO BE GETTING CLOSE NOW.
OH BOYS
WELCOME TO THE END OF THE WORLD, PALS...

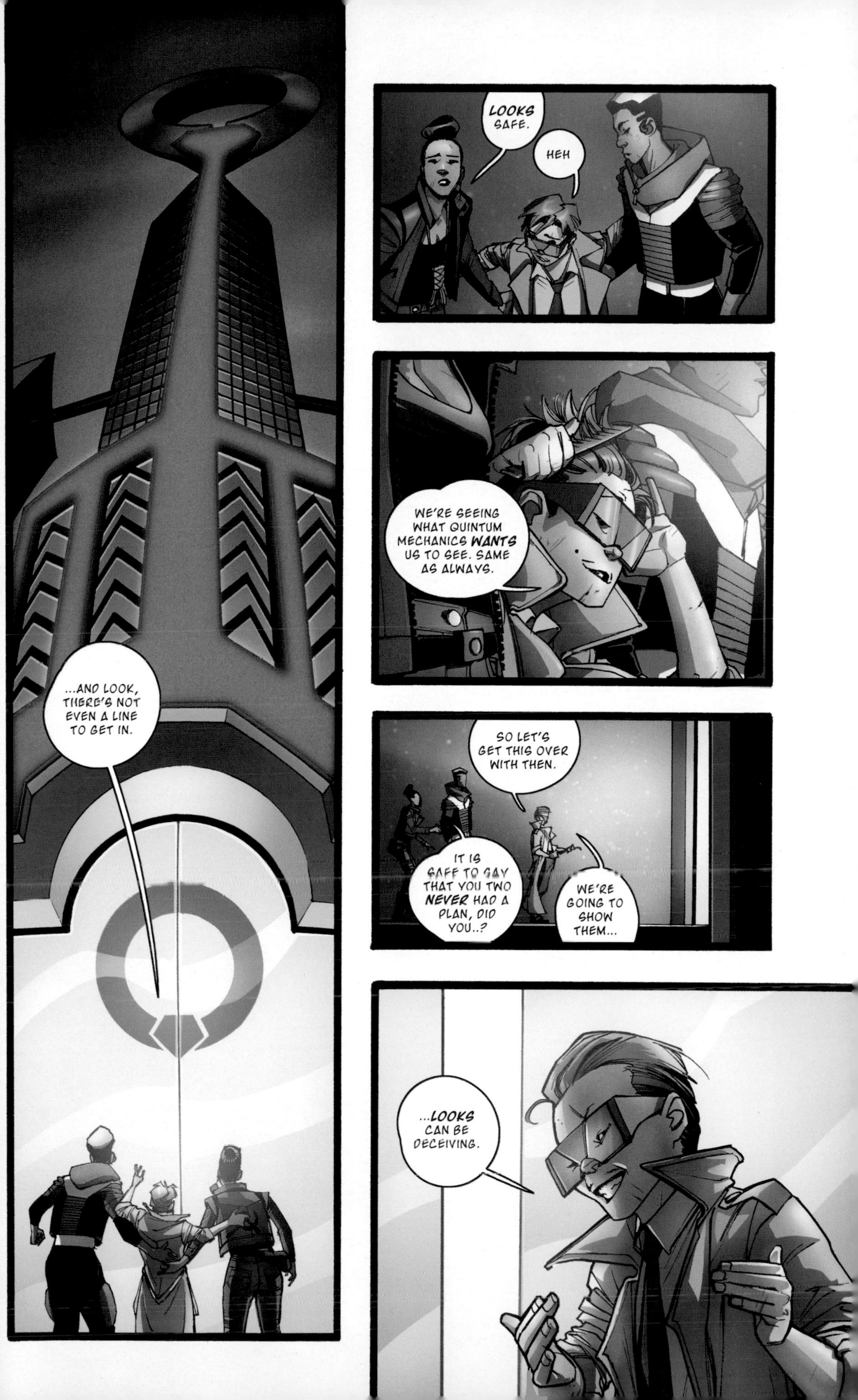
...AND LOOK, THERE'S NOT EVEN A LINE TO GET IN.
LOOKS SAFE.
HEH
WE'RE SEEING WHAT QUINTUM MECHANICS WANTS US TO SEE. SAME AS ALWAYS.
SO LET'S GET THIS OVER WITH THEN.
IT IS SAFE TO SAY THAT YOU TWO NEVER HAD A PLAN, DID YOU..?
WE'RE GOING TO SHOW THEM...
...LOOKS CAN BE DECEIVING.

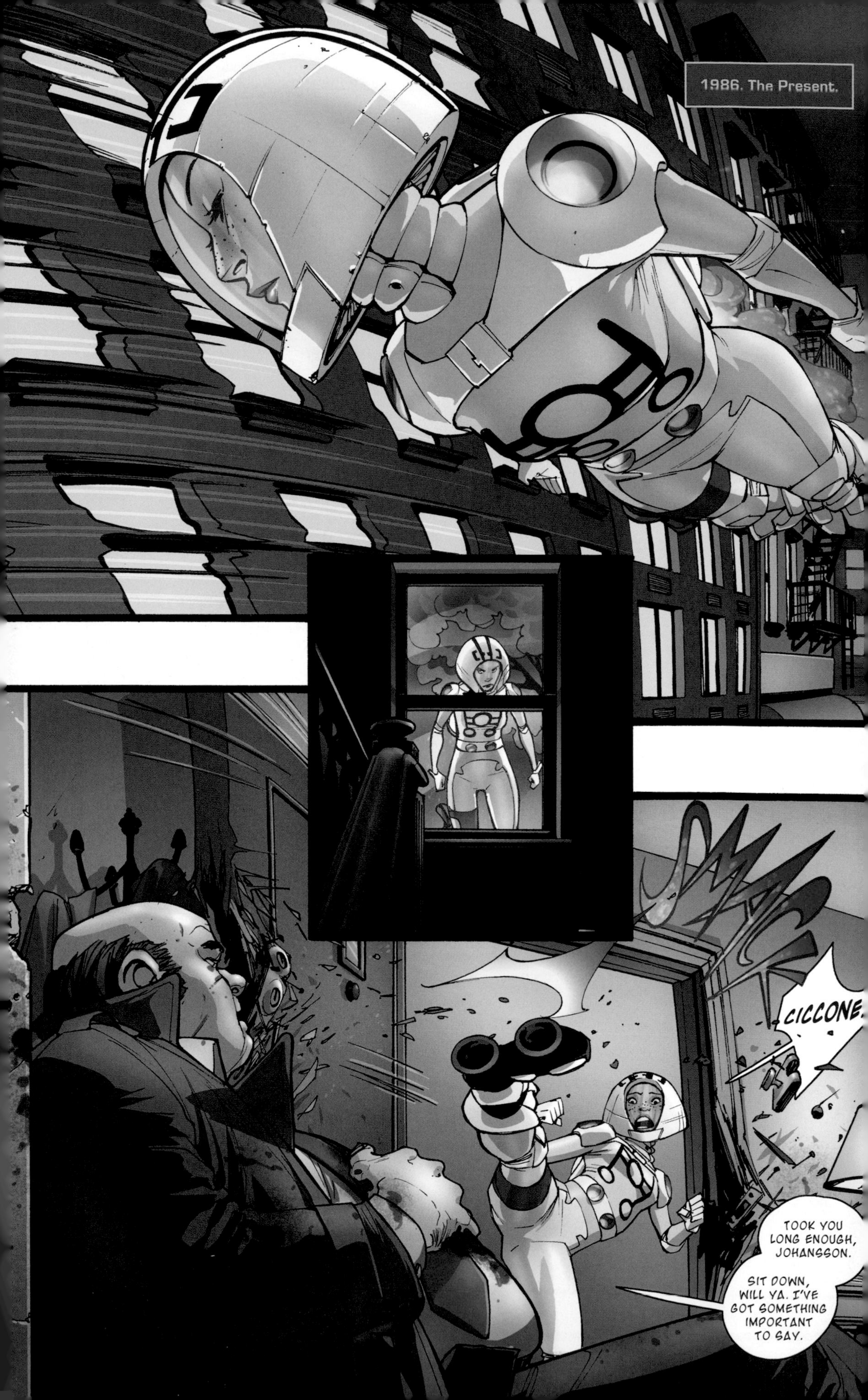
1986. The Present.
SMASH
CICCONE.
TOOK YOU LONG ENOUGH, JOHANSSON.
SIT DOWN, WILL YA. I'VE GOT SOMETHING IMPORTANT TO SAY.

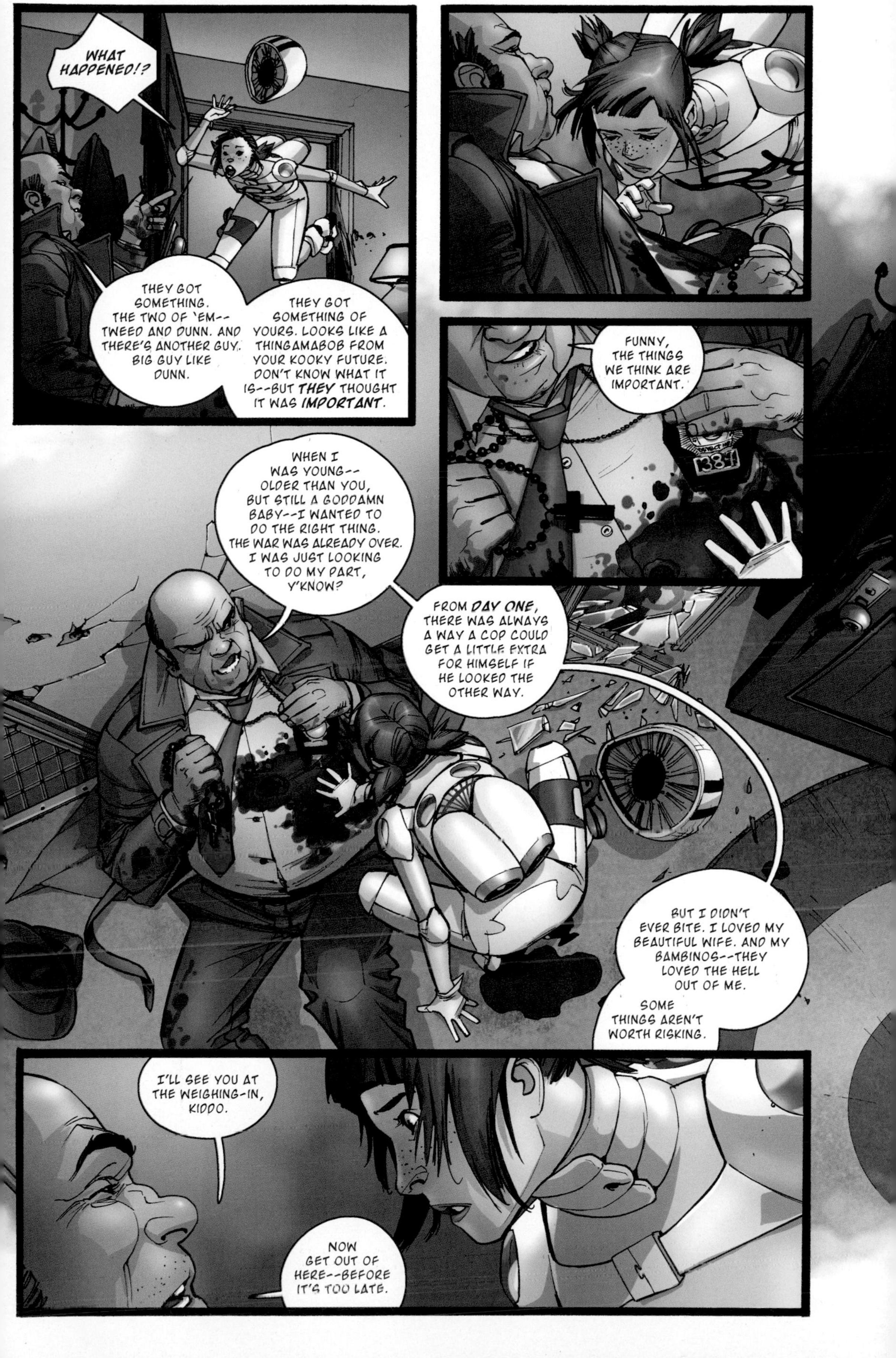
WHAT HAPPENED!?
THEY GOT SOMETHING. THE TWO OF 'EM--TWEED AND DUNN. AND THERE'S ANOTHER GUY. BIG GUY LIKE DUNN.
THEY GOT SOMETHING OF YOURS. LOOKS LIKE A THINGAMABOB FROM YOUR KOOKY FUTURE. DON'T KNOW WHAT IT IS--BUT THEY THOUGHT IT WAS IMPORTANT.
FUNNY, THE THINGS WE THINK ARE IMPORTANT.
WHEN I WAS YOUNG--OLDER THAN YOU, BUT STILL A GODDAMN BABY--I WANTED TO DO THE RIGHT THING. THE WAR WAS ALREADY OVER. I WAS JUST LOOKING TO DO MY PART, Y'KNOW?
FROM DAY ONE, THERE WAS ALWAYS A WAY A COP COULD GET A LITTLE EXTRA FOR HIMSELF IF HE LOOKED THE OTHER WAY.
BUT I DIDN'T EVER BITE. I LOVED MY BEAUTIFUL WIFE. AND MY BAMBINOS--THEY LOVED THE HELL OUT OF ME.
SOME THINGS AREN'T WORTH RISKING.
I'LL SEE YOU AT THE WEIGHING-IN, KIDDO.
NOW GET OUT OF HERE--BEFORE IT'S TOO LATE.

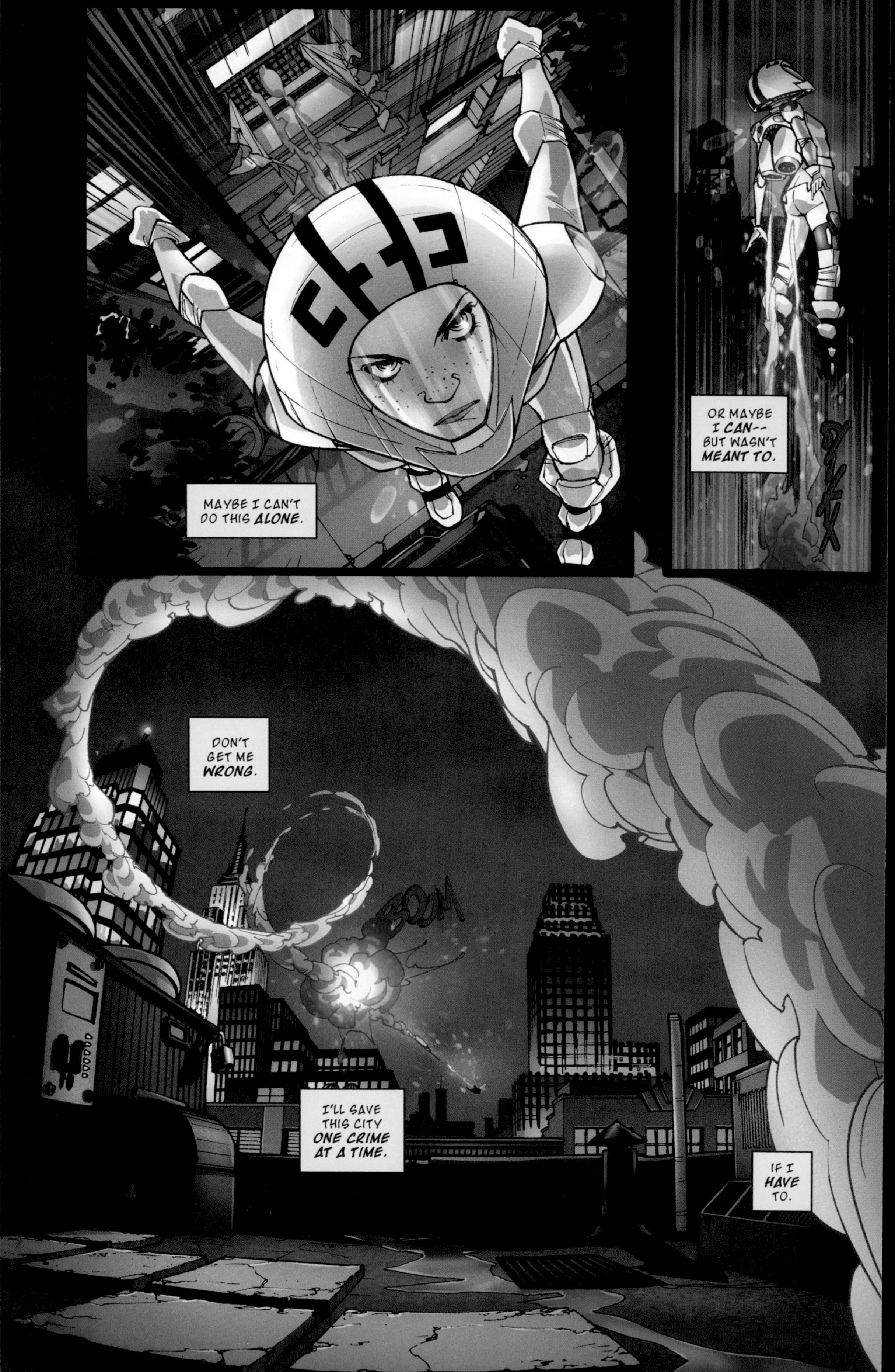
MAYBE I CAN'T DO THIS ALONE.
OR MAYBE I CAN-- BUT WASN'T MEANT TO.
DON'T GET ME WRONG.
BOOM
I'LL SAVE THIS CITY ONE CRIME AT A TIME.
IF I HAVE TO.

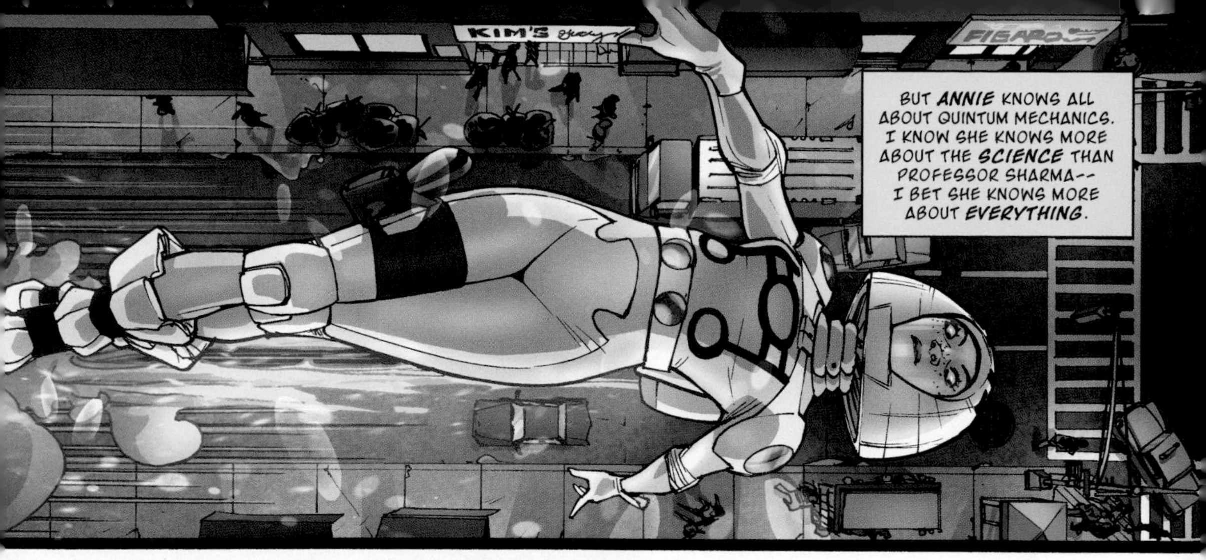
KIM'S
FIGARO
BUT ANNIE KNOWS ALL ABOUT QUINTUM MECHANICS. I KNOW SHE KNOWS MORE ABOUT THE SCIENCE THAN PROFESSOR SHARMA-- I BET SHE KNOWS MORE ABOUT EVERYTHING.

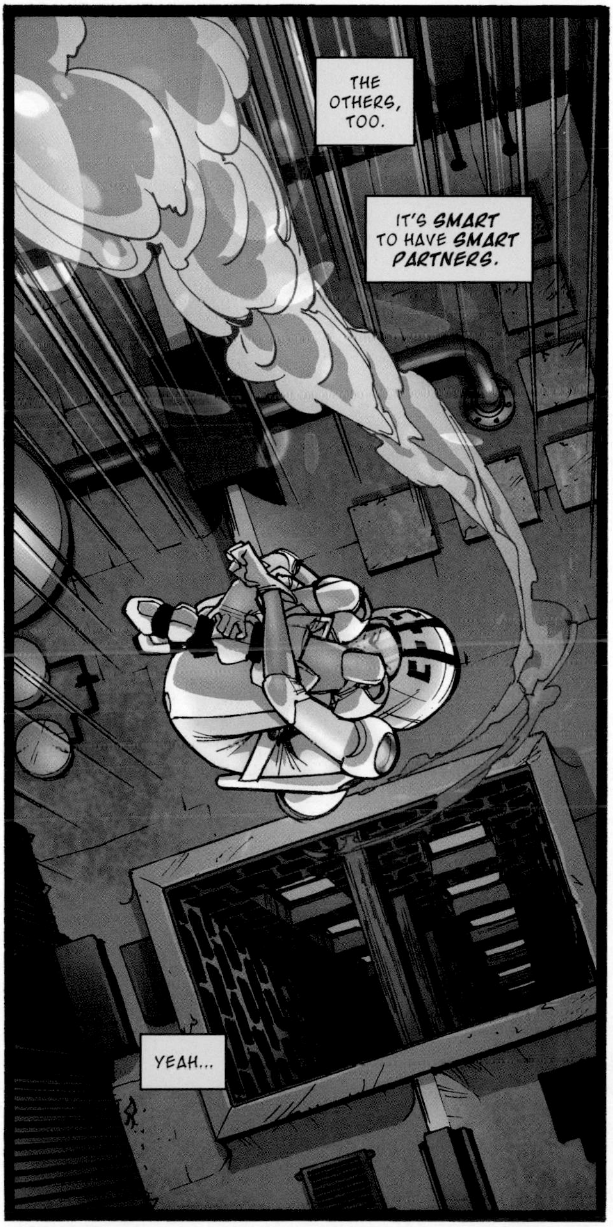
THE OTHERS, TOO.
IT'S SMART TO HAVE SMART PARTNERS.
YEAH...

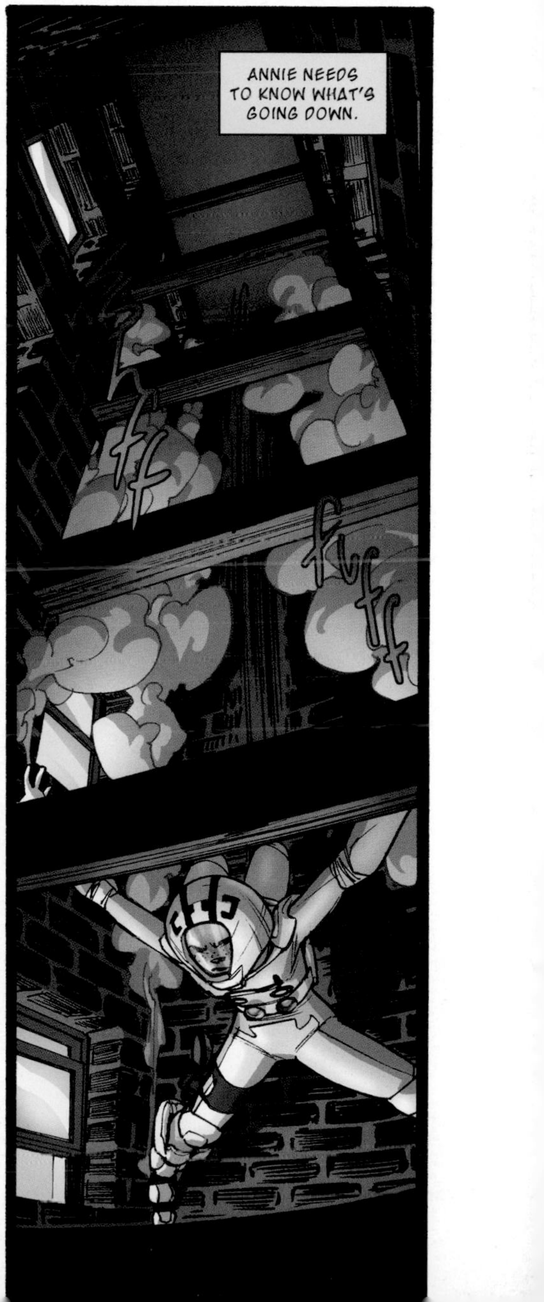
ANNIE NEEDS TO KNOW WHAT'S GOING DOWN.

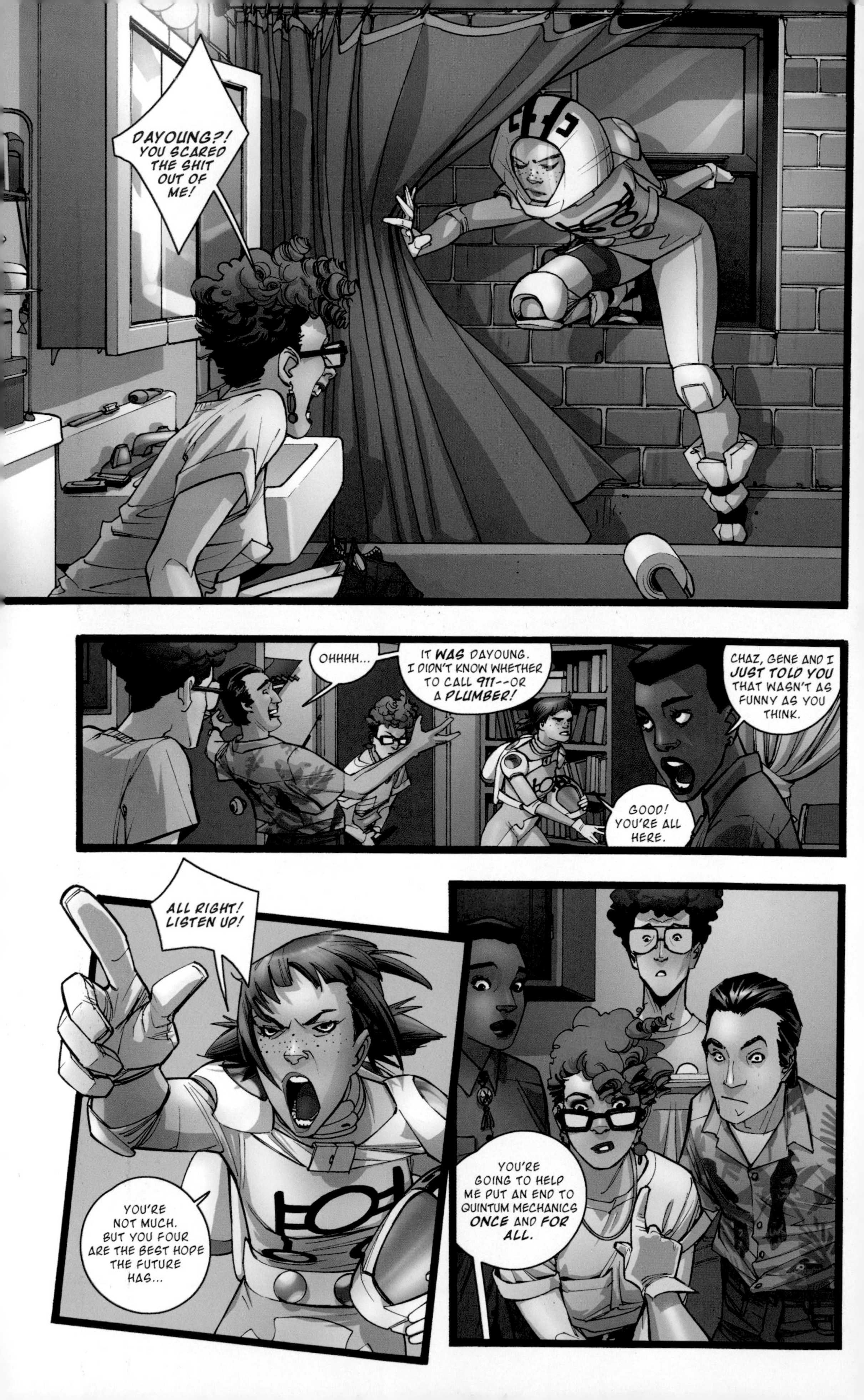
DAYOUNG?! YOU SCARED THE SHIT OUT OF ME!
OHHHH...
IT WAS DAYOUNG. I DIDN'T KNOW WHETHER TO CALL 911--OR A PLUMBER!
CHAZ, GENE AND I JUST TOLD YOU THAT WASN'T AS FUNNY AS YOU THINK.
GOOD! YOU'RE ALL HERE.
ALL RIGHT! LISTEN UP!
YOU'RE NOT MUCH. BUT YOU FOUR ARE THE BEST HOPE THE FUTURE HAS...
YOU'RE GOING TO HELP ME PUT AN END TO QUINTUM MECHANICS ONCE AND FOR ALL.

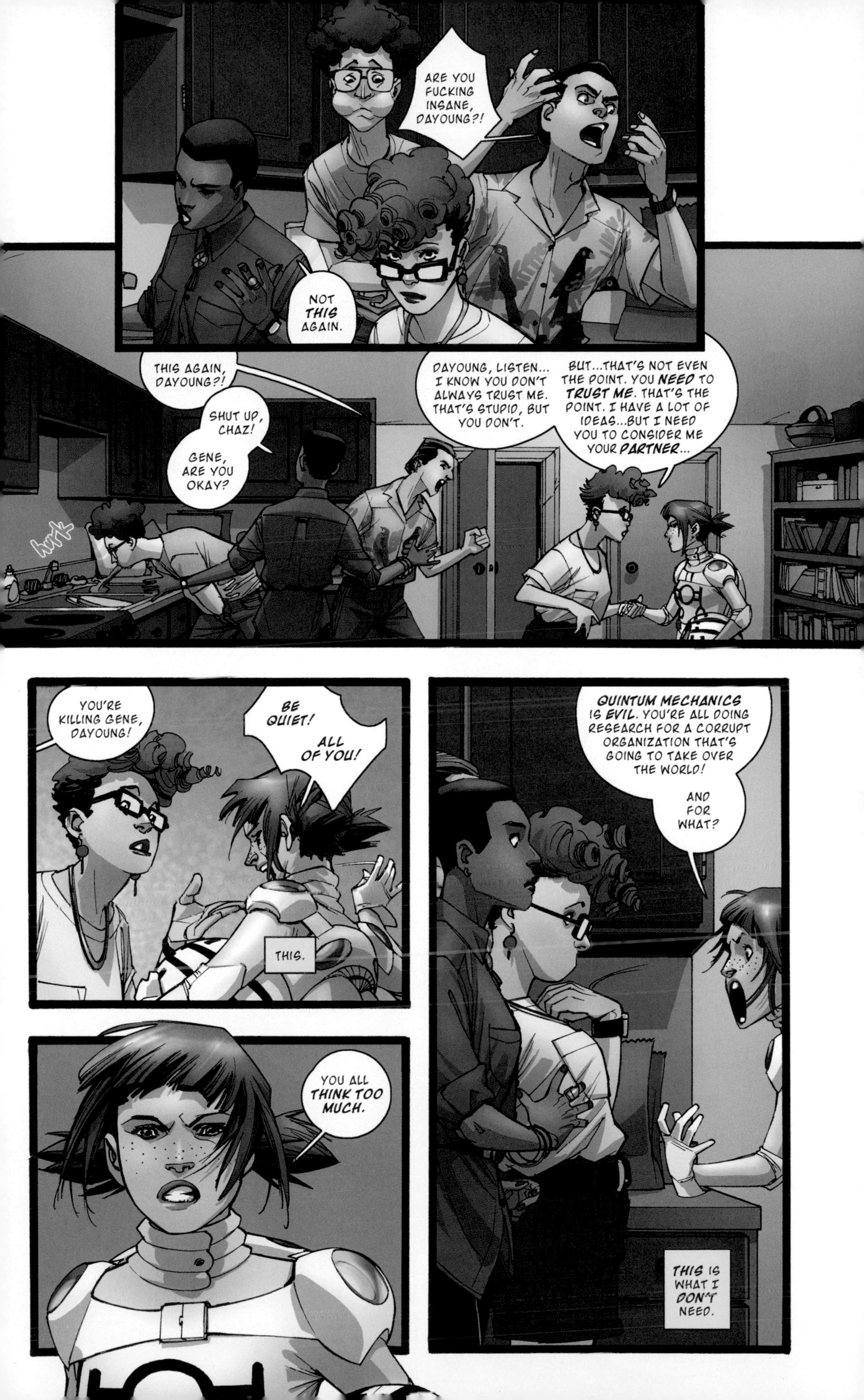
ARE YOU FUCKING INSANE, DAYOUNG?!
NOT THIS AGAIN.
THIS AGAIN, DAYOUNG?!
SHUT UP, CHAZ!
GENE, ARE YOU OKAY?
DAYOUNG, LISTEN... I KNOW YOU DON'T ALWAYS TRUST ME. THAT'S STUPID, BUT YOU DON'T.
BUT...THAT'S NOT EVEN THE POINT. YOU NEED TO TRUST ME. THAT'S THE POINT. I HAVE A LOT OF IDEAS...BUT I NEED YOU TO CONSIDER ME YOUR PARTNER...
YOU'RE KILLING GENE, DAYOUNG!
BE QUIET!
ALL OF YOU!
THIS.
QUINTUM MECHANICS IS EVIL. YOU'RE ALL DOING RESEARCH FOR A CORRUPT ORGANIZATION THAT'S GOING TO TAKE OVER THE WORLD!
AND FOR WHAT?
THIS IS WHAT I DON'T NEED.
YOU ALL THINK TOO MUCH.

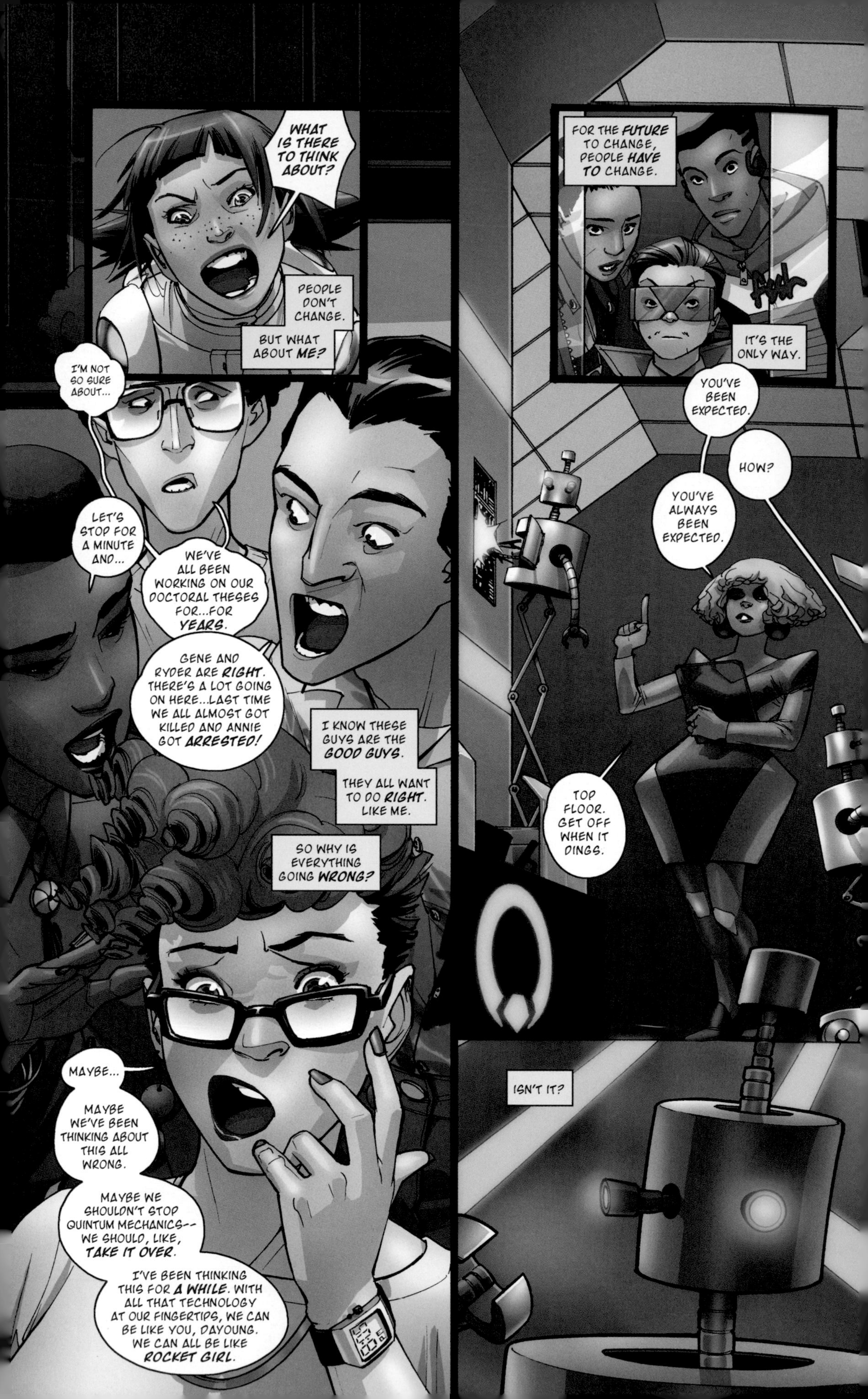
WHAT IS THERE TO THINK ABOUT?
PEOPLE DON'T CHANGE.
BUT WHAT ABOUT ME?
I'M NOT SO SURE ABOUT...
LET'S STOP FOR A MINUTE AND...
WE'VE ALL BEEN WORKING ON OUR DOCTORAL THESES FOR...FOR YEARS.
GENE AND RYDER ARE RIGHT. THERE'S A LOT GOING ON HERE...LAST TIME WE ALL ALMOST GOT KILLED AND ANNIE GOT ARRESTED!
I KNOW THESE GUYS ARE THE GOOD GUYS.
THEY ALL WANT TO DO RIGHT. LIKE ME.
SO WHY IS EVERYTHING GOING WRONG?
MAYBE...
MAYBE WE'VE BEEN THINKING ABOUT THIS ALL WRONG.
MAYBE WE SHOULDN'T STOP QUINTUM MECHANICS--WE SHOULD, LIKE, TAKE IT OVER.
I'VE BEEN THINKING THIS FOR A WHILE. WITH ALL THAT TECHNOLOGY AT OUR FINGERTIPS, WE CAN BE LIKE YOU, DAYOUNG. WE CAN ALL BE LIKE ROCKET GIRL.
FOR THE FUTURE TO CHANGE, PEOPLE HAVE TO CHANGE.
IT'S THE ONLY WAY.
YOU'VE BEEN EXPECTED.
HOW?
YOU'VE ALWAYS BEEN EXPECTED.
TOP FLOOR. GET OFF WHEN IT DINGS.
ISN'T IT?

Chapter 9_Foregone >>

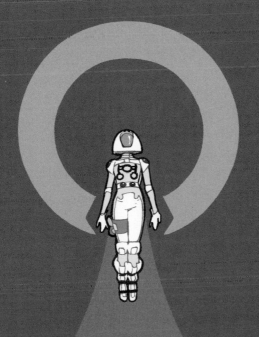

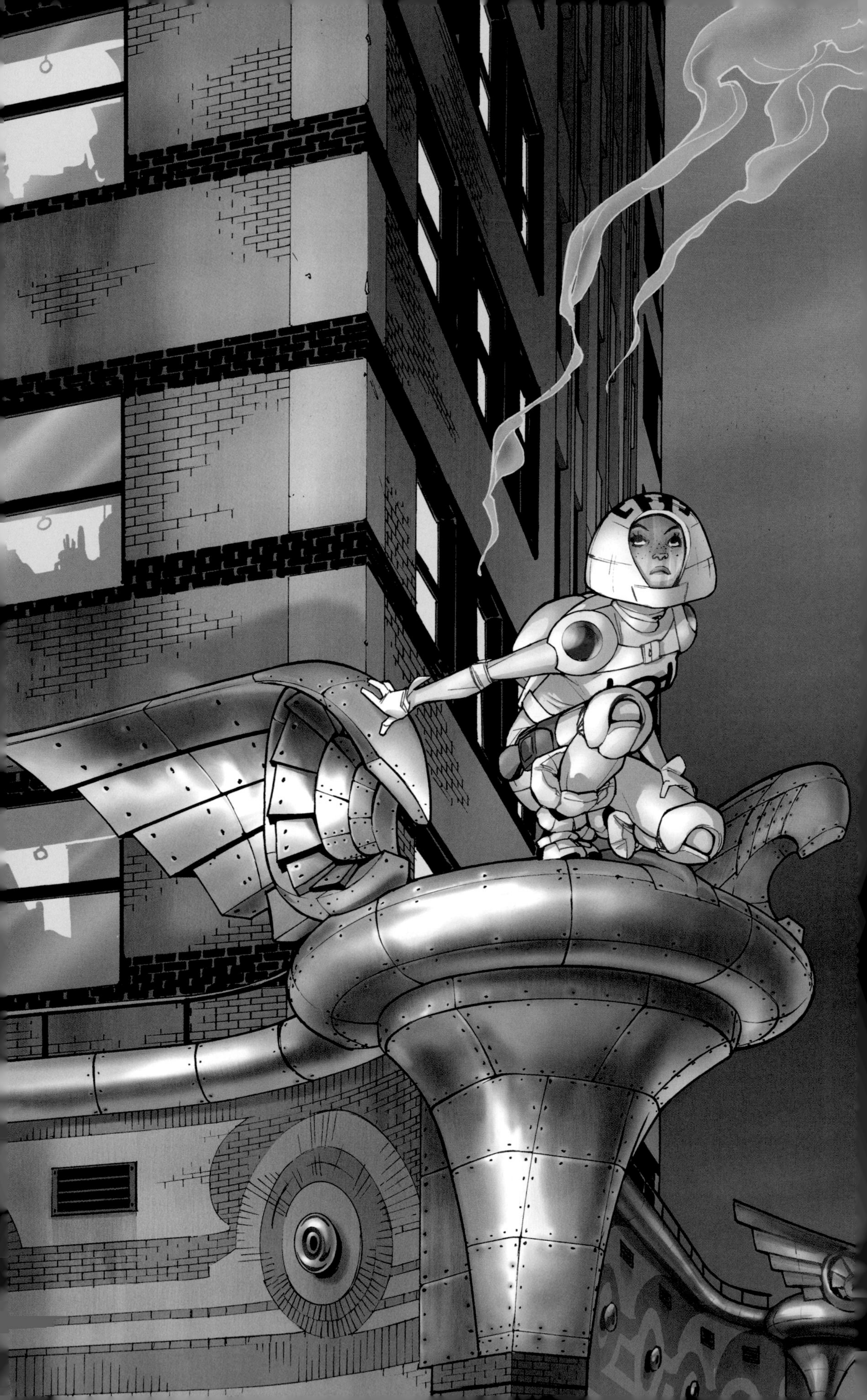

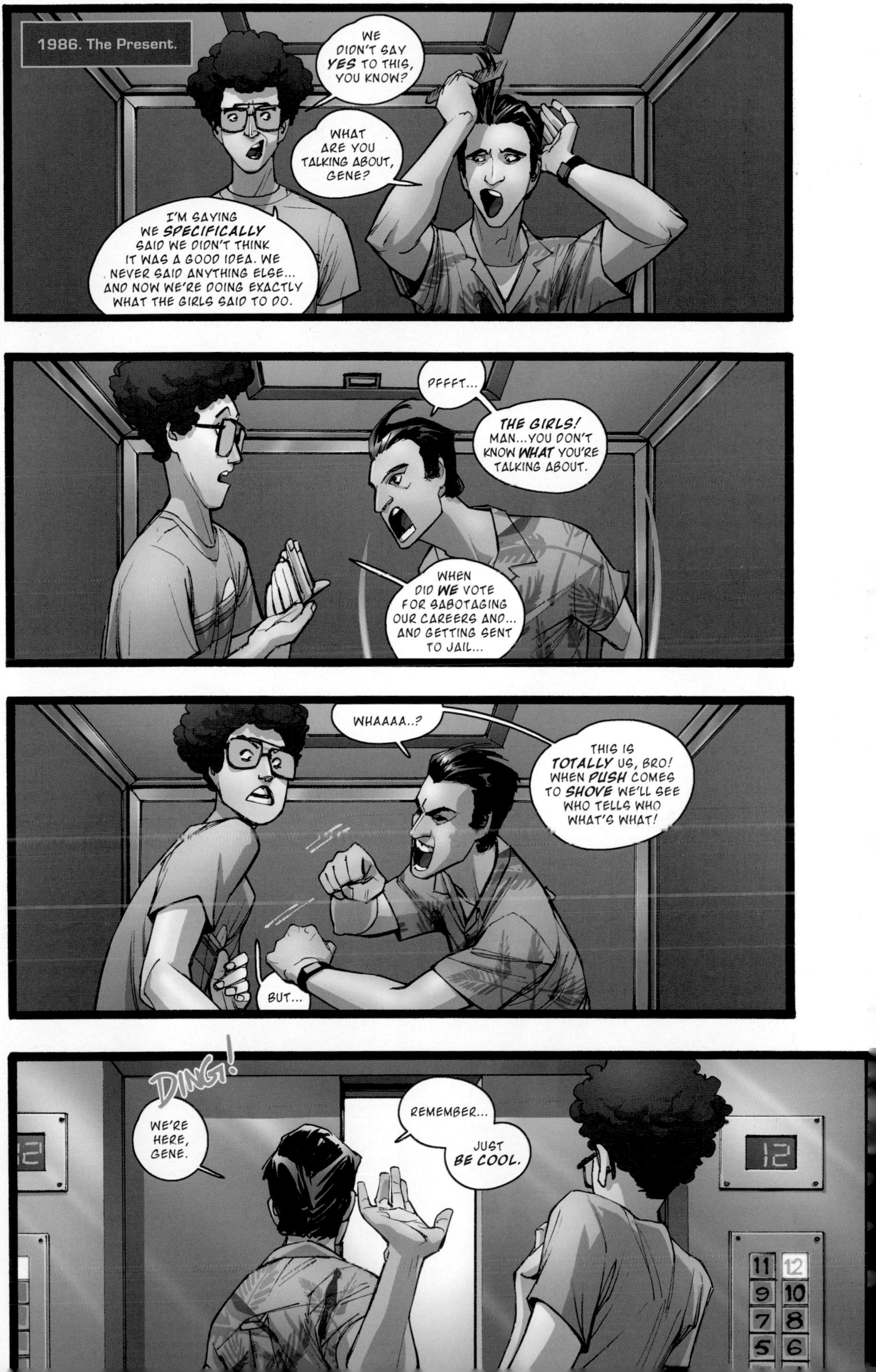
1986. The Present.
WE DIDN'T SAY YES TO THIS, YOU KNOW?
WHAT ARE YOU TALKING ABOUT, GENE?
I'M SAYING WE SPECIFICALLY SAID WE DIDN'T THINK IT WAS A GOOD IDEA. WE NEVER SAID ANYTHING ELSE... AND NOW WE'RE DOING EXACTLY WHAT THE GIRLS SAID TO DO.
PFFFT...
THE GIRLS! MAN...YOU DON'T KNOW WHAT YOU'RE TALKING ABOUT.
WHEN DID WE VOTE FOR SABOTAGING OUR CAREERS AND... AND GETTING SENT TO JAIL...
WHAAAA..?
THIS IS TOTALLY US, BRO! WHEN PUSH COMES TO SHOVE WE'LL SEE WHO TELLS WHO WHAT'S WHAT!
BUT...
DING!
WE'RE HERE, GENE.
REMEMBER...
JUST BE COOL.
12
11
12
9
10
7
8
5
6

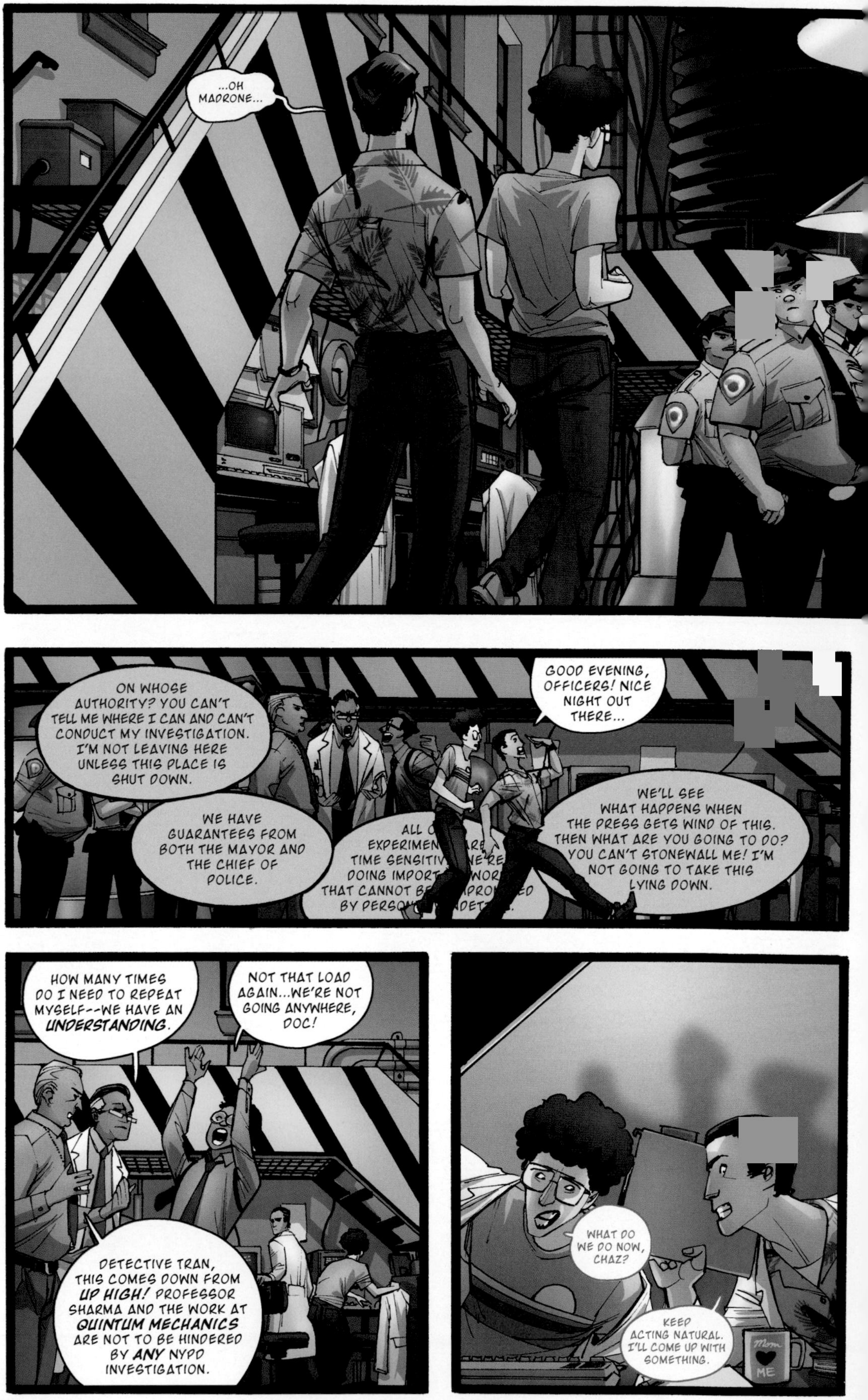
...OH MADRONE...
ON WHOSE AUTHORITY? YOU CAN'T TELL ME WHERE I CAN AND CAN'T CONDUCT MY INVESTIGATION. I'M NOT LEAVING HERE UNLESS THIS PLACE IS SHUT DOWN.
WE HAVE GUARANTEES FROM BOTH THE MAYOR AND THE CHIEF OF POLICE.
GOOD EVENING, OFFICERS! NICE NIGHT OUT THERE...
WE'LL SEE WHAT HAPPENS WHEN THE PRESS GETS WIND OF THIS. THEN WHAT ARE YOU GOING TO DO? YOU CAN'T STONEWALL ME! I'M NOT GOING TO TAKE THIS LYING DOWN.
HOW MANY TIMES DO I NEED TO REPEAT MYSELF--WE HAVE AN UNDERSTANDING.
NOT THAT LOAD AGAIN...WE'RE NOT GOING ANYWHERE, DOC!
DETECTIVE TRAN, THIS COMES DOWN FROM UP HIGH! PROFESSOR SHARMA AND THE WORK AT QUINTUM MECHANICS ARE NOT TO BE HINDERED BY ANY NYPD INVESTIGATION.
WHAT DO WE DO NOW, CHAZ?
KEEP ACTING NATURAL. I'LL COME UP WITH SOMETHING.
MOM ♥ ME

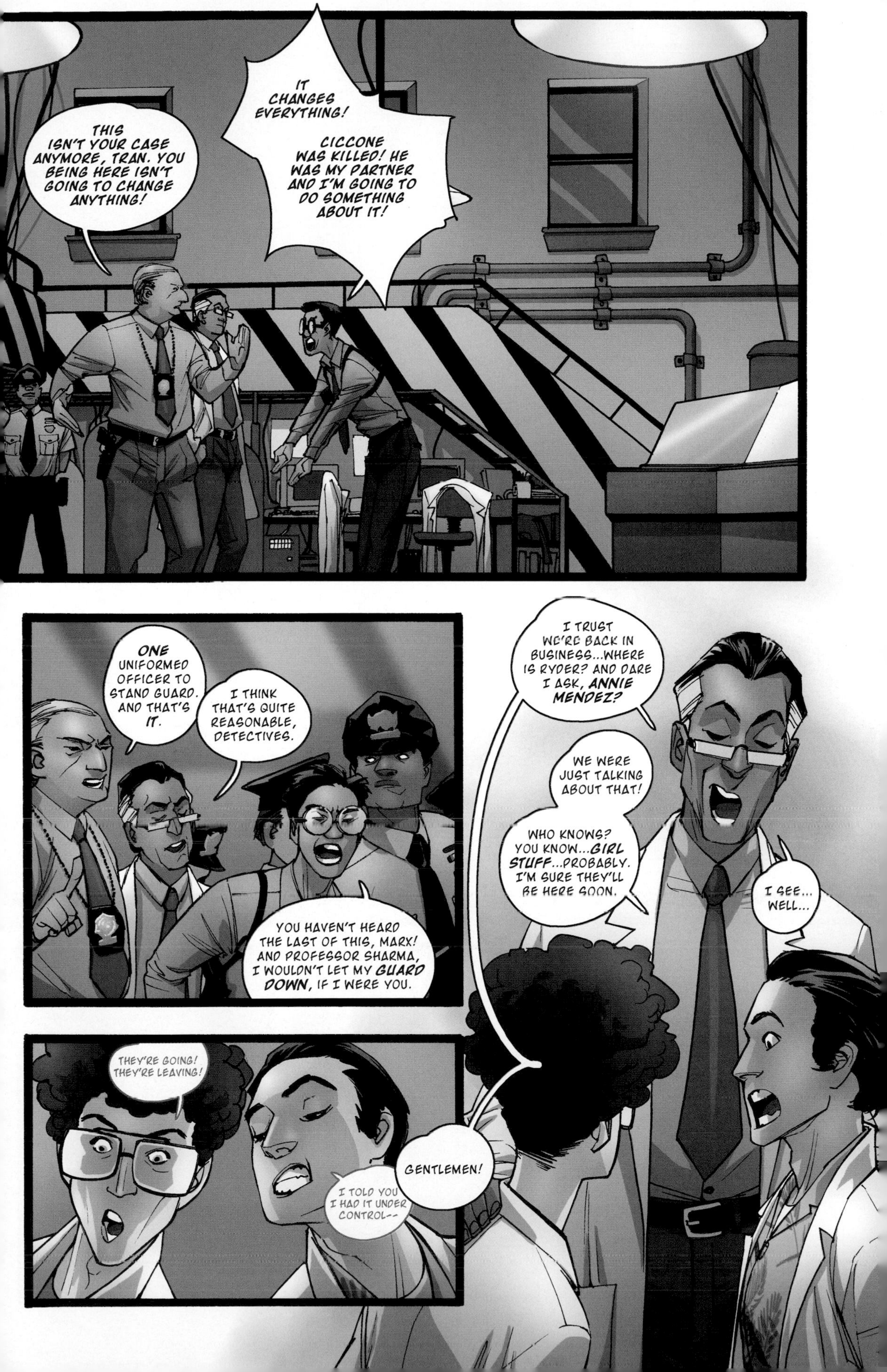
THIS ISN'T YOUR CASE ANYMORE, TRAN. YOU BEING HERE ISN'T GOING TO CHANGE ANYTHING!
IT CHANGES EVERYTHING!
CICCONE WAS KILLED! HE WAS MY PARTNER AND I'M GOING TO DO SOMETHING ABOUT IT!
ONE UNIFORMED OFFICER TO STAND GUARD. AND THAT'S IT.
I THINK THAT'S QUITE REASONABLE, DETECTIVES.
YOU HAVEN'T HEARD THE LAST OF THIS, MARX! AND PROFESSOR SHARMA, I WOULDN'T LET MY GUARD DOWN, IF I WERE YOU.
THEY'RE GOING! THEY'RE LEAVING!
I TOLD YOU I HAD IT UNDER CONTROL--
GENTLEMEN!
I TRUST WE'RE BACK IN BUSINESS...WHERE IS RYDER? AND DARE I ASK, ANNIE MENDEZ?
WE WERE JUST TALKING ABOUT THAT!
WHO KNOWS? YOU KNOW...GIRL STUFF...PROBABLY. I'M SURE THEY'LL BE HERE SOON.
I SEE... WELL...

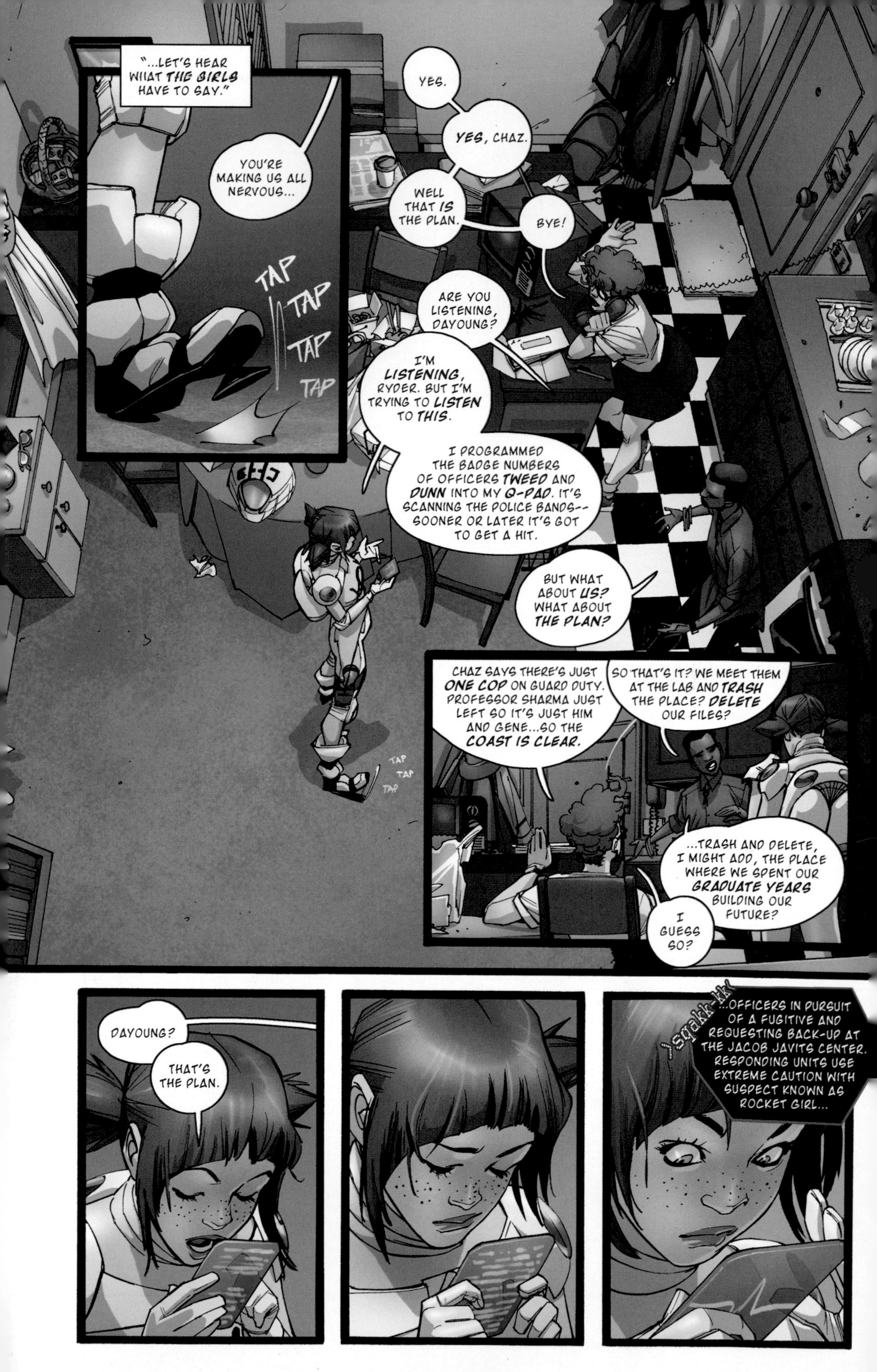

"...LET'S HEAR WHAT THE GIRLS HAVE TO SAY."
YOU'RE MAKING US ALL NERVOUS...
TAP TAP TAP TAP
YES.
YES, CHAZ.
WELL THAT IS THE PLAN.
BYE!
ARE YOU LISTENING, DAYOUNG?
I'M LISTENING, RYDER. BUT I'M TRYING TO LISTEN TO THIS.
I PROGRAMMED THE BADGE NUMBERS OF OFFICERS TWEED AND DUNN INTO MY Q-PAD. IT'S SCANNING THE POLICE BANDS-- SOONER OR LATER IT'S GOT TO GET A HIT.
BUT WHAT ABOUT US? WHAT ABOUT THE PLAN?
TAP TAP TAP
CHAZ SAYS THERE'S JUST ONE COP ON GUARD DUTY. PROFESSOR SHARMA JUST LEFT SO IT'S JUST HIM AND GENE...SO THE COAST IS CLEAR.
SO THAT'S IT? WE MEET THEM AT THE LAB AND TRASH THE PLACE? DELETE OUR FILES?
...TRASH AND DELETE, I MIGHT ADD, THE PLACE WHERE WE SPENT OUR GRADUATE YEARS BUILDING OUR FUTURE?
I GUESS SO?
DAYOUNG?
THAT'S THE PLAN.
sqakk-kk
...OFFICERS IN PURSUIT OF A FUGITIVE AND REQUESTING BACK-UP AT THE JACOB JAVITS CENTER. RESPONDING UNITS USE EXTREME CAUTION WITH SUSPECT KNOWN AS ROCKET GIRL...

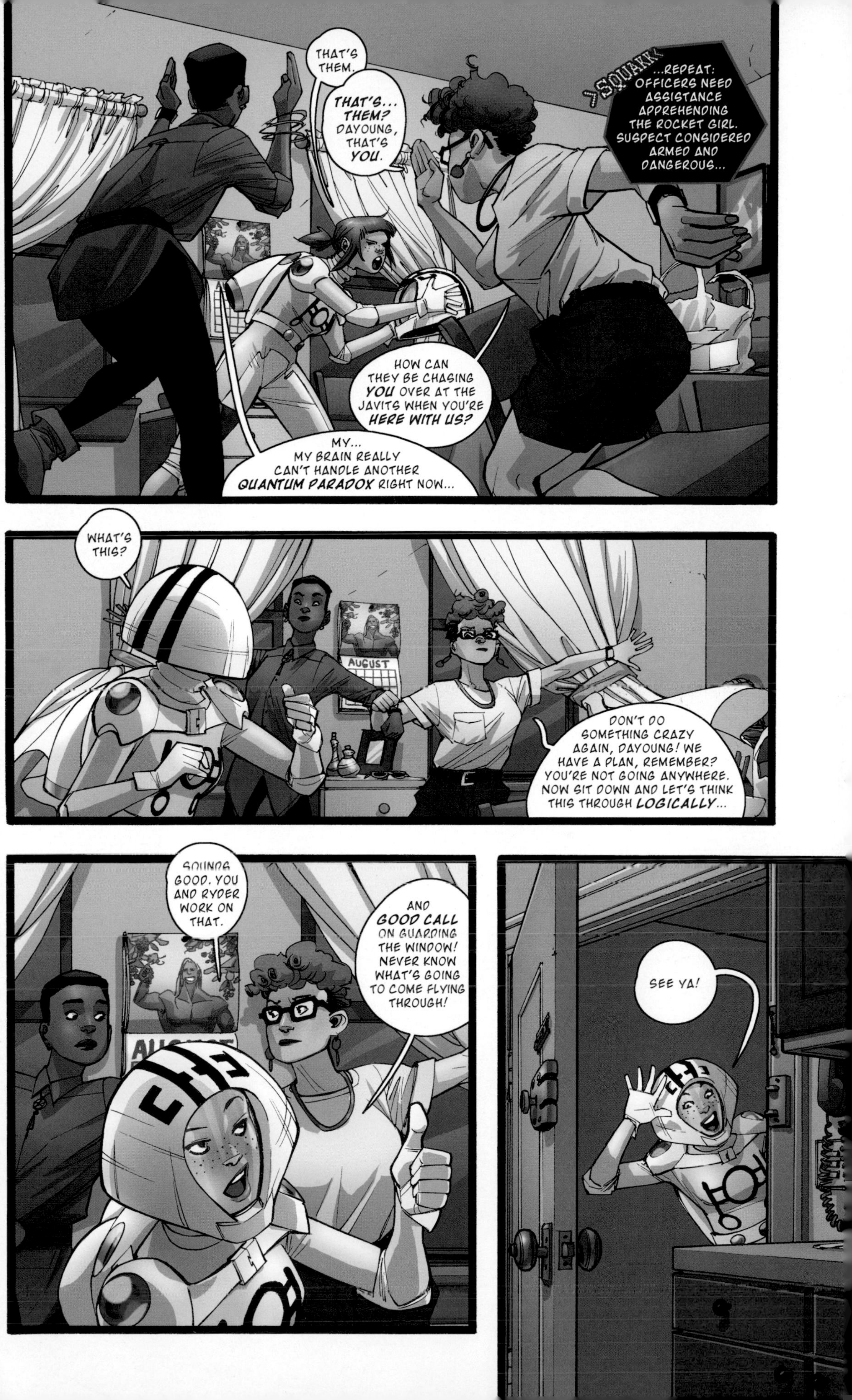
THAT'S THEM.
THAT'S... THEM? DAYOUNG, THAT'S YOU.
SQUAKK
...REPEAT: OFFICERS NEED ASSISTANCE APPREHENDING THE ROCKET GIRL. SUSPECT CONSIDERED ARMED AND DANGEROUS...
AUGUST
HOW CAN THEY BE CHASING YOU OVER AT THE JAVITS WHEN YOU'RE HERE WITH US?
MY... MY BRAIN REALLY CAN'T HANDLE ANOTHER QUANTUM PARADOX RIGHT NOW...
WHAT'S THIS?
AUGUST
DON'T DO SOMETHING CRAZY AGAIN, DAYOUNG! WE HAVE A PLAN, REMEMBER? YOU'RE NOT GOING ANYWHERE. NOW SIT DOWN AND LET'S THINK THIS THROUGH LOGICALLY...
SOUNDS GOOD. YOU AND RYDER WORK ON THAT.
AND GOOD CALL ON GUARDING THE WINDOW! NEVER KNOW WHAT'S GOING TO COME FLYING THROUGH!
SEE YA!

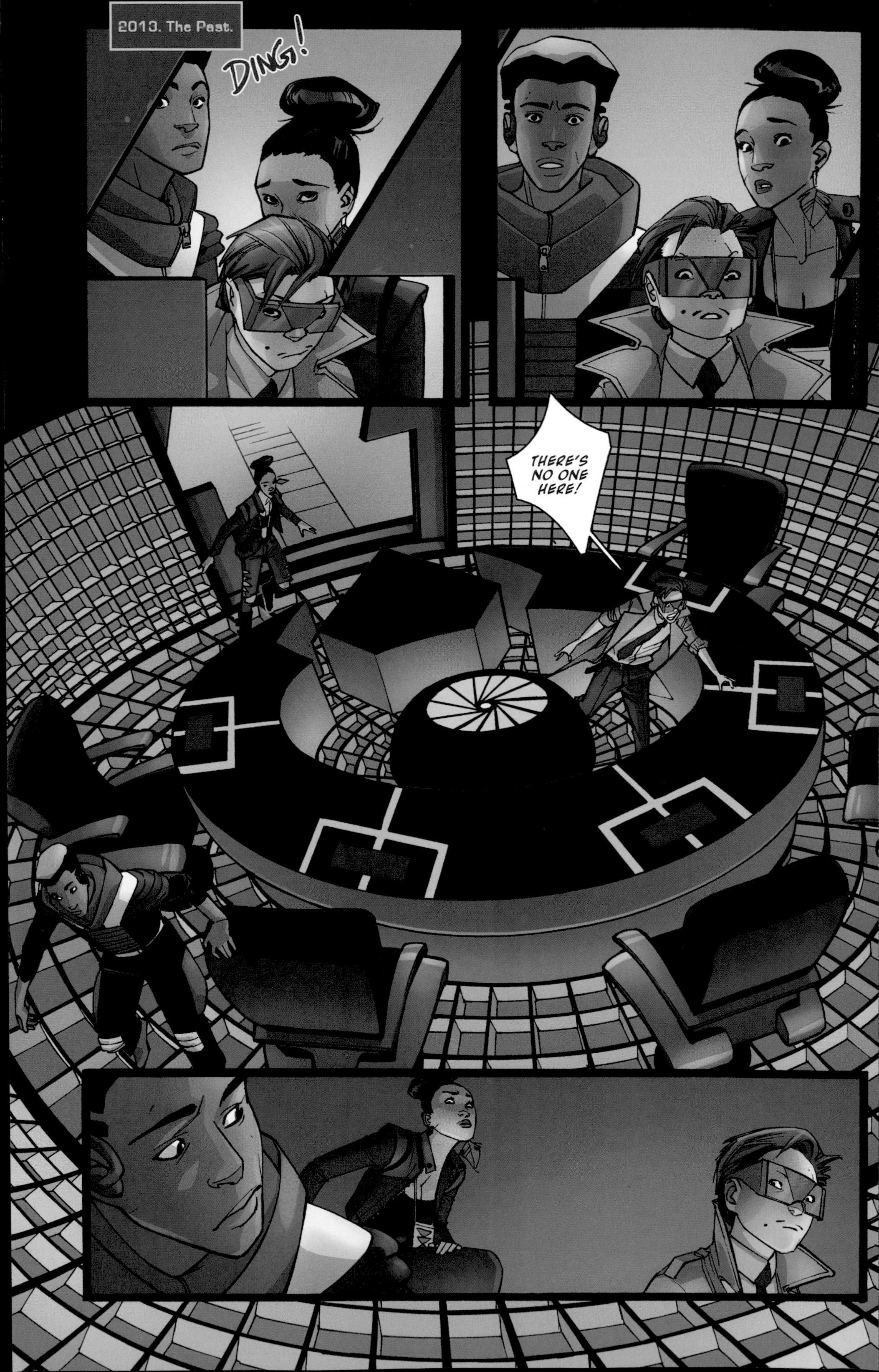
2013. The Past.
DING!
THERE'S NO ONE HERE!

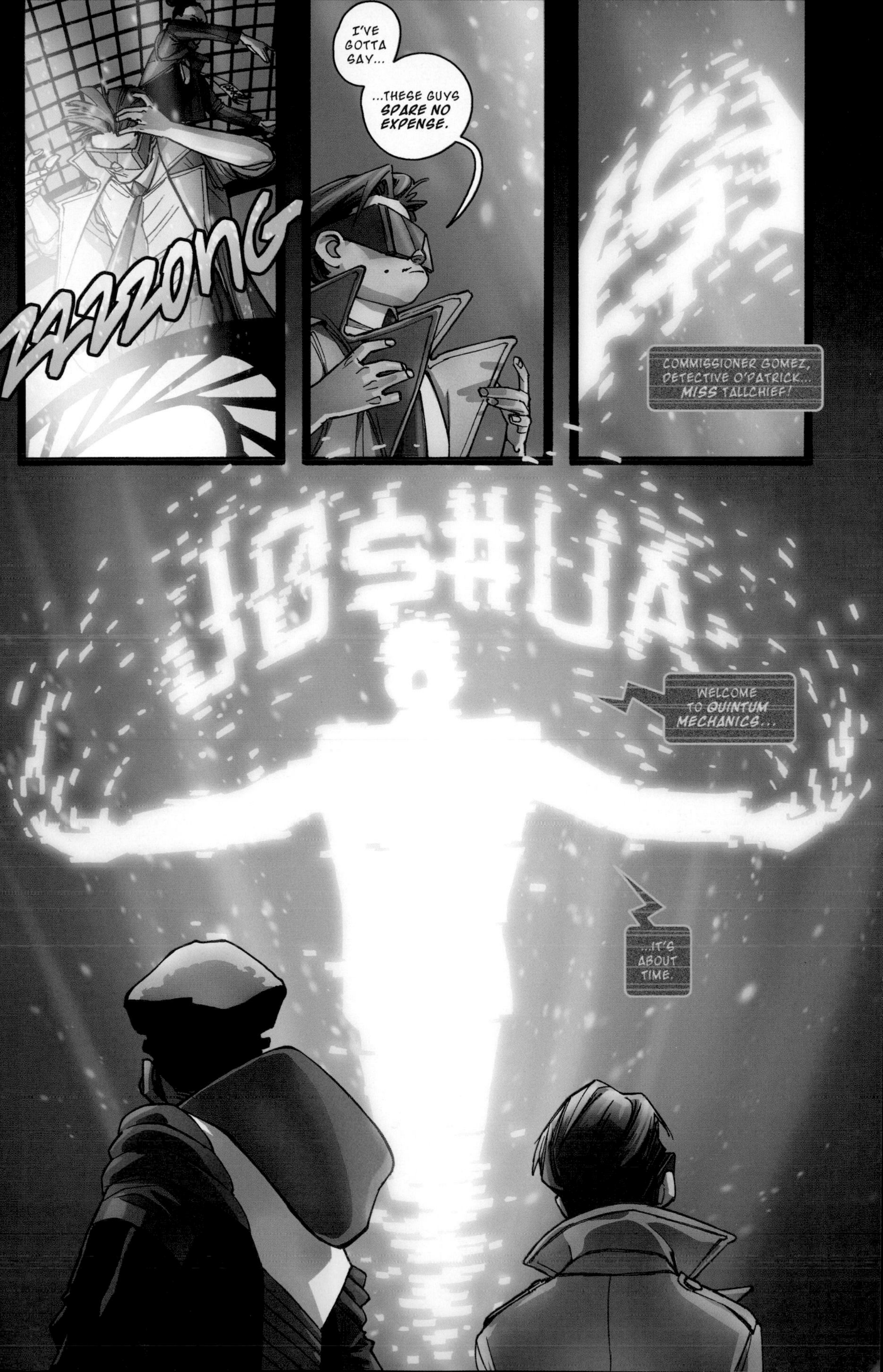
ZAZZONG
I'VE GOTTA SAY...
...THESE GUYS SPARE NO EXPENSE.
COMMISSIONER GOMEZ, DETECTIVE O'PATRICK... MISS TALLCHIEF!
JO$#UA
WELCOME TO QUINTUM MECHANICS...
...IT'S ABOUT TIME.

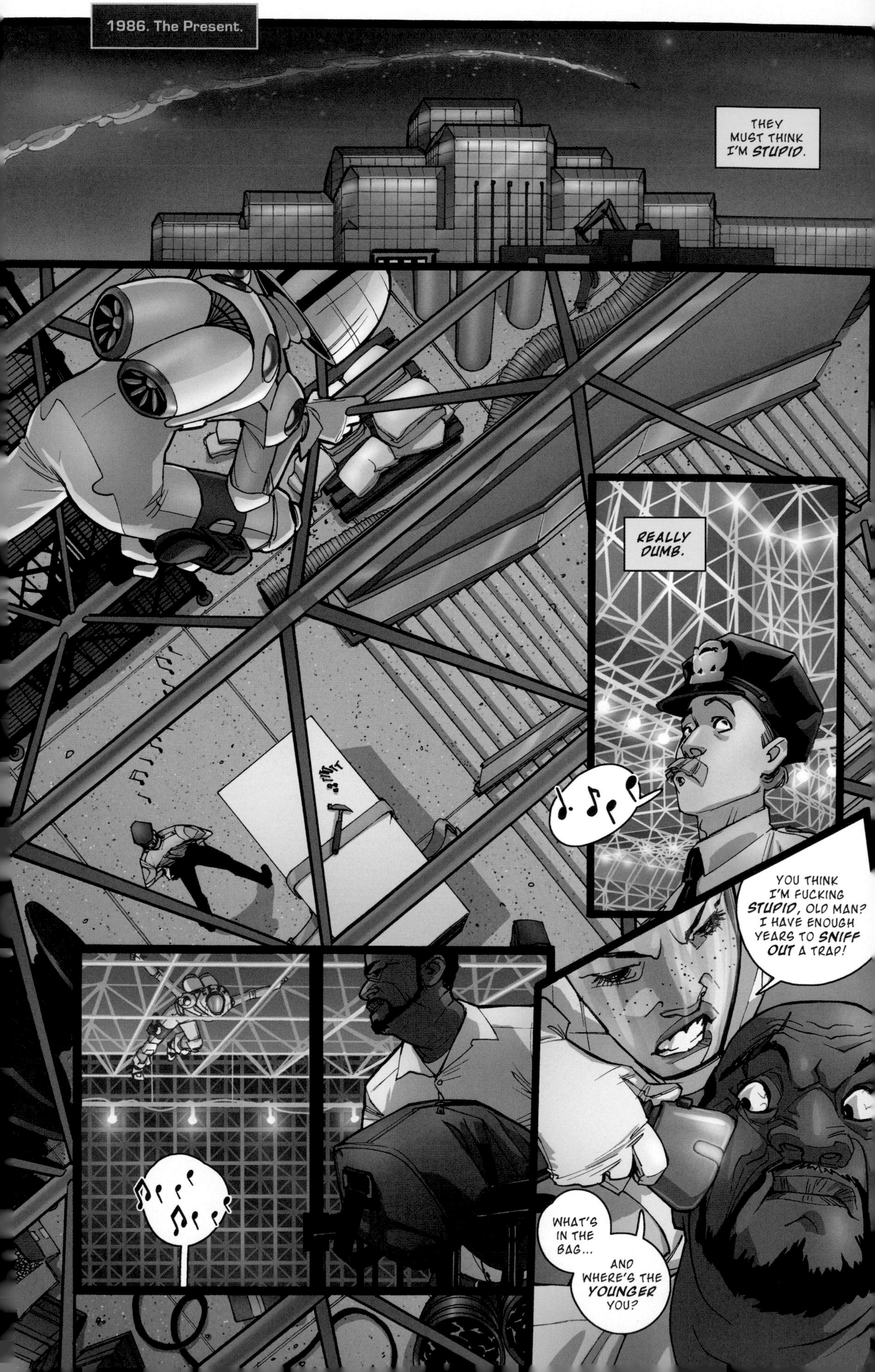
1986. The Present.
THEY MUST THINK I'M STUPID.
REALLY DUMB.
YOU THINK I'M FUCKING STUPID, OLD MAN? I HAVE ENOUGH YEARS TO SNIFF OUT A TRAP!
WHAT'S IN THE BAG...
AND WHERE'S THE YOUNGER YOU?

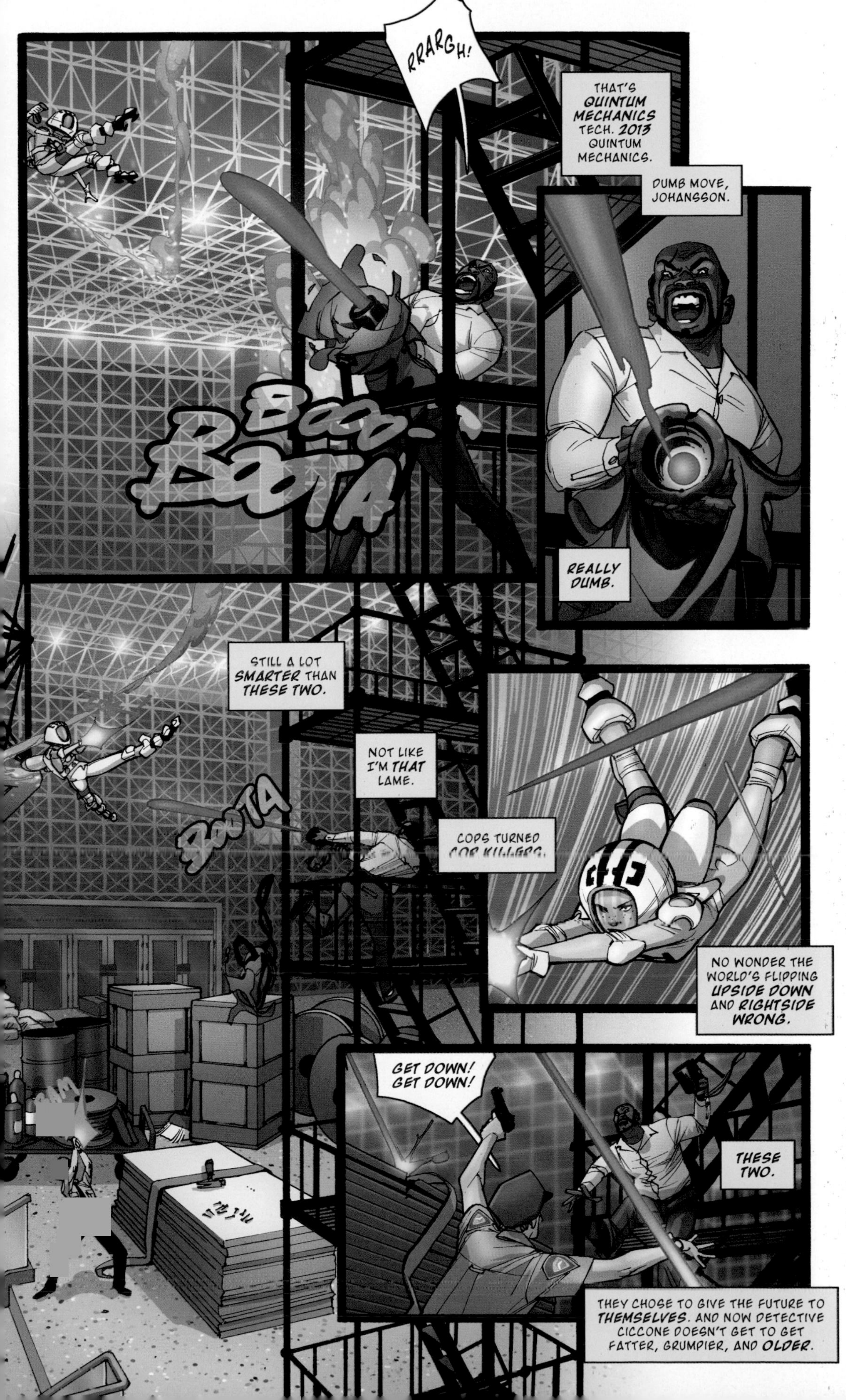
RRARGH!
THAT'S QUINTUM MECHANICS TECH. 2013 QUINTUM MECHANICS.
DUMB MOVE, JOHANSSON.
BOOO-BOOTA
REALLY DUMB.
STILL A LOT SMARTER THAN THESE TWO.
NOT LIKE I'M THAT LAME.
BOOTA
COPS TURNED COP KILLERS.
NO WONDER THE WORLD'S FLIPPING UPSIDE DOWN AND RIGHTSIDE WRONG.
GET DOWN! GET DOWN!
THESE TWO.
THEY CHOSE TO GIVE THE FUTURE TO THEMSELVES. AND NOW DETECTIVE CICCONE DOESN'T GET TO GET FATTER, GRUMPIER, AND OLDER.

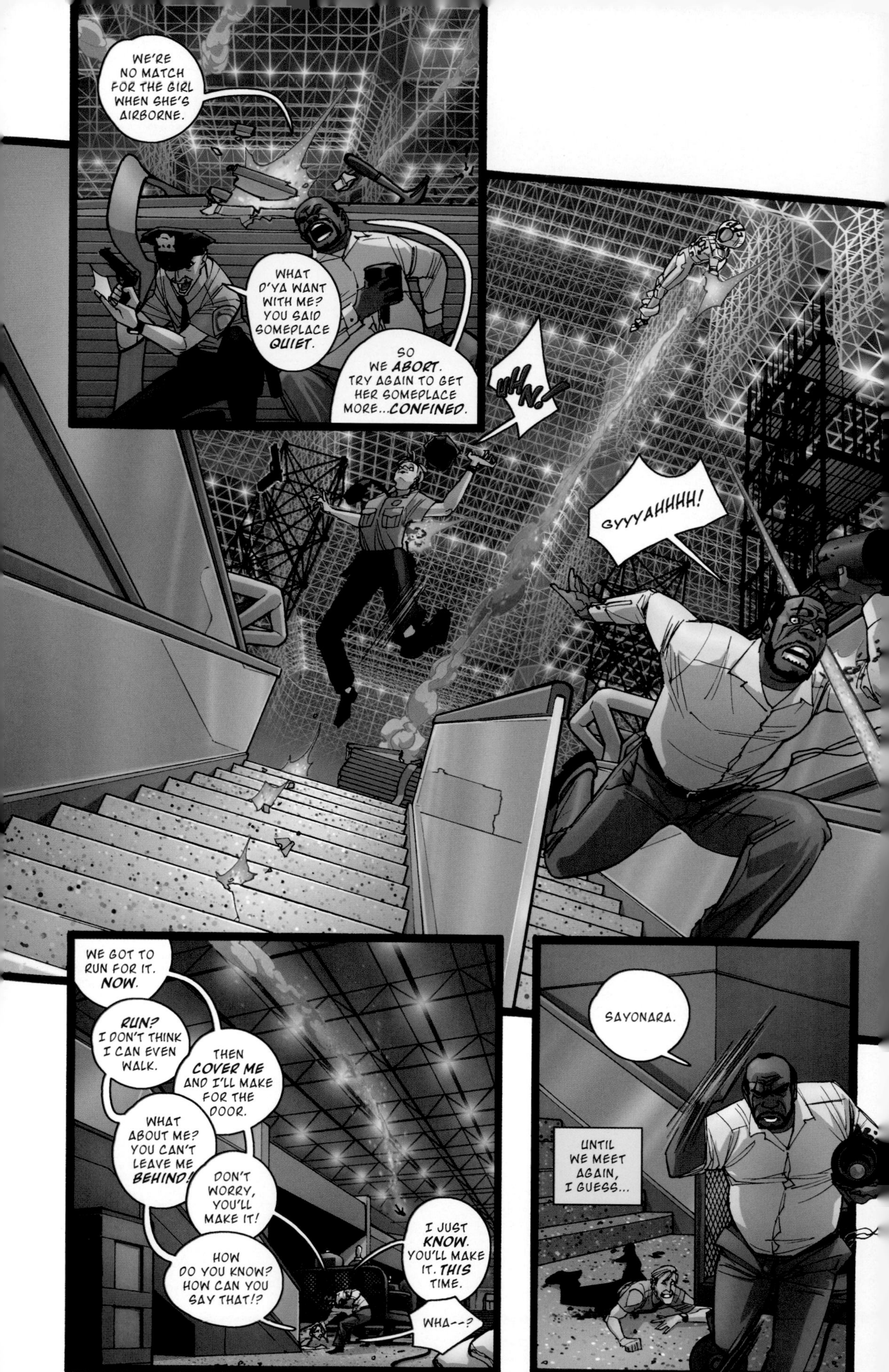
WE'RE NO MATCH FOR THE GIRL WHEN SHE'S AIRBORNE.
WHAT D'YA WANT WITH ME? YOU SAID SOMEPLACE QUIET.
SO WE ABORT. TRY AGAIN TO GET HER SOMEPLACE MORE...CONFINED.
UHN!
GYYYAHHHH!
WE GOT TO RUN FOR IT. NOW.
RUN? I DON'T THINK I CAN EVEN WALK.
THEN COVER ME AND I'LL MAKE FOR THE DOOR.
WHAT ABOUT ME? YOU CAN'T LEAVE ME BEHIND!
DON'T WORRY, YOU'LL MAKE IT!
HOW DO YOU KNOW? HOW CAN YOU SAY THAT!?
I JUST KNOW. YOU'LL MAKE IT. THIS TIME.
WHA--?
SAYONARA.
UNTIL WE MEET AGAIN, I GUESS...

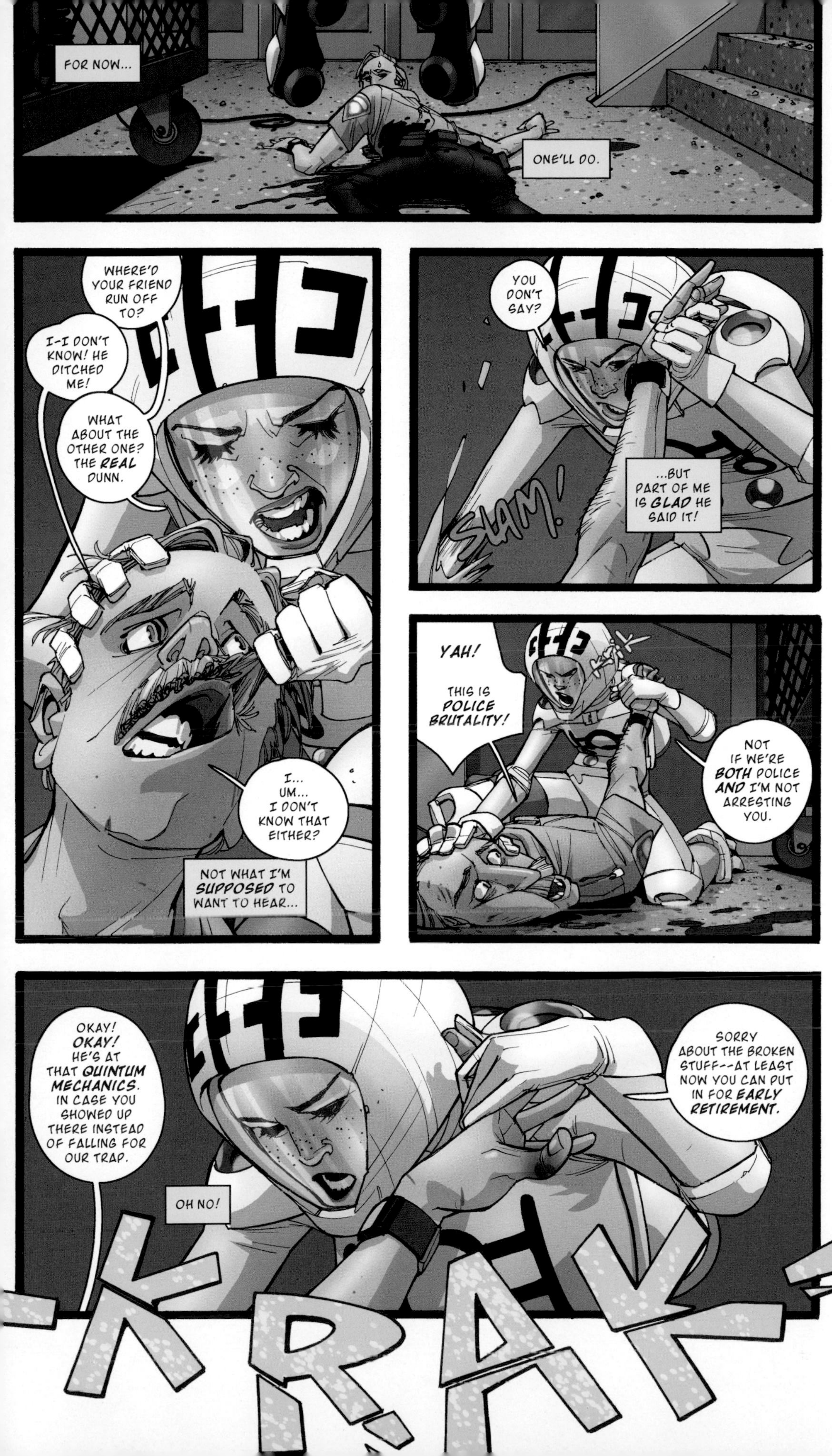
FOR NOW...
ONE'LL DO.
WHERE'D YOUR FRIEND RUN OFF TO?
I-I DON'T KNOW! HE DITCHED ME!
WHAT ABOUT THE OTHER ONE? THE REAL DUNN.
I... UM... I DON'T KNOW THAT EITHER?
NOT WHAT I'M SUPPOSED TO WANT TO HEAR...
YOU DON'T SAY?
SLAM!
...BUT PART OF ME IS GLAD HE SAID IT!
YAH!
THIS IS POLICE BRUTALITY!
NOT IF WE'RE BOTH POLICE AND I'M NOT ARRESTING YOU.
OKAY! OKAY! HE'S AT THAT QUINTUM MECHANICS. IN CASE YOU SHOWED UP THERE INSTEAD OF FALLING FOR OUR TRAP.
SORRY ABOUT THE BROKEN STUFF--AT LEAST NOW YOU CAN PUT IN FOR EARLY RETIREMENT.
OH NO!
KRAK

2013. The Past.

CUTE.

SO DID THEY SEND YOU UP FROM MARKETING? WE WERE HOPING TO TALK TO SOMEONE IN CHARGE--

WHY DID YOU DO THIS?

WHERE'S DAYOUNG?

WHY DID...I?

YOU WERE THERE, LESHAWN. YOU KNOW AS WELL AS I THAT THERE WAS NO STOPPING HER...

WELL...YOU DON'T KNOW AS WELL AS I, BUT YOU KNOW WELL ENOUGH.

ENOUGH!

WHAT'S GOING ON WITH THE CITY? WHO TURNED OUT THE LIGHTS?

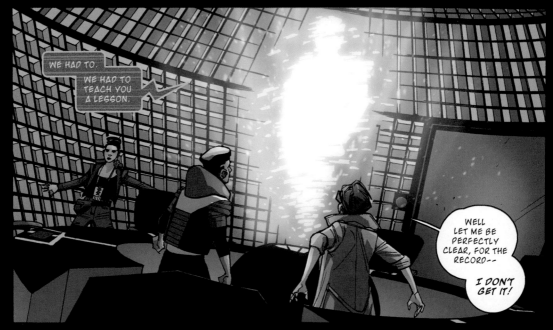

WE HAD TO. WE HAD TO TEACH YOU A LESSON.

WELL LET ME BE PERFECTLY CLEAR, FOR THE RECORD--

I DON'T GET IT!

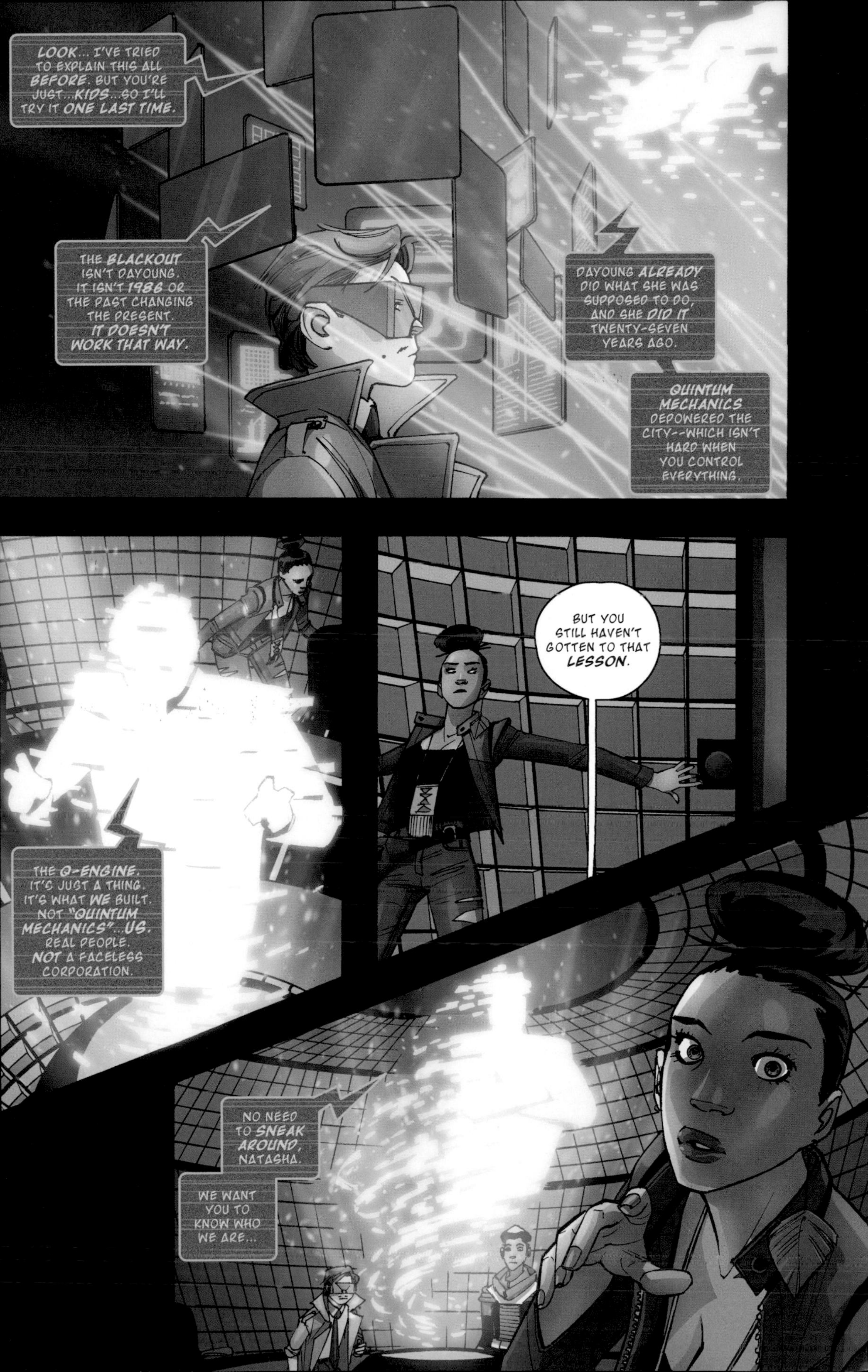
LOOK... I'VE TRIED TO EXPLAIN THIS ALL BEFORE. BUT YOU'RE JUST...KIDS...SO I'LL TRY IT ONE LAST TIME.
THE BLACKOUT ISN'T DAYOUNG. IT ISN'T 1986 OR THE PAST CHANGING THE PRESENT. IT DOESN'T WORK THAT WAY.
DAYOUNG ALREADY DID WHAT SHE WAS SUPPOSED TO DO, AND SHE DID IT TWENTY-SEVEN YEARS AGO.
QUINTUM MECHANICS DEPOWERED THE CITY--WHICH ISN'T HARD WHEN YOU CONTROL EVERYTHING.
BUT YOU STILL HAVEN'T GOTTEN TO THAT LESSON.
THE Q-ENGINE. IT'S JUST A THING. IT'S WHAT WE BUILT. NOT "QUINTUM MECHANICS"...US. REAL PEOPLE. NOT A FACELESS CORPORATION.
NO NEED TO SNEAK AROUND, NATASHA.
WE WANT YOU TO KNOW WHO WE ARE...

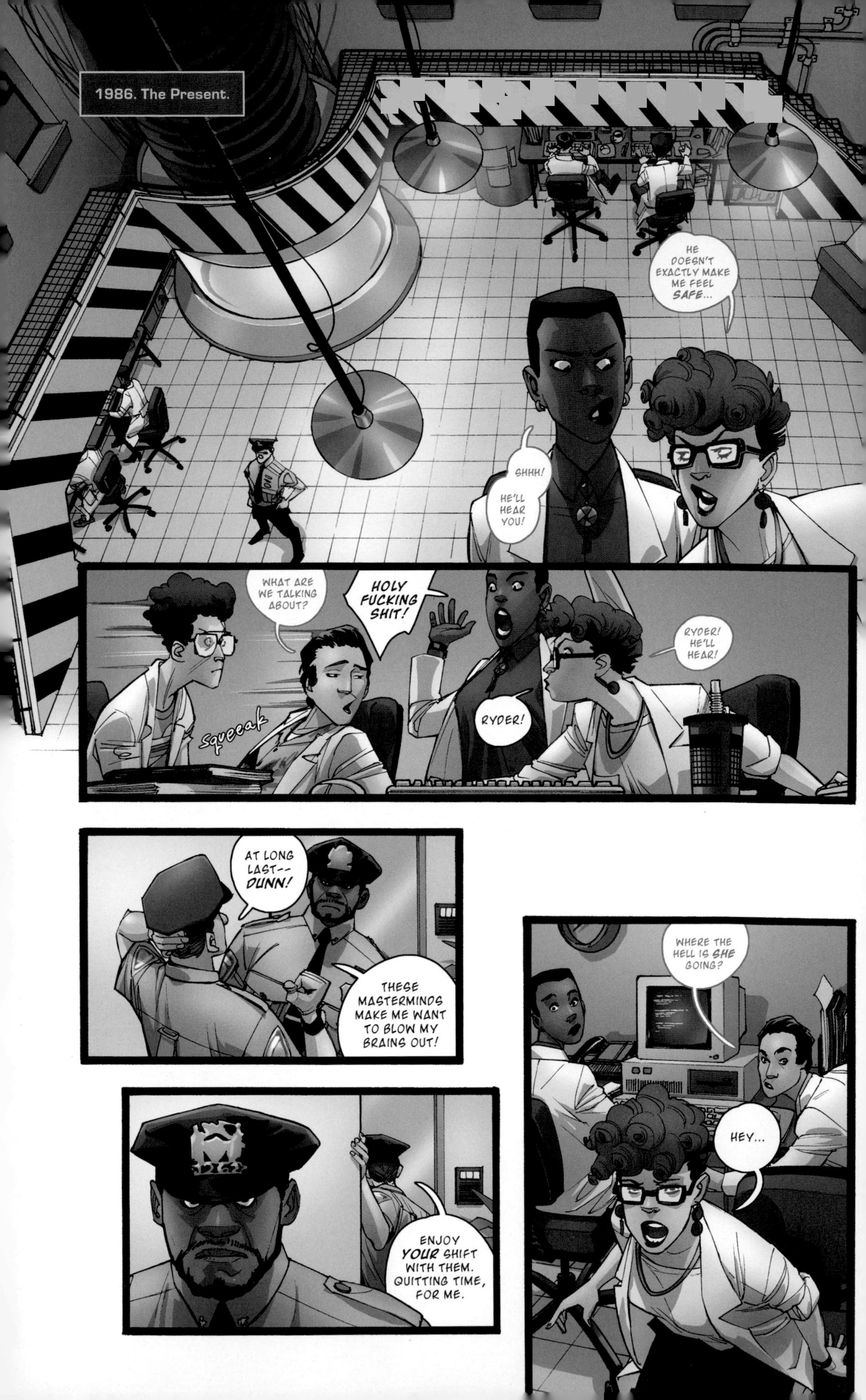
1986. The Present.
HE DOESN'T EXACTLY MAKE ME FEEL *SAFE*...
SHHH! HE'LL HEAR YOU!
WHAT ARE WE TALKING ABOUT?
HOLY FUCKING SHIT!
Squeeeak
RYDER!
RYDER! HE'LL HEAR!
AT LONG LAST-- *DUNN!*
THESE MASTERMINDS MAKE ME WANT TO BLOW MY BRAINS OUT!
ENJOY *YOUR* SHIFT WITH THEM. QUITTING TIME, FOR ME.
WHERE THE HELL IS *SHE* GOING?
HEY...

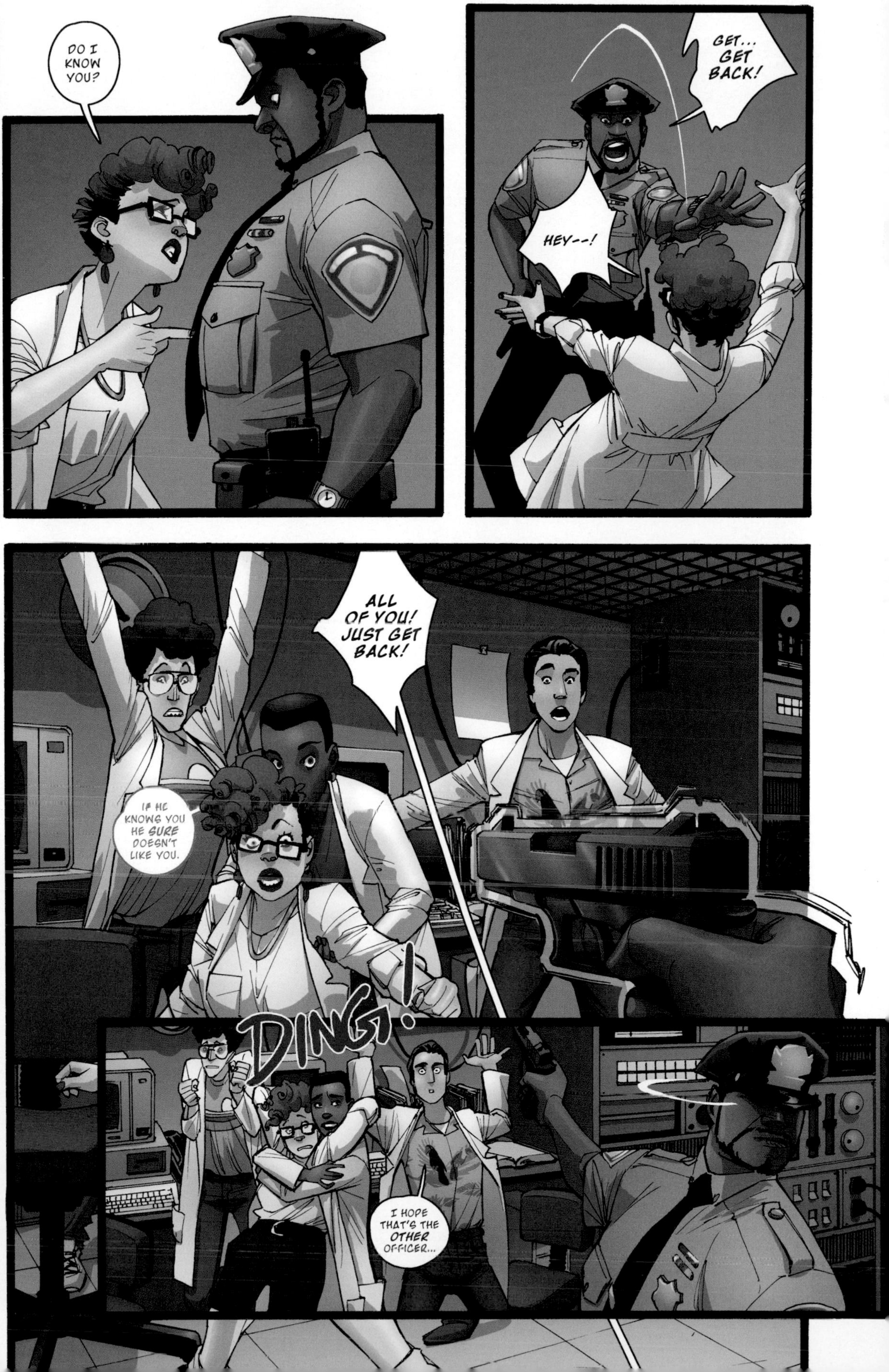
DO I KNOW YOU?
GET... GET BACK!
HEY--!
ALL OF YOU! JUST GET BACK!
IF HE KNOWS YOU HE SURE DOESN'T LIKE YOU.
DING!
I HOPE THAT'S THE OTHER OFFICER...

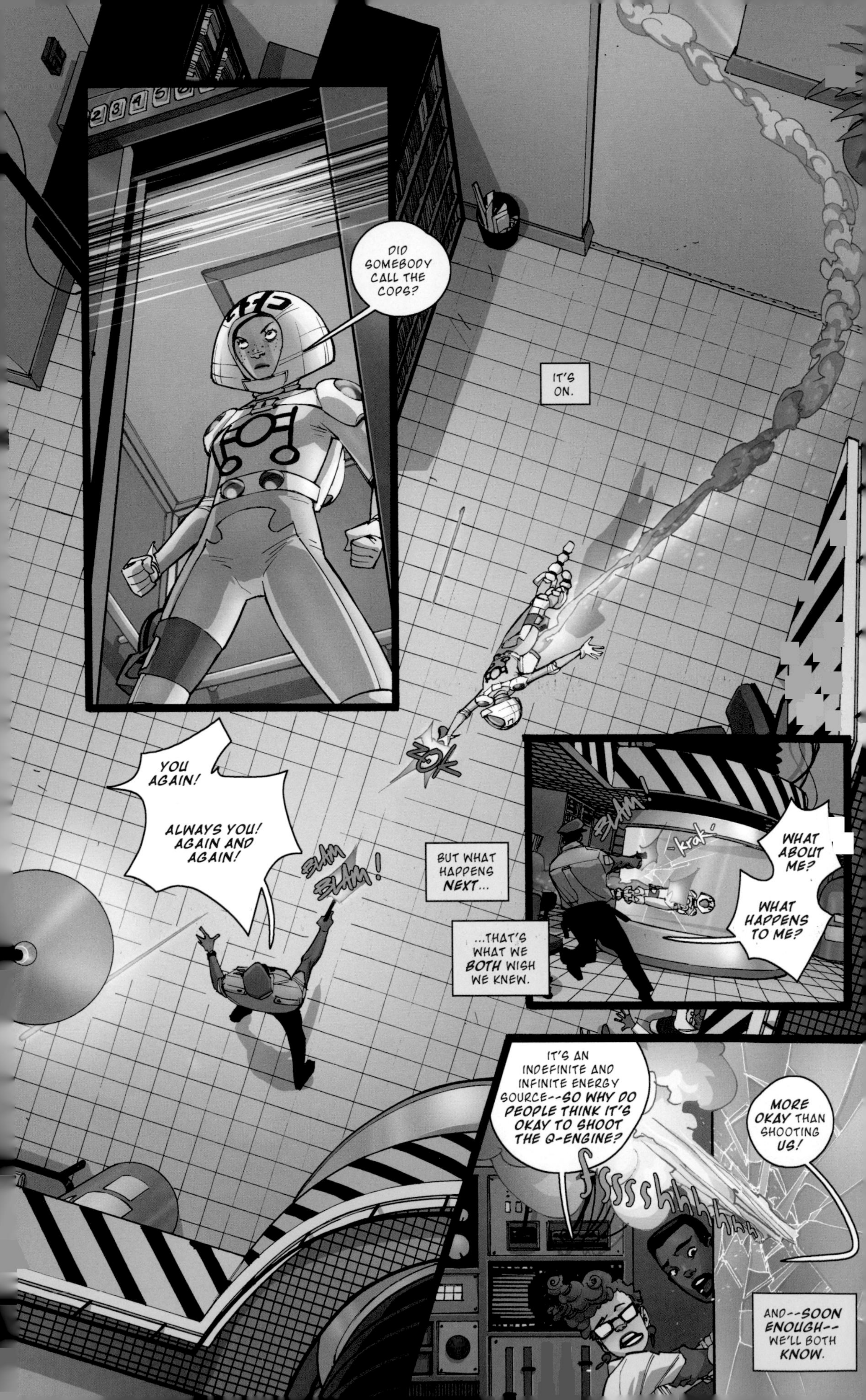
DID SOMEBODY CALL THE COPS?
IT'S ON.
ZOK
YOU AGAIN!
ALWAYS YOU! AGAIN AND AGAIN!
BLAM BLAM!
BUT WHAT HAPPENS NEXT...
...THAT'S WHAT WE BOTH WISH WE KNEW.
BLAM!
-krak-
WHAT ABOUT ME?
WHAT HAPPENS TO ME?
IT'S AN INDEFINITE AND INFINITE ENERGY SOURCE--SO WHY DO PEOPLE THINK IT'S OKAY TO SHOOT THE Q-ENGINE?
MORE OKAY THAN SHOOTING US!
fsssshhhhhhh
AND--SOON ENOUGH--WE'LL BOTH KNOW.

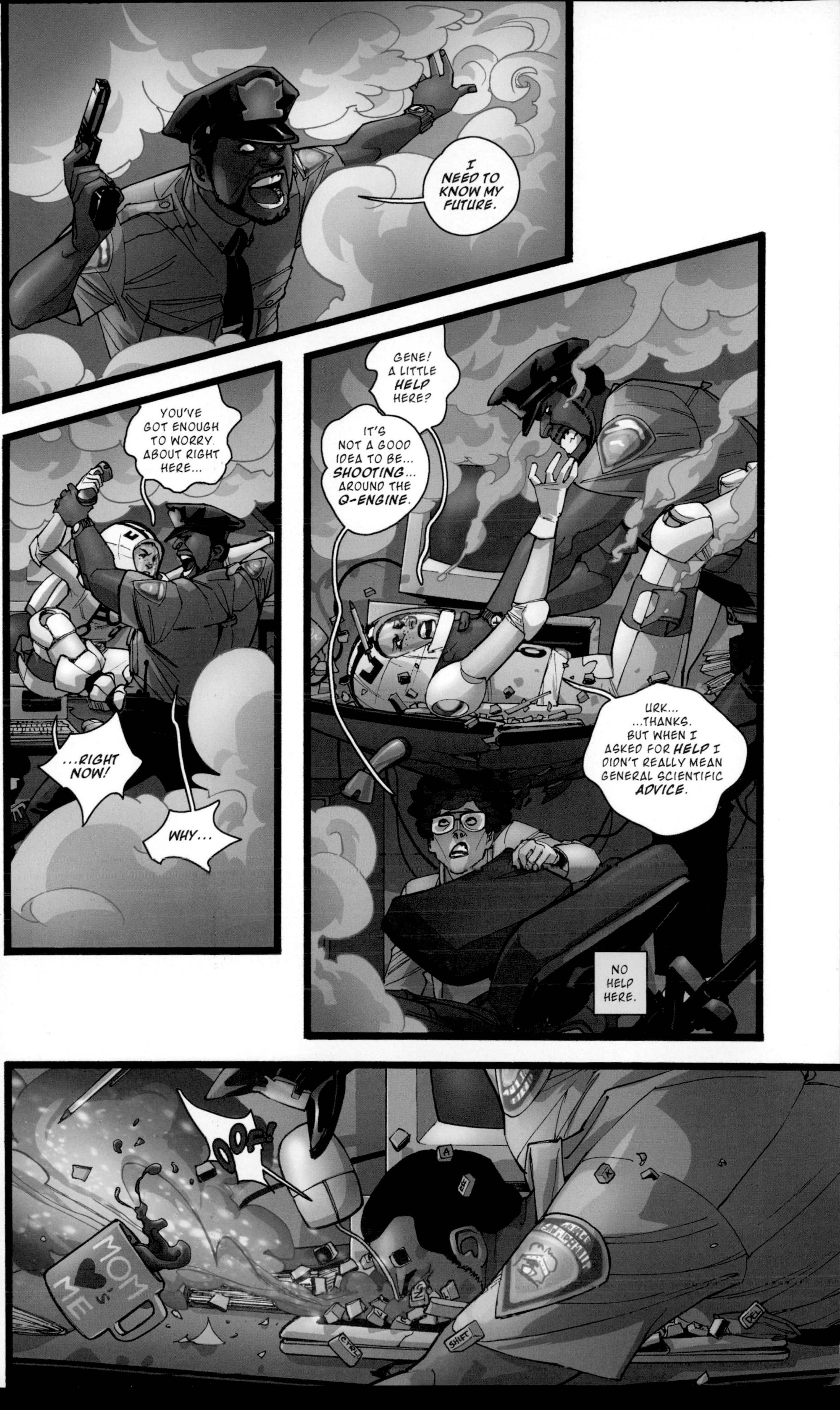

I NEED TO KNOW MY FUTURE.
YOU'VE GOT ENOUGH TO WORRY ABOUT RIGHT HERE...
...RIGHT NOW!
WHY...
GENE! A LITTLE HELP HERE?
IT'S NOT A GOOD IDEA TO BE... SHOOTING... AROUND THE Q-ENGINE.
URK... ...THANKS. BUT WHEN I ASKED FOR HELP I DIDN'T REALLY MEAN GENERAL SCIENTIFIC ADVICE.
NO HELP HERE.
OOF!
MOM ME

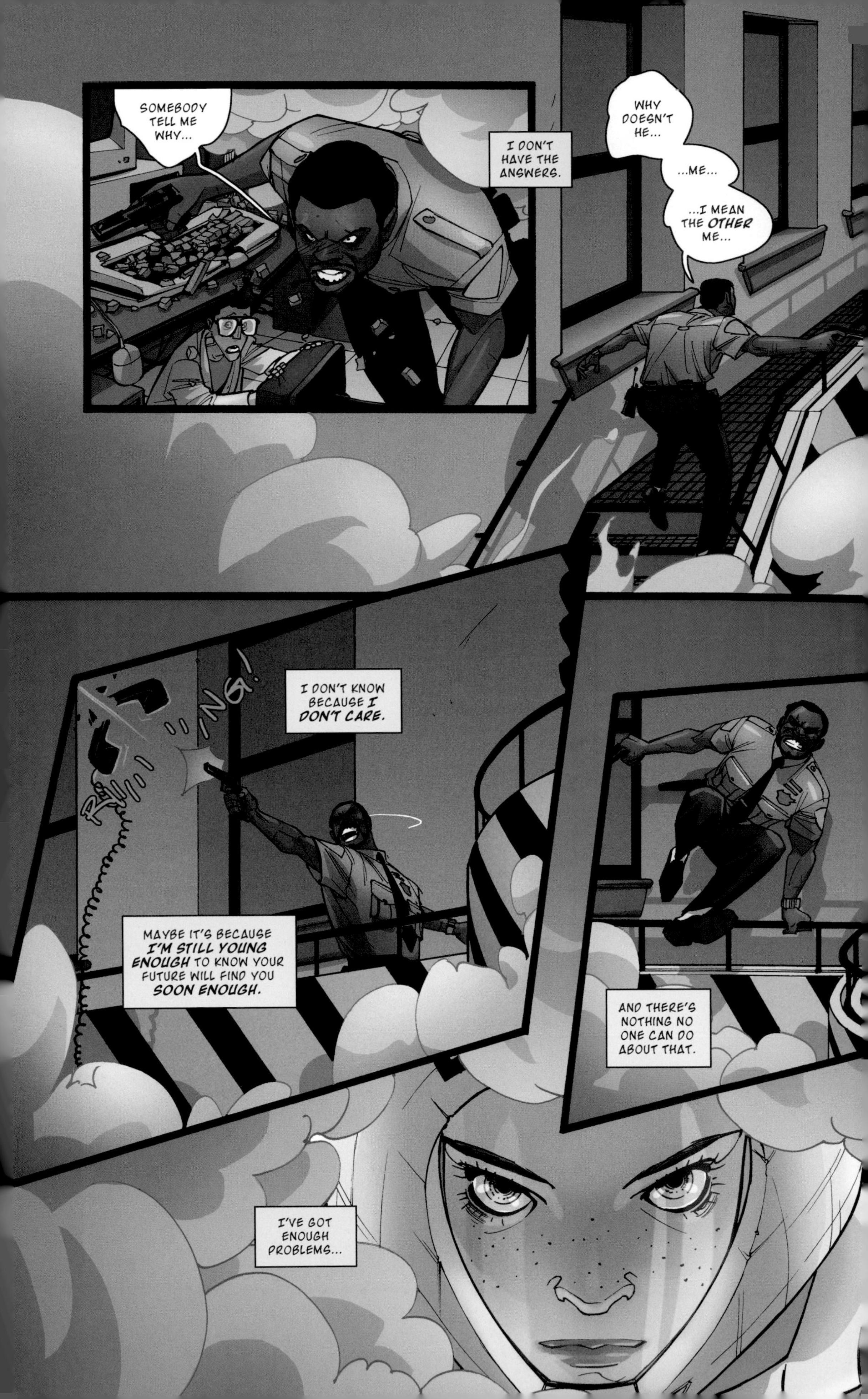

SOMEBODY TELL ME WHY...
I DON'T HAVE THE ANSWERS.
WHY DOESN'T HE...
...ME...
...I MEAN THE OTHER ME...
I DON'T KNOW BECAUSE I DON'T CARE.
MAYBE IT'S BECAUSE I'M STILL YOUNG ENOUGH TO KNOW YOUR FUTURE WILL FIND YOU SOON ENOUGH.
AND THERE'S NOTHING NO ONE CAN DO ABOUT THAT.
I'VE GOT ENOUGH PROBLEMS...

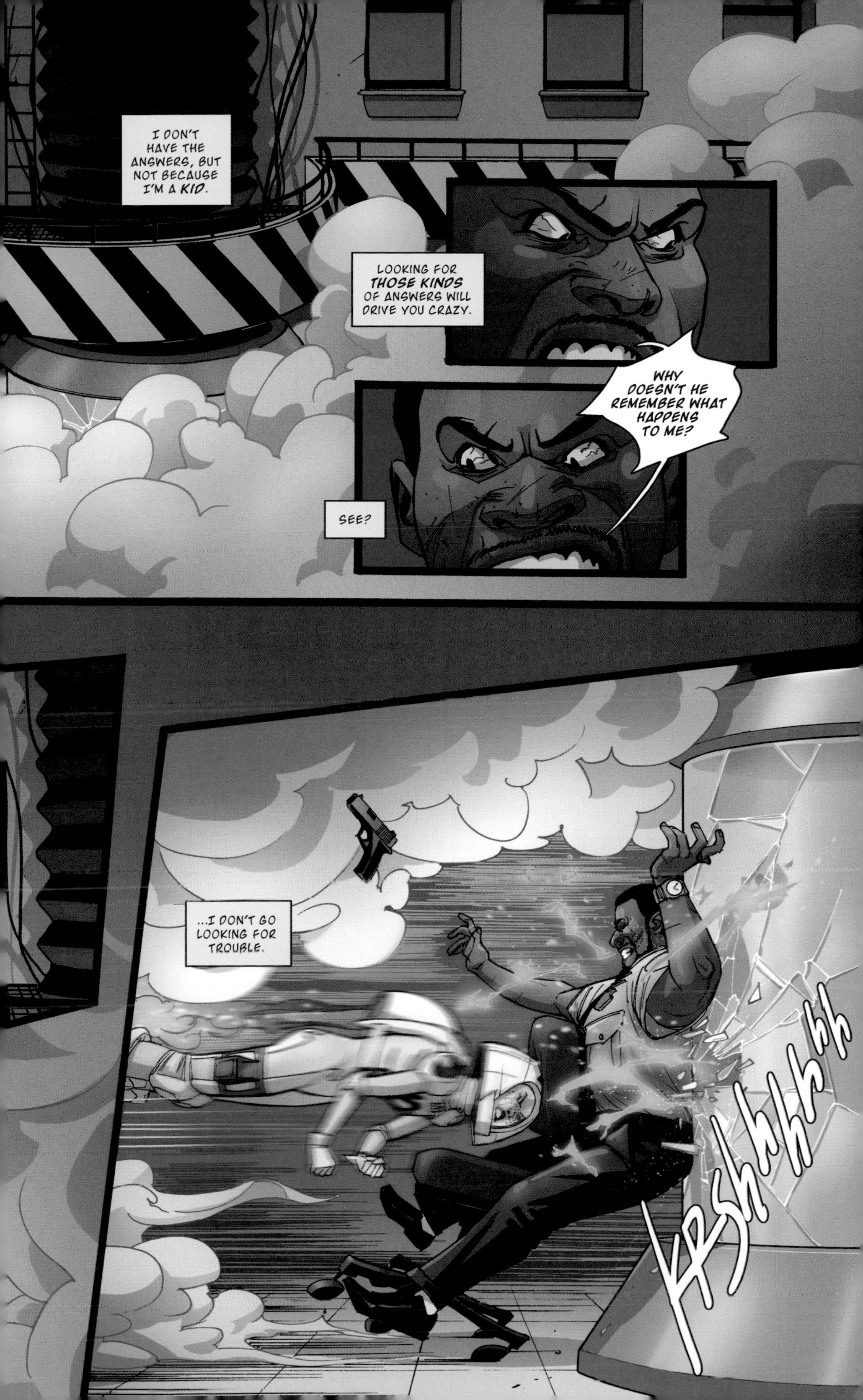
I DON'T HAVE THE ANSWERS, BUT NOT BECAUSE I'M A KID.
LOOKING FOR THOSE KINDS OF ANSWERS WILL DRIVE YOU CRAZY.
WHY DOESN'T HE REMEMBER WHAT HAPPENS TO ME?
SEE?
...I DON'T GO LOOKING FOR TROUBLE.
KRSHhhhhhh

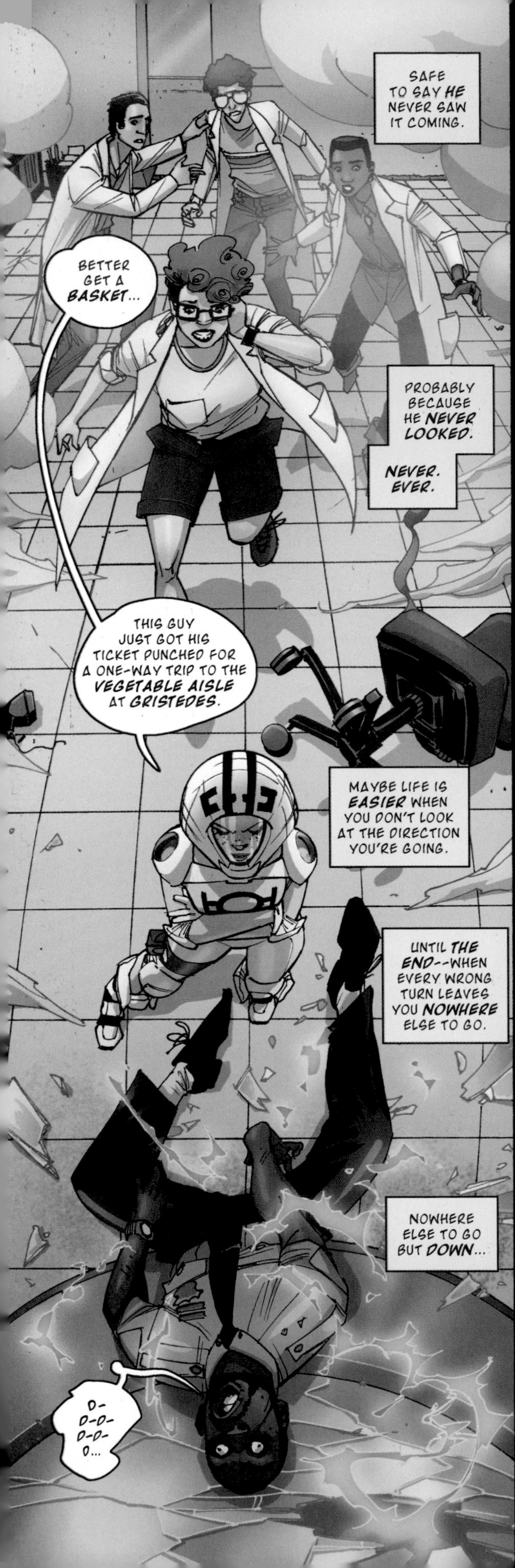
SAFE TO SAY HE NEVER SAW IT COMING.
BETTER GET A BASKET...
PROBABLY BECAUSE HE NEVER LOOKED.
NEVER. EVER.
THIS GUY JUST GOT HIS TICKET PUNCHED FOR A ONE-WAY TRIP TO THE VEGETABLE AISLE AT GRISTEDES.
MAYBE LIFE IS EASIER WHEN YOU DON'T LOOK AT THE DIRECTION YOU'RE GOING.
UNTIL THE END--WHEN EVERY WRONG TURN LEAVES YOU NOWHERE ELSE TO GO.
NOWHERE ELSE TO GO BUT DOWN...
D- D-D- D-D- D...
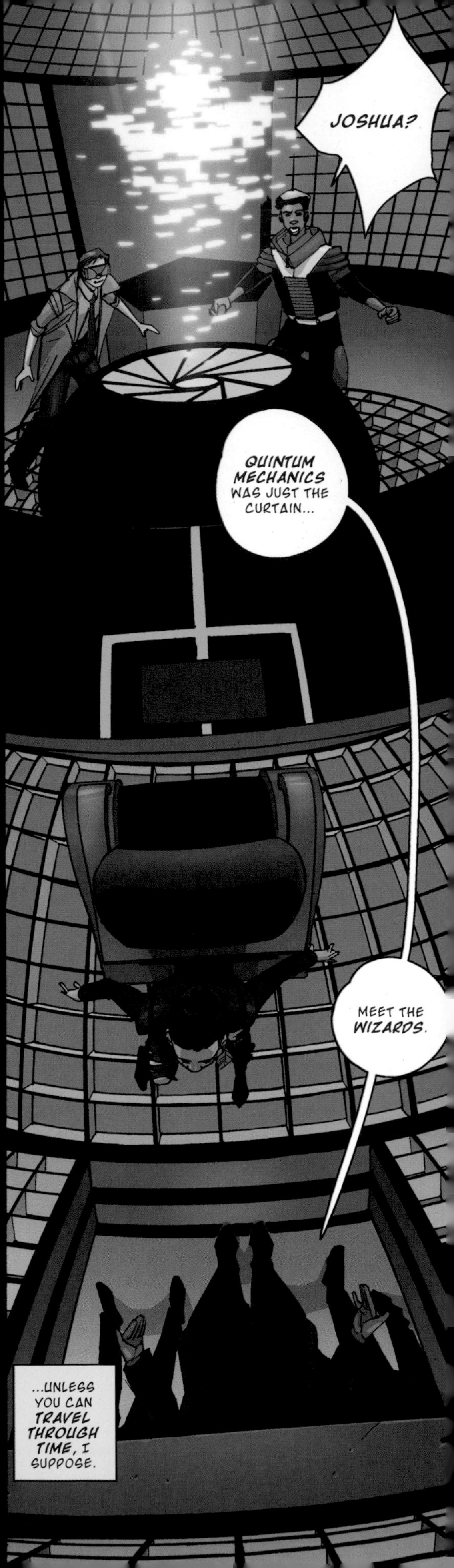
JOSHUA?
QUINTUM MECHANICS WAS JUST THE CURTAIN...
MEET THE WIZARDS.
...UNLESS YOU CAN TRAVEL THROUGH TIME, I SUPPOSE.

Chapter 10_Only the Good...>>

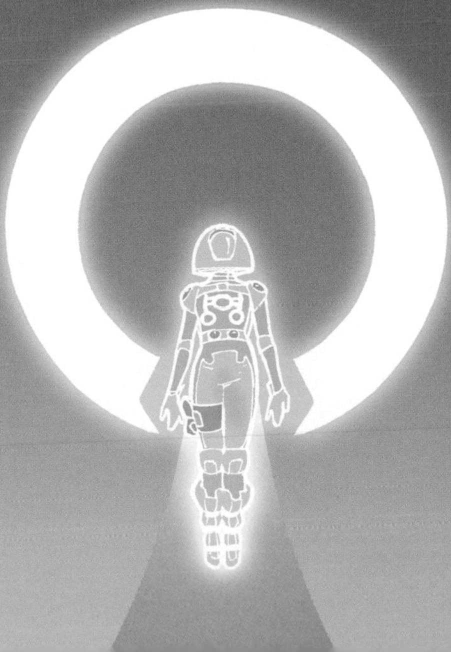

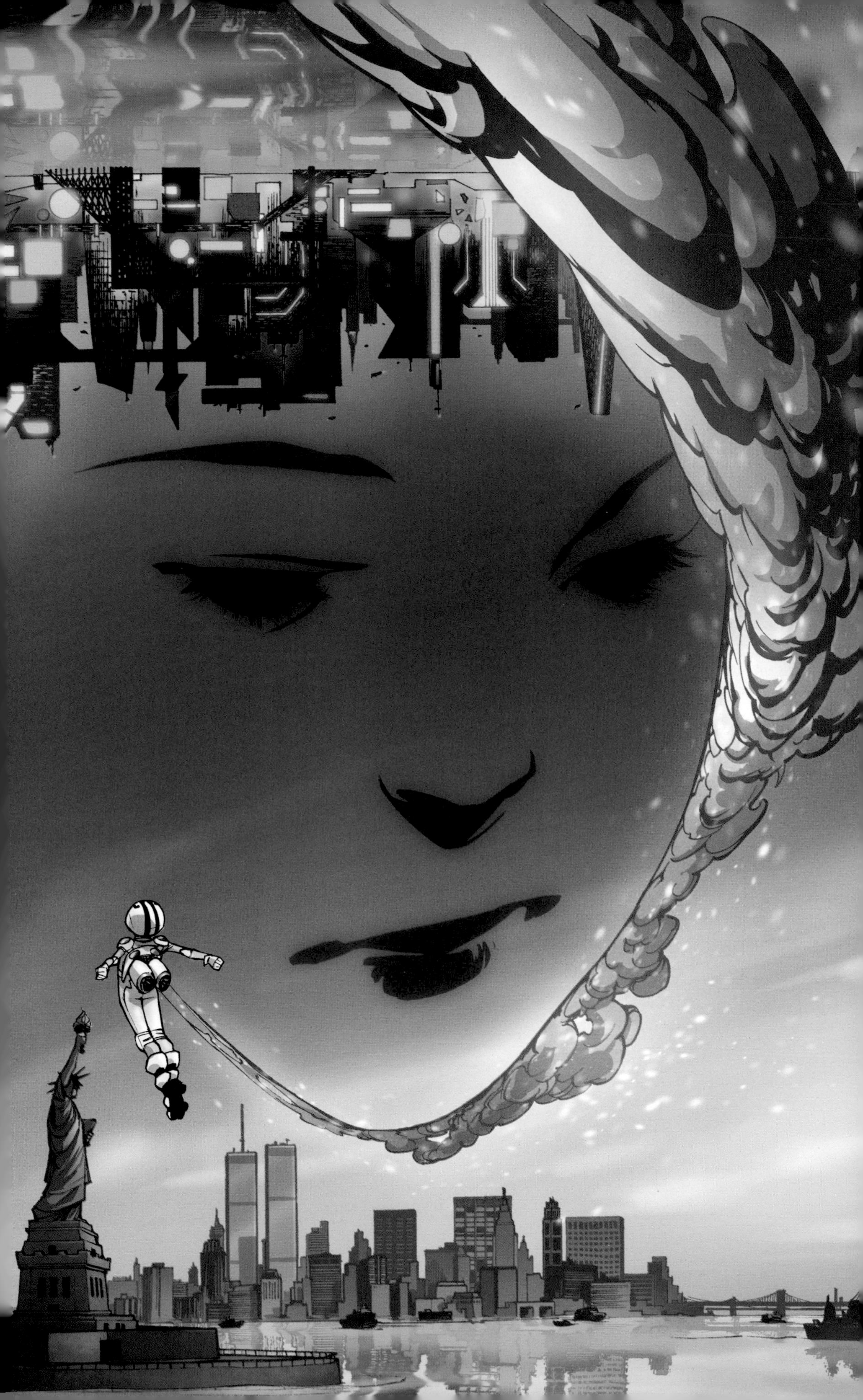

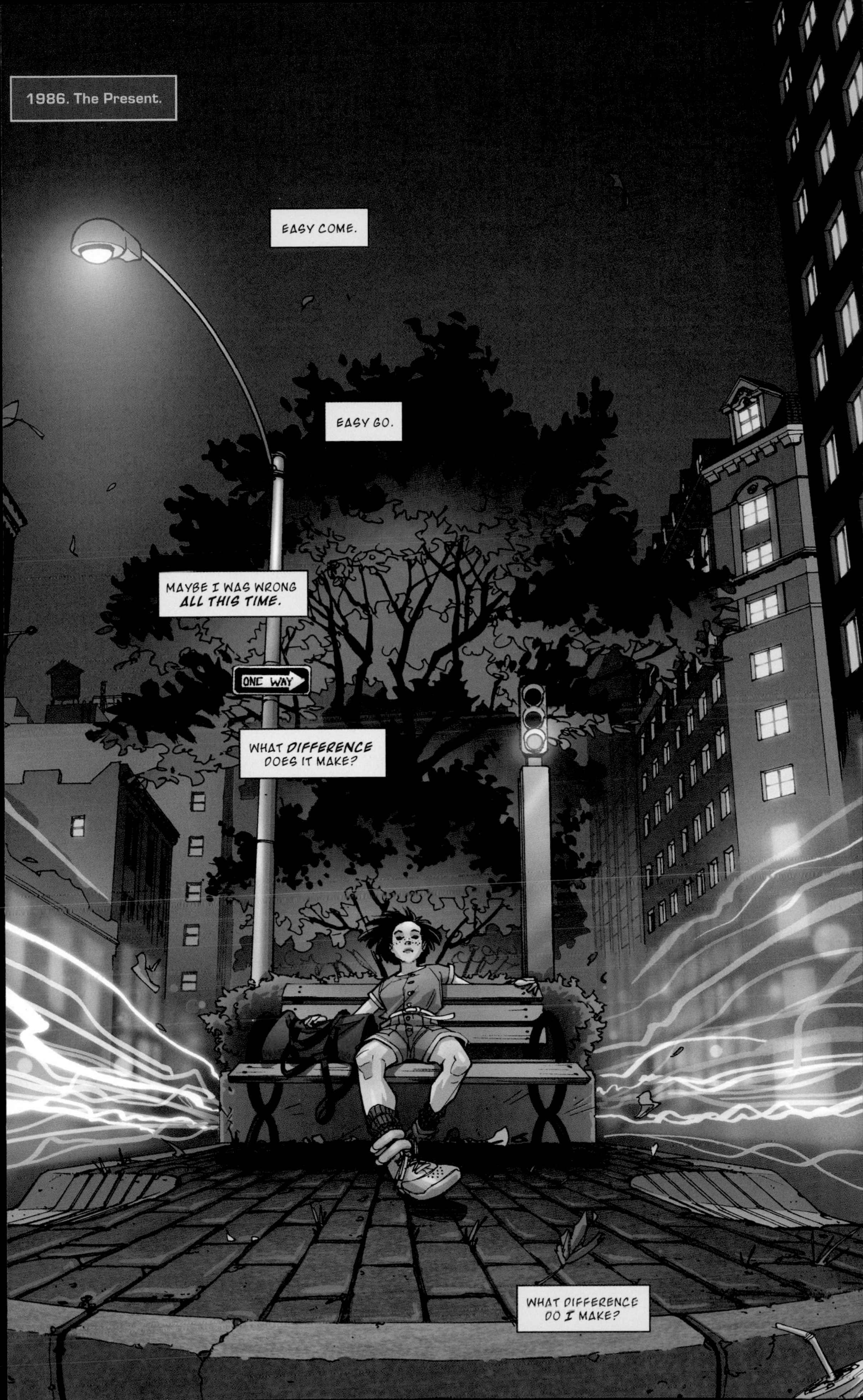
1986. The Present.
EASY COME.
EASY GO.
MAYBE I WAS WRONG ALL THIS TIME.
ONE WAY
WHAT DIFFERENCE DOES IT MAKE?
WHAT DIFFERENCE DO I MAKE?

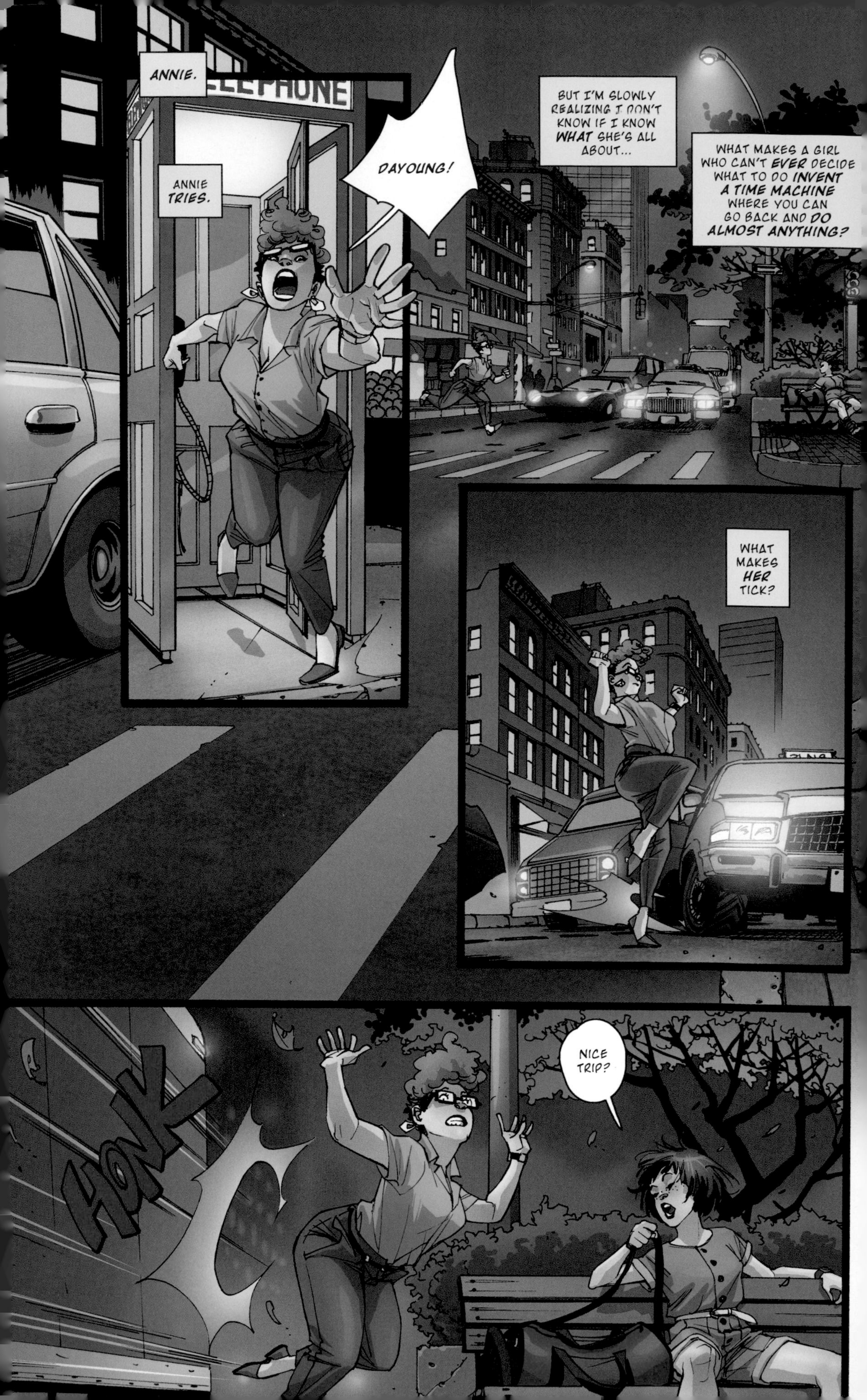
ANNIE.
TELEPHONE
ANNIE TRIES.
DAYOUNG!
BUT I'M SLOWLY REALIZING I DON'T KNOW IF I KNOW WHAT SHE'S ALL ABOUT...
WHAT MAKES A GIRL WHO CAN'T EVER DECIDE WHAT TO DO INVENT A TIME MACHINE WHERE YOU CAN GO BACK AND DO ALMOST ANYTHING?
WHAT MAKES HER TICK?
HONK
NICE TRIP?

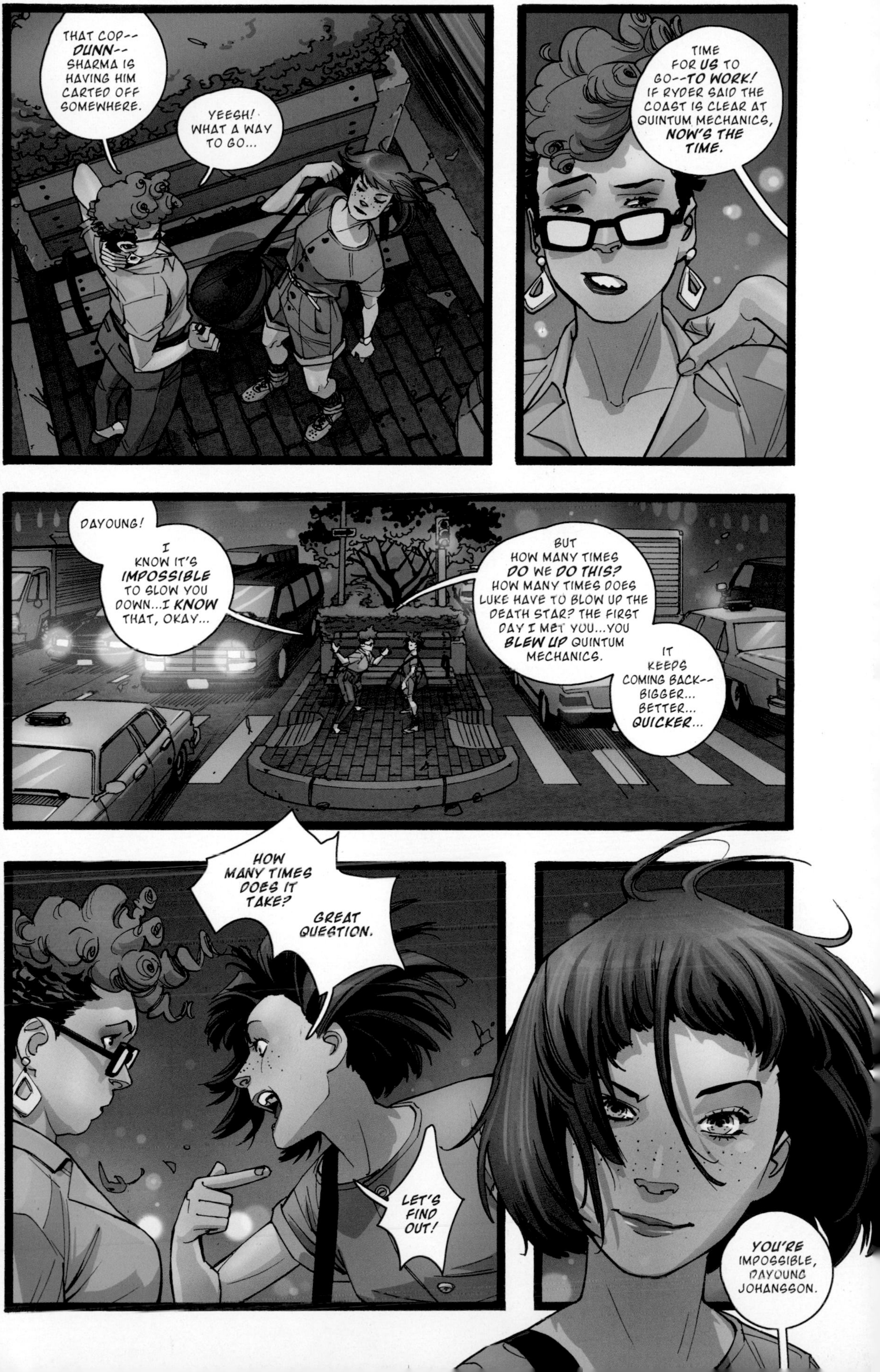
THAT COP--
DUNN--
SHARMA IS HAVING HIM CARTED OFF SOMEWHERE.
YEESH! WHAT A WAY TO GO...
TIME FOR US TO GO--TO WORK! IF RYDER SAID THE COAST IS CLEAR AT QUINTUM MECHANICS, NOW'S THE TIME.
DAYOUNG!
I KNOW IT'S IMPOSSIBLE TO SLOW YOU DOWN...I KNOW THAT, OKAY...
BUT HOW MANY TIMES DO WE DO THIS? HOW MANY TIMES DOES LUKE HAVE TO BLOW UP THE DEATH STAR? THE FIRST DAY I MET YOU...YOU BLEW UP QUINTUM MECHANICS.
IT KEEPS COMING BACK--BIGGER... BETTER... QUICKER...
HOW MANY TIMES DOES IT TAKE?
GREAT QUESTION.
LET'S FIND OUT!
YOU'RE IMPOSSIBLE, DAYOUNG JOHANSSON.

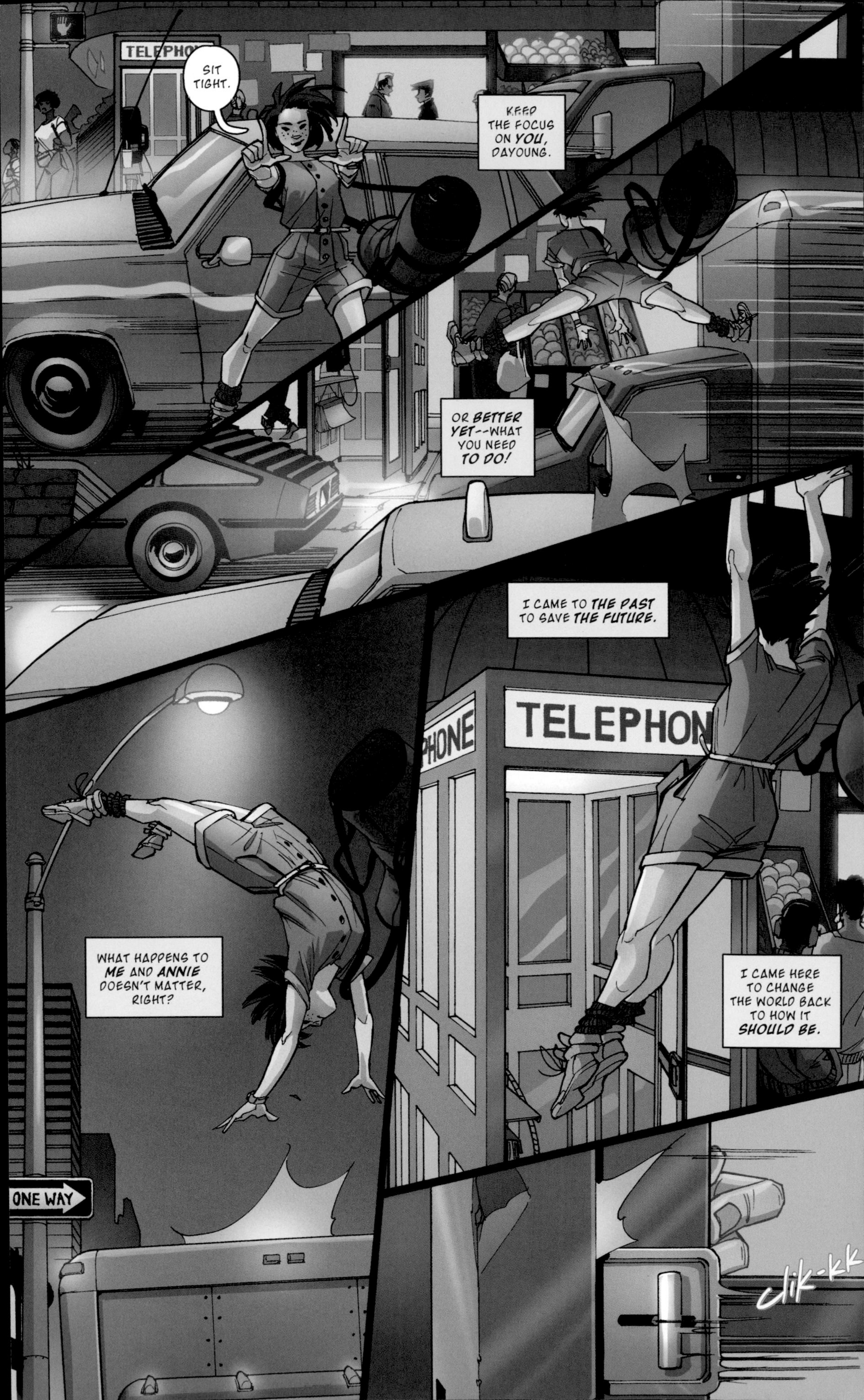
TELEPHON
SIT TIGHT.
KEEP THE FOCUS ON YOU, DAYOUNG.
OR BETTER YET--WHAT YOU NEED TO DO!
I CAME TO THE PAST TO SAVE THE FUTURE.
TELEPHON
PHONE
WHAT HAPPENS TO ME AND ANNIE DOESN'T MATTER, RIGHT?
I CAME HERE TO CHANGE THE WORLD BACK TO HOW IT SHOULD BE.
ONE WAY
clik-kk

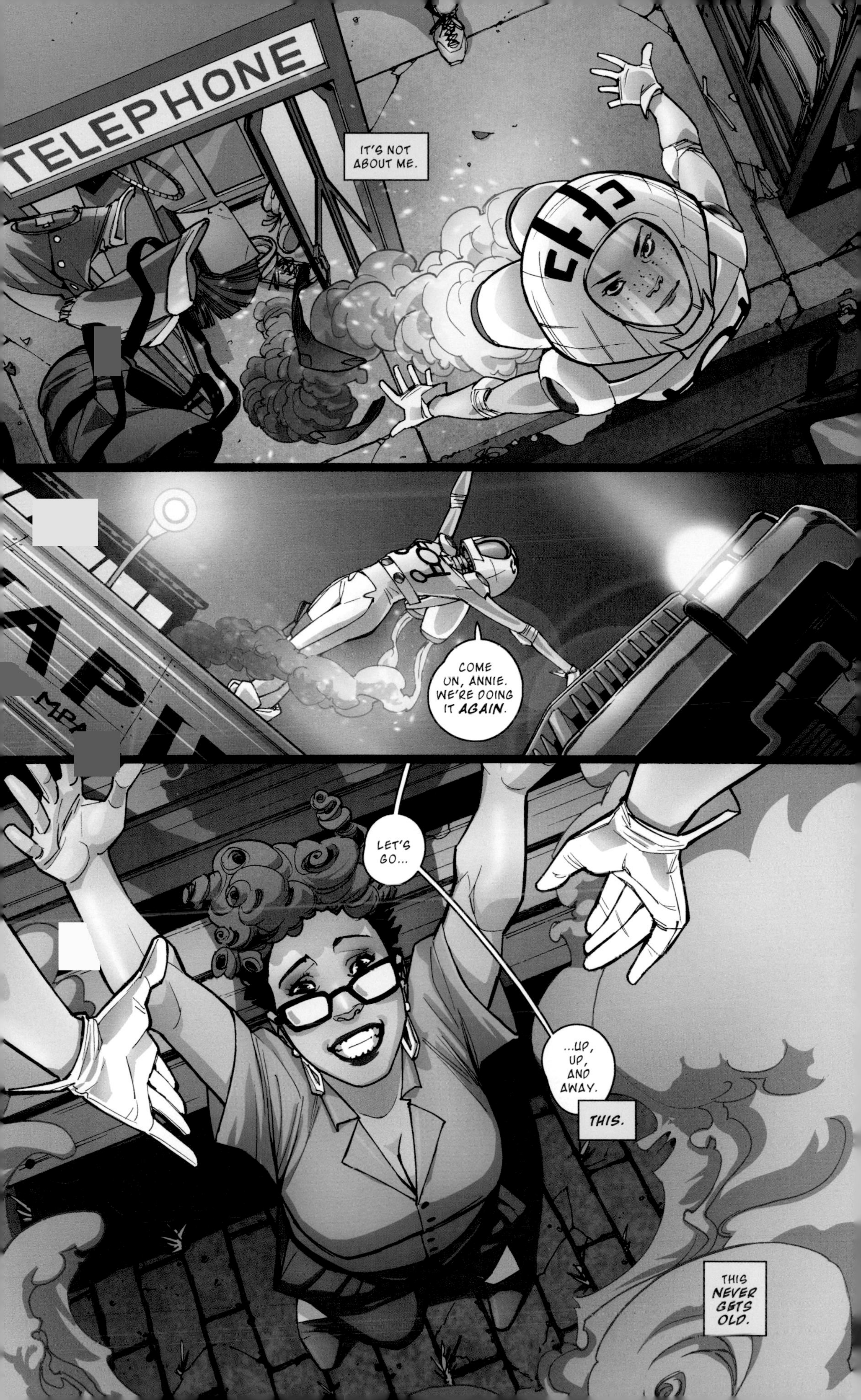
TELEPHONE
IT'S NOT ABOUT ME.
COME ON, ANNIE. WE'RE DOING IT AGAIN.
LET'S GO...
...UP, UP, AND AWAY.
THIS.
THIS NEVER GETS OLD.

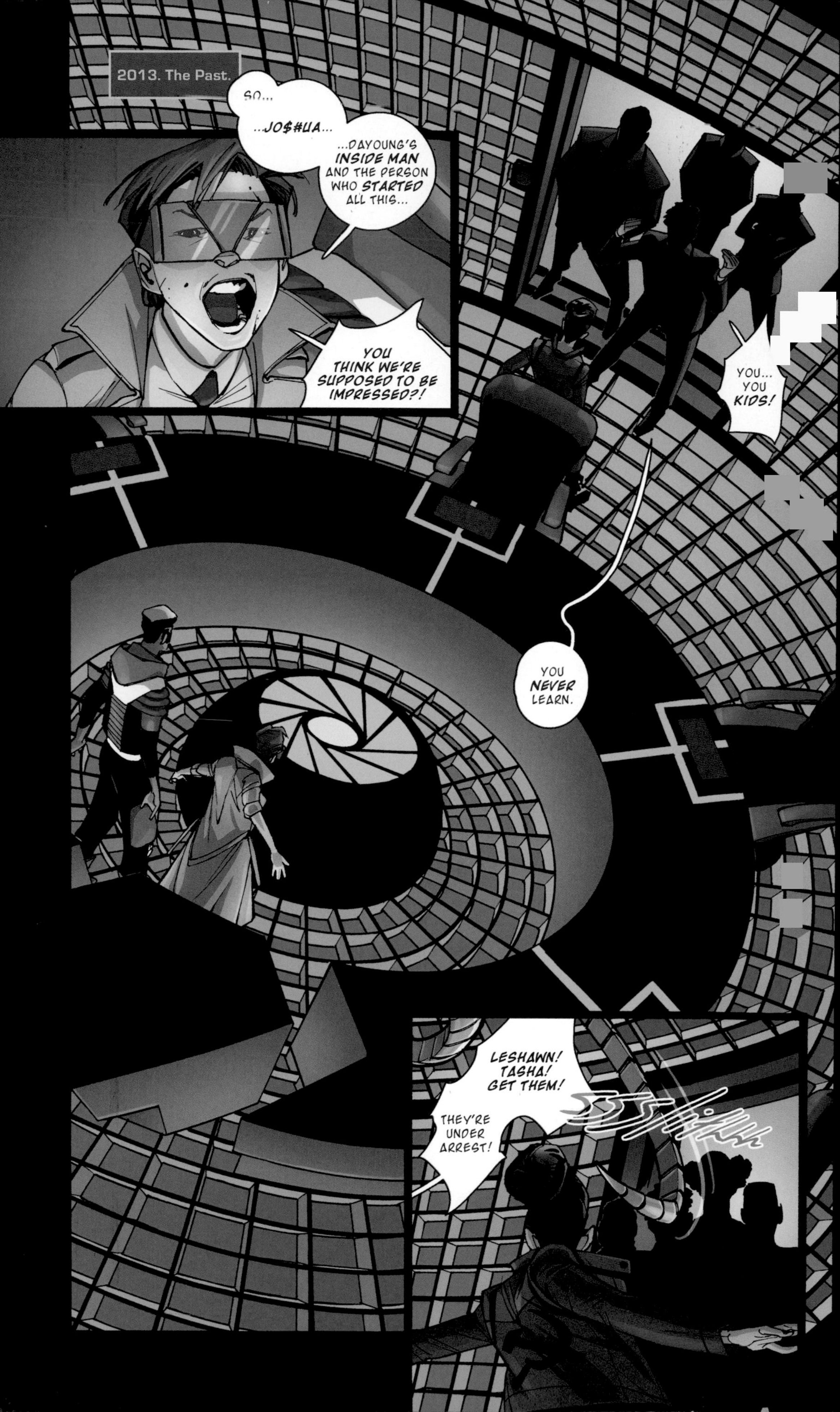
2013. The Past.
SO...
...JO$HUA...
...DAYOUNG'S INSIDE MAN AND THE PERSON WHO STARTED ALL THIS...
YOU THINK WE'RE SUPPOSED TO BE IMPRESSED?!
YOU... YOU KIDS!
YOU NEVER LEARN.
LESHAWN! TASHA! GET THEM!
THEY'RE UNDER ARREST!
SSSHHH

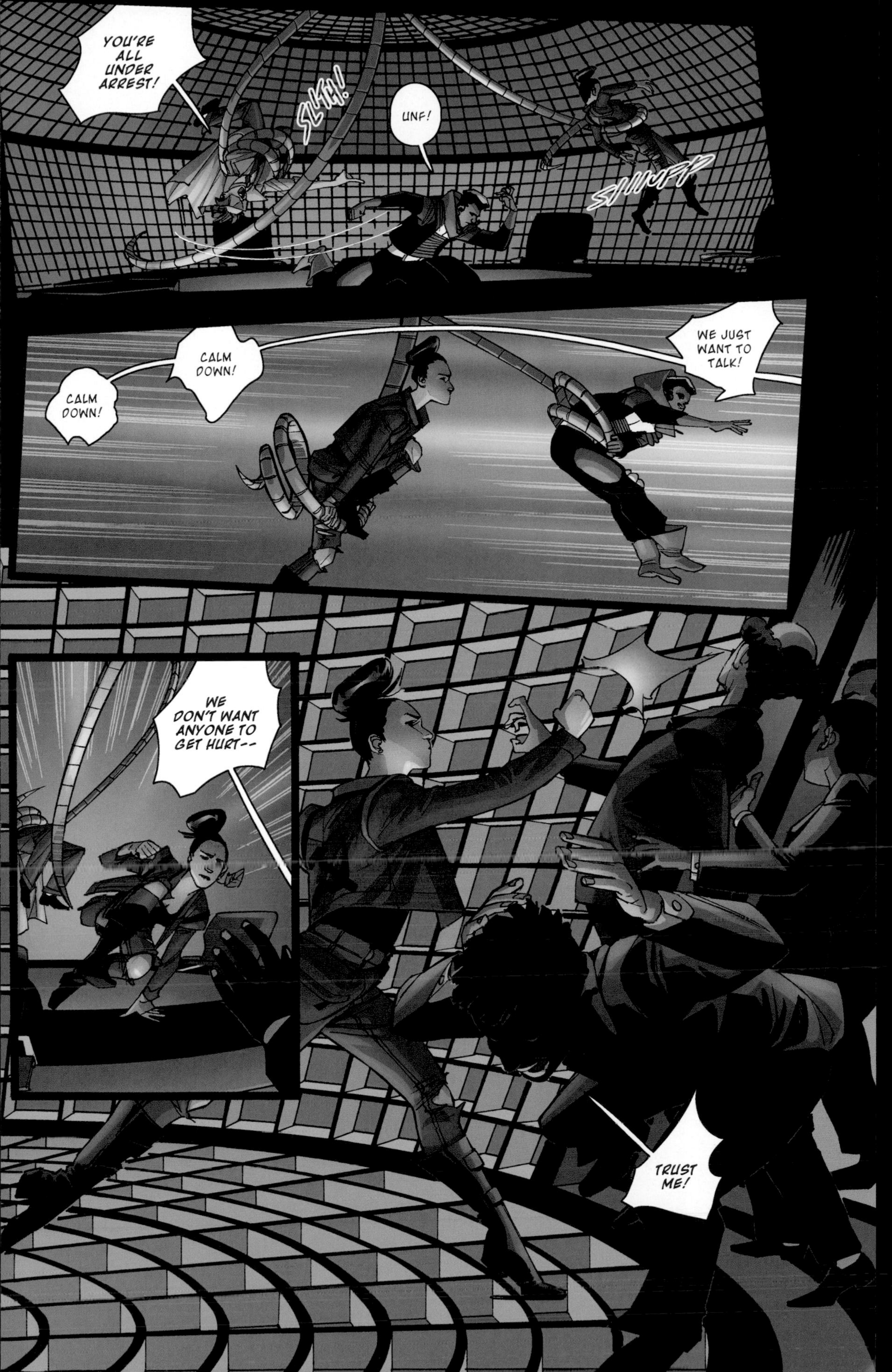
YOU'RE ALL UNDER ARREST!
SLKK!
UNF!
SHUNFF!
CALM DOWN!
CALM DOWN!
WE JUST WANT TO TALK!
WE DON'T WANT ANYONE TO GET HURT--
TRUST ME!

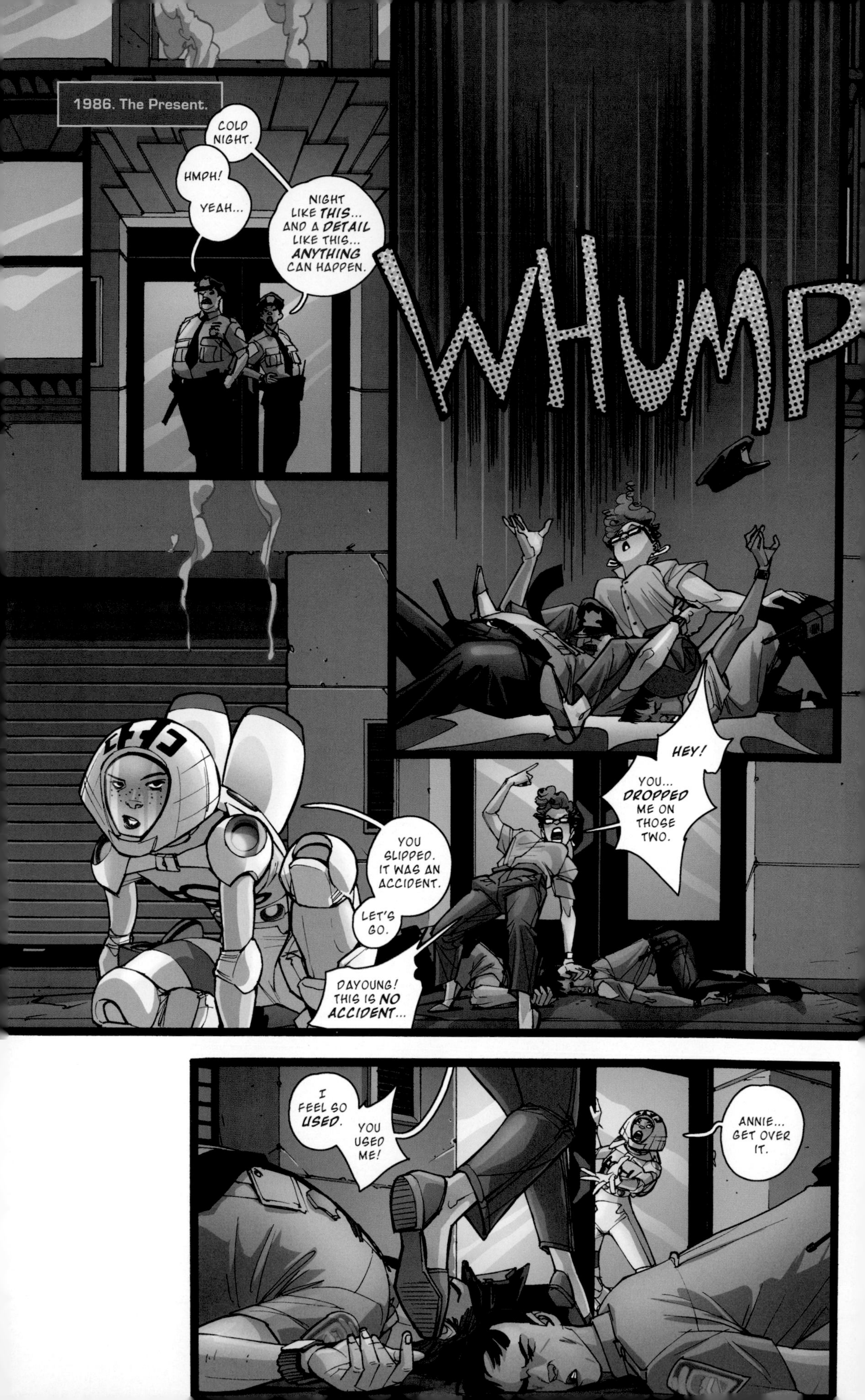
1986. The Present.
COLD NIGHT.
HMPH!
YEAH...
NIGHT LIKE THIS... AND A DETAIL LIKE THIS... ANYTHING CAN HAPPEN.
WHUMP
HEY!
YOU... DROPPED ME ON THOSE TWO.
YOU SLIPPED. IT WAS AN ACCIDENT.
LET'S GO.
DAYOUNG! THIS IS NO ACCIDENT...
I FEEL SO USED.
YOU USED ME!
ANNIE... GET OVER IT.

WHAT ARE YOU *DOING?*

I *THOUGHT* WE SHOULD BACK IT ALL UP!

THAT WAY I CAN ANALYZE IT-- FIND OUT WHO, AND WHEN... AND *WHY.*

NO, ANNIE!

BUT...

NO MORE "BUTS". THIS IS WHAT WE'VE GOT TO *DO...*

...WE'VE GOT TO DESTROY *ALL* THE RECORDS. IT'S TOO RISKY TO KEEP *ANYTHING.* I'M TELLING YOU, THE QUINTUM MECHANICS EXECUTIVES *WILL* FIND IT--*IF* THERE'S SOMETHING TO FIND.

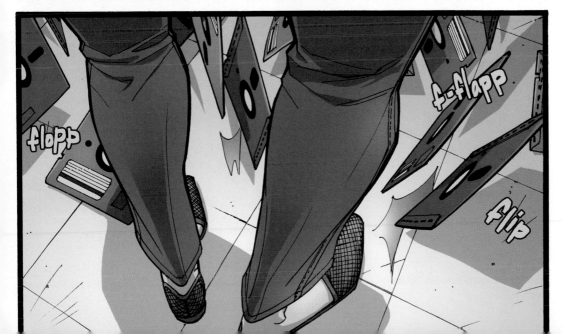

flopp

f-flapp

flip

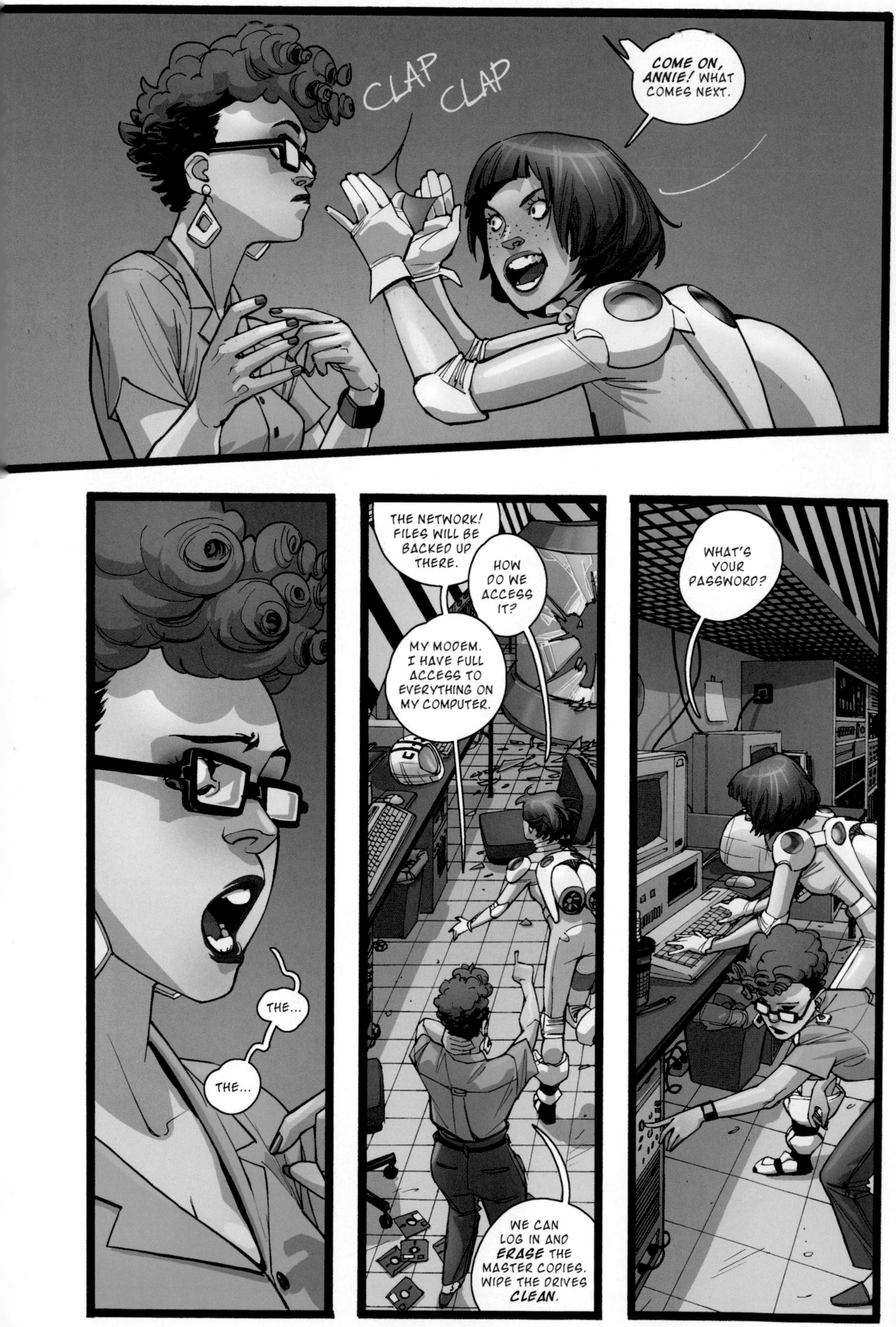
CLAP CLAP
COME ON, ANNIE! WHAT COMES NEXT.
THE...
THE...
THE NETWORK! FILES WILL BE BACKED UP THERE.
HOW DO WE ACCESS IT?
MY MODEM. I HAVE FULL ACCESS TO EVERYTHING ON MY COMPUTER.
WE CAN LOG IN AND ERASE THE MASTER COPIES. WIPE THE DRIVES CLEAN.
WHAT'S YOUR PASSWORD?

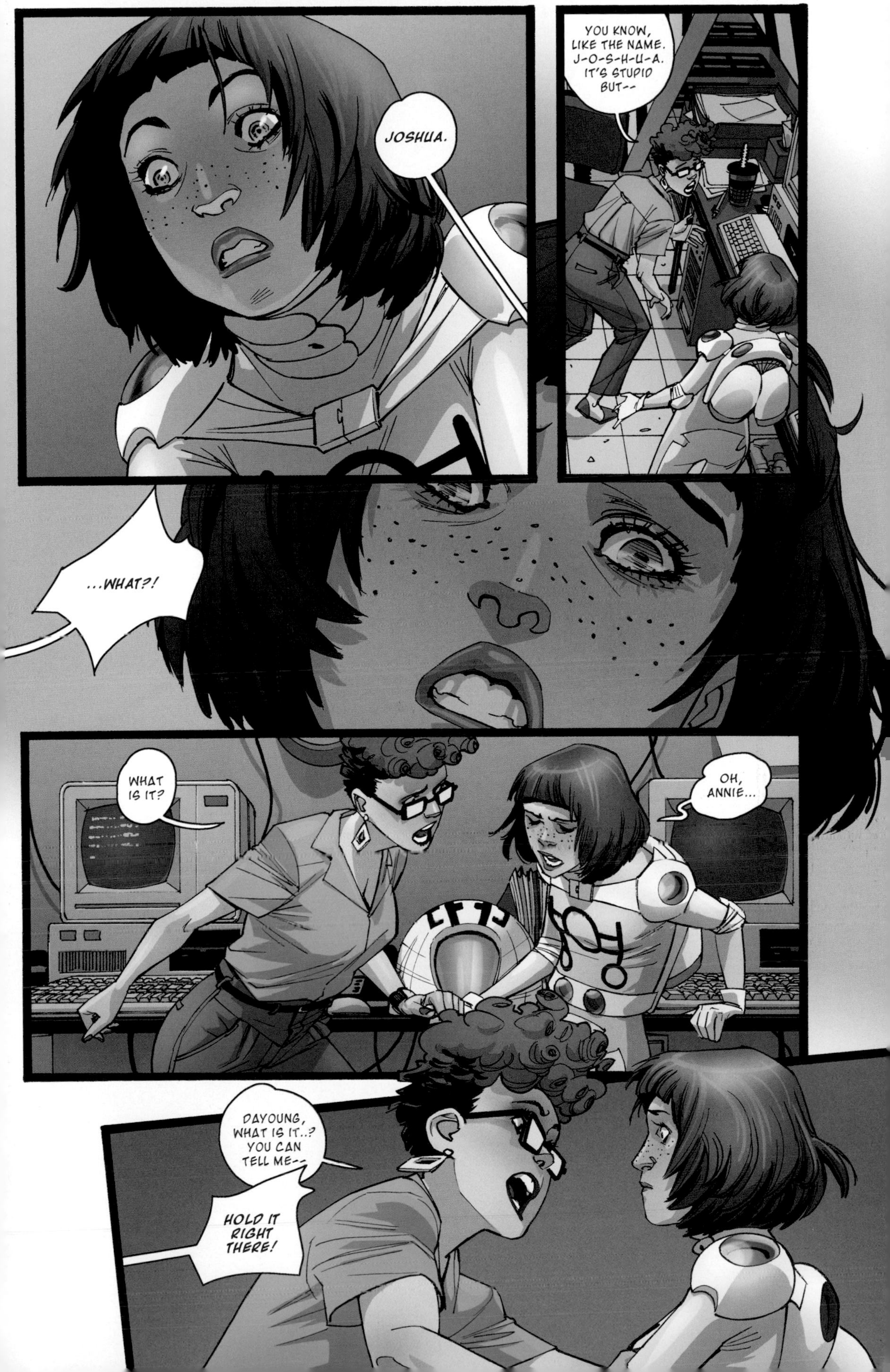
JOSHUA.
YOU KNOW, LIKE THE NAME. J-O-S-H-U-A. IT'S STUPID BUT--
...WHAT?!
WHAT IS IT?
OH, ANNIE...
DAYOUNG, WHAT IS IT..? YOU CAN TELL ME--
HOLD IT RIGHT THERE!

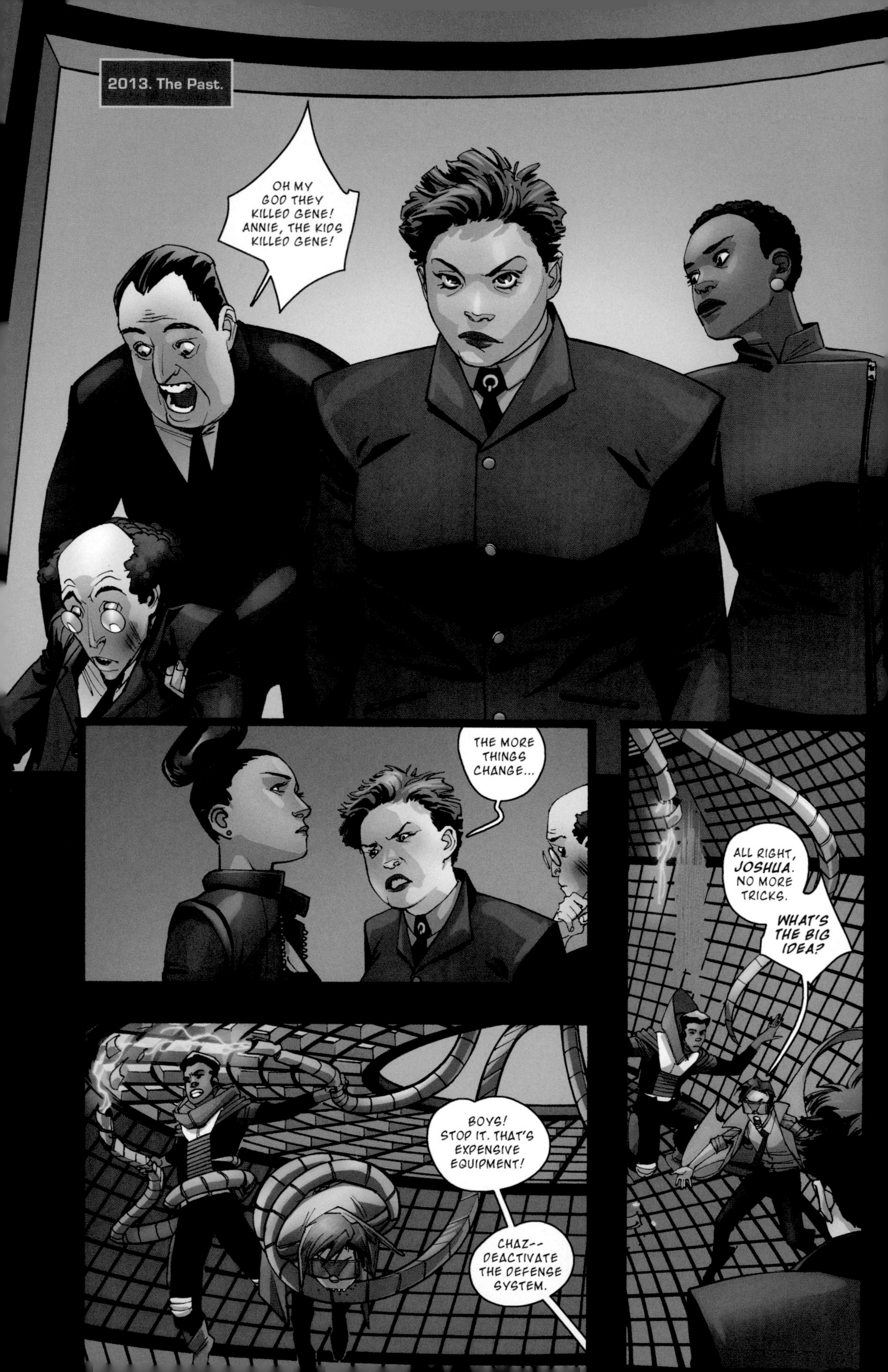
2013. The Past.
OH MY GOD THEY KILLED GENE! ANNIE, THE KIDS KILLED GENE!
THE MORE THINGS CHANGE...
ALL RIGHT, JOSHUA. NO MORE TRICKS.
WHAT'S THE BIG IDEA?
BOYS! STOP IT. THAT'S EXPENSIVE EQUIPMENT!
CHAZ-- DEACTIVATE THE DEFENSE SYSTEM.

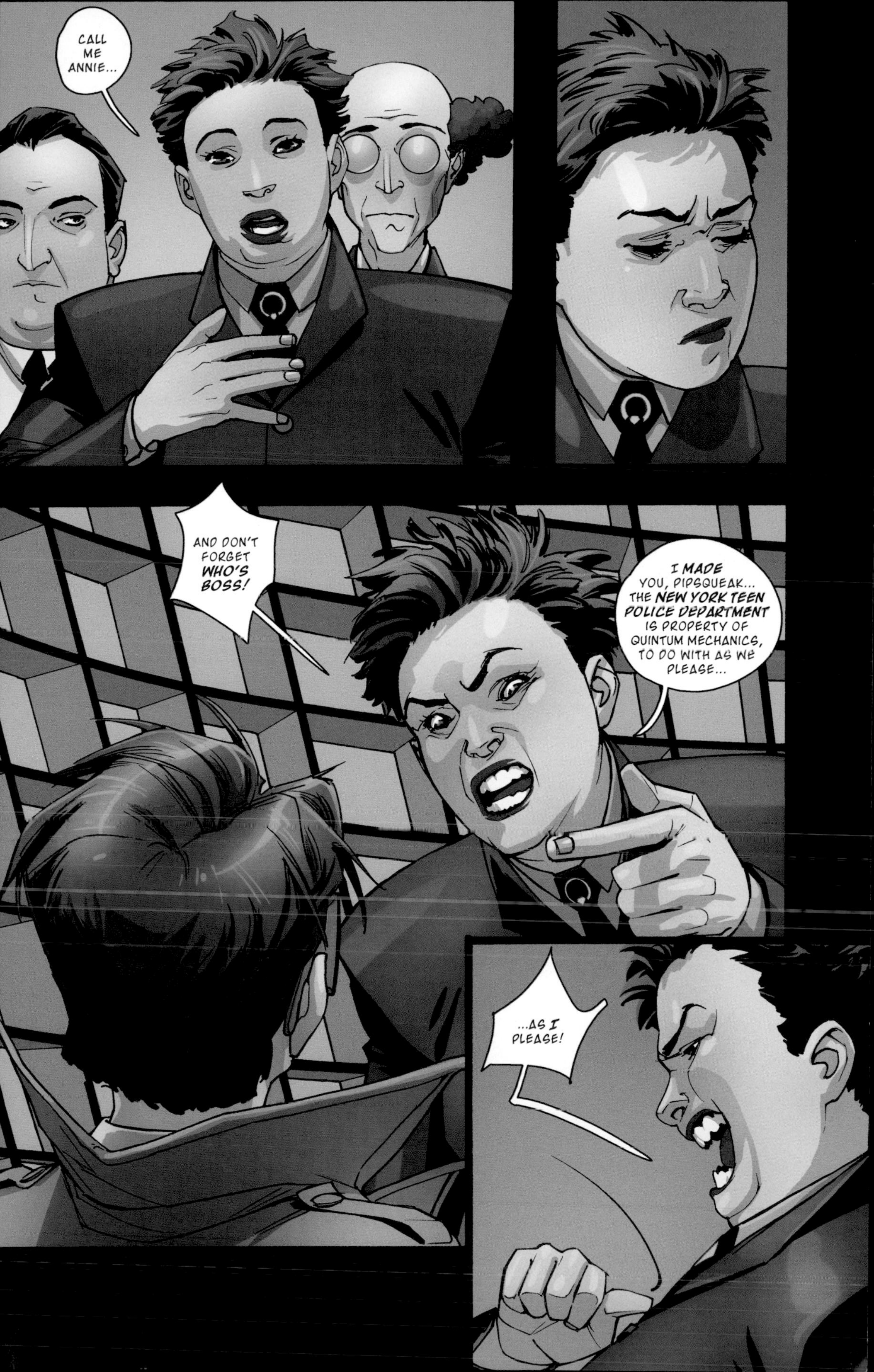
CALL ME ANNIE...
AND DON'T FORGET WHO'S BOSS!
I MADE YOU, PIPSQUEAK... THE NEW YORK TEEN POLICE DEPARTMENT IS PROPERTY OF QUINTUM MECHANICS, TO DO WITH AS WE PLEASE...
...AS I PLEASE!

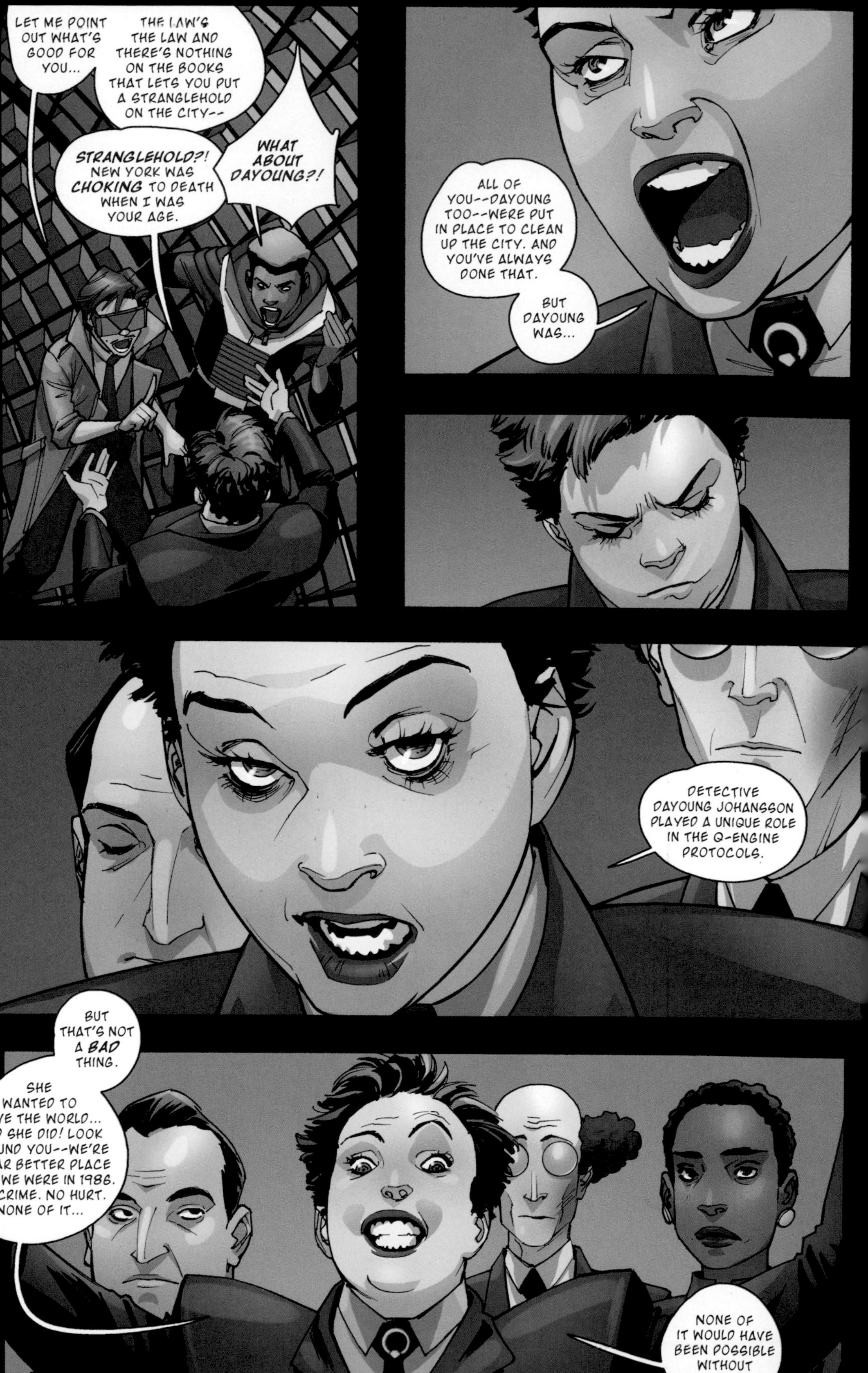
LET ME POINT OUT WHAT'S GOOD FOR YOU...
THE LAW'S THE LAW AND THERE'S NOTHING ON THE BOOKS THAT LETS YOU PUT A STRANGLEHOLD ON THE CITY--
STRANGLEHOLD?! NEW YORK WAS CHOKING TO DEATH WHEN I WAS YOUR AGE.
WHAT ABOUT DAYOUNG?!
ALL OF YOU--DAYOUNG TOO--WERE PUT IN PLACE TO CLEAN UP THE CITY. AND YOU'VE ALWAYS DONE THAT.
BUT DAYOUNG WAS...
DETECTIVE DAYOUNG JOHANSSON PLAYED A UNIQUE ROLE IN THE Q-ENGINE PROTOCOLS.
BUT THAT'S NOT A BAD THING.
SHE WANTED TO SAVE THE WORLD... AND SHE DID! LOOK AROUND YOU--WE'RE IN FAR BETTER PLACE THAN WE WERE IN 1986. NO CRIME. NO HURT. NONE OF IT...
NONE OF IT WOULD HAVE BEEN POSSIBLE WITHOUT DAYOUNG.

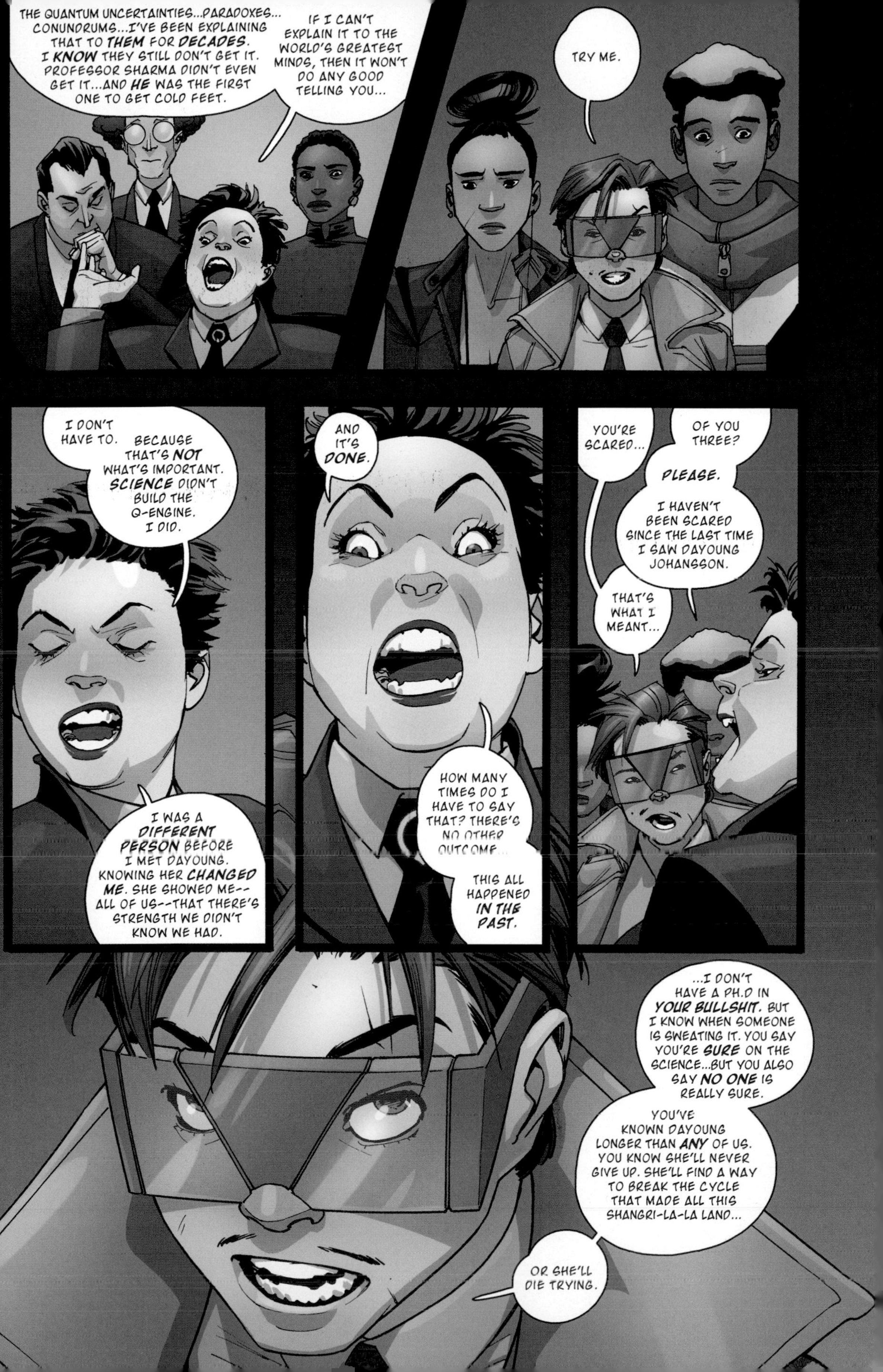
THE QUANTUM UNCERTAINTIES...PARADOXES... CONUNDRUMS...I'VE BEEN EXPLAINING THAT TO THEM FOR DECADES. I KNOW THEY STILL DON'T GET IT. PROFESSOR SHARMA DIDN'T EVEN GET IT...AND HE WAS THE FIRST ONE TO GET COLD FEET.
IF I CAN'T EXPLAIN IT TO THE WORLD'S GREATEST MINDS, THEN IT WON'T DO ANY GOOD TELLING YOU...
TRY ME.
I DON'T HAVE TO.
BECAUSE THAT'S NOT WHAT'S IMPORTANT. SCIENCE DIDN'T BUILD THE Q-ENGINE. I DID.
I WAS A DIFFERENT PERSON BEFORE I MET DAYOUNG. KNOWING HER CHANGED ME. SHE SHOWED ME--ALL OF US--THAT THERE'S STRENGTH WE DIDN'T KNOW WE HAD.
AND IT'S DONE.
HOW MANY TIMES DO I HAVE TO SAY THAT? THERE'S NO OTHER OUTCOME...
THIS ALL HAPPENED IN THE PAST.
YOU'RE SCARED...
OF YOU THREE?
PLEASE.
I HAVEN'T BEEN SCARED SINCE THE LAST TIME I SAW DAYOUNG JOHANSSON.
THAT'S WHAT I MEANT...
...I DON'T HAVE A PH.D IN YOUR BULLSHIT. BUT I KNOW WHEN SOMEONE IS SWEATING IT. YOU SAY YOU'RE SURE ON THE SCIENCE...BUT YOU ALSO SAY NO ONE IS REALLY SURE.
YOU'VE KNOWN DAYOUNG LONGER THAN ANY OF US. YOU KNOW SHE'LL NEVER GIVE UP. SHE'LL FIND A WAY TO BREAK THE CYCLE THAT MADE ALL THIS SHANGRI-LA-LA LAND...
OR SHE'LL DIE TRYING.

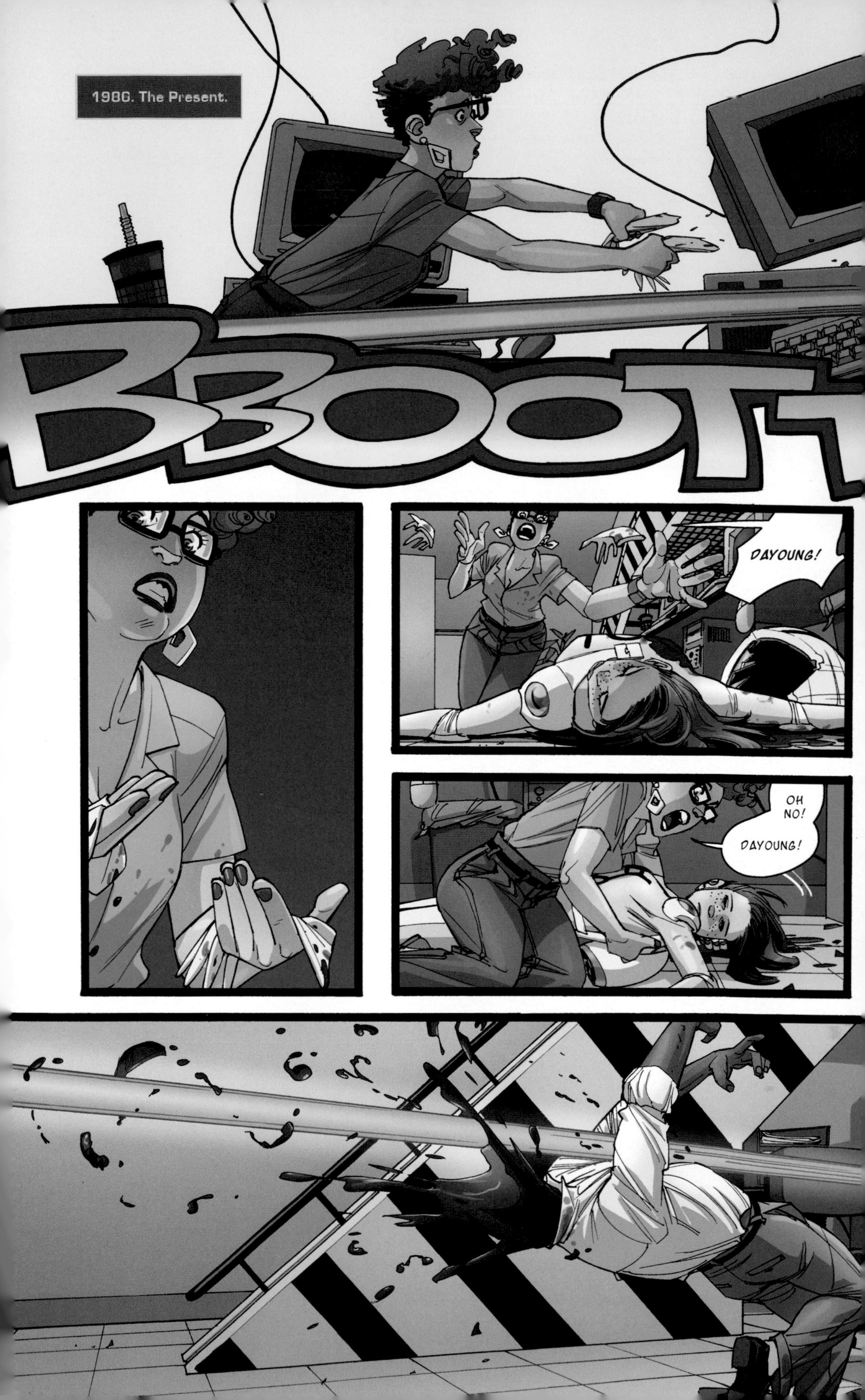
1986. The Present.
BBOOTT
DAYOUNG!
OH NO!
DAYOUNG!

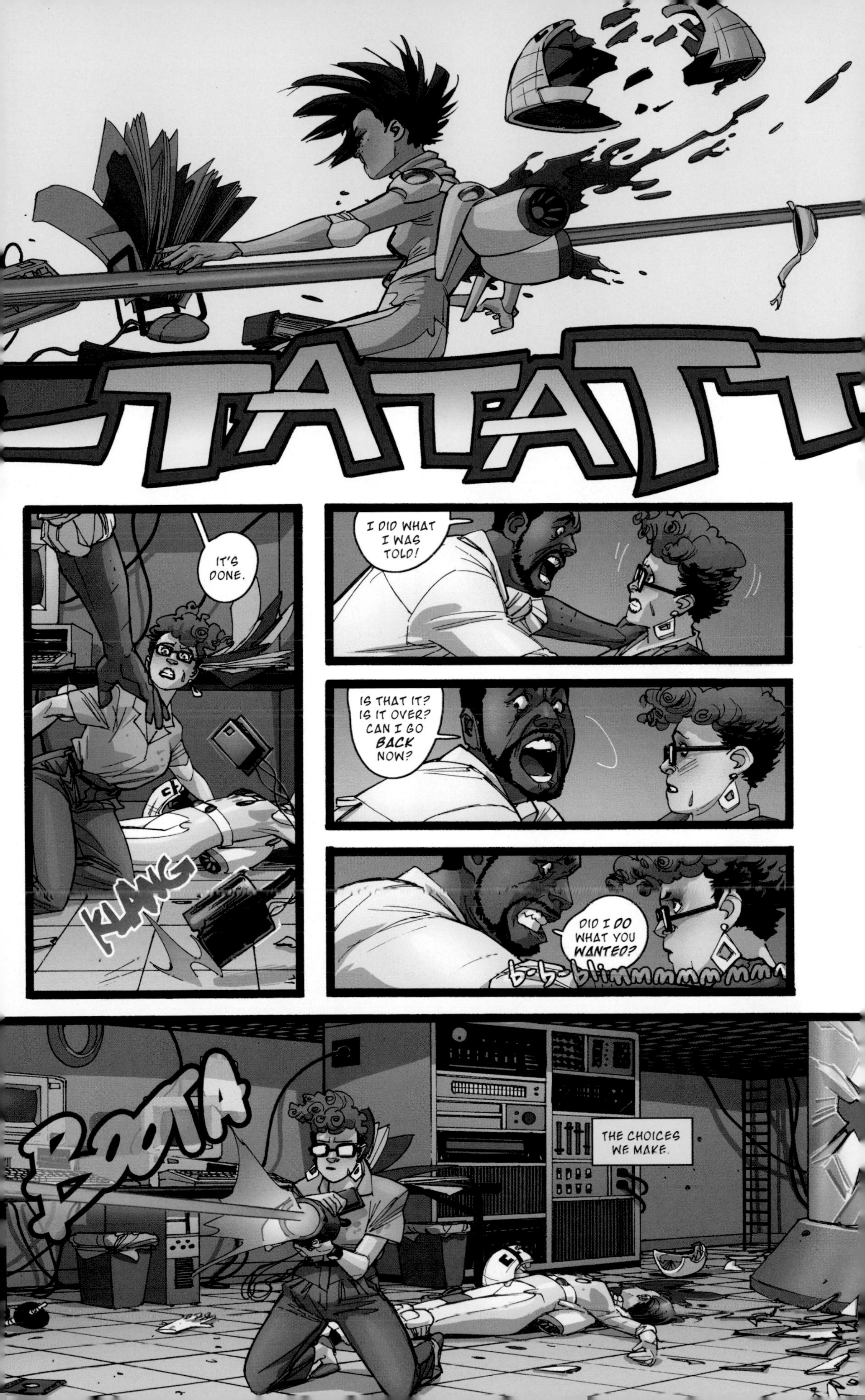
TATATT
IT'S DONE.
KLANG
I DID WHAT I WAS TOLD!
IS THAT IT? IS IT OVER? CAN I GO BACK NOW?
DID I DO WHAT YOU WANTED?
THE CHOICES WE MAKE.

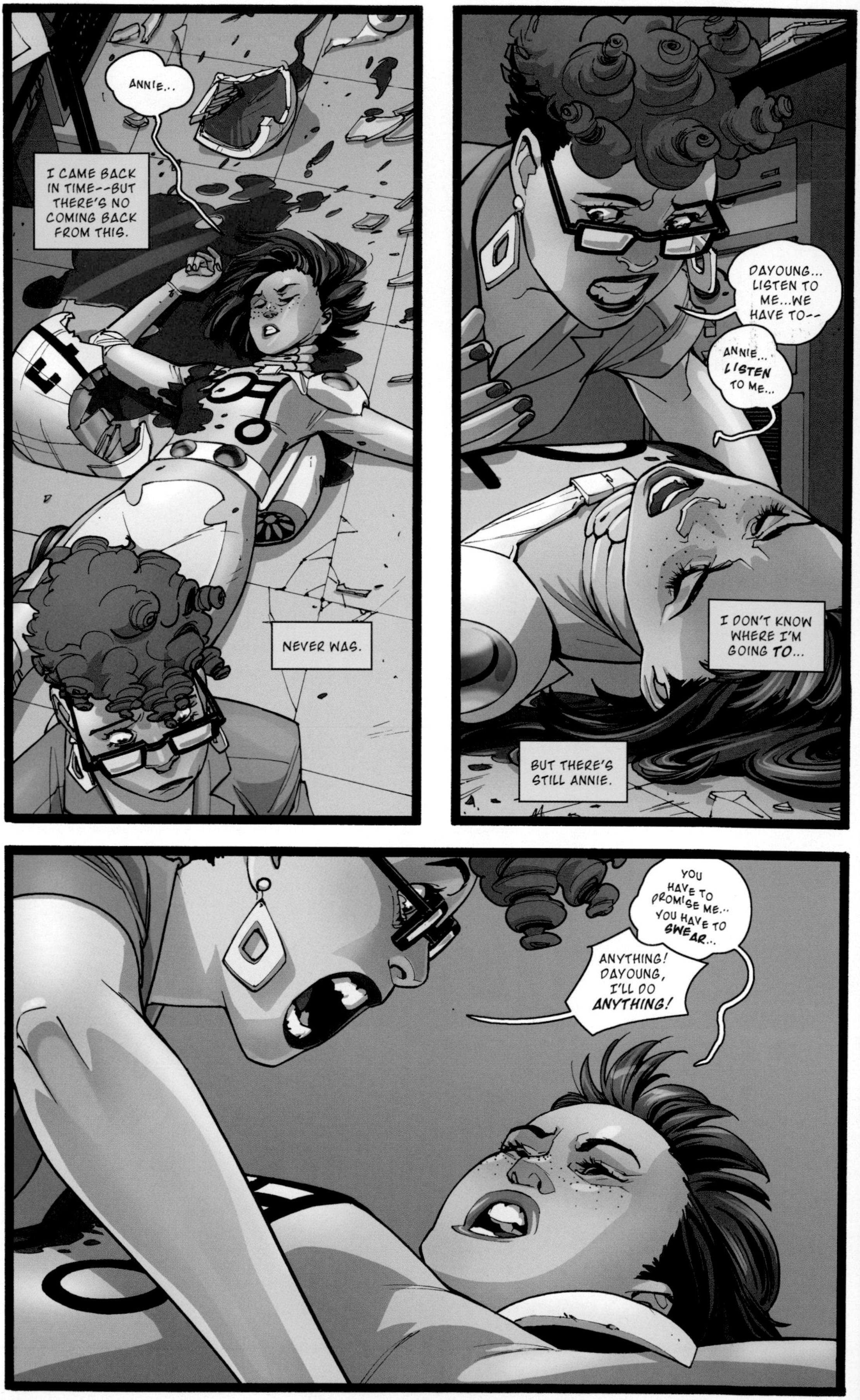
ANNIE...
I CAME BACK IN TIME--BUT THERE'S NO COMING BACK FROM THIS.
NEVER WAS.
DAYOUNG... LISTEN TO ME...WE HAVE TO--
ANNIE... LISTEN TO ME...
I DON'T KNOW WHERE I'M GOING TO...
BUT THERE'S STILL ANNIE.
YOU HAVE TO PROMISE ME... YOU HAVE TO SWEAR...
ANYTHING! DAYOUNG, I'LL DO ANYTHING!

REMEMBER.. DON'T THINK.
DAYOUNG..?
SWEAR!
THINKING IS NO GOOD FOR ANNIE MENDEZ.. YOU OVERTHINK EVERYTHING..
THE DIFFERENCE BETWEEN RIGHT AND WRONG IS SIMPLE.
DESTROY THE Q-ENGINE...DON'T TRY TO CHANGE THE WORLD--IT'LL ONLY CHANGE YOU.
SHHHHH
I-I PROMISE, DAYOUNG. I SWEAR.
...ANNIE...
THERE'S RIGHT.
AND THERE'S WRONG.
JUST LIKE I'VE ALWAYS SAID.

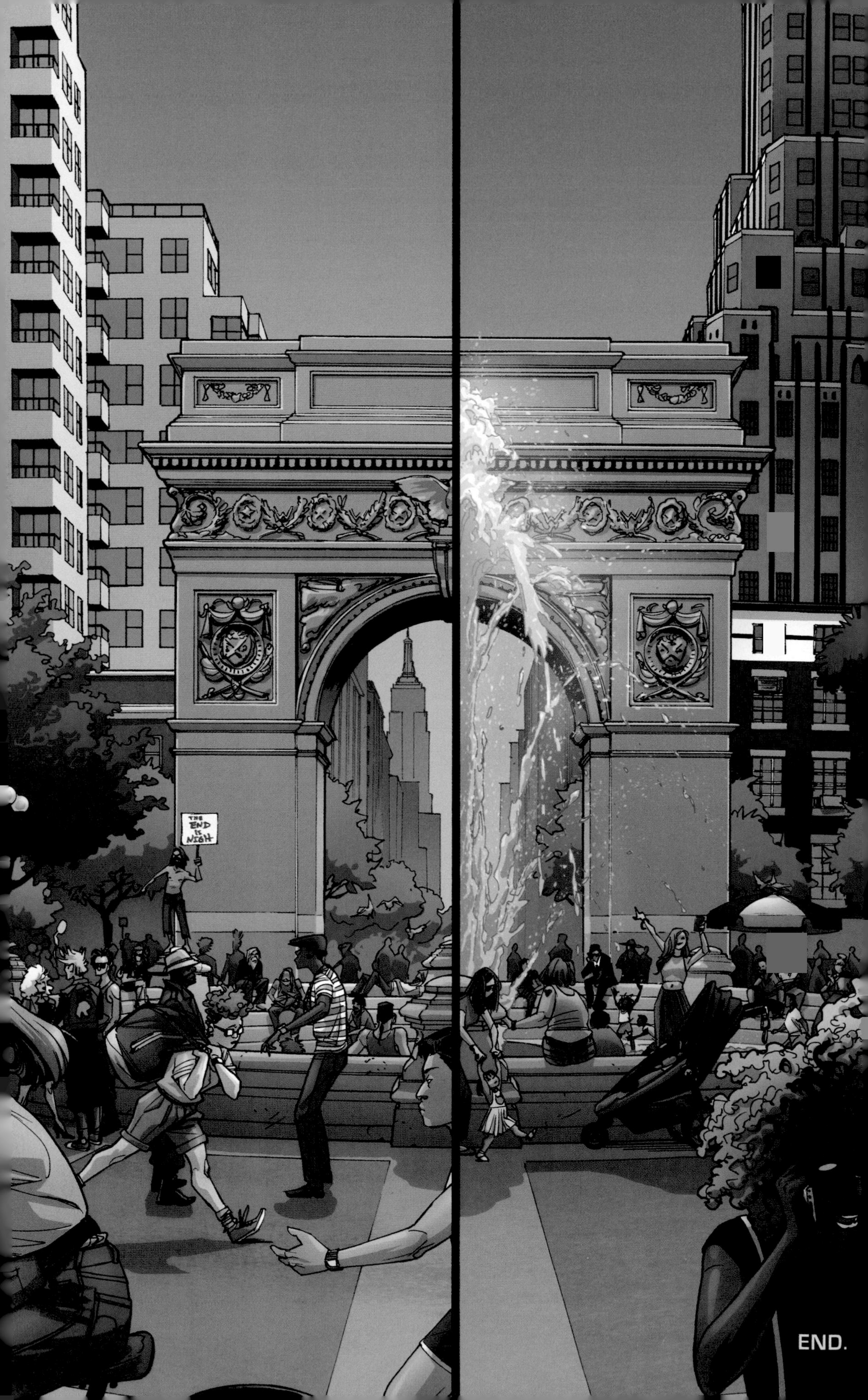
THE END IS NIGH
END.

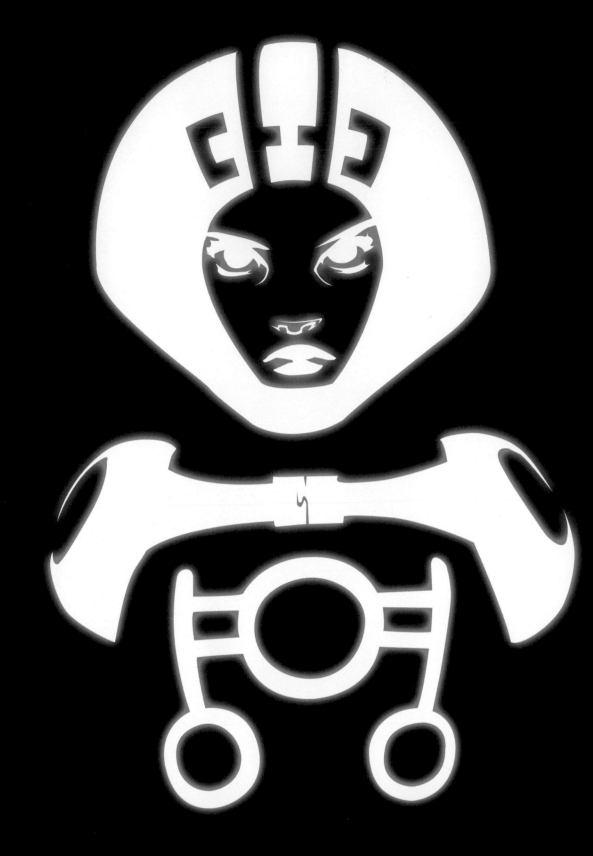

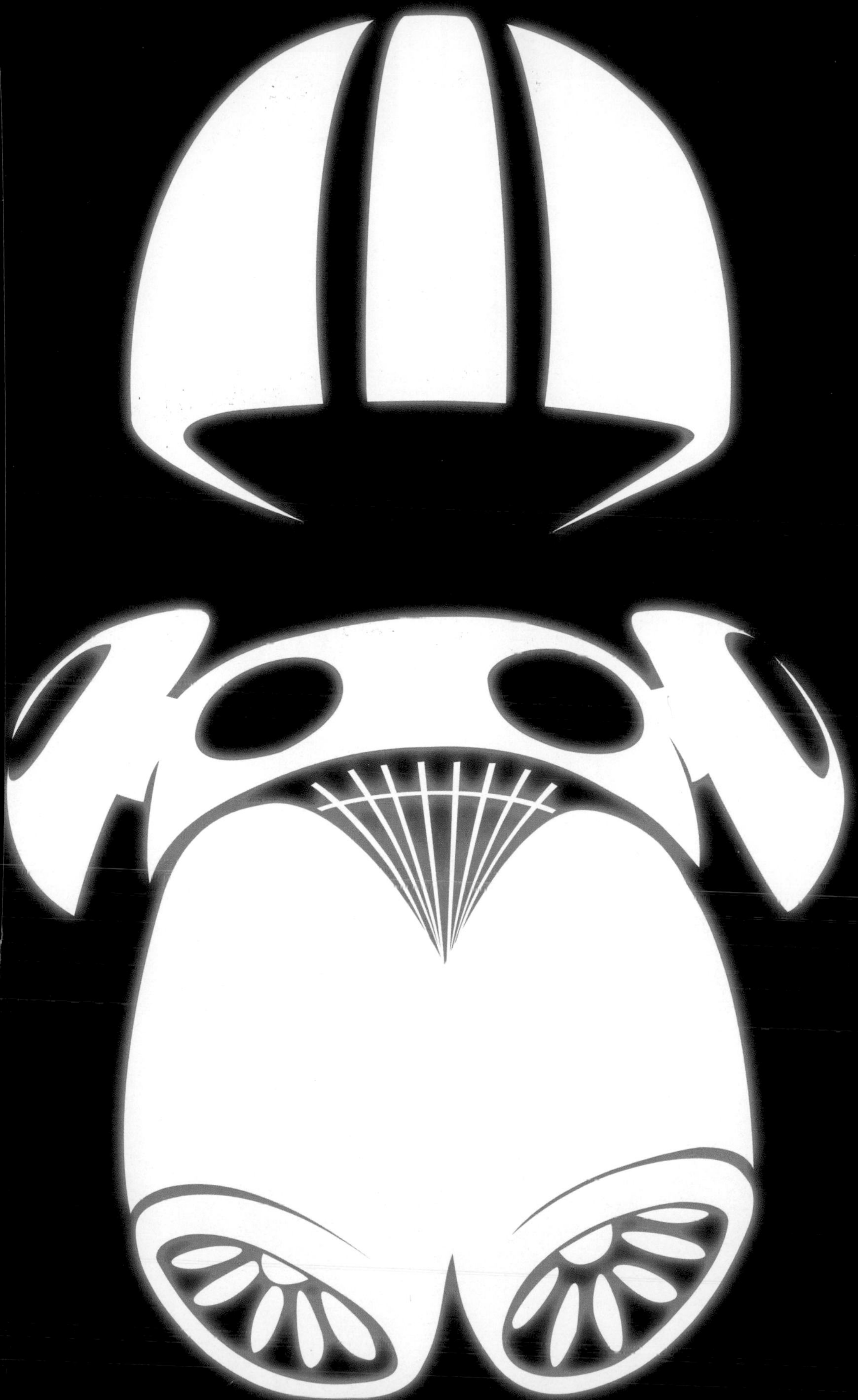

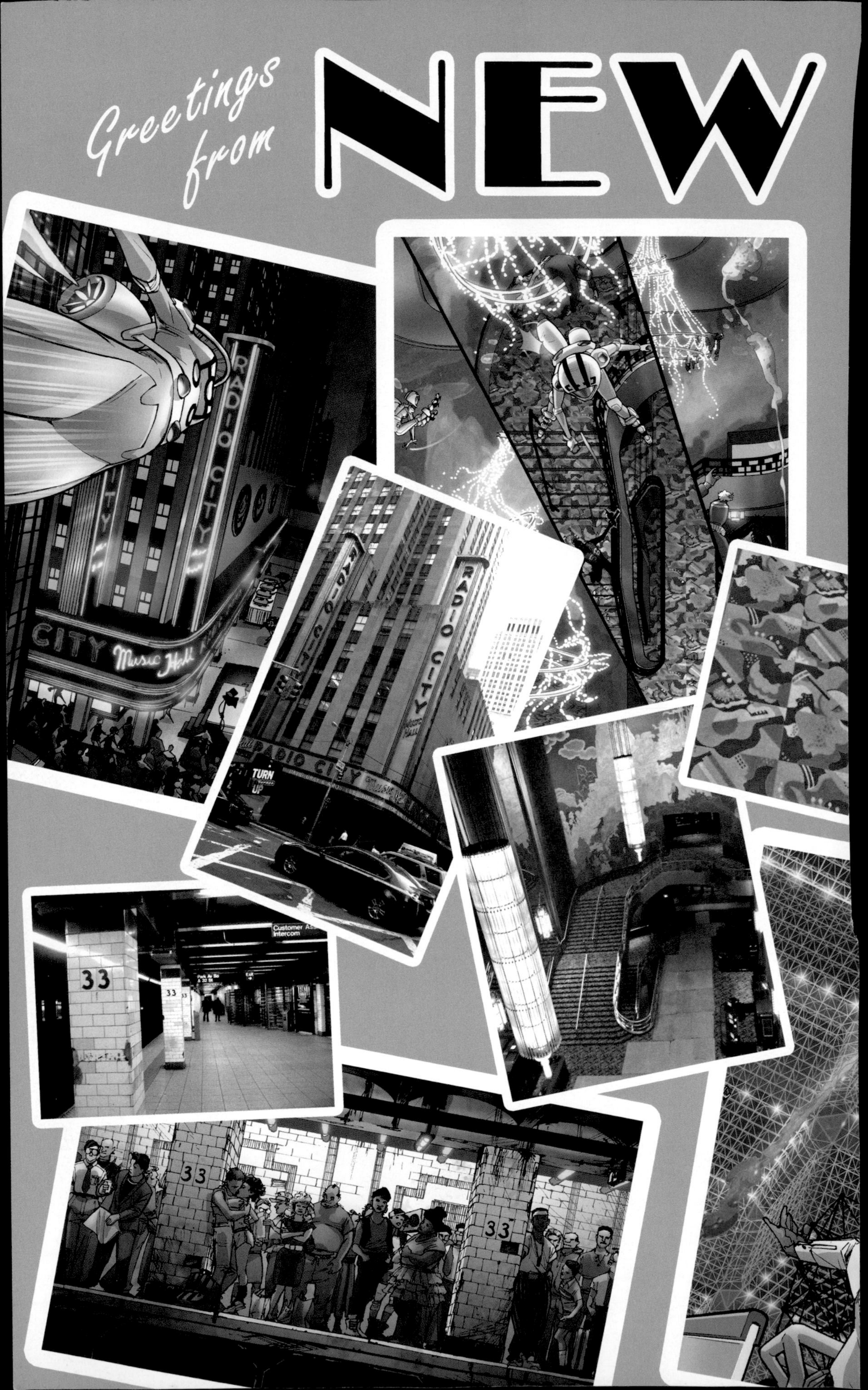

Greetings from
NEW
RADIO CITY
CITY Music Hall
RADIO CITY
TURN UP
33
Customer Assistance Intercom
33
33
33

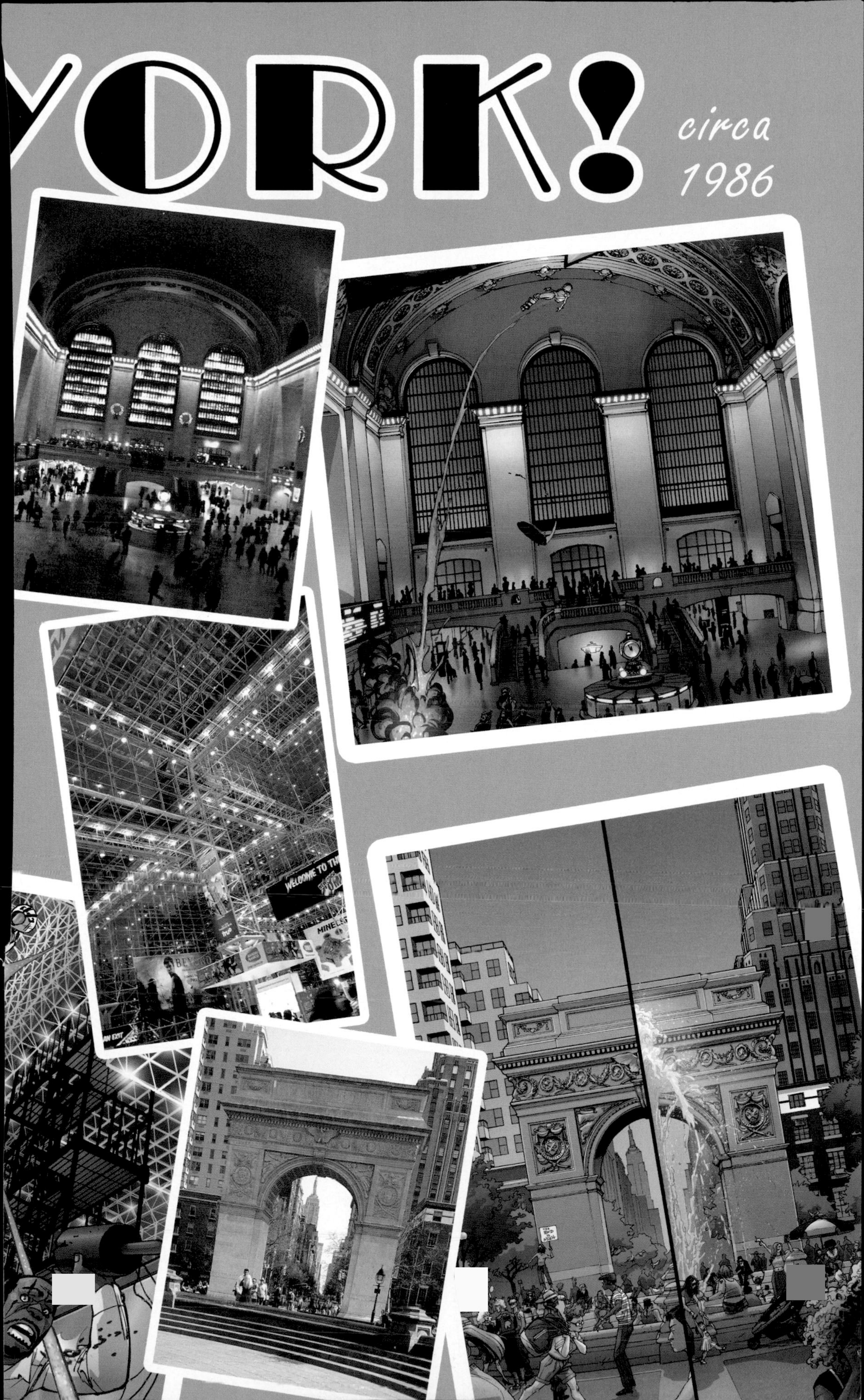
YORK!
circa 1986
WELCOME TO THE

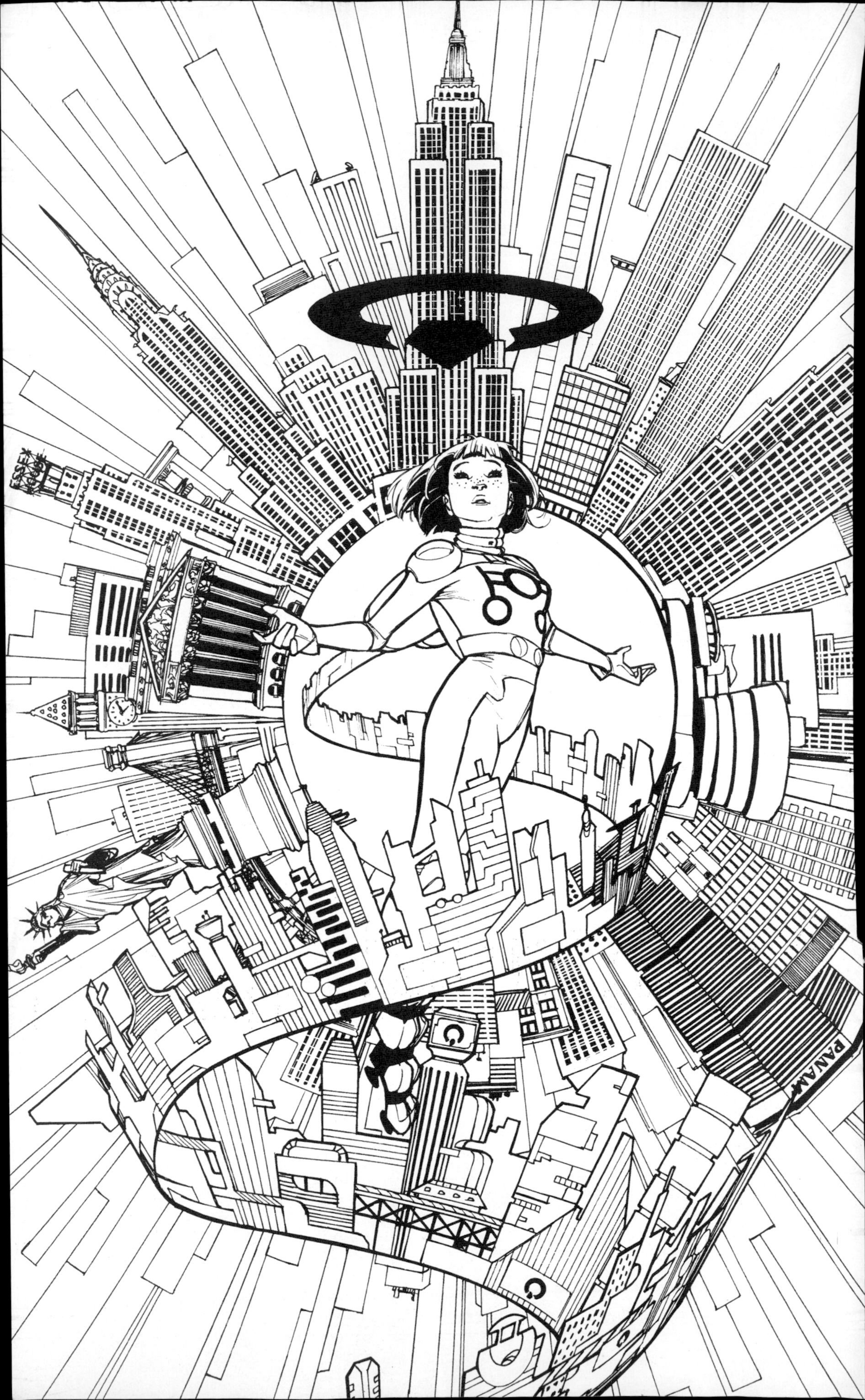
PANAM

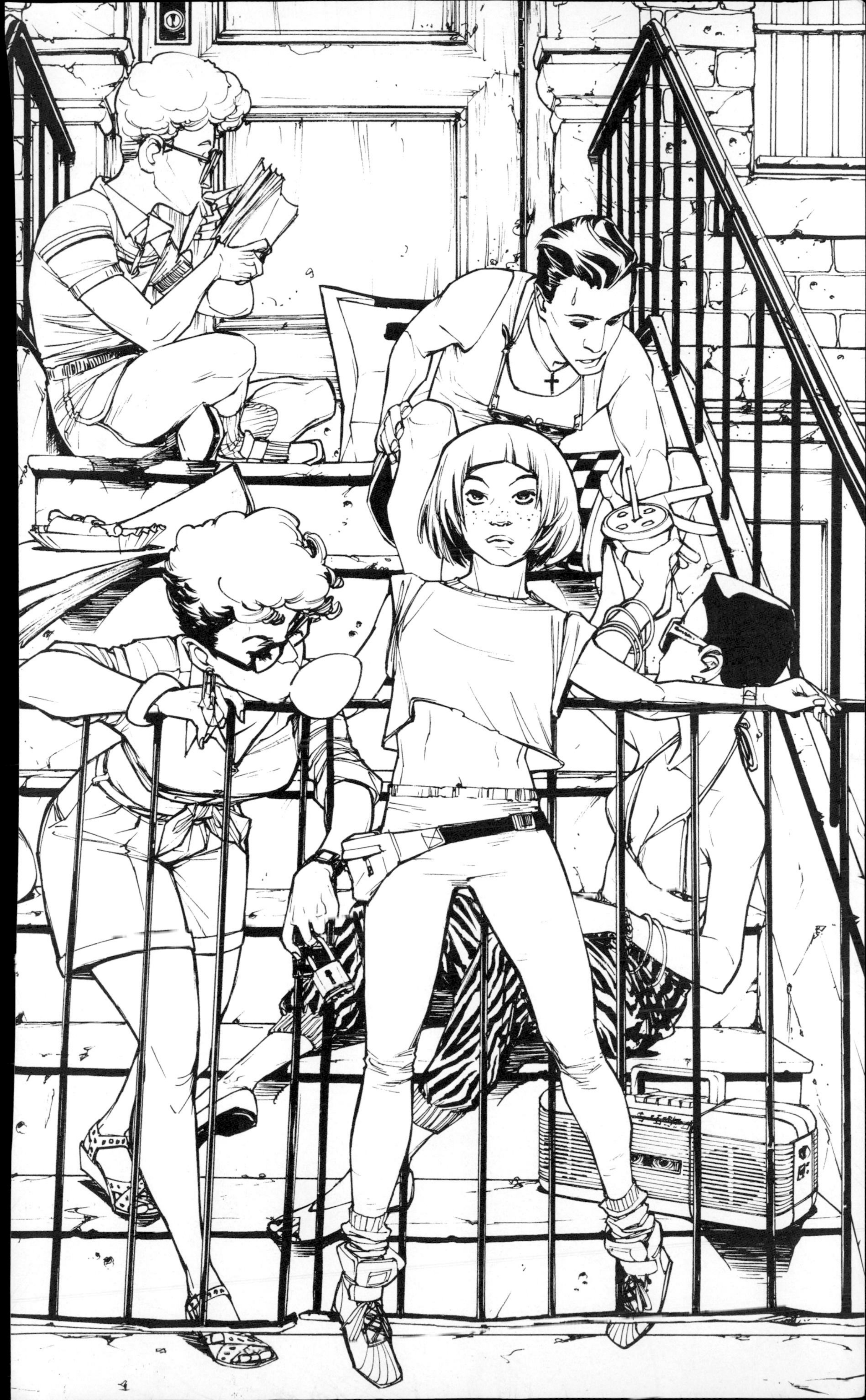

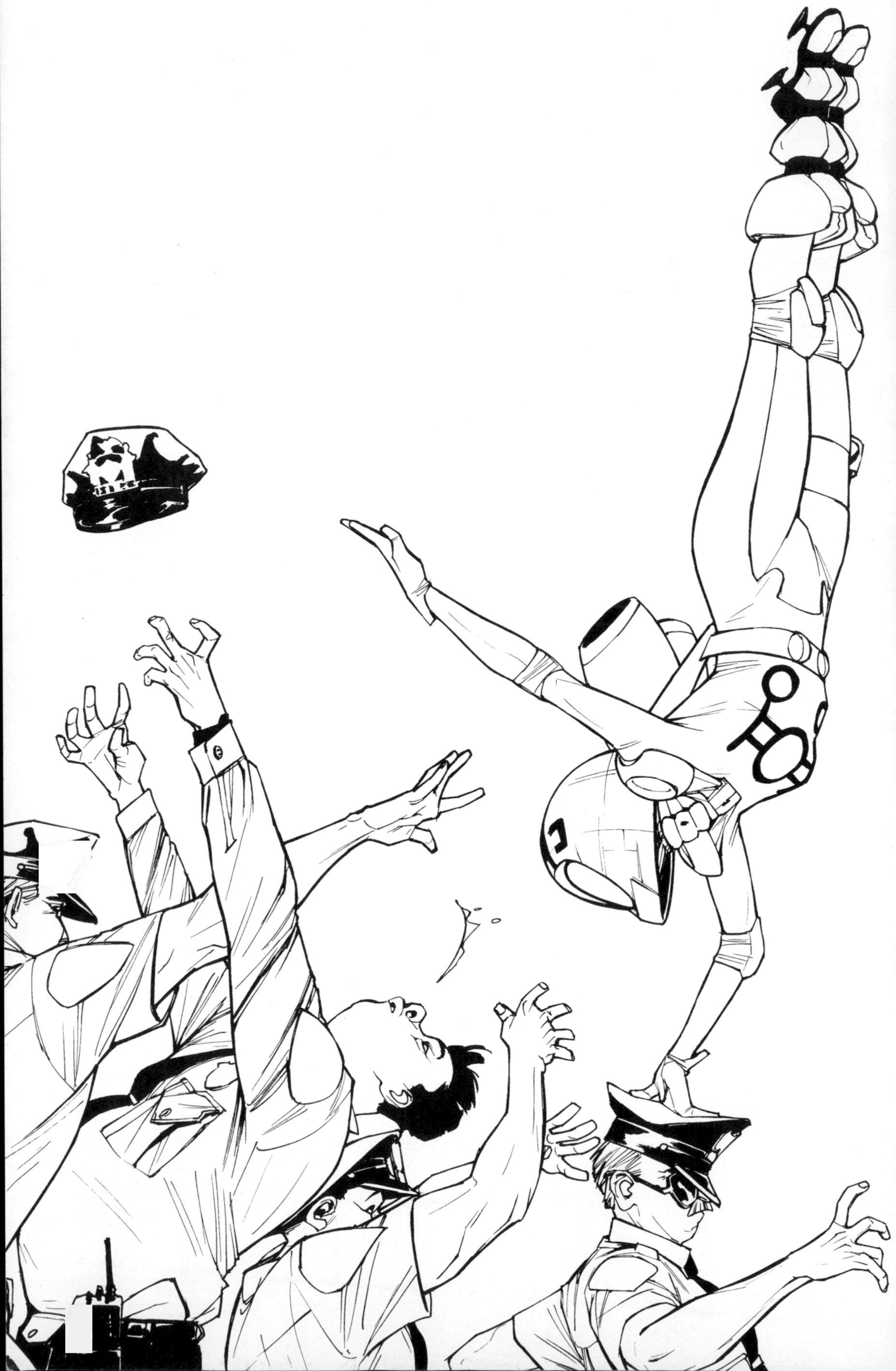

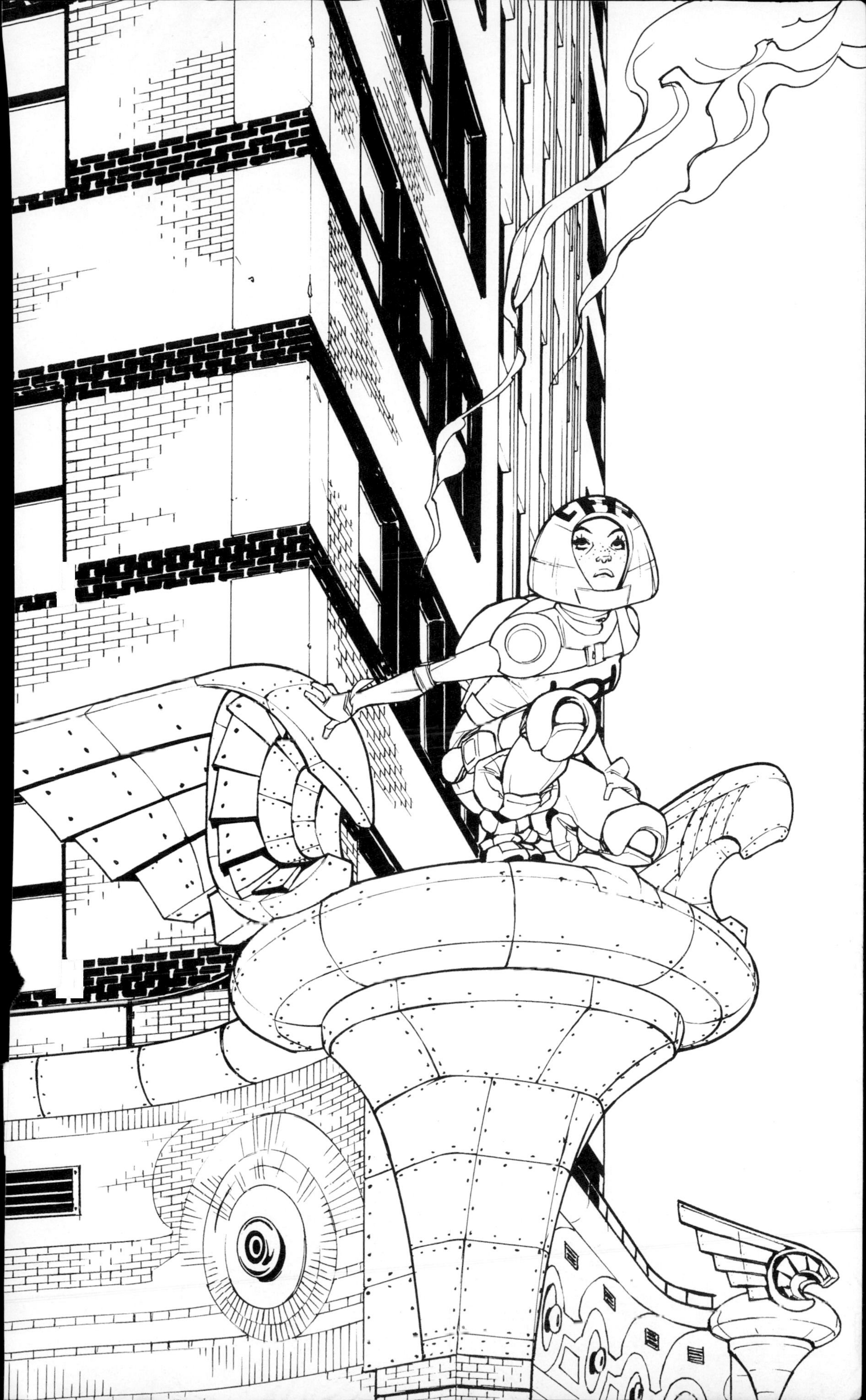

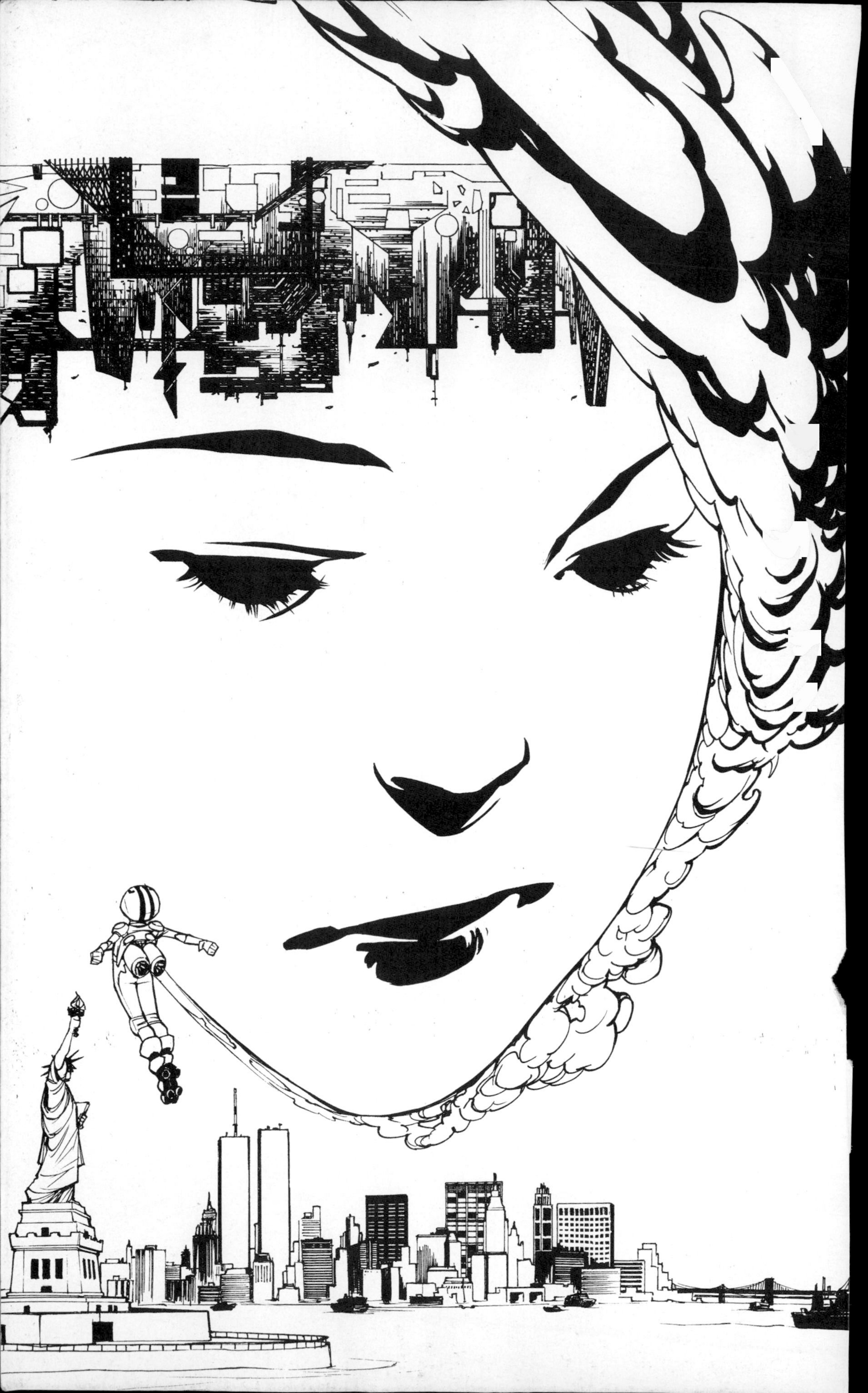